"The realistic underbelly of *Article 5* is what makes this dystopian tale a haunting read and incredibly engaging. The high-stakes and seemingly impossible escape for the heroine brings forth a tone similar to films *Midnight Express* and *Full Metal Jacket*. Simmons' debut solidified her place within the YA community as a true dystopian force."

—The CW Atlanta

"[A] fun read . . . a good amount of adventure and action."

—*Wired* on *Article 5*

"*Article 5* can be compared to Lauren Oliver's *Delirium* in terms of the control of emotions and morality imposed by society. Ember's feelings of helplessness are palpable. The story is well written, and the descriptions are vivid. Fans of dystopian books will love this debut novel, the first in a series."

—*School Library Journal*

"Paints a picture of a world that could easily be our future. [Simmons'] fluid writing creates an easy-to-read story that opens the eyes of readers to what the loss of civil liberties could entail. This book is a must-have for all young adult collections." —*VOYA*

"The new world imagined here is legitimately terrifying. The pacing and emotions . . . will keep readers eagerly turning the pages, keen to follow Chase and Ember to a hopefully happy end. The chemistry between Chase and Ember is excellent, and the plentiful action, high stakes, and deliciously angst-laden love story will please readers."

—Bulletin of the Center for Children's Books on *Article 5*

"Will be enjoyed by young people captivated by post-apocalyptic reads. *Article 5* is a suspenseful, action-packed novel that is sure to keep you on the edge of your seat. I recommend it to high school students and mature middle schoolers who enjoy imagining what life might be like if the wrong people were in power."   —*Portland Book Review*

"Simmons has put plenty of heart into her characters, so readers will want to follow them to the next book. But the momentum seems to be with the FBR. Watch out, guys."
                                        —*Booklist* on *Breaking Point*

"Suspenseful and immediate. Whom to trust and how far are rarely clear. Some interesting moral questions about pragmatism and violence arise, and no easy answers are given. The strongest of the series' three volumes, with a tense and harrowing climax."   —*Kirkus Reviews* on *Three*

"[A] vivid read."   —*Children's Bookwatch* on *Three*

BOOKS BY KRISTEN SIMMONS

Article 5
Breaking Point
Three
The Glass Arrow

THREE

KRISTEN SIMMONS

TOR®
TEEN

A TOM DOHERTY ASSOCIATES BOOK
NEW YORK

This is a work of fiction. All of the characters, organizations, and events portrayed in this novel are either products of the author's imagination or are used fictitiously.

THREE

A Tor Teen Book
Published by Tom Doherty Associates, LLC
175 Fifth Avenue
New York, NY 10010

www.tor-forge.com

Tor® is a registered trademark of Tom Doherty Associates, LLC.

The Library of Congress has cataloged the hardcover edition as follows:

Simmons, Kristen.
    Three / Kristen Simmons.
      p. cm.
    "A Tom Doherty Associates Book."
    ISBN 978-0-7653-2960-8 (hardcover)
    ISBN 978-1-4299-4803-6 (e-book)
    1. Government, Resistance to—Fiction.   2. Fugitives from justice—Fiction.
3. Science fiction. I. Title.
  PZ7.S591825Thr 2014
  [Fic]—dc23

                                        2013026344

ISBN 978-0-7653-2963-9 (trade paperback)

Tor Teen books may be purchased for educational, business, or promotional use. For information on bulk purchases, please contact the Macmillan Corporate and Premium Sales Department at 1-800-221-7945, extension 5442, or write to specialmarkets@macmillan.com.

First Edition: February 2014
First Trade Paperback Edition: January 2015

Printed in the United States of America

0 9 8 7 6 5 4 3 2 1

FOR JOANNA

There would be no Three *without* Article 5,
and no Article 5 *without you.*

CHAPTER

1

THE dream was changing. Even asleep I sensed it.

Before, it had been my mother and me, linked arm in arm, drawn down the center of our deserted street by the same violent destiny: home and soldiers and *blood*. Always blood. But now there was something different. Off. Needling at me like a riddle I couldn't figure out.

The asphalt was still broken. Our neighborhood waited, silent and haunted, each condemned front door posting the Statutes like a warning of the plague. Above, a pale, flat sky spanned from shoulder to shoulder, and I was alone.

And then beside me, where my mother should have been, Chase appeared.

Not the Chase of now, but the boy I'd met long ago—messy black hair and the curious, daring eyes of an eight-year-old, white socks winking from beneath the jeans he'd already outgrown. He darted down the lane and I ran after him, giggling.

He was fast; every time I swiped at him, he escaped, my fingertips always just inches away from his billowing T-shirt. His laughter filled me with something warm and forgotten, and for a time, there was nothing but joy.

But the sky began to bruise, and the carefree way he kicked

a rock down the middle of the road suddenly worried me. He was too young to know what was happening—that this place wasn't safe anymore. With urgency, I reached for his hand.

Curfew, I told him. *We have to get home.*

But he fought me.

I tried to pull him along, but it was no use; his little hand was slippery in my grasp. The failing light tightened my fear.

They were coming. I could feel their footsteps inside my chest.

Darkness came, black as coal and just as thick, until I could no longer see the houses and all that remained were the innocent boy beside me and the broken street we stood upon.

A soldier approached, his uniform neatly pressed, his slim, agile build too familiar, even at a distance. His golden hair gleamed, a halo in the moonless night.

I knew how this part went, but my heart still thumped all the way down to my stomach. I tried to push the boy back, to keep him away from the man who'd killed my mother. *You will not touch him*, I told Tucker Morris, but no sound came from my lips. Still, the cry echoing in my head seemed to infuse Tucker with speed, and suddenly he was upon us, three feet away, aiming a gun directly between my eyes.

I screamed for the boy to run, but before I could turn to do the same, my gaze found the man's face.

It wasn't Tucker. Before me was a different soldier, one with pallid skin and eyes long dead, and a hole in his chest that wept blood. One we'd killed to escape the hospital in Chicago.

Harper.

I gasped, tripped, and fell backward. And left the boy beside me exposed to the weapon.

Harper shot, a sound that made the world quake and the

street break open. And when it stopped, the little boy lay motionless, a fist-sized hole punched through his rib cage.

I woke with a start, braced to fight. The image of the soldier—Harper—who Chase had shot while we'd been rescuing Rebecca from the Chicago rehab hospital faded, but left a sticky residue, making it impossible to fall back asleep.

My breath evened out, and as it did I registered the sounds of sleep: heavy breathing and the occasional snore. The hard floor beneath my back served as a reminder that we'd taken shelter in an abandoned house, a break from the beach where we'd slept the last three nights. The heavy moon, nearly full, peeked in a glassless window and helped my eyes adjust to the dark. Chase's space beside me was empty.

I untangled the beach towel from around my legs. Six sleeping bodies were scattered around the room. People like me, who had come to the coast in search of the safe house—the only known refuge for those escaping the FBR's oppression—only to find it destroyed. By some miracle, tracks had led away from the wreckage and a small team of us had followed them south, leaving those who'd been injured in the attack on Chicago behind. They waited for us in a mini-mart outside the blast radius, vulnerable with only a few healthy fighters to defend them and a meager ration of food and supplies.

It took several beats to shake off the dream and remember that Tucker wasn't with us, that he'd gone with the carriers three days ago to tell the other resistance groups what had happened to the safe house. They were supposed to make contact once they reached the first post. We were still waiting to hear from them.

No matter how much I wanted him gone, I couldn't breathe while he was out there, despite the help he'd given us over the past few weeks. At least when he was close I could keep tabs on him. Now it felt like I'd dropped a knife with my eyes closed, with only the hope that the blade wouldn't land in my foot.

Someone was mumbling. Probably Jack, one of the survivors from the Chicago resistance. He hadn't been right since the Moral Militia had bombed the tunnels and we'd all nearly been buried alive. His lean body spanned out like a star in the entryway while a guy from Chicago named Rat, every bit as short as Jack was tall, lay on his side just beyond him. Sean had fallen asleep against a weathered sofa, head sagging, palms open on his lap as if in meditation. Behind him, Rebecca curled across the cushions, the metal crutches in her arms taking the place of the boy who so obviously wanted to be there.

Though she should have stayed behind with the injured at the mini-mart, Rebecca had insisted on forging ahead. The pace was hard on her body but she didn't complain. That worried me. It was like she was trying to prove something.

The other two that stretched into the dining room were from the Chicago resistance, and hadn't given up hope that their families had somehow lived through the attack on the safe house, that they'd managed to escape and flee south.

From outside came the sound of twigs snapping. I rose silently and wove through the bodies to the open door. The air smelled strongly of salt and mold, both fresh and dirty at the same time. From over the sandbank whispered the ocean, the ebb and flow of the waves, the hush of the long grass between the beach and this decrepit seaside village where we'd made camp. It was called DeBor-something. The "Welcome to . . ." sign had fallen victim years ago to someone's target practice; little copper punctures distorted the right side.

Once, DeBor-something had been posh; the gates that blocked out the poor had fallen, but were still there, stacked beside the burned security booth. There had been riots here during the War, like in a lot of the richer communities. What remained of the empty Easter egg–colored beach houses were ruins: scaffolding stretching like burned, blackened fingers into the sky, foundations half-collapsed on their weathered stilts, walls muted by layers of white salt and sand, and gagged by crisscross boards that blocked what remained of their windows. Somewhere close a rusted screen door slapped against the frame.

From the bottom porch step came another delicate snap. It was only Billy, all sharp elbows and shoulder blades, hunched over his knees. He was peeling the bark off a stick, and hadn't seemed to notice my arrival.

A frown tugged at the corners of my mouth. If Billy was on watch it was near dawn. He'd relieved Chase earlier in the night. But Chase wasn't here; the towel he'd slept on had been tossed near the window beside a trash bag that held our only possessions—two cups, a rusty kitchen knife, a toothbrush, and some rope we'd harvested from the wreckage.

Billy didn't so much as shift as I tiptoed across the porch to sit beside him.

"Quiet night?" I asked cautiously. He gave me a one-shouldered shrug. The red light of a CB radio we'd harvested from one of the carriers' trucks blinked on the step between his electric-taped boots. It was metal, and half the depth of a shoebox. Not as convenient as a handheld, but it was strong enough to connect to the interior.

At least, we thought it was strong enough. The red light was supposed to glow green when we had an incoming call, but had yet to do so.

My gaze lifted back to Billy. He'd been quiet since we'd been reunited in the safe house ruins. I knew he held out hope that

Wallace, the one-time leader of the Knoxville resistance—and more important, his adopted father—was still alive, that he was among the survivors we tracked. But that was impossible. Wallace had burned to death in the Wayland Inn. We'd all seen it go down.

"There's some canned stew left," I offered. Hunger gnawed at my own stomach. Rations were running thin. He grimaced and kept picking the bark off that stick with his fingernails, as though it was the most fascinating thing in the world.

Billy could hack into the MM mainframe. A stick wasn't all that interesting.

"Okay. Well. One of the guys found spaghetti noodles, did you—"

"Did I say I was hungry?"

Someone sleeping near the front door stirred. Billy lowered his chin back to his chest, hiding his defiant brown eyes under a greasy curtain of hair.

The silence between us strained. He'd lost a parent; I knew how that felt. But it wasn't like we'd killed his father.

Not like we'd killed Harper.

A sudden chill crept over my skin, despite the balmy temperature.

"How long has Chase been gone?" I asked.

He shrugged again. Irritated, I stood, and made my way around the side of the house toward the beach, hoping Chase had gone in this direction. The grass was thinner to the right so I took that path, and winced when the climb up the dune sent a burning jolt up my shins. My legs had become their own war zone: purple and yellow bruises from the Chicago blast, blisters from my boots, and dime-sized welts on my ankles and heels from the gravel that had worked its way into my socks.

But when I reached the top of the embankment, my pain was forgotten.

A burst of stars reflected off the black ocean, pure and bright as diamonds, with no competition from the lights of a city or base. The exact line where the water met the shore was hidden in the darkness, but its murmur was as constant as a heartbeat.

The vastness of it swallowed me. The cool, fresh air played with the ends of my hair, in the absentminded way my mother used to when we would talk. It was times like these I missed her most—the quiet spaces, when no one else was around. When I closed my eyes, it was almost like she was back.

"Still no tracks. Not since yesterday morning," I said aloud, hoping she could hear me. I didn't know if that was how things worked. All I knew was that I wished I could hear her answer back, just one more time. I twisted my heels in the sand. "No word from our people at the mini-mart. Chase thinks their radio is probably dead. It was on its last legs before we left." I sighed. "No word from the team we sent to the interior, either."

Each of us that was searching for the survivors took a shift carrying the radio, anxious to hear news from the other resistance posts. No one spoke the truth: that our team could have been captured. That the chances that anyone had made it out of the safe house were slim. That our friends, our families, were all gone.

"I don't suppose you could tell us if anyone survived," I said. "Guess that would be cheating."

I opened my eyes and tilted my chin skyward in search of any sign of the bombs that had destroyed our sanctuary. But the stars were silent.

Before the War, I'd been so used to the noise I hadn't even heard it. Cars, lights, the hum of the refrigerator. *People*. People everywhere—passing by in the street, talking on their phones, calling for their friends. When the Reformation Act decreed that the power be shut off for curfew, the nights got quiet. So quiet you could hear thieves breaking into houses two streets over, hear the sirens and the soldiers that came to arrest them. So quiet you could hear your heart pound and every creak in the floor as you hid under your bed hoping they didn't come get you, too.

The silence didn't scare me anymore. I welcomed it because it had strengthened me, made me more aware. But times like this I would have given anything to bring back the noise. To shout at the top of my lungs, *I am still here, you haven't beaten me!* To tell everyone who could still sleep soundly because they were convinced the MM was at best our saving grace, and at worst a necessary evil, what had happened to me, and what they'd done to my mother.

A compression in the sand behind me pulled me from my thoughts. I spun toward the tree to my left, and strained my eyes into the darkness, gripping a fork in my pocket that I'd picked up in the street earlier.

"Who's there?" I called after a moment.

A familiar shape emerged from under the canopy of dew-soaked leaves. "I didn't mean to interrupt."

Relief rose within me, right along with the heat in my cheeks. I should have made sure no one was listening before launching into a one-sided conversation.

"Are you spying on me, Chase Jennings?" I planted my fists on my hips.

He chuckled. "Never."

The sand shifted with each step that brought him closer, and for an instant the night behind Chase wavered, and he was back in the ruined remains of the safe house, digging through piles of broken wood and bent metal with his bare hands. Destroyed, just as the safe house had been destroyed, because his uncle was gone, because his last hope for our shelter was gone. But as quickly as it had come, the vision dissolved, leaving my throat swollen and my hairline damp.

I shook it off.

I couldn't see him clearly until he was even on the embankment an arm's length away. The black hair that grew so quickly was already fringing over his ears, and his jaw was scruffy from days of not shaving. He wore just a white T-shirt that seemed to glow in the moonlight and soot-stained jeans, torn through the knees, that frayed at his bare feet. His boots were tied together by their laces, and hung from one hand.

And just like that, I forgot the images that had clouded my mind. I forgot how I'd woken or what I'd dreamed. Something stirred inside of me, simmering with each moment his dark, glassy gaze held mine.

"Hi," he said.

I smiled. "Hi."

We hadn't been alone much in the last three days, and when we had, Chase had been consumed by the search. He'd been a million miles away.

He didn't feel so far away now.

I reached for his waistband, threaded a finger through the belt loop, and pulled him closer.

His shoes made a muted clunk as they dropped to the ground. His fingertips rose to my face and brushed along my cheekbones, his skin rough but his touch soft. They inched down the nape of my neck, down my spine, drawing me in as they came to rest around my waist.

I held my breath, aware of his hips against my stomach and the fluid way his shoulders rounded beneath my palms as he lowered his face to mine. I arched into the space between us so there was no longer him and I, but one. One form in the darkness. One breath, in and out.

His lips skimmed over my lips, side to side, as if memorizing their shape, innocent at first, but then something more, until the world beyond us dropped away. His eyes drifted closed and his embrace grew tighter and stronger, as if he could gather me inside of him.

My hands slid up the back of his shirt and traced the puckered skin from a scar on his lower back. He tensed in that way he did when he remembered things he didn't want to.

The cloud that crawled over the moon hid his face. Sometimes it felt like the past was pulling Chase one way while I was pulling him the other.

Sometimes the past won.

I found the spot where the strong cords of his neck met his shoulder and kissed him there, in the place I knew would always distract him. His breath expelled in one hard rasp.

"You taste like salt." I tried to make my voice steady, to give him something to hold on to. "You need a bath."

His muscles loosened by the slightest degree. "Maybe you should take one with me." I felt his grin against my neck. "Make sure I don't cut any corners."

My stomach fluttered. "Maybe I will."

He went still. I giggled. But the thought of us together, like that, made my mouth dry.

"What are you doing out here?" I asked after a moment.

He straightened, and my cheek found its place on his chest.

"Couldn't sleep." He paused. "My head's not right." I heard his sigh, and the scraping sound of knuckles dragging along his unshaven jaw. My fingers laced behind his waist to lock him against me.

"You could tell me about it," I tried.

He broke away, and though I tried to hold on, it was clear he needed space. Apart, I felt the cold for the first time since I'd come to the beach. The air around us had shifted and now felt somber and humid.

In the quiet that followed, my dream returned: Chase as a child, stretched out over the ground, bleeding. A prickle of unease crawled through me. I wished I could read his mind; then maybe I'd know what to say to help him instead of feeling so powerless.

"He was never going to come with us—that soldier. Whatever his name was." The words burst from him with enough force to make me jump.

"You mean Harper."

His gaze shot to mine, the question clear.

My stomach dropped. Had we really never used his name? I'd heard it a hundred times a day in my mind—over and over, like a whip coming down on my back. But Chase and I hadn't said it out loud once. We hadn't talked about what had happened in Chicago at all, and I wanted to. We *needed* to. We couldn't keep pretending like it never happened.

He fell back a step.

"Harper was the soldier," I said quickly. "The one at the rehab center in Chicago. The one we . . . you know."

Shot.

His expression changed. His whole posture changed. Became tortured and twisted in a way I hadn't seen since he'd told me how my mother had died. The reminder was enough to make my stomach hurt.

"His name was Harper?"

"I . . . saw his name badge." My arms crossed over my chest. I forced them down to my sides.

Chase retreated toward the house where we'd made camp, and when I pursued he held up a hand. Something close to panic swelled in my chest. The sand beneath my feet seemed to quake.

"Chase, I—"

He turned. A forced smile flickered over his face, then went dim. "We need to keep moving. If it rains again today we'll lose any chance of finding the others."

"Wait . . ."

"It's my uncle," he insisted, as though I'd somehow implied that we should stop tracking the survivors. My shoulders rose.

"He took me in after my mom and dad were gone," Chase explained, as if I didn't know. As if I wasn't *there* when his uncle had come to pick him up after the car accident had killed his parents. "He's the only family I've got left, Ember."

His words felt like a slap. "What about me?"

"He's my *uncle*," Chase said again. As if this explained everything.

"He left you when you were sixteen," I said. "In a *war zone*. He taught you to fight and to break into cars and then he left."

The words hung between us. Instantly I wished I could take them back. We didn't even know if his uncle Jesse had been at the safe house, much less if he was still alive. Regardless what he'd done, Chase cared for him, and it did no good to pick apart his memory.

"It wasn't his fault," Chase responded, focusing on the water. "He did what he had to do."

A different past returned then: a hill above a gray stone base, sour tendrils of white smoke spiraling to the sky, a gun in my hand.

I'm a damn good soldier. I did what needed to be done.

My knuckles were white peaks, nails sharp in my palms.

Tucker Morris had said those words right after confessing to my mother's murder. Chase couldn't use them; he was nothing like Tucker. He knew not everything could be excused.

But at the same time, I understood why Chase tried. If he slowed down, every disappointment, every pound of shame, weighed on him like a man in quicksand. And so he never stopped. He barely slept. He pushed on. Like he could keep running forever.

I swallowed the lump in my throat. "You did what you had to do, too."

The air was misting, heavy with the coming dawn, and in the dying starlight I could make out the shadows under his eyes, the damp ring around the collar of his shirt, and his fists, balled in his pockets.

Tentatively, I reached for his shoulder. Hard muscles flexed beneath my palm a second before he flinched away.

"We should go," he said, avoiding my eyes. "We've got to get an early start."

My hand fell, empty, to my side.

Come back to me, I wanted to say. But he was the boy in my dream, running away, and as much as I tried to hold him he slipped from my grasp.

"All right," I said. "Let's wake the others."

CHAPTER
2

CHASE was right; rain was coming.

The night was lit by a straight, pink scar on the horizon, and from it rose a ghost of the sun, muted and pale yellow. The air became palpable, thick to breathe, slick on our skin. Nearly as heavy as Chase's silence.

I wished I'd never said the name Harper—that I'd never even seen it on his stupid ID badge. I tried to banish it from my mind, but the harder I tried, the more I could see him. His crisp blue uniform. The high flush in his cheeks. The young soldier who'd nearly joined us in that Chicago rehab hospital before he'd gotten scared. I hated that he'd gotten scared. I hated that he'd blocked our path, and threatened to turn us in, and raised his gun. That he'd *made* Chase shoot him, because Chase never would have done that if he hadn't been forced to.

It was Harper's own fault he was dead.

The black tentacles of guilt that had snaked around my chest eased their hold. But in their place, something slippery remained.

I told myself it wasn't right to think that way. That despite being a soldier, Harper was flesh and blood, just like us.

Just like Tucker. Who'd redeemed himself several times over, but who'd still killed my mother.

I shook my head to clear it. Traveling down that road just made me crazy. This was a war—just as much as the War that had brought it. And if Harper had chosen the right side, he'd still be alive. At least for now.

I still wasn't sure where that left Tucker.

By the time we'd reached the house the others were already stirring and I was glad for the distraction. They packed quickly as there wasn't much to pack, and with only a few mumbled words we moved out, heading south in the same direction we'd been traveling since we'd seen the tracks three days ago. Time was ticking—we'd told the injured we'd return to the mini-mart with a report within five days. Our return trip would be quicker without the search, but we were still cutting it close.

Every indentation in the sand was scrutinized. Every piece of trash that floated in the shallows was inspected. One of them would be the sign we needed: a footprint, or a discarded can from someone's meal. No one wanted to return to the mini-mart with nothing to show. But an hour passed, maybe more, and there was still no evidence of survivors.

When it was my turn to carry the radio, I kept it in the trash bag over my shoulder so it wouldn't get wet when the rain finally came. With the responsibility came paranoia; convinced I would miss the call, I checked the box every few minutes, but the red light had yet to flash green.

It was the smell that reached us first. The breeze had turned in anticipation of the storm, and carried on it a putrid, dead stench.

"What *is* that?" Billy finally asked, pulling the sweat-ringed neck of his T-shirt over his nose and mouth.

No one answered.

We slowed. Chase, Jack, and Rat took the lead, though Chase was the only one not to draw a gun from the back of his belt. Beside me, Sean put a warning hand on Rebecca's shoulder, but she ignored him, leaning heavily on her crutches and shuffling onward through the sand.

Jack gagged. "Fish," he called. "*Dead* fish."

Billy and I moved up to see, but the closer I got to the front, the more nauseating the stench became. Taking Chase's cue, I buried my nose in the crook of my elbow, and then stopped short as a sudden breeze swept aside the fog.

The sand here wasn't fine and white as it had been, but black, painted by waves of sticky oil during high tide. It pooled in every divot in the ground, gleaming and pearlescent, even without the bright light. Littered all across our path were animals coated in it. Fish, turtles, sea creatures I didn't recognize. Birds, white feathers tarred and matted, beaks open, eyes blank. Not even the bugs ate them.

It went on for miles.

I fought the urge to vomit; the bile in my throat tasted like rotting things. I imagined what it must feel like to choke on oil. How it would slosh in my lungs and coat the walls of my stomach, sleek and poisonous. A warning to turn back shook through me, but all that remained behind us was more death.

I glanced over to Chase, who stared forward, and I could feel his pity for all these living things lost.

"Sick," whispered Billy.

We stood in reverent shock for only a moment more, and then with a deafening roar of thunder, the sky broke open.

IF there were tracks in the sand they were swept away by the storm, so we moved inland and scoured the brush and trees beside the beach in search of bits of torn clothing, campfire remains, anything to show that someone had passed through. But the raindrops fattened, and it didn't take long before our clothing was drenched. The clatter drowned out the noise. It wasn't until Chase was standing before me, pellets of water bouncing off his bare arms, that I noticed he was trying to tell me something.

"I said Rebecca's falling behind again," he repeated as I checked the red blinking light on the radio for the umpteenth time. "Sean's got to take her back to the mini-mart."

He was the only one besides Sean and I that kept tabs on Rebecca. At first the others had given her wide berth, like she was bad luck, but now her presence was starting to wear on them. She wasn't as mobile as the rest of us, which made her a liability. Most hadn't even bothered to learn her name.

I glanced back the way we'd come, sore because he had a point—Rebecca should have stayed back, despite how much I wanted to keep her in my sight. The last time we'd been apart she'd been hurt, and this was the only way I could guarantee her safety. Still, though searching was slow work, her speed was half ours, especially through the brush and knotted roots off the beach. She wasn't going to be able to keep up much longer.

When I turned back Chase was gone, having disappeared through the mist. A frown tugged at my mouth; he was clearly worried. Somehow Rebecca had become his responsibility, too.

Billy was nearby, and I grabbed his sleeve to get his attention.

"Have you seen Rebecca or Sean?"

He glanced around impatiently. "They were behind me earlier."

The water ran in rivulets from the tips of my hair, and I shoved it back from my face and held a hand up like a visor above my eyes. Only gray surrounded us; the low light made even the trees lose their color.

I shoved through the underbrush back the way we'd come. The mud puddles deepened in the gaps between the trees and every sloshing step soaked my socks. The beach was to my right; surely Rebecca hadn't waded through the oil and dead animals. To my left the grass grew tall and thick, and it struck me that any number of things could be living within it.

Rebecca could be hurt within it.

"Becca!"

Sean's call drifted over the slimy, wet field. Sweeping both hands in front of me to clear the way, I surged forward.

"Sean! Where are you?" I was glad the rain was still loud. Though we hoped to find survivors, we didn't know who lurked in the evacuated Red Zone. For the past few days we'd stayed as quiet as possible so we wouldn't attract unnecessary attention.

Finally I saw him—head and shoulders above the grass that tickled my neck. He spun frantically, still calling for Rebecca.

"What happened?" I asked when I reached him.

"She was right behind me," he said, a muscle in his jaw bulging. The water matted his darkened hair and streamed down his face.

We pushed forward ten more feet, then twenty, until the grass gave way suddenly to an open, single-lane street. Rainwater cascaded down thick cracks in the asphalt, and weeds, some as tall as me, grew from the potholes. Boarded-up houses, all with a similar brick front, lined the opposite side.

Before I could make myself move, Sean had yanked me down into a crouch. Anyone could be hiding in those houses, aiming a shotgun through one of those busted windows. Maybe even one of the survivors we were tracking.

I searched the windows first, then the spaces between the buildings. Every door was marred by a Statute posting. Even the rain couldn't peel them from the wood.

"There!" Sean pointed up the road to where a solitary figure stood on the center yellow line. Before I could stop him he was running, and with one final glance around I followed, eyes trained on the houses for movement. As we neared, the staggering gait became familiar, and two silver crutches came into view.

Sean didn't slow as he hauled Rebecca out of the street. A short scream of surprise burst from her throat, and then she was fighting him, falling in a heap in the wet grass. Mud splashed over her clothes and freckled her face.

"What's wrong with you?" Sean yelled. "We've got to keep off the roads, I told you that."

Rebecca pulled herself up into a seated position, legs splayed out before her. She'd lost her crutches in the fall, and where they usually fastened to her forearms were raw, bleeding patches of skin. I bit back a cringe.

"Afraid I'll get hit by a car?" She stared at him defiantly, cheeks stained, arms open to the empty street behind us.

"Yeah, Becca. That's what I meant."

"Stop it," I said, inserting myself between them. "You never know who's hiding in places like this. That's all he's trying to say."

"He's trying to say I'm a child. *That's* all he's trying—"

"Maybe if you'd stop acting like—"

"Sean!" I turned on him, pointing up the road. "Go find the others. We're right behind you."

Sean laced his hands behind his neck, then slammed them down in frustration. "Fine." A moment later he disappeared through the grass and rain.

A deep breath to summon patience, and I squatted beside her.

"Let me see your arms."

She kept them locked to her body, gaze still pinned in the direction Sean had taken off. Her lower lip quivered.

I rubbed at the tightness in my chest. "He's just worried about you."

"He hates me," she said, so quietly I almost missed it.

I grabbed her crutches, needing something to busy my hands. Rebecca didn't have to say it, but I knew she blamed us for her misery. I told myself for the hundredth time that she was better off with us than the FBR, that we wouldn't cart her around or put her on display to dissuade citizens from corruption. But seeing her sitting in a mud puddle, arms bright with sores, not even attempting to shield her face from the rain, I couldn't help but doubt myself.

That didn't mean I was going to let her quit.

"Get up," I told her. "Enough with the pity party."

"Excuse me?"

"You heard me. Get up."

She balked, and when I didn't back down she snatched the crutches from my grasp. Barely a wince came from her lips as she fastened the braces around her forearms.

"That's not exactly easy in case you haven't noticed," she said.

I knew it wasn't. I knew it was killing her and I ached to fix it, but I also knew if she was going to survive out here she couldn't give up.

I fought the sympathy eating away at my insides and cocked an eyebrow. "Neither is sneaking out of a locked facility every night to fool around with a guard."

Her ice blue gaze widened. "Ember . . ."

"You have to go back to the mini-mart." I shifted. "Sean will take you. . . ."

"*Ember.*" She pointed to the trash bag I'd set on the ground beside us. "The radio!"

The red light was flashing green—the mouth of the bag had opened when I'd set it down and now the box sent a pale jade reflection onto the black plastic. Instantly, I snatched up the whole package, flooded with the need to answer, but knowing I couldn't. The rain would ruin the machine.

"Come on." I only took a second to weigh the consequences, and then sprinted toward the nearest house with the radio latched tightly to my chest, unwilling to miss this first connection with Tucker's team. As far as we knew, they were the only ones who could tell the posts what had happened to the safe house.

Once under the shelter of the stone entranceway, I hurriedly removed the silver box from the bag then set it on the dirty cement. Beads of water gathered on the top of the metal and I tried in vain to wipe them away with my wet shirtsleeve.

Rebecca arrived, huffing. Unaccustomed to moving that fast with crutches, she bumped into the wall, but held on before falling.

"Do you know how to use that thing?"

"Yes." In theory. I wished one of the others were here; even though Chase had walked me through the steps I'd never actually used a CB radio before.

"Then answer! Hurry! You're going to miss it!"

"Keep a lookout," I told her.

I unhooked the black handheld microphone, untangling the coiled cord from around the handle. The light stopped flashing.

"No." I made sure the knob was dialed to the frequency we'd agreed to use and pressed the button labeled RECEIVE TRANSMISSION, praying I wasn't too late.

"Hello?" I tried. "Are you there? Hello?"

"What happened?" Rebecca asked.

"Come on." I pressed the button to accept the call again. Again. "Please be there."

"Take your time, why don't you," came the muffled voice of my mother's killer.

I sat back on the damp pavement, exhaling in one hard breath. A deep scowl had etched into Rebecca's face.

"Well it took you long enough to call." My throat tightened, as it always did when I spoke to Tucker Morris. "Everything going all right?"

"Yeah." He hesitated. "So far so good. Sorry I couldn't call earlier. Had some trouble getting a connection."

There was heaviness in his tone, telling me that something bad had happened. We couldn't discuss it over the open radio. Even though this was an old frequency the MM didn't use anymore, it wasn't secure. They could always be listening.

"So how is it out there?" I doubted much had changed in the few days we'd been away from the cities, but if anything big had happened, we wouldn't have known. Our CB radio wasn't strong enough to eavesdrop on any FBR frequencies, and there wasn't a news station reporting close enough to pick up a signal. It was easy to feel disconnected out here in the Red Zone.

"Oh, you know," he said. "No one wants to starve in peace and quiet. They've all got to moan and groan about it."

"Then maybe they should come with you," I said. Join the resistance. Stop complaining and do something.

"Ha," he said dryly. "Then what would they have to whine about?"

The truth was few people fought the MM because they were scared. It took something big—something like reform school, and losing your mother—to push through the fear to anger. That was when you could fight back.

"We went through this place yesterday, though that was different," Tucker continued. "They had a sign at the front of the street that said, get this, it was a 'compliant neighborhood.' It was like they were proud of it or something. The place looked good—what we saw of it anyway. Nice-looking houses. We even saw a bunch of little kids in school uniforms."

A compliant neighborhood? I wanted to gag. I wondered if they were bigots or just liars. How could a community embrace the Statutes? It baffled me, got under my skin. If everyone knew the MM was executing people for violations to their precious moral rules, they wouldn't be so quick to boast their pride. Unless they were scared of course.

I changed the subject. "How are the others? Tired of driving?" The carriers used aliases, but I wouldn't risk saying even those aloud.

"Fine. They're just . . . visiting with old friends. We should get to Grandma's house tomorrow. We already crossed over the river." He snorted. "Now we just have to get through the woods."

Over the river and through the woods, to grandmother's house we go.

I smirked at his chosen code name for the first post and sagged against the wall. They'd made it over the Red Zone border. At least that much was going right. Rebecca, who'd turned to watch the street, glanced back over her shoulder.

"My mom used to sing that song," I said. She'd loved the holidays. For a moment, I could smell the pungent pine air fresheners she would spray around Christmastime to make the house smell "festive."

I didn't know what I was thinking, bringing her up now. If not for him, she'd still be here.

"Mine too," he said.

I wrapped the coiled cord absently around my finger, picturing a woman singing to a young boy. It was tough to imagine that someone had loved Tucker like my mother had loved me. I wondered if she was alive. If she was proud of him. If she could forgive everything he'd done because he was her son. I stared at the radio, wishing I'd missed the call after all, but somehow unable to end it at the same time.

"What about you?" he asked. "Find what you were looking for?"

The concern in his tone took me by surprise.

"Not yet," I said, stifling the sudden urge to tell him I was beginning to think we were wasting our time. "We're going to keep looking."

He was quiet for a while.

"I'll call back tonight around curfew. We should be at Grandma's by then."

Curfew was at dusk. He was farther west than us, but it should have been around the same time.

"We'll be here." I clicked the button one more time. "Be careful."

"You too."

The light switched from green to red.

BY the time we caught up with the others, they'd cleared the main drag of the next small town and had begun their initial search of the area. We entered the street behind a two-pump gas station that had been closed in the War, and took shelter from the rain in a small diner that had been stripped clean and now served as a home to a family of raccoons. The radio felt like it weighed a hundred pounds over my shoulder. I was ready to pass it on.

The seating area had been almost completely cleared out, and what was left showed evidence of riots. Only charred skeletons remained of the booths along the walls, and the vinyl floor was blackened and heaped with shattered glass and firewood. It had been a long time since I'd been to a restaurant—during the War, before my mom had lost her job. I couldn't remember what kind of food we'd eaten, but whatever it was they'd brought too much, and we'd sent back half. Such a waste.

My eyes landed on three faded hash marks, scratched into the wooden counter, and immediately I thought of Three, the mysterious head of the resistance that oversaw the smaller branches, the group that was supposed to help us organize against the MM. Sean had told us about it at the Wayland Inn in Knoxville. Rumor was Three was supposed to operate out of the safe house. If they had, they were gone like the rest of it, along with any hope for change.

I stared at the marks again, wondering when they'd been made. Wondering if they were just scratches or something more.

The flimsy kitchen door hung by one clasp, and when I pushed inside, a twisted jungle gym of overturned tables and rusted wires was revealed. A line of cabinets were anchored on the wall. The doors were all open, the insides gutted what looked to be a long time ago. If there had been any survivors from the safe house, they wouldn't have gotten any help here.

"Why don't you rest," I told Rebecca, sitting now on a round seat fastened in front of the bar. "I'll come back and get you before we move on."

"I'm fine," she said in the same petulant tone Billy had used with me earlier that morning. Then, with a pointed look, she rose and backed through the exit.

I resolved to stop trying to be helpful.

The rain had begun slashing sideways, bending the tall palm trees that were already weighted by dead, untrimmed fronds. I stomped my feet; slowing down had spiked a chill straight to my bones. There was something haunting about this place. The salt in the air and the white sand on the asphalt. The heady combination of mold and wild, tropical plants. It was nothing like home.

We kept to the side of the main street, searching for some sign of the others, but they must have gone farther than I'd anticipated. Chase had to be somewhere close; he never would have disappeared without me. Had I been alone, I would have hurried—the wind was less forgiving as the clustered shops gave way to widely spaced homes—but Rebecca was confined to a shuffle.

Down the road something moved, its true shape indistinguishable through the rain. At first I thought it was one of our companions, hunched over a trash can or a discarded piece of furniture, but as we neared the dark shape broke apart into pieces and started creeping in our direction.

"What is that?" Rebecca had lifted her hand to block the rain.

Animals. I didn't know what kind. I squinted only long enough to see they'd picked up their pace before the instinct to bolt raged through me.

"Let's go." I tried to sound calm, but my voice pitched with urgency.

Rebecca couldn't run, so I ducked under her arm, half carrying, half dragging her toward the nearest shelter: a small, one-story home tucked back on a long strip of property. Her body tensed, making it harder to hold on to, and when we hit the gravel drive, I slipped and we tumbled to the ground. The radio, still in the bag, swung off my shoulder and out of my grasp. Rebecca shrieked; her crutches detached from her arms, flung into the brick siding of a one-car garage with a clang. From behind me came a growl, then the gnash of teeth. Desperation pierced through the buzzing in my brain. We weren't going to make it to the door.

A cross between a scream and a sob burst from her throat as she suddenly jerked backward. She clawed into the gravel, arms working frantically to propel her body forward.

"Rebecca!" I swiped her hand but she was yanked out of reach again.

Blood pumping, I scrambled up and lunged for the crutches. My fingers found an edge of metal and I spun around, brandishing it before me like a blade. Beyond its protection were our attackers—dogs, domestic once, but now feral, bone-thin, and pockmarked with scabs. Their leader, a split-eared German shepherd, stalked us in a low crouch, fangs bared and snarling. Another had sunk his teeth in Rebecca's pant leg and was shaking his head from side to side as if trying to tear the limb free. The fabric ripped, and she heaved herself under me.

Without another thought, I hauled back and swung the crutch as hard as I could. It connected with a crack to the side of the leader's head, eliciting a pained yelp and then a moan so pathetic it made my jaw ache. The growls from the others ceased, and in those seconds something wound in the back of my shirt and yanked me away.

Chase's chest pressed against my back, and over my shoulder his arm stretched out, pointing a gun in the direction of the dogs. His other arm wound around my waist and before I could find my balance he was dragging me up the porch steps. Sean was already there with Rebecca, and when I glanced back into the driveway, I saw the other crutch half submerged in a muddy puddle of water. The dogs were gone, as if they'd never been there in the first place.

I shook myself from Chase's hold and fell to my knees beside Rebecca. The house shielded us from the wind, the awning from the sky, and as the tremors faded I realized I had become a sponge, unable to hold any more water. It dripped off me from the tips of my hair to my matted lashes, from my elbows and my fingertips and the jeans that now stuck to my legs.

Chase surveyed me carefully, but his eyes widened as they lowered, and he purposefully looked away. Quickly, I pulled the shirt away from my skin, realizing it was now painted on, the outline of my bra as clear as a print on the fabric.

"The radio," I said with a wince. "I dropped it." I hoped it wasn't broken. Chase nodded and went to find it before I could make my trembling legs move down the steps.

"Did it bite you?" Sean was feeling his way down Rebecca's leg, but she slapped his hand away as he neared the ankle. The denim that had been torn away revealed the heavy plastic supports she wore beneath her pants.

"It didn't break the skin," she said. Her face was pale as death, her eyes still roaming over the yard searching for the pack of dogs.

Chase bent to retrieve the crutch, which now bowed like a tree in the wind. Guilt swamped through me. Walking was hard enough for my roommate when both of her crutches were in working order.

He glanced warily at Sean, who looked at the bowed metal like it had just crushed his hopes and dreams. But instead of being upset, Rebecca clasped her hands over her mouth, and began to giggle hysterically.

I tried to keep my face even, but after a moment the same crazy laughter bubbled up inside of me, too.

"Sorry," I managed. I tried to hold my breath. I didn't know what was so funny.

After a shared look of confusion with Sean, Chase went to bring back the radio and other crutch.

"If you wanted a puppy, you should have just told me," muttered Sean as he started reshaping the one I'd bent.

Chase's brow was furrowed as he returned to the porch. He handed Rebecca the metal brace and removed the radio from the bag. The metal box now had a dent in the top, but the red light was still flashing, and the cord for the microphone was still connected. I sighed, relieved.

"It was my fault, going so far ahead. We'll stick together from now on," Chase said, tucking the radio back inside the bag.

I forced my mouth to straighten. "I had it covered."

"Yes," he said with a reluctant smirk. "You did."

Rebecca cleared her throat. "We were so far behind because the other team called."

Chase looked to me, brows raised. While I told them what Tucker and I had discussed, he watched me closely, seeming to read my reactions more than listen to my words. I didn't tell him I'd brought up my mom; I didn't have to. He knew the conflict I faced every time I spoke to Tucker.

"Well, that sounds awkward," said Sean.

"Thanks," I said. He gave a short chuckle and threw his arm around my shoulder, just for a second until he caught Rebecca's hurt expression and quickly stepped away. I tried to remember the last time I'd seen him touch her so easily and couldn't.

When my pulse had finally slowed, and Rebecca was back on her feet—if somewhat crookedly—I followed the others inside. It seemed strange that they didn't have to break the lock. It was the first house we'd come across where the door was already open.

Even in the rain the stench that burst from within was unbearable. I hiked up the collar of my shirt around my nose, fighting the urge to throw up, and tried not to think about the oil spill on the beach.

The front living room was completely preserved in its original state, evoking such a strong pang of nostalgia my chest clenched. The couch may have been covered by a thin skin of dust, but the pillows were still at perfect angles, and on the coffee table in front of it were three pre-War magazines, the pages warped and faded, but still readable.

I could imagine a steaming mug of Horizons hot chocolate on the table.

A wax candle, flame flickering.

My mother, toes curled under the back cushion.

I was vaguely aware of Chase, rifling through the kitchen, and the sound of drawers opening and closing.

I picked up one of the magazines and flipped through the pages, looking at the pictures of happy women, sexy women, clad in swimsuits and revealing clothes the FBR would later ban as immoral. There were articles on the pages; I didn't read them, just scanned the print. It had been so long since I'd read something not sanctioned by the MM.

"WHERE'D you get that?"

My mother grinned, her eyes bright with mischief. She flipped through the pages of the worn magazine as though she was really interested, not just trying to get a rise out of me.

"Might have picked it up from one of the ladies at the soup kitchen." She pursed her lips.

"Might have," I repeated with a frown. "You know we've got an inspection coming up." The MM hadn't been through in almost a month. We were running on borrowed time. Every day this week I'd checked the house before and after school to make sure nothing contraband was lying around.

"Oh, live a little," she said, rolling up the magazine and smacking me on the arm. "You wouldn't believe the stuff they used to write in these things." She wiggled her eyebrows.

Don't ask. Don't ask.

"What kind of stuff?" I asked.

Her smile was triumphant. "Oh, you know. Just your run-of-the-mill treason."

MAKEUP tips. Gossip about movie stars. And sometimes mixed in, political stories about the rise of the Federal Bureau of Reformation. Concerns about President Scarboro's moral platform, and what that meant for women's rights and religious freedom. The writers snuck those stories in between glamorous photo shoots and new fashions. They never advertised them on the front covers. They must have known the danger of what they were writing, even then.

"What are you looking at?" Rebecca asked.

I fought the sudden urge to keep it for myself and take it with me. The memories were too sharp: going home after the arrest, learning that all my things had been taken by the MM. My best friend Beth had managed to snag only a few items—one of my mother's magazines that we'd later lost in the tunnels in Chicago among them. It seemed wrong to take this now, when it could mean so much to someone who might one day come back.

Still, it hurt to hand it over to Rebecca.

I winced at the tracks my boots left over the carpet and

wandered down the hallway toward the back rooms, bypassing the kitchen.

The bedroom door squeaked as I pushed it open. Just inside was an antique wooden dresser, covered with a doily and a small silver comb. I cringed at my reflection in the round mirror atop it—my cropped hair flat and fading back from black to brown, my skin too pink from the sun.

And then, beside me in that reflection, I saw the two bodies lying on the bed, and screamed.

CHAPTER
3

DEAD. Inhuman. Brown shells of skin and lips drawn back into leathery snarls. Holes where there should have been eyes. Painted skeletons dressed up in moth-eaten clothes.

My heel caught in a floor rug and I stumbled backward into the wall. It knocked the wind out of me, or maybe I didn't have any to begin with, because when I tried to swallow another breath I couldn't.

The bodies were moving now, coming alive on their floral comforter. A whispering, scuttling sound, and the clothing shifted. I was paralyzed, my muscles frozen. I'd landed near the foot of the bed, and watched in horror as a faded pink house slipper twisted slightly on its boney ankle and then slid off an old weathered foot as if pulled by some invisible hand.

From the slipper erupted a legion of roaches, each the length of my thumb, flowing like lava from a volcano.

I scrambled backward into the hallway, then leaped to my feet. Chase appeared, saying my name, but I couldn't hold on to it. I stared past him through the door, to Sean, who'd arrived moments after Chase, now grimacing over the bodies. They weren't moving. It was the roaches that were moving. Hundreds of them. They were everywhere.

I jolted back, swiping my hands down my arms, shaking out my hair. My skin itched like they were on me, under my clothes and on my neck and in my shoes. *Get them off get them off get them off.*

Chase grabbed my face between his hands, and finally my gaze locked on his. There was a steadiness there that grounded me and slowed my pulse.

"Why are they here?" I asked, suddenly angry at them—the dead people. They shouldn't have scared me. I'd seen worse. *Much* worse.

"Let's go get some air," he said.

I peeled his fingers away.

"Why didn't they clear out like everyone else?" There wasn't any sign of violence; it was like they'd laid down to sleep and not woken up, and for some reason this bothered me even more.

"I don't know."

"They should have evacuated." The government had cleared this area years ago.

I swiped at my arms again, feeling the tickle on my skin.

"Maybe they didn't want to." He chewed his bottom lip, looking into the room.

His words shifted my fear to something more solid, something stronger. I'd had it backward. These people hadn't given up, they'd made their stand. Maybe that was all we really got: a choice to control our own fate.

"I hate roaches," Sean was saying. "They'll eat anything, you know. Glue. Trash. Fingernails. They even eat each other. Roach cannibals. Disgusting."

Chase gave him a look. "Sean."

"They can survive without their heads. I bet you didn't know that."

"Sean," said Chase. "Let it go."

"Right."

Behind them something had caught my eye. On the floor, where the shoe had landed, a strip of silver peeked out from beneath the thin bedspread. Chase stepped aside when I gave his forearm a small squeeze.

"There's something under the bed," I said.

Sean, pale and damp with sweat and rain, gave a grunt and motioned toward the bodies.

"After you," he said "I like my fingernails just fine where they are."

Mouth pulled tight, Chase kicked the shoe out of the way and then swept his leg beneath the mattress, knocking out a tarnished silver box the size of a briefcase but twice as thick, with a combination lock. Roaches crawled up his legs and he hastily brushed them to the floor.

I asked, "What do you think it is?"

"Something good," said Sean. "Otherwise it wouldn't be locked."

Chase knelt and tried to pry it open, but to no avail. The contents inside slid and clanked together as he carried it out into the hallway, where the stench was not so intoxicating.

"Maybe we should leave it," I said, feeling suddenly like we were desecrating a tomb. Chase had kept a wooden box in his old house filled with memories of his life before the War: pictures of his family, his mother's wedding ring, which I knew he still carried in his front pants pocket. The thought of someone rifling through his things like we were about to do here made something pinch inside of me, but it wasn't enough to stop.

"No way," said Sean, taking the case. He spun the tiny rusted numbers, but the box remained firmly closed.

Chase rubbed the back of his neck. "Might be something worth trading."

"Might be something worth keeping." Sean glanced up to where Rebecca was now peeking around the doorframe. "Pain meds or something."

"Might be filled with more cockroaches," I said. Sean's hands snapped back. He gagged, and then reached for the case again.

"Just bugs," he muttered. "Men aren't afraid of bugs. Not even if they have tiny little heads and giant shiny bodies."

Voices outside distracted us from our find and drew us to the front door, where a figure appeared in the rain. Though Jack waved from the garage, I was reluctant to step down into the driveway. The pack of dogs was still absent, but that didn't mean I didn't feel them, lurking in the shadows.

"Looks like they found something," said Rebecca. She placed an assortment of cups she'd gathered from the kitchen on the railing, where each immediately began filling with rain water. I grabbed one and rinsed my mouth clean of the sour taste that had gathered there, grateful Rebecca had thought of it.

"They're not the only ones," I muttered.

Jack, grimacing against the weather, carried a wooden crate toward the house. It was heavy from the looks of it; he rested it against one hip as he heaved it through the rain. Billy followed, his T-shirt clinging to his pale, skinny chest. In our rush toward shelter, we hadn't even thought to search the garage.

"Not bad, huh?" asked Billy, dropping his freight onto the warped deck. Inside the box were a dozen rusty cans of food. My eyes grew wide; my empty stomach rejoiced.

"It's a Horizons truck," said Jack. He didn't seem happy about it. He didn't seem happy about anything since Chicago had fallen—not that there'd been much to celebrate. "All the other houses on this street have been stripped clean."

Rat was the last to arrive, an enormous green raincoat slung over his shoulders. He stroked the sleeves smugly.

"Can we drive it?" I asked. Rebecca could ride inside while we searched the beach.

"Not unless you have four spares," said Billy. "The tires are flat."

Chase scratched the back of his head. "The town's cleaned out. What's a supply truck doing here?"

"Who cares," said Jack, puncturing a can of peaches with his knife. Rust crumbled off the top. The juice dribbled down his stubbly chin as he slurped up the contents.

"No, he's right," I said. "Why are we the first to find this stuff? It's like it was restocked after the evacuation." I'd never seen so much food left in one place. No one I'd met would leave a Horizons truck unchecked unless it had been guarded by government workers.

I glanced back toward the bodies on the bed and shivered.

"Maybe Wallace restocked it," said Billy.

Chase and I shared a worried glance.

"He hijacked tons of Horizons trucks in Knoxville." Though Billy shrugged, his eyes had brightened. "Maybe he knew we were coming," he added quietly.

I wasn't sure what to say. The cans had clearly been here for years.

"Or maybe he's dead," said Jack bluntly. He motioned toward the garage. "Didn't I tell you to get that other box?"

I scowled at him as Billy slumped and headed back into the rain.

"What?" he asked. "Like you're not all thinking it."

"Shut up, Jack," I said.

I didn't know who had left the food, but it couldn't have been the safe house survivors. They wouldn't have had a chance to gather supplies before the bombs hit—they'd be scavenging, just like us.

"Looks like you found something, too," said Rat. Behind me, Sean was in the midst of swinging the lockbox into the side of the house. It hit the side of the house with a *thunk*.

Just over his shoulder, beside the front door, was a single black metal number marking the address. It was coated with a thick layer of rust and corroded around the edges.

Three.

Chase nodded toward the door. "It was guarded by a couple of stiffs."

Rat scrunched up his pointy nose. "Still juicy?"

"No," I said, wanting to rid the image from my mind forever.

Sean shook the box, and from within came a metallic clatter. "I tried messing with the combination. Maybe we should just shoot it open."

"Three," I said aloud. The others paused, and faced me.

"There's four numbers," said Sean.

Chase saw what I had seen. "Then try zero, one, one, one. Or three zeros, and then a three," he said.

Sean did. The latch clicked open.

Inside was a handgun and a box of ammunition. We all stared in awe for a full beat before Jack reached to retrieve it. He pulled back the slide; there was already a round in the chamber. The consequent click made me jump.

"Your pal stashed this here, too," Jack told Billy, who'd returned with another box. "He's inside waiting for you."

Billy glanced through the door, red in the face. Chase gave the Chicago leader a hard look as Rat chuckled.

"Leave him alone," Chase warned. His focus turned back to the gun. "Ember's right, someone's been here. Whoever left the gun did it recently."

"Why do you say that?" Sean asked.

"The slide's clean, no catch," he answered. "Unless someone just wiped it down, there's no way the dust and humidity wouldn't have clogged the mechanism."

Jack's brows lifted. He tapped the side of his temple with the barrel of the gun.

Time stopped.

"Always thinking, aren't you?" He snapped his fingers at Billy, and then shoved the gun in his direction. "No hard feelings, right Fats?" He'd called Billy this since they'd met.

Hesitantly, as if waiting for a joke, Billy took the gun, then fitted it into the back of his waistband, the way Chase did.

Jack laughed, and said, "Who's the big man now, huh?" My teeth ground together.

"Think it was them?" asked Sean. "Three?"

I stepped back to the doorway, giving Jack a wide berth. My blood began to hum as I traced the "3" with my fingertips. A Horizons truck of supplies. A gun, hidden in a house marked by the same sign of the resistance. These things had been left for someone.

I remembered what Sean had told me weeks ago in Knoxville—that the carriers received messages from Three at the safe house to take to the other branches. Rumor was that their base was in the same location, but no one seemed to know for sure. Maybe it was a coincidence, but what if Three had used this house as a checkpoint of sorts? A place to stash their supplies? Someone had clearly been here recently, which meant that someone from Three might still be alive, and if so, we needed to find them. If the resistance branches could unify we could strike back at the MM, and we needed Three's intelligence to do so.

Rat and Jack were mumbling something to each other warily.

"What?" I asked. "If they survived, they can help us."

"Like they helped us in Chicago?" spat Jack. "We had Three contacts scattered around the city. In uniform, even. And where were they when the tunnels fell, huh?"

My shoulders rose defensively. Sure, Three was illusive, but I'd never heard anyone in the resistance openly talk bad about them.

"We're all on the same side," I said.

"Don't kid yourself, sweetheart," said Jack. "Three's on their own side."

Thunder cracked, and white lightning split the sky. The rain slashed against the roof. In the distance, thunder rumbled, on and on, like it would never stop.

Maybe Jack was right. Even if Three had survived, hope that they would help was probably just a dream. We couldn't even find the tracks that had left the safe house ruins, much less the rebel kings.

When the final two guys on our team had returned from checking the other houses, I told them all about Tucker's call. That seemed to ease some of the tension. Because Tucker had already spoken to me, they decided I should be the one to continue to answer, that way in case anyone was listening they wouldn't know how many were in our group. Despite Chase's silent reservations, I wrapped the radio back up in plastic and hoisted it over my shoulder.

We moved on after that. I followed Billy, who made his way down the center street, a dinner plate held over his head like a halo, blocking the rain. The handle of the gun rested against his lower back, molded beneath his wet T-shirt.

We spread out for the remainder of the afternoon, spearing through the woods, tromping through the sand. The sky drew back to a thin layer of white, and my clothes grew tough and chafed my skin. Blisters crowned my feet, but we didn't rest. Slowing would have turned the questions from a whisper to a shout: Where were we going? Who would we find? Chase felt it, too. He didn't have to say anything; I could see it in the way his fists clenched, the way his gaze rested on nothing, always moving.

As we entered an old state park, the beach gave way to swamps and marshland. Twisted trees blocked our path, their white roots like long, spindly fingers diving below the murky water. We carved a single-file line down a trail forged long ago and abandoned before the War, slapping at the mosquitos that buzzed in our ears as our heavy footsteps crashed through the brush.

Our party thinned. Rebecca and Sean had fallen behind again, and to keep them connected to the others, Chase and I slowed our pace, isolated in the middle of the train. We weren't about to leave our friends defenseless, but we couldn't lose track of the others, either.

When it seemed the path had been completely lost, we rested beside a stream to wait for Sean and Rebecca. The light was dimmer beneath the trees, and a curtain of vines and foliage created an isolated cove. We sat on moss-covered rocks and split a can of oily tuna and powdered mashed potatoes, silent, but for our thoughts. I nearly cried with relief when I took off my shoes to shake out the sand and dipped them in the cool, clear water.

After a while Chase rose and waded in. Facing away, he squatted low to dip his hands in the stream. He took a drink. Then pulled his shirt off over his head.

My cheeks warmed. I thought I should avert my eyes but I couldn't look away; he knew I was here, but still it felt like I was intruding on something private. There was something different about him—in the bow of his head and the way his arm fell slack—that made my heart ache.

He stood, wrung out the shirt that he'd dipped in the water, and scrubbed it over the back of his neck. The muscles of his shoulders shifted, rolled, made winged blades as he lifted his arms. A raised scar cut from the side of his ribs to his spine. The light that filtered through the trees glinted off the metal handgun tucked in the waistband of his jeans.

Before I could stop myself I was moving forward, shocked back to reality by the sound of the splashing water around my ankles.

He turned to face me, his emotions guarded. I swallowed, aware of how his eyes moved between my eyes and my lips.

A beat passed. Then another.

"How'd you get that scar?" I asked.

One brow arched.

I flattened my palm over his back. At my touch he siphoned in a sharp breath and twisted away, shaking out his shirt. It couldn't have hurt him. Was he embarrassed? Of the way he *looked?* It seemed impossible.

I placed my hand on it again. This time he stilled.

"I know it's from the MM." I felt the rough skin, the ridges, tracing the map of his body. And waited.

"Two months in I tried to run." A hint of a smile touched his lips. "There was this girl at home. The kind that made you want to try." His smile melted. "I got caught in a fence. Then I got caught by a guard."

My chest tight, my fingertips rose climbing his back, drifting over his shoulder to the puckered scar on his bicep, where he'd taken a knife in my defense outside a sporting goods store. He shivered, watching my hand.

Lower. Goose bumps raised the dark hairs of his forearm. I

lifted his knuckles, tracing the cuts and indentations, following the half circle around the back of his thumb.

"And here?"

"My first fight in the FBR," he said, voice strained. "The guy bit me."

"Like this?"

Gently, I lifted his hand to my mouth. And bit down on the calloused flesh of his thumb.

His eyes shot to mine, so dark I couldn't see his irises. There was one weightless moment, the suspension just before the fall. And then a voice rang out through the woods.

"Over here!"

It was Billy—not too far away. A flush crept over my skin as Chase twitched in surprise, then shoved his shirt back over his head. My feet had sunk into the silt and pebbles, making it hard to move. It took some time to get our shoes back on, but after we did the seconds caught up, and we raced upstream to where Billy and the guys from Chicago had gathered.

At first I just saw the animal—a dark, filthy mutt. Pulse spiking, I scanned the area, ready for an attack from the rest, but they were nowhere to be seen. This one was probably an outcast. Closer, I could see its mangy fur, and how its belly was only half the circumference of its rib cage. It was clearly starving.

The dog had managed to step though a can, getting its paw stuck on the sharp, clean edge of the lid as he'd attempted to pull it out. It hurt him; he whined pitifully, then growled, and then whined again. I watched with a cringe as he tried to chew off the trap and found the metal barely rusted. It hadn't been here long.

"I wouldn't if I were you," Chase told Billy when he crouched down and whistled. A low growl emanated from the animal.

"You're *not* me," Billy returned, fire in his glare. "I don't walk away when something needs my help."

Chase dragged a hand over his jaw but remained silent. I wondered if he could still see the flames tearing down the roof of the Wayland Inn, swallowing Wallace whole.

Rat chased the dog away before Billy could approach it, and crouched to pick another recently opened can off the ground. He tossed it to Jack.

"Let's keep moving," I said.

"They're close," said Billy. "They've got to be close. Why do we have to be so quiet? They probably think we're an FBR tracking team or something. We need to call out to them, let them know we're on their side."

Jack was turning in a slow circle, eyeing the bushes as though something might pop out at any moment. The hairs on my neck prickled.

"You ever met the kind of people that live in the Red Zone, Fats?" he asked. "They're not the type you invite to dinner."

Billy groaned. "This is a waste of time! If the survivors don't know we're here, they're just going to keep running!"

"Keep it down, kid," said Rat dismissively. But part of me agreed with Billy. If there were survivors, they were either running from us scared, or not aware that we were pursuing them.

Billy pulled the gun from his belt.

"No," he said. "I'm sick of you all acting like I'm some stupid kid. Wallace and me were running Knoxville while you guys were still in your pathetic blue uniforms."

My pulse was pounding. "Billy, put the gun down. He didn't mean anything by it."

"Shut *up*, Ember." His voice cracked. "Stop telling me what to do!"

Chase stepped in front of me. A sudden image of the young soldier in the rehab hospital flashed in my mind. Harper—scared, unable to decide whether he should turn us in or let us go. Billy was close to tears, his eyes were tinged with red, and his shoulders were twitching.

"What do you think we should do?" Chase asked. "Tell us, and we'll talk it over."

"This." Billy tilted his chin up and shouted. "Hey!" He swallowed a deep breath. "*Is anybody out there?*"

Jack lunged toward him, but stopped cold when Billy lifted the gun. Blood screamed in my ears. Behind me, I heard Sean swear. Everyone went very still.

Billy raised the gun overhead. He fired once. Twice. The sound shattered the silence. Nearby birds took flight, their wings making a jumbled *thwap* sound. I hadn't realized I'd ducked until the warm mud oozed between my fingers. Rebecca whimpered somewhere behind me.

"Put it down, Billy," ordered Chase.

"Or what?" Billy's voice was eerily calm. He did lower the gun, but there was something different about him, something that gave me chills.

He placed the gun in his waistband and gave me a strange look, as if I were the crazy one because I was on the ground.

No one asked him for the gun.

"You're nuts, you know that, Fats?" asked Jack. He cracked a smile for the first time since before the tunnels had fallen. "You would have liked it in Chicago."

"Yeah," Rat said with a nod. "Yeah, he would have."

We moved on.

CHAPTER
4

IT was just after sunset when the second transmission came through. We had practically collapsed in the small clearing, collectively famished and exhausted. I'd tried to connect with the mini-mart again, but no one had answered. Either the battery in their radio had finally crashed, or they'd simply turned it off to save power.

When the blinking red light on the transceiver turned green, the others jumped into action. They gathered around where I knelt, creating a canopy of faces that looked down on me expectantly. With a surge of adrenaline, I unraveled the cord to the handheld microphone, dialed the knob to the correct frequency, and pressed the RECEIVE TRANSMISSION button.

"Go ahead. We're all here."

A wave of static came over the line.

"Is it too redneck to say you look sexy operating a radio?" Chase said quietly enough so that only I could hear. I was glad to see some of the worry erased from between his brows.

"You should see what I can do with a nightstick."

He smirked, both of us remembering the time I'd clocked him in the side while swinging blindly to defend us from thieves.

The expression disappeared as Tucker's voice came over the line.

"Find anything yet?"

The marshland was alive with the buzz of insects and the croaking of frogs, and the others tightened the circle around the radio and me so they could hear.

I pressed the button on the microphone. "Not yet. Did you get to Grandma's house?"

"They should be in Virginia," said Chase. "That's where they said they were heading first. Somewhere near Roanoke." Sean nodded.

"Yeah. But she's not home."

The anxiety settled over us, heavy and palpable. My mind flashed to the Wayland Inn burning, to the Chicago tunnels bombed. Was our team's first stop already discovered, or was there simply no one there?

"What's that mean, not home?" asked Jack. He gestured for me to hurry up. "Ask already."

"Where is she?" I asked.

"Not sure," Tucker answered. "The house is still there, but no one's inside. Our friend with the dental problems went to ask some questions."

"Truck," said Jack. "That has to be who he's talking about." Truck, the big musclehead carrier we'd met in Chicago, was missing a few of his front teeth. He and Jack were friends.

"How long has he been gone?" I asked. Chase nodded his encouragement.

There was a long pause. So long I thought maybe the line had been disconnected.

"Awhile. He said he'd be back by now. The other driver went to look for him."

Tubman, the other carrier who we'd met in Knoxville. This seemed like a bad plan—Truck and Tubman were the people who carried messages between the resistance posts. If they were gone, the rest of the team wouldn't know where to go.

"Something's wrong," said Rat.

"Any signs of trouble?" I asked.

Another pause.

"Got to go," Tucker said hurriedly. "I'll call tomorrow at dawn."

"Wait. What's going on?"

The line went dead. After a moment, I let the microphone fall into my lap. For a few seconds, no one said anything, then everyone spoke at once.

"Should have gone with them," Jack was saying.

"Bad idea," said another guy. "They'll be strung up for this, you know they will."

I had a sick feeling in my stomach. Chase took the microphone from my lap and wound the cord around the handle.

"What do you think?" I asked.

He shook his head, his expression dark. "I think we need to move on."

He was right; exhausted as we were, it did no good sitting around stewing over Tucker's call. We had to press on, even if it was only to verify there was no one who'd survived. We had to get back to the mini-mart. People were still depending on us. I kept the radio close though, just in case Tucker decided to call back.

At the end of the clearing was a raised walkway—left over from the national park—that crossed over a marsh to the woods on the other side. The boards were rickety, missing in chunks, and the handrails were mostly disintegrated.

Billy climbed the first step. It groaned beneath his weight.

"Hey, Fats," said Jack. "Send a lightweight to test the bridge. You break it, no one's getting across."

Billy stepped back, grinning. "Rat, you're up."

Something stirred in the water. When I held my breath I swore I could hear the snap of jaws.

Rat swore. "Why don't we just go around?"

"Scared the swamp monster's gonna get you?" chided Billy. "Bunch of babies."

It was Rebecca that had spoken. She pushed between Billy and Sean and hoisted herself up the steps, relying mostly on her braces. Sean went after her, but when he grabbed her arm she shook him off.

"See?" She was breathing hard when she reached the top, and shoved the sweaty hair back from her forehead. "It's fine."

I bounced on my heels, waiting for Sean to follow, but he didn't. He grumbled something I couldn't make out, but stayed put as she took a few careful steps out over the water.

I wanted her to stop, for someone else to do this. It was risk enough without her stiff legs and uneven gait; she wasn't even strong enough to react if her footing gave way. This wasn't the right time to prove herself, and I was just about to go after her myself when I saw the grim determination in her face. She needed this.

It took a great deal of restraint to hold myself back. I scarcely breathed as I watched her take each careful step over the rickety boards. She made it ten feet, then twenty, and then went farther, and farther, until she was halfway across. There, she stumbled, and I bit down hard on my lower lip as one leg fell through a gap to her knee. A board came loose and splashed into the water below, but before any more followed, she caught herself on the braces, and hoisted herself back up. She took another step, as if it had never happened.

I almost cheered. Somehow this had become a test, and she was beating it.

"Looks like gimpy's useful after all," said Jack.

"Yeah, as gator bait," snickered Rat. Billy's shoulders jostled as he laughed along.

I was so infuriated that I didn't see Sean lunge across me to tackle Jack until it was too late.

Too late to shove myself out of the way, I was sideswiped by a stray punch and fell back, scraping my hands on the pebbly ground. Beside me, Sean pummeled Jack with his fists, his face contorted with rage. When Chase tried to intervene, Rat and one of the others shoved him off to the side, and soon they were shoving each other, exchanging heated words.

"Stop!" I tried to rise but a scream, high and terrified, drew my attention back to the bridge to where Rebecca was now fifty yards out. I feared she'd fallen, but she was still upright—at least until a moment later, when she collapsed against the boards and curled into a ball.

"Rebecca!" I called, but Sean had already detached himself from Jack and was scrambling up the stairs. I followed him up the first two steps before the wood bowed and gave way beneath his right foot. He grabbed the guard rail, barely staying upright. Pieces of mushy wood splashed in the water, eight feet below him.

Rebecca screamed again, and my blood ran cold.

Something was wrong. From where I was I could see her, hugging an upright post, her head down close to the deck. A moment later a crack split the air; its reverberations slapped off the water.

Someone was shooting at us.

"Ambush!" I heard Jack yell. I tore my horrified gaze away

from Rebecca, stuck on the walk, to search for Chase in the sudden commotion behind me. I couldn't find him.

Male voices, raised in confusion, belted out conflicting orders. Ducking low, I sprinted back toward the woods, dropping the bag with the radio in my rush to find cover. Rat, face pale with panic, shoved past me, sprinting down the trail in the direction we'd come. I dove behind a fallen tree, and flipped onto my belly to peer out from beneath it. Chase was across the clearing, back pressed to a tree trunk. His gun was drawn and his face tilted skyward, and I braced myself for the possibility that the MM had found us and sent their bombs.

There was too much coverage from the canopy of leaves for a clear view of the darkening sky. The shadows had grown long and deep and played tricks on my mind.

Gunshots followed, yanking my gaze back to the ground. Three, in quick succession: *Pop! Pop! Pop!*

Rebecca screamed again. Sean was trying to crawl toward her, but he was too heavy—the planks beneath him kept breaking.

"Hold on!" he shouted to her.

I was light enough to follow her; it had to be me.

I strained my eyes for any sign of our attackers. Was it soldiers? We could have come across anyone here in the swamps—holdouts from the evacuation, refugees, even the survivors. In the failing light no one would be able to see anything. I cursed Billy for firing his gun earlier in the afternoon. He'd given our attackers the advantage. He'd drawn whoever it was right to us.

In the clearing our belongings were scattered across the ground. Billy lay in the center, curled in a ball, arms wrapped around his head. Jack had ducked behind the walkway's broken steps. He fired his weapon in the direction of the swamp.

The reeds were moving, the water rippling to the shore. The whole marsh seemed to bend to the breeze making it impossible to tell where our attackers hid, but from the sound of the sloshing water they were close, maybe twenty yards away. Moving closer by the second.

And then a black, shapeless shadow clinging to a support beam below the bridge burst over the edge of the deck and wrapped itself around Sean. I made out the figure of a man, and the flash of something metal, but before I could scream for Sean to watch out he dragged them both into the swamp with a huge spray of water. There was a struggle, and the black murky shell bubbled and churned, and finally went still. Sean didn't surface.

I opened my mouth to call his name, but no sound came out. One breath, two, and I heaved myself up. Something whizzed by, implanting in the dirt right in front of me, and I staggered back. I looked down, but all I could see was a small gray pebble.

I hit the ground hard, Chase's body sheltering mine.

"Get back," he growled in my ear.

A male cry, and from under Chase's arm I saw a body fall. Jack. In his surprise, he released the gun, which went skidding across the ground in my direction. He landed on his side. A knife was lodged in his leg, and he grimaced at it for one full second before baring his teeth and pulling it free with a grunt and the sickening sound of tearing skin.

The light was fading, aiding the ambush. The hollow clacking of reeds came from the water and was met by the crash of breaking branches behind us in the woods.

Two, then three shadowed bodies sprung from the bushes and leaped on Jack, taking him by surprise. Our attackers were shrouded in dark clothes, their faces caked with mud so that they blended with the night. One kicked him hard in the chin and he fell back, out cold.

We were surrounded.

Chase leaped up and ran toward the water, where a limp figure was being dragged through the brush at the shoreline. I thought I caught a glimpse of the blue printed T-shirt Sean had been wearing earlier. A moment later there was a splash, and Sean was crawling weakly toward dry ground.

Rebecca's name ripped from my throat, but was met with no response.

Grabbing Jack's arm, I tried to pull him backward into the trees, but he was too heavy. Desperately, I crawled forward, fingers digging through the sand for his gun. It had to be close—I'd seen it fly this way. Someone jumped over me. A second later Billy cried out in pain.

My hands closed around something thin and metallic. Not the gun—my fork.

And then I froze. A cold, blunt barrel pressed against the back of my head. Legs straddled me, boots near my hips.

"Get up."

I gripped the fork tightly. My gut turned to ice.

A fist wound into the back of my shirt, and heaved me up like I weighed no more than a child, the man's thick forearm wedged under my chin, momentarily cutting off my air supply. A bright white frame outlined my vision. I gasped.

"Hold!" he called into the dark. Something muffled his words; did he wear a mask? I could feel the stoop in his posture—he had to be a foot taller than me. He smelled rank—of mud and sewage.

I turned the fork in my grasp. Points down.

Gradually the fighting stalled. My captor must have been their leader.

"Why are you following us?" he asked.

I bucked against him and tried to tuck my chin beneath his arm. "Get your hands off—"

His grip tightened.

"Survivors," I gasped. "We're looking . . . for survivors . . . from the bombs . . ."

"Let her go."

I could see only Chase's shadow, but knew the sound of a slide chambering a round.

My captor twitched. "Come closer," he said.

"Shoot him," rasped Jack. "Shoot him now!" He huffed as someone hit him in the gut.

Chase took a step forward, the roll of his boots over crackling leaves deafening to my ears.

"Let her go."

I couldn't see his face, so I knew he couldn't see mine. My only hope was that he would be ready.

I lifted my arm, and with all my strength slammed the fork down into the man's hip. With a grunt of pain he released me and fell back, and in that second Chase charged and took him to the ground.

They scrapped, rolled, a black mass of shadows in a night gone quiet. With a sharp intake of breath, Chase was thrown to the dirt beside me. For a moment I thought he'd been injured—he didn't rise. He didn't *move*. He leaned back on his elbows, eyes wide with shock.

The man rose before us, taller than Chase, gripping his hip with a wince. His clothing and skin were painted with mud; his eyes were glowing black beads. In his hand was a screwdriver, not a gun. The blunt end protruded from his fist.

Hot blood spiked through my veins. I crouched low, ready to pounce, eyeing the fork still lodged in the side of his thigh as it bobbed with each tiny movement of his leg. He removed it with a hiss and dropped it on the ground.

With the back of his hand the man yanked down the filthy bandana that now hung crookedly off of one ear. A clean patch of skin was exposed, gleaming with sweat.

My mouth gaped open.

A twisting snake tattoo stretched from the right side of his collar to just below his jaw, and though it had been years since I'd seen his face, it was one I would never forget.

"Did you stab me with a fork?" asked Chase's uncle.

CHAPTER
5

"CHASE can stay with us. He doesn't even know you!"

My mother's grip tightened around my shoulders. She breathed out my name, almost a warning but too soft.

"He knows me, don't you, nephew?" Chase's uncle leaned against our living room wall as if to hold it up. He probably could, too. He was big enough. "I came to your birthday party."

Chase stood in front of the couch, where he'd been for the last fifteen minutes, since Jesse had arrived. He was still wearing the green T-shirt he'd had on when the cops had told him his parents and sister had been in an accident, two days ago. It was wrinkled now; the collar was all scrunched up.

"I was five," he mumbled, staring at the feet that had grown two sizes since summer. "That was nine years ago."

"Well. Time flies when you're having fun." Jesse flicked back his long, loose hair, and beneath it appeared the black ink tattoo of a snake, twisting up his neck.

I stared at it. "Chase's mom said you went to jail."

"Ember." My mother tried to pull me back, but I jerked away and attached myself to Chase's lanky arm. He looked down at me with a small smile, but the arm I was holding tightened against his body as I squeezed.

Jesse grinned. Grinned like I was funny or something. It made my stomach hurt. I didn't like him at all.

My mother cleared her throat. "We're both attached to Chase, Mr. Waite. We'd be happy to work something out so he can finish school with his friends."

Jesse snorted. "No offense, lady, but he's better off with family."

CHASE and Jesse stared at each other, just as shocked at finding each other as I was.

"What are you doing here?" I finally blurted.

This seemed to snap Jesse out of his trance, and he gave a quick order to his team to withdraw.

His dark eyes found mine. They were similar to Chase's in shape, but hard and cold. His hair was still long, and matted with mud and twigs, as if he'd lived out in the wilderness for years.

"I know you," he said. "You're the neighbor girl."

The neighbor girl. I wished I still had the fork.

He shook his head as if to clear his thoughts and offered Chase a hand. After a moment's hesitation, Chase took it, and found himself smashed in Jesse's embrace. His arms hung loosely at his side, then surrounded his uncle's back, not quite touching him.

"My nephew!" Jesse called into the now silent night. I stood by awkwardly as Jesse pulled Chase back and laughed. "You came. You remembered."

"Remembered?" I asked.

"I told him about this place—well, the safe house. You remember, nephew? I saw you in Chicago. I told you to come here if you got in trouble." Jesse laughed.

I'd forgotten that was how Chase had originally learned of the safe house. He'd run into Jesse during his FBR training in

Chicago. Later, Chase would try to convince me my mother was there waiting. If we'd made it there then, we might be dead now.

Chase's front half was now covered with mud from Jesse's clothes. Though his mouth cracked open, he had yet to say anything. For a brief moment, he met my gaze, and I was reminded of that same, weak smile he'd offered all those years ago, before Jesse had taken him away.

As if suddenly remembering, Chase fished something out of his pocket. I caught a glint of metal from the small silver ring a second before he stuffed it back inside.

"Who *are* you?" asked Billy, approaching from behind me.

Jesse sobered. "We were at the safe house." He held his arms out wide. "We're all that's left."

Immediately the night erupted with questions. More people came from the bushes. Men, women, even a few children. More than twenty of them.

"We were looking for you," Chase croaked. "We followed your tracks."

"Thought you were soldiers come to finish the job," said Jesse. "Hence the warm welcome. Can't see anything in this swamp." When he grinned his teeth stood out in sharp contrast from his dirty skin.

"I told you guys," said Billy.

"Ma?" called Jack, blood dripping down his leg as he hoisted himself to a stand. "Anyone know Sherri Sandoval?"

Billy began shoving through the crowd. "Wallace?"

While the others reunited, a man whose face was still half covered in mud approached me. The radio, or what was left of it, was cradled in his arms. He handed it to me in four separate pieces.

"Sorry," he said. "I think some of it's still back there in the grass."

I looked at the shambles—the cord was severed, the microphone cover ripped off and the wires within sticking out in all directions. The transceiver box caved in at the middle, as though someone had stepped on it. I'd give it to Billy to see what he could do, but I already knew it wasn't going to be fixed.

"Do you have a radio?" I asked the man.

He shook his head. "Everything went down with the safe house."

The first resistance post our team was meeting was empty, Truck was missing, and Tucker was on his own. Why was it so impossible for more than one thing to go right at the same time?

I left Chase and Jesse to their reunion and turned toward the walkway. The moon reflected off the water and provided enough light to show the two figures out in the middle of the swamp. A girl with blond hair, wrapped in the arms of the boy who loved her.

Sean had finally found Rebecca.

WE built a fire that night in a large meadow west of the marsh where we'd made camp. The survivors had food—not a lot, but more than the three cans of peaches we had left. Accustomed to life in the Red Zone, they'd killed a boar in the woods during the storm. An old man with matted gray hair cleaned and cooked it.

In the dark and covered with mud it had been impossible to gauge who was present, but once the fire had been lit and the grime had been wiped clean, we were able to size each other up.

Twenty-three had survived the safe house's demolition. Twenty-three out of nearly three hundred. Chase's uncle was the only family member present, but two women matched the descriptions given to us by their brothers, back with the injured at the mini-mart.

The mood was somber now. Others shared what news they had, but Billy sat by himself away from the fire, using the excuse of fixing the CB radio as a reason to be alone. In a way I was glad I didn't have to look for my mother. My hopes of meeting family on the coast had been laid to rest long ago.

"How'd it happen?" I heard Chase ask Jesse.

Jesse shook his head, his snake tattoo seeming to slither in the flames. I sat cross-legged on the ground a cautious distance away. Behind me, Rebecca laid across the grass, her head on Sean's thigh. He combed her hair behind her ear, oblivious to all else.

"Don't really know," said Jesse. "I was out hunting when I heard it—a whistle, like those firecrackers we used to set off in the summer when I was a kid. And then it was like the War all over again. The shaking and the screaming . . ." He trailed off. "And then the quiet. You remember."

I shuddered, remembering the collapsing tunnels when the resistance had been bombed in Chicago. The way the earth had nearly swallowed us.

"I remember," said Chase.

"Found the others in the wreckage," Jesse said. "A couple on the beach. A couple hiding out in the woods. That guy over there." Jesse pointed to a man sitting alone, staring blankly into the flames. "He carried his dead wife around for half the day. Thought she was just knocked out."

"Please," hissed a woman, rocking a child. "Please, can't you talk about something else?"

I'd had enough, too. I rose and wandered to the other side of the circle, passing a girl who sat with her back to the fire. She was draped in enormous clothes, her bare feet stretched out before her. I was so surprised by her pregnant belly that I nearly stumbled.

"Sarah?"

"Oh!" She shimmied up to her knees and grabbed my hands. "You made it!"

The last time I'd seen her in Knoxville her face had been bruised and swollen, and we'd been loading her into the back of the carrier's truck to send her to safety. I tried to remember when that had been. It felt like months, but it had just been a couple of weeks. After finding what remained of the safe house, I'd been sure she was gone.

I smiled. The marks to her face had faded, leaving pretty dimples. Seeing her gave me hope.

"How did you . . ."

She motioned with her chin over her shoulder. "Jesse. I was out for a walk when it happened. He found me on the beach and brought me with him. He saved us."

I looked back to Chase and his uncle, thinking I might have been too quick to judge him. It had been a long time ago that I'd met him, and this world had a way of changing people.

Billy stalked by on his way toward the food, but when he saw us talking he slowed. I motioned him over. To my surprise, he joined us.

"Nobody's got a radio," he said. "I thought I might be able to salvage parts and rig something strong enough to connect to the interior, but . . ." He shrugged.

Maybe it was better Tucker's team couldn't reach us. Since only twenty-three people had survived, it wasn't like we had a lot of good news to share.

When I looked over at Sarah, she was straightening her sweater. Billy glanced up, then shoved aside his greasy hair.

I'd forgotten they'd never met. "Billy, this is Sarah."

He waved awkwardly. Neither of them spoke.

"Okay," I said, hiding a smile. "I'm going to check on the food."

We didn't have plates or utensils, but it hardly mattered. The old man who'd cooked the boar cut off chunks with a butterfly knife and handed me a piece on a broad, heart-shaped leaf. There was only enough for two grisly bites, but it was better than nothing. I took another piece for Chase.

He was still sitting on the grass with his arms draped loosely around his knees. His slumped posture and tapping heel made me tense. He took the food with an absent nod and scooted over to make room.

"Everything okay?" I whispered, sitting beside him.

Jesse jabbed into the fire with a stick and grinned. "My nephew and I were just talking about the good old days."

"Oh?"

Chase stared into the fire. "Nothing important."

"Come on," said Jesse. "Tell her about that time you stuck up that guy inside the pharmacy."

Chase glanced at me, then looked away.

Jesse laughed. "He goes into the place shakin' like a leaf, knife ripping a hole through his shirt pocket. First-time jitters had him so worked over." Chase smirked, but his heel was digging into the dirt. I bit down on the inside of my cheek. "He came back outside, no meds, no knife. Nothing but a black eye the pharmacist gave him." Jesse was doubled over now, wiping a tear from his eye. "Boy, were you soft back then."

I knew Chase's education during the War had been unique; he'd stolen cars and learned to fight—things that had kept us alive. But I'd never heard the details of how he'd learned. I didn't think I wanted to hear them from Jesse's perspective.

"Not soft anymore." Chase slung a broken branch into the fire.

Jesse stalled, and leaned back against a felled tree trunk. The dried berries he flicked into the fire popped like tiny gunshots.

"Is that right," he said quietly. "So you're a man now."

I didn't understand what they were talking about at first, but the pain was coming off of Chase in waves, and it wasn't hard to figure out he was thinking about Harper again, and what had happened in the hospital in Chicago.

The flush hit my cheeks like a slap. "*That* doesn't make you a man," I said.

"It does in this world," said Jesse. He sized me up with his gaze. "I saw you with that fork, neighbor. Would you have had the courage to stick it in my heart?"

I didn't realize I was leaning forward until I felt my elbow bump Chase's. "I got it in your leg, didn't I?"

A slow, dangerous smile spread across Jesse's face. It made me wonder what he'd done that had forced him to go into hiding.

I looked to Chase to back me up, but he was staring through the flames as though he wasn't even listening. I placed my hand gently on his knee. He shuddered, as though waking from a dream, and wiped his palms on his jeans. Jesse watched us curiously.

Across the fire, Jack's tall form stooped to talk to a small gathering of survivors. After a few moments, he rose and moved to Billy and Sarah. Billy stood and made his way to another group as Jack limped in our direction.

We stood. Jack picked at his teeth. What looked to be a T-shirt was tied around his leg.

"Rat's gone missing," he said. "A few of us are going back to the bridge to see if he's there."

It wasn't until then that I remembered that Rat had raced past me in the attack. I'd assumed he'd returned once the fight was over, but apparently he had not.

"He went through the woods," I said, leaving out the part that he'd been running scared. "I saw him during the fight."

"Your *uncle* probably stabbed him. Accidently, of course." Jack tightened the bandage around his leg, then spat into the fire. The flames hissed back at him.

"It was a mistake," said Chase flatly.

"A mistake," Jack repeated. "You choking back there, was that a mistake, too?"

I knew he was talking about the attack—I could still hear his call for Chase to shoot Jesse—but that didn't explain the venom in his tone. My arms crossed over my chest.

"Something you want to say, Jack?" Chase took a step closer.

Jack's lips drew back into a thin line. "If you're not too busy with your family reunion, maybe you could look for our man."

Chase's fingers tapped against his thigh, and I reached for his forearm, feeling the muscles flex beneath my hold.

Jack looked to where we touched, and then back at Jesse. His eye twitched. Without a word, he stalked off toward the bridge. I tried to ignore the punch of sympathy when his shoulders sagged; not until that moment did I remember him calling for his ma—Sheri something. It wasn't the first time I'd wondered why he hadn't gone with the others from Chicago back to the resistance bases. I figured he'd been burned by the tunnel collapse, scared to go back to the cities, but now I realized he'd hoped someone would be waiting for him out here in the wilderness.

When I turned back, Chase had already torn a strip off his sleeve and tied it around the end of a stout branch to make a torch. He dipped it into the flames, and it crackled as it caught, creating a small glowing ring to light our way.

"Good luck," said Jesse, hardly moving.

"Thanks," muttered Chase.

The woods were dark, and even with the torch held high, the shade swallowed most of the light. We tracked north, cutting sideways through the brush, calling for Rat every few minutes. I stayed near Chase as the echoes of our voices distorted in the woods, coming back like the whispers of strangers, but whenever I got too close he pulled out of reach. I thought of Rebecca—the way she'd looked on that wobbly bridge, the straightness of her back as she'd walked away into the unknown, as if she'd never turn around. A chill shivered over my skin.

"Jack was right," Chase said when we reached the stream. "I choked."

I stepped closer into the halo of light, hating the doubt I saw in his face.

"It ended up being your uncle. It's a good thing you didn't shoot him." I tried to sound convincing, but my lack of enthusiasm for Jesse was shining through.

"It won't happen again," he said. I wasn't sure who he was trying to convince.

So you're a man now, Jesse had said.

I stopped and snagged the back of his shirt before he could walk away.

"You didn't buy all that stuff Jesse was saying, right?" I took a step closer. "I mean, I know he's your uncle, but he doesn't really know you."

Chase shoved his free hand in his pocket. "He knows me better than you think."

"Because he taught you how to steal? Because, why?" I swallowed the lump in my throat. "He shot someone, too?"

Chase exhaled through his teeth.

"Because he knows what it's like digging food out of Dumpsters," he said. "And because he was there when the bombs hit Chicago, and when people went crazy and started looting and fighting and things you don't even want to know."

I forced my eyes to stay on his. "How do you know I don't? You never talk about it."

"I'm more like him than I'm like you," he said, faster now. "I was stealing cars when you were sitting in high school, do you know that? You think the FBR was the first beating I ever took? Or ever *gave*?"

"So you're big and bad, is that it?" The toes of my boots bumped his as I stepped into his shadow. "You don't scare me, Chase, so stop trying to."

He made a sound of disgust and took a step back, staggering and then catching his balance at the last moment. We were standing on an embankment, and when he dropped the torch it extinguished in the water below with a hiss. He stared after it into the darkness.

"I shot Harper," he said. "He almost came with us and I shot him."

"I was there." I saw that hole in the soldier's chest, saw the blood pooling on the floor. "He never would have come."

"Is that what you tell yourself?" he asked. "You know what I tell myself? That he fired first. That it was self-defense." He screwed his thumb into his temple as if to dislodge the memory.

"It *was* self-defense."

"I don't understand you," he said, suddenly quiet. "Everyone else gets it. Jesse got it. My parents. Even *Tucker* got it."

The hurt slashed through me. "Everyone else gets what?"

"That it's me." He looked as if he'd finally figured out what everyone else had known all along. "I screw up everything."

I stood in shocked silence, the air between us thick enough to cut.

"You don't mean that."

He didn't say anything. I would have rather him been angry.

I lifted my hands to hold his face, to make him meet my eyes, but he twisted away. My arms fell slack at my sides.

"I'm not scared of you," I said. "No matter what you say."

I turned, the tears blurring my vision. It was too dark anyway without the torch, and not more than three steps later I slipped, and slid down the embankment into the streambed, rolling once I hit the bottom.

Cold water needled my sensitive skin. The rocks scraped my knees but my chest landed on something soft. My fingers fanned over thin, soaked material, and as I pushed myself up my elbow grazed a patch of hair.

All the air in the world seemed to disappear.

"Ember!"

I rolled to the side and grasped Chase's outstretched hand, jolting out of the water, clawing into the mud and roots below the stream's high bank. The bile rose, sharp and biting in my throat.

"Hey!" Chase sloshed back into the stream and flipped over the body. He crouched, feeling for a pulse, but there was none. I'd already known there wouldn't be.

"Who . . ."

"Rat." Chase stood, swore. "He must have fallen off the bank. Hit his head."

Without a light he could have tripped over the tree roots and plunged the three feet straight down into the stream. Now his skin was bloated and blue in the starlight, and his eyes were dull and blank and lifeless.

He'd died alone. And as I looked at Chase, I saw fear come to life. He stared at the body, frozen, dark stains of water climbing up his pant legs as he stayed ankle deep in the stream.

He'd lost everyone and everything. And if I let him, he would push me away just so he wouldn't have to wait to lose me, too.

"We have to move him," I said. "I'll help you."

CHAPTER
6

I SHIVERED by the fire, knees locked to my chest. The humid air had taken a bitter edge, and my wet clothes clung to my skin. Chase nudged my boots closer to the flames with his toe, watching Jack pace back and forth on the opposite side. Thirty feet behind him, in the woods, they'd buried Rat in a shallow grave.

"Sean said I'd find you over here." Rebecca eased herself down beside me, falling the last six inches with a huff of breath. She placed her braces between us, a solid silver line.

The damp wood crackled. I stared at it, wishing it would stave off the chill inside me.

"Was it awful?" she whispered after a while. "Being the one to find him?"

I glanced her way, noting how she purposefully avoided my gaze. Another kind of cold wormed its way deep in my stomach.

"It was terrible," I said. "I wouldn't wish it on anyone."

Her small mouth twisted into a frown.

"At least it's over," she said quietly.

"For me?" I asked. "Or for him?" I pictured her again, hobbling down the walkway over the murky swamp. If she had fallen in we may not have been able to reach her in time. I had a bad feeling she'd known that when she'd started.

She acted as though she hadn't heard me, but I knew she had. She picked at the grass, one blade at a time, tearing it into little pieces, and I stared at her, fighting the image of her small body lying motionless in the water as Rat's had been. Of her hair, silver in the moonlight, fanning around her head.

I wanted to ask *why?* And *how could you?* And to tell her never, ever to do anything like that again. But I couldn't, because I knew why she had, and that scared me just as much.

"At dawn we're going back to the mini-mart," Jack announced, breaking my train of thought. I turned back to where he'd paused, his face shadowed and dangerous in the red glow of the embers. "We told them we'd be back in five days; tomorrow our time's up."

There was no way we'd make it back in one day. Two maybe, if we didn't break for sleep, but probably three.

"*You* go back then," said the old man who'd cooked the boar. His silver hair feathered out below his ears and he patted it down anxiously. "I'm not going back there. Not ever."

"What about my brother?" asked one of the people from Jesse's group, a lanky girl who believed her brother was laid up in the mini-mart.

"Well we can't stay here." Sean came to stand beside Chase. "What're we going to do? Build tree houses? Live off the land?" Rebecca shifted.

"We've been doing all right that way," objected another man from the safe house. His clothes were covered in grime; he must have been in the party that attacked us. He looked to Chase's uncle, as if expecting backup, but received none.

It struck me that Jesse's seniority hadn't been determined by age; several people here were older than him. He was younger than Chase's mother, maybe only thirty-five. Based on the way he was kicked back against a felled log like this was nothing more than a camping trip, I wasn't sure how he'd been made their leader. He didn't look like the type who wanted to be in charge of the big decisions.

"Looks like you've been doing just great," said Jack. "Least Rat cut out before hearing his folks were part of the ash stuck to the bottom of his boots."

Several people voiced their disapproval.

"He made his choice," said Jesse. The others quieted. "Don't put that on us."

"Maybe I was just putting it on you," Jack said, pointing across the flames.

Jesse took a slow breath. "It wouldn't be the first time someone did."

I rose to my feet. Jack snorted in disbelief, staring coldly at Chase's uncle.

"What *is* your plan?" Curious eyes turned my way.

Jesse stoked the fire, casual as ever. "You're looking at it." He didn't even glance up.

"We can't keep running—eventually we'll run out of land. I learned at least that much in school," Sean said.

"There are lots of empty towns around here. We'll just start over. Build a new safe house," said a woman.

Billy snorted. "You don't have any protection. You tried to take us out with a couple guns and a few kitchen knives. The soldiers have bombs, in case you forgot."

"Forgot?" Sarah asked, pushing herself off the ground. "How could we forget?" She stalked away from him and he watched her go, scratching his head.

"We'll make them pay for it," Billy added. That strange look came over him again, like in the woods when he'd fired the gun into the air. As if the answer was clear as day, and he couldn't understand why no one else understood.

I did understand, though I wasn't sure it helped anything. As much as I tried to focus on our current situation, I wanted the MM to pay. For the safe house. For my mother. For every Statute that had shoved the lot of us out into the wilderness.

"That's the spirit." Jesse laughed mockingly, causing Billy to hunch over his knees. "I'll tell you what, kid. You find a way to rally the people, I'll be right behind you."

"We need a permanent location," interrupted Chase. "Regroup. Refuel. We can't bring our hurt people here."

"What we need is to send a team back," pressed Jack.

"Spread us thin, you mean," said the old man. "Take the strongest of us and leave the rest to fend for themselves. We got kids here, you know." He jabbed a thumb over his shoulder to where three children slept in the grass.

The tension built steadily, each person that spoke up trying to pull the group their way, then biting back at those who disagreed. Their voices rose, waking a little girl, who began to cry. Soon, others were standing, shoving each other and threatening more. All but Jesse, who continued to stare into the fire, unfazed.

"What about Three?" I called, loudly enough that those closest could hear. A few stopped, eyeing me suspiciously, but the boys from Chicago grumbled.

"Forget about it already," said Jack.

"Quiet." Jesse's voice boomed in the night. "What about Three, neighbor?"

Chase glanced back at me and nodded slightly. He was thinking, as was I, of the house in the town we'd passed, and the guarded supplies within.

My palms grew damp. I wasn't chilled at all anymore; the pressure of their stares warmed me considerably.

"Three what?" asked one of the survivors.

This struck me as odd: the rumors we'd heard of Three were that they were based at the safe house, yet none of the survivors apart from Jesse seemed to have any clue what I was talking about.

If Three's base was somewhere else, they might still be out there. They might still be able to fight back. For a moment, the gaping hole I felt in my chest whenever I thought of the safe house seemed to close a little. Alone, we could only scratch at the MM's defenses, but with Three, I felt like we had a real chance of getting their attention.

"We found supplies in the last town," I started uncertainly. "I—we—thought that maybe someone else could have put them there. Someone who survived the blast."

Jesse's gaze was heavy, and unconsciously I moved closer to Chase.

"No one else survived," said Sarah bleakly.

"There are rumors of a settlement down the coast," said Jesse finally.

Stunned silence.

"It's old," continued Jesse. "I'm not sure it's even still there." He stared forward, as if mesmerized by the flames. "Tomorrow we'll head further south. If we don't find them in two days, you're free to take your team back to the safe house. Or what's left of it."

"We're free to?" snorted Jack. "What makes you think—"

"Two days?" interrupted the girl whose brother was still missing. "What about the people you left behind? My brother needs—"

"What do you think?" I whispered to Chase while the others began to argue again. "We're supposed to be back by then."

He nodded, rubbing a crease between his brows with his thumb. "But if we find a settlement, that could mean food, medical supplies . . ."

"Three," I said. He nodded.

"Maybe Three."

As guilty as I felt about stranding the injured, the prospect of finding Three was too big to pass up.

"Just two days," I said. "If we haven't found a radio by then, we go back. Agreed?"

Jesse's eyes traveled from Jack to Chase and lastly to me. He didn't look to his people; maybe he already knew they'd follow his lead.

"Fine," said Jack.

"Agreed," said Jesse.

WE left at dawn.

The morning was much like the days before, only now we weren't looking for empty cans or footprints, we were looking for signs of a permanent settlement, and there weren't just nine of us, there were twenty-six. We could spread out, cover ground faster. With so many to offer protection, we even took our chances on the highway that ran down the coast toward Charleston, South Carolina. There Rebecca and Sarah could walk with more ease, and Jack, nursing the knife wound in his thigh, could hobble slowly behind them.

I watched Rebecca as closely as I could. Something told me not to leave her alone, and every time she branched from the group, I was there, keeping her company. If she noticed what I was doing, she didn't say anything about it.

Jack and a few of the others from Chicago rallied in the back. Their whispering did not go unnoticed. More than once when I neared, their conversations ended abruptly. I worried they didn't mean to keep their word—that they'd attempt to take control, or simply disappear, and after the way we'd been received by the survivors, we couldn't risk more dissension. The silence frayed my nerves. Today's path had been quiet, but there was a prickling at the base of my neck. It felt like we were being watched.

In the early afternoon the bright scent of oranges drew us into an abandoned grove. The trees were weighed down with fruit, and below on the grass were the rotting remains of those that had fallen.

We weren't the only tenants. Squirrels, mice, deer, and cats fled when we approached. In the sky, hawks circled. Hunters, watching from above.

Chase had spent the morning scouting our path, but found me once we stopped. As he approached, I busied myself picking oranges, still keeping one eye on Rebecca across the lane, dozing beneath a tree. In our search I'd been able to distract myself from what had happened last night with Rat, and what had happened before in the woods. But now those things hung between us, heavy and impossible to ignore.

He stood just beyond the reach of the tree, fiddling with something in his hand, as if waiting for me to stop. When I did, he took a quick breath, like he was about to dive into cold water, then stepped beneath the shade, having to adjust his position until he found a place he could stand without hitting his head on the branches.

"I'm sorry," he said.

"For which part?" I hadn't meant to be snide, but the words

still came out that way. When he slumped I placed the oranges I'd gathered at my feet and wiped the juice off my hands onto my jeans.

"The part where I was an idiot," he said, clearing his throat. "I don't want to scare you. Ever."

He opened his hand, and in his palm was a yellow flower—like a rose, but smaller. When I looked at it, he unfurled my fist and placed it within.

I prodded the tender petals—those that had survived his grasp. Most were bent or torn, but it was still beautiful. Something fluttered inside when I imagined him finding it and carrying it for me.

"I think I might be broken." He didn't look up.

I moved closer, feeling his sadness wash over me.

"We're all broken," I said. "We just have to put each other back together."

My loose fist holding the flower came to rest in the center of his chest, locked between us. He leaned down, his forehead touching mine. His eyes closed.

"What if I'm too far gone?"

"Then I'll find you," I said. "And I'll bring you back."

HE told me about the first time he'd had to steal food, and the days after Jesse had left him in the wreckage. Stories from the War. At first he didn't release my hand, and eyed me cautiously, waiting for some sign to stop, but after a while the words began flowing more freely, and as we split an orange he told me funny things, too, about the doomsday prophesiers and the all-night card games he'd play with the other kids at the Red Cross Camps. Before long, we'd polished off another orange, and then a third. We were laughing when Sean ducked under the branches. I shot to my feet, realizing I'd lost track of the time.

"Becca—have you seen her?" Sean's hair spiked in all different directions, as though he'd been pulling on it.

I stepped out from beneath the boughs into the alley between the rows of trees, dread balling in my stomach. Rebecca had been sleeping here just minutes ago, but in my distraction she'd managed to disappear. From the look on Sean's face I didn't have to ask what he was thinking; I wasn't the only one who'd gotten a bad feeling from her stunt on the bridge.

"She can't be too far," Chase said. "She was just here a few minutes ago." It comforted me that he'd been watching her as well.

Sean threw back his head and groaned.

We split up, each taking a different direction through the grove. Behind me, I could still hear the others in our group, but the deeper I headed into the trees, the more muffled their voices became. Soon, there was no more than the cry of the birds and the crunching of the twigs and fallen leaves beneath my feet.

"Rebecca?"

A sudden movement to my left startled me. I twisted, shoes slipping on a piece of black, rotten fruit, and I caught my balance on a low-hanging branch. When I looked again, there was nothing but the gray-brown base of the tree, and a metal crutch leaning against it.

"Rebecca?" My words were muffled by the thick cover. I grabbed the single brace, searching for any sign of her.

A noise from behind had me spinning around, and I found myself looking at a boy whose face was streaked with mud and half hidden behind a wild brown nest of hair. His clothing was odd: he wore no shirt or shoes, and around his hips hung a pleated skirt that stopped just above his bony knees. He wasn't one of the survivors; I had no idea where he'd come from.

"Hello," I said.

He didn't respond. He stared at me, eyes too round, as though he was forcing them open as wide as he could.

"How old are you?" It was a stupid question, and I wasn't sure why I asked.

He held out his hands, making the number seven. My brows pulled together. I would have pegged him at twelve, at least.

"Where is your family?" I asked.

His eyes roamed lower, to Rebecca's silver brace, still in my grip. I stood it up immediately, realizing it probably looked like I was preparing to swing it at him.

"It's my friend's. Have you seen her?" I touched my hair. "She has blond, *yellow* hair. She's about my height."

He turned, and began to run.

"Hey!" I took off after him, deeper into the trees. He was sure-footed in this terrain and gained ground quickly. Finally, I stopped, frustration boiling inside of me. There had been a flicker of recognition in his face when I'd asked about Rebecca, I hadn't made that up.

A branch broke behind me and I turned, a short yelp of surprise bursting from my throat as two more boys—shirtless and smeared with mud like the other one—threw something at me. Trying to block whatever it was, I released the crutch and within seconds my arms and torso were ensnared. When I jerked back, they yanked forward, and I collapsed in a heap.

They'd caught me in a net like I was some kind of animal. It twisted around my legs; the harder I struggled, the tighter the string cut into my neck and face.

"What are you doing?" I shrieked. "Let me go!"

The two boys gathered the end of the net over their shoulders, turned away, and proceeded to drag me over the bumpy ground. The smell of rot and wet soil filled my nostrils as I flipped and my face came in contact with the earth. Through squinting eyes I looked up and saw the boy I'd been chasing keeping pace beside us. He grinned at me with yellow, crooked teeth. I swung to try to kick him, but only managed to flip my-self over again.

"Help!" I shouted. "Help!"

The two boys pulling me stopped. They were older, maybe thirteen, and emaciated. Their ribs rose from the skin, leaving a hollow well where their bellies belonged. They both wore the same stained beige pants, shredded at the ends, and much too tight. An assortment of feathers were tied in their hair.

The boy on the right wheeled back and kicked me in the side. My arms were latched above me by the net; I couldn't even protect myself. The air whooshed out of my lungs and I gasped for breath.

"Shuddup," he said.

They didn't take me far. Soon I heard other voices: Rebec-ca's strident order to be let go and another boy telling her not to move.

I was released in front of my old roommate, who was seated with her legs stacked on their sides in a narrow clearing be-tween two rows of trees. Her face was tight with fury. I forced myself up, but only managed to rest on my elbows as the net had now bound my arms behind my back. A second later, some-one was tossed over the top of me, and the air was once again smashed from my body.

"Sean!" Rebecca cried. He rolled off, rubbing the side of his head, where a thin trickle of blood smeared down his temple.

"Little bastards," he grumbled. There were now three more of them. Eight, counting those who had been here with Re-becca.

Behind us, an argument was ensuing, and I rolled over to

my other side to see Chase surrounded by five more wild boys, all pointing handmade spears in his direction. The look on his face was a mixture of confusion and irritation. When he saw me, his eyes darkened, and a snarl drew back his lips. He attempted to get close, but one of the boys kicked him behind the knees, and with a grunt he fell forward.

"Please tell me you still have a gun," said Sean.

Some of the boys had gathered between us, gasping in delight and exchanging high fives. Based on Chase's expression, the firearm had made it into the wrong hands.

A shot rang out, a deep boom that echoed off the trees. It wasn't the sharp clap of a handgun, but something larger and more powerful, coming from the direction where we'd entered the grove—where the others in our party had stopped to rest.

I didn't remember any of the survivors having a rifle.

Around us the boys had frozen, scarcely breathing, all facing the origin of the sound. At the second shot, they ran, their steps almost silent as if they'd taken flight.

The four of us were left alone in the grove.

"That doesn't sound good," said Sean.

My ears rang as I struggled to get free of the net. Whatever had spooked the boys was still here. In the distance, shouts of confusion filtered between the trees, a haunting warning of the danger just beyond our sight.

Chase reached me, untangling my legs. I winced when the thin strings tightened around my upper body. He bared his teeth and ripped the net, until finally I was able to wriggle out. I scratched the tattered pieces from my skin as if they'd been part of a giant spiderweb and stared down the alley for signs of who had fired those shots.

"That was the survivors, right?" Rebecca asked nervously.

Chase gave me a grim look. *Someone else.*

Sean had been in the midst of helping Rebecca up, but stopped suddenly and let her slide to the ground. She gripped his calves as he stood over her, struggling to see what had caught his attention.

I followed his gaze. Over Chase's shoulder, something black and metallic glinted off a slice of sunlight peeking through the trees.

The barrel of a rifle.

"Chase," I whispered.

As he turned, I stood slowly, shoulder to shoulder with Sean. Chase rose on my other side, his back to me. His waistband, where he'd held a standard issue FBR gun, was empty. I cursed the boys under my breath.

The leaves to my left rustled, and a man wearing a loose tan tunic and cropped pants stepped out into the light. He was cleaner than the boys, with neatly trimmed ginger hair, and old enough to be their father. A shotgun was wedged against his shoulder, aimed at the four of us.

And then they were everywhere. Men. Women. A dozen. Two dozen. More. Some were on horseback. They formed a circle around us and tightened rank, until Chase, Sean, and I were locked in a triangle over Rebecca.

"We should have stayed in reform school," Sean muttered behind me.

CHAPTER
7

WE were ushered up the lane behind the man with the orange hair. He didn't say anything. None of our captors did, but their guns spoke for them, and soon we had rejoined the rest of our party.

More men and women, dressed in the same uniform outfits, had surrounded the others. There was no evidence of the boys—no nets on the ground or pointed sticks. These people were definitely from a different group, and judging by the way they'd rounded up our people, we didn't concern them in the least.

It looked as if we were the last to arrive. Sarah stood behind Billy. Both of them appeared unharmed. Jack was railing a woman for confiscating a set of knives he'd collected. Beside me, Chase craned his neck, probably looking for his uncle. I couldn't see Jesse, but the group was packed so densely it was difficult to tell who was there.

"If you could lay down any other weapons you might have, that would be appreciated."

A man stood before us wearing the same strange, loose clothing—a baggy beige shirt and straight, cropped pants that looked like they'd been hand-patched from someone's old sheets. On his feet were boots, their laces held together by black electrical tape. He spoke without any sense of urgency, as if he had all the time in the world.

As we drew closer, I could see that his chocolate-colored hair was streaked white around the temples, and that his blue eyes were both intense and somehow familiar. At first I thought his face was dirty, but as Chase and I pulled to the front of the pack I could see the scars: a smattering of pink scratches and hooks across both cheeks.

He watched Chase and me, drawing us out of the crowd, and though I wanted to sink back into the others, I stood my ground.

Several men stepped forward, looking exceedingly more dangerous than their leader. Billy reluctantly gave up the gun we'd found at the house and slowly placed it on the ground.

"You won't need those weapons," Jesse bellowed from the center of the group. "We got refugees and children. A pregnant girl and a lame one, too. We're not here to stir trouble."

I huffed at Jesse's assessment of Rebecca, and Sean muttered something I couldn't make out. Beside me, Chase exhaled, out of relief or disappointment, I didn't know.

The man froze, then reanimated as Jesse, previously hidden within the folds of the group, emerged. They appraised each other with a strange kind of challenge in their gazes—Jesse's brows raised as if amused while the leader of the strangers pulled absently at his bottom lip.

"I find that most folks who tell me that usually intend the opposite." The scars on his jaw flexed as he spoke.

Jesse scratched a hand over his chest. "Guess you'll have to take my word for it."

The man turned to where Chase and I stood. His head tilted in curiosity.

"Looks like it's your lucky day," he said. I suspected he was talking about the boys who'd trapped us, but I didn't feel particularly lucky. Then his gaze returned to the group, a slight frown pulling at the corners of his mouth. He was silent for a long moment, and in it I held my breath, feeling too exposed and vulnerable.

"Are you really all that's left?" When no one answered, he nodded gravely. "So it's true. The safe house is gone."

AS the guards lowered their weapons the circle buzzed with whispers. My own blood was humming. How long had they tracked us? We'd scouted the area and posted perimeter guards each night—the possibility of us being watched without knowing it was unnerving.

"My apologies for our lack of hospitality," said the man. "These days it's better to be cautious."

"Who are you?" Chase's voice was raised in suspicion. His hand found mine and tightened.

"They're from the settlement—the one in the South that Jesse was talking about—right?" asked Sarah. She smiled broadly, one hand on her round belly.

"Long as they're not with those crazy kids," Sean said.

The man's mouth twitched.

"I can assure you the boys you encountered are not part of our group, despite our invitations," he answered, leading Sean to stand a little straighter.

This bothered me; I wasn't sure I could trust anyone who spoke of those devil children kindly. Still, I wondered how they'd gotten out here, and who, if anyone, watched over them.

"My name is Aiden DeWitt," the man continued. "We're friendly, despite what it may look like. If you come with me I can offer you a place to stay, food, and protection."

Another surge of whispers. His name was familiar, but I couldn't place it.

"It's the scars," I heard Billy say to someone beside him. "That's why I didn't recognize him. His mug shot must have come up a hundred times on the mainframe."

I remembered then. Aiden DeWitt. *Dr.* Aiden DeWitt. He was one of the five suspects thought to be in collaboration with the sniper, as was I. Instantly, I was back in the Wayland Inn, listening to the FBR report as Wallace adjusted the radio: *Dr. Aiden Dewitt, responsible for the murders of five FBR officers during a routine home inspection.* And then I was on the street, outside the blood donation bus in the Square in Knoxville, and my photo was posted beside his. He'd looked younger when it was taken, maybe forty, and his face had been smooth and free of scars.

News of his attack on the MM and his escape was all the gossip at the soup kitchen five years ago. The crime had occurred someplace in Virginia. My mother even wondered if he might run west, toward our town. As much as the act frightened her, I think she thought of him as a hero. I wondered what she'd think if she knew I was here now, before him.

"Why should we trust you?" Chase asked. "Weren't you just shooting at us?"

"Common mistake," said Jack sarcastically.

DeWitt took a step closer. "Because you're out of other options, Jennings."

Chase's hand gripped mine so hard I winced. My mouth went dry.

"How do you . . ."

DeWitt lowered his gaze to mine. "How do I know you? I know many things." He was speaking softly now, but those closest could still hear. "I know you two need protection now more than ever."

An ice-cold finger of fear traced up my spine.

"You're them," said Sean. "Or him. Whatever. You're Three."

A hand closed in the back of my shirt, and I was surprised to see Rebecca over my shoulder staring evenly at Dr. DeWitt. Seeing her brave like that made me stand taller.

"All in good time," said DeWitt. He backed away without further explanation, then turned and began to walk toward the main road where we'd entered the grove.

"That's ominous," commented Sean.

We followed DeWitt anyway.

It became apparent as we were herded after the doctor that the debris on the far side of the grove had been placed there deliberately. The junked cars and old washing machines on either side of the street created a sieve, one that grew tighter and tighter until we were forced to walk only two or three abreast with those on horseback flanking us. It was a human trap, a strategic move to capture any wanderers between two defensible rows, and though we followed him blindly, I couldn't help but feel impressed.

In front of me, Sarah latched herself to Billy's arm and leaned against him, feet dragging. He glanced back at me, cheeks red, and then trained his eyes straight ahead.

"Any ideas how he knows us?" I asked Chase under my breath.

"One or two," he answered. "But no clue what he plans to do with it."

"Maybe he's just showing off," whispered Sean over my shoulder. "Trying to get in your heads."

"It worked," I said. Nothing good had ever come of Chase or I being recognized.

The road gave way to a fenced area barricaded with parts of cars and houses and mounds of rock and brick and surrounded by a moat that ran the length of the fence like an empty river. Only one narrow strip of ground led to a gate, and it was blocked by a metal sheath and sheltered by an ancient, hunching oak, its branches dripping with gray moss.

As we approached, Dr. DeWitt slowed. I waited with bated breath as he turned to face us, hoping for a proclamation that this was indeed a resistance base.

"We call it Endurance," he said. "Named by our first settlers—a small band of criminals and freaks hunted by the Bureau."

At his callous tone, I felt myself smirk, because he was talking about *us*—all of us, himself included.

"You're tired," DeWitt said. "Hungry. Hurt and angry. We can help you."

Though his words were encouraging, I found myself frowning. There was more to this than DeWitt was letting on— Wallace hadn't been nearly so hospitable when we'd been brought to the resistance base in Knoxville. Three was made up of the most illusive rebels in the country, it made sense that they'd surrounded us and aimed guns at our chests. Offering us food and shelter without even verifying our story didn't fit.

"What about the Bureau?" called the old man from the group of survivors. "What if they send their bombs again?"

A sympathetic smile stretched the scars on DeWitt's face. "Inside these walls you don't have to fear the Bureau."

"What's the catch?" I asked.

Dr. DeWitt glanced up, and as I followed his gaze I saw the gunmen, half a dozen of them, seated in slings in the trees on either side of the gate. Their clothing was the same as the others, only camouflaged to blend in with their surroundings. I wondered how many trees we'd passed that held the same silent watch.

"Only that you protect our secret," said DeWitt. "And that you work. Everyone contributes in Endurance."

With a clank and a squeal of metal, the gate pulled back, revealing an open field, split down the middle by a dirt path. On one side were gardens—rows and rows packed with leafy greens and crawling vines. Bushy plants I didn't recognize, and bright red tomatoes, their tender leaves trembling in the breeze. Against the far wall, men and women, dressed like De-Witt but with broad straw hats, picked sickle-shaped beans hanging from trellises made of old doors and chairs. It was enough to fill my eyes with tears and make my stomach grumble in eager anticipation.

On the opposite side of the path the grass dipped down into a pond, and anchored to the shore by iron posts were two men attending to large mesh boxes. They looked up, but did not seem surprised by our arrival. *Fish*, I heard people whisper. They were harvesting fish. And ahead were pens of chickens, sheep, and goats. Those tending them leaned against the fence, welcoming us with nods and the occasional wave.

Too astounded to do anything but gasp, we entered without a backward glance. Past the gardens and the pond was a white barn. There were horses inside—brown with black noses and manes, dapple gray, and even one that was white with glassy blue eyes. They ran to the fence as we approached, and we all laughed as they huffed and stomped and smacked their lips, expecting treats.

Joy streaked through me, overriding the suspicion. It was better than what I'd hoped the safe house would be. It was better than anywhere I'd ever seen.

"These people are going to eat us," Sean muttered behind

me. "Or use us for fish bait. Or horse food. Something. This is way too good to be true."

If I hadn't wanted it to be true so badly, I might have agreed with him. But since we'd been inside, the guards had holstered their weapons and were trailing the group, joking with one another as if we weren't there at all.

Finally we approached a wide, one-story brick building that stretched back from a simple white stone foyer. A cement pillar rose on each side of the entranceway. They'd once been part of an arch, but now were the connecting points for long clothes-lines from which hung drying wildflowers and braided strings of withered vegetables. Over a boarded front door was painted one word: LODGE. Far to the right a crooked metal pole emerg-ing from the ground had been bolted to the side of the build-ing. It stretched ten feet above the roof.

"This was a school," said Dr. DeWitt. I got the impression that he'd been talking for a while, but I'd been too awestruck to hear anything. "Now we call it the Lodge. We eat here, store food and supplies. Most everything we grow ourselves."

He held the door, and with an impressed glance at each other, Chase and I followed the crowd inside.

It was much like the elementary school I'd gone to—a long hall with classrooms lining the right side and big windows on the left. Their mismatched shutters were cast open and the breeze that entered was tinged with the scent of the livestock across the pasture. The walls—decorated with charcoal draw-ings of stick figures and houses—were bathed in sunlight.

The sound of children's voices floated down the corridor, easing the remaining tension in my chest. We came to an open door, and the classroom inside was bright and colorful. There were children of all ages sitting in plastic chairs attached to L-shaped desks like I'd used in school. The older ones, probably near twelve or thirteen, helped the younger ones, who wore just the straw-colored tunics that exposed their little legs. In the back, one boy sat alone, staring at us with a sour look on his face.

On the walls were clusters of water-wrinkled magazine photos. Cityscapes, smiling women wearing the tight clothes of the old days, and even pictures from the War—crushed buildings, yellow smoke, and people running. The images chilled me—a reminder of our bloody past, viewed from a failing television in my old living room.

I was reminded again of my mother. *You wouldn't believe the stuff they used to write in these things.* I almost smirked, thinking of her story in one. She would have liked that. And even if only one person read it, and it made them stop and think, or maybe even fight back, it would have been worth it.

A woman with a short crop of black hair and skin the color of coffee wrote on a chalkboard at the front of the room.

"That's Ms. Rita," said Dr. DeWitt. "She's on the council. Her daughter Jana's next door with the infants." He smiled at Sarah.

"What's the council?" Chase asked.

The doctor looked at him for the first time since he'd recognized us in the grove.

"The council is made up of members who vote on the direction of Endurance. Van Pelt, he works the fields. Panda's our head cook, and Patch Connor trains the fighters."

"And what do you do?" asked Jesse a bit rudely.

DeWitt took a slow breath. "Whatever I can to help the cause."

My heart beat faster. I was certain now that the rumors of Three's presence at the safe house had been false. This was their base, and clearly, DeWitt was someone of importance here. It appeared our luck had finally turned.

I was just about to move on when I saw the words Ms. Rita had written across the board: "Article 3."

The class recited in unison, "Whole families are to be considered one man, one woman, and children."

Instantly I was back in reform school, sitting in a stiff wooden chair, wearing an itchy wool uniform. The scars on my hands I'd been given there throbbed, and I fought back the urge to march into that classroom and tear up the Statute circulars I now saw in the hands of each one of the children.

"She's teaching the Statutes?" I asked.

"We need to know our enemies," answered DeWitt.

"They're kids," I tried to reason. "They should be reading books and learning, I don't know, spelling. History."

Jesse gave me an odd look. "This *is* their history."

I flexed my hands from their tight fists. In public school I'd learned math and science; I'd read novels and poems. And then my sophomore year they'd taken the Bill of Rights from the curriculum as if it never existed and posted the Statutes in the hallways and told us that if there was ever a hope our country could rebuild after the War, we needed to comply. Now I doubted there was anyone left who didn't know what the Moral Statutes were.

"Things have changed since I went to school," I said.

Jesse snorted. "And you're young. How do you think I feel?"

As he limped ahead of me, I couldn't help but feel a little bad for sticking the fork in his leg.

We stopped at the cafeteria, but the hallway continued on around the bend. Two guards, like those that had hidden in the trees, blocked that path.

DeWitt stood before them. "The north wing is off-limits except by permission of the council. If you all will find a seat in the cafeteria, I'm sure I can talk our cook into throwing together something for you to eat."

"What's in the north wing?" asked Billy.

"Weapons depository," answered DeWitt. I had a feeling guns and ammunition weren't the only things these guards were protecting.

"But we get our own weapons back," prompted Billy.

DeWitt smiled, but didn't answer.

"Sir, our injured made camp near the safe house wreckage," said Chase. "They'll be running out of supplies soon."

In my admiration of the compound, I'd completely forgotten about the rest of the group, fending for themselves at the mini-mart. The guilt settled between my shoulder blades as I awaited DeWitt's response.

DeWitt continued through the threshold into the cafeteria. "We'll look into it," he said.

"We also need a radio," I said. "Ours was damaged, and part of our group is supposed to make contact sometime around sunset."

"I'll see what I can do."

"Thank you," I said. "The last we heard, some of our people might be missing." For some reason, I stopped myself before telling him Tucker's team had found the first resistance post abandoned.

DeWitt nodded. "Eat," he said. "Everything else can wait." With that, he departed, leaving Chase and I exchanging skeptical looks.

A HALF hour later we were in the cafeteria, crowded around a long table fixed with green circular stools attached to its base, like we'd had in my middle school. As it was, most of the men either sat on the table itself or faced away so they could stretch out their long legs. Rebecca and I crammed next to each other, and for an instant my heart felt like it was being twisted, because I remembered how Beth and I used to swap our lunches in a place like this.

Behind the cafeteria was a playground, and through the open door a few children played on the old rusted equipment. Beyond them, six mismatched ovens were visible—they'd been gutted, their insides filled with fires. A dozen people bustled around these stoves while two others managed a central fire pit. I didn't know what they were cooking, but it smelled so delicious my stomach growled.

Across the table, a few seats down, Chase was talking to Jesse. Though Jesse's hair was long, and his scruffy beard fuller, the similarities between them were eerie. The way they sat, facing out with their elbows on their knees, and how their eyes moved over everything, always vigilant, even if you could never see it in their expressions. Jesse leaned back and scratched a hand over his skull, something I'd seen Chase do a hundred times.

"He's taller than I thought," said Rebecca.

My attention snapped back into focus. "Who?"

She snorted. "Chase, of course."

I nodded. He was tall. Taller than most men by several inches, with the exception of Jesse, though thinner than before. Now that I thought of it, I'd always seen him split everything evenly, even though he should have needed more.

"Sean told me how he came for you at the reformatory," she said. "And how he turned himself in to the FBR to find you when you got caught."

"Sean's not so different," I said.

"No," she acknowledged. "He's not."

"How could you leave him?" I asked, suddenly angry. "Don't pretend you don't know what I mean. I saw you on that bridge. You knew he wouldn't be able to follow you."

I tried to turn away from her, but my legs were trapped between the table's bars.

"I knew," she said. "I knew after the first step he couldn't follow."

"Then why?" I demanded. "You could have been hurt!"

"I already am hurt."

She leaned against me, head on my shoulder, and tentatively, I rested mine atop hers. Her hair was matted with sweat and smelled a little, but she was alive and I was grateful for that.

"You're going to get better."

"You sound *so* sure," she said with a sad smile.

I opened my mouth to object, but she continued. "Do you know how hard it is to look at someone and know they blame themselves for what happened to you?"

She looked up then, meeting my eyes, and I did. I knew exactly, because it was my fault she was hurt, my fault she was out here. I turned my head and my gaze came to rest on Chase's back, bowed down by the weight of the burdens he carried.

"I don't want you to go," I said.

She squeezed my arm. "I'm not going anywhere."

WE ate a meal like I'd never eaten before—not even when I was home, and my mother had a job before the War had started. A man named Panda with buzzed hair and a list of names tattooed on his forearms served us goat meat and sweet potatoes and leafy green kale and carrots. There were chunks of nutty, coarse bread we dipped in honey, and oranges from the orchard and as much fresh water as we could drink.

I ate myself sick; I wasted nothing. And when my plate was clean a lanky boy with skin so tan it was nearly the color of red clay asked me if I wanted more and I said yes because the memory of hunger was just as sharp as the real thing.

When I was able to lift my eyes off my plate I spotted Jesse across the table. He'd barely touched his food. The boy with the tan skin made his way toward him, and as I watched he tripped, then caught himself. He hadn't spilled anything, but he turned around just the same and sped back to the kitchen, embarrassed.

I tracked him, wishing DeWitt would resurface from wherever he'd hidden. Now that I'd eaten, I wanted to know how he'd recognized Chase, and what he'd meant when he said we needed protection more than ever.

I rose when Chase appeared behind me.

"Sean's convinced they're poisoning us to use our bodies as hog's feed," he said. "But that didn't stop him from licking his plate clean." He rubbed a hand absently down his throat.

"I thought Three was supposed to be, I don't know, *scary*," I whispered. "They look like farmers, not fighters."

"Who said we can't be both?"

The voice behind me made me jump. Even Chase looked surprised; the noise from the kitchen had distracted him. Behind me, Dr. DeWitt smiled, his blue eyes bright with amusement.

"So you *are* Three," Chase said.

A little girl that had joined us from Jesse's group tugged on DeWitt's tunic. One of the women who'd been tending to her stood back a few steps, and encouraged her to ask him a question.

"Can I go play?" she asked without looking up.

For a moment he didn't move. Then, slowly, he squatted before her and brushed the hair from her face.

"I hear your name's Justine, is that right?"

I took a good look at her now, brunette, with pretty round eyes. I realized I hadn't taken the time to learn the children's names. Or any of the survivors' names, for that matter. Better not to get too close. But maybe here things could be different.

The girl nodded, wiping the crumbs off her dirty sweater.

"Pretty name," said DeWitt. "I'll tell you what. You've got ten minutes to have as much fun as you can. Then you have to wash up and go to bed."

"But . . ."

"Nine minutes and fifty seconds," he said. She pouted for another two seconds, then raced out the door, two other children on her heels.

"Will can show you to your sleeping quarters," DeWitt told the group, motioning to the boy who'd tripped while serving dinner. "The council has decided a formal introduction to the camp can wait until tomorrow."

The thought of being paraded around made me nervous. We didn't even know how many people lived in Endurance.

"Did you talk to them about our people?" Chase asked. Across the table, Jesse flicked back his greasy hair.

"One step at a time," said DeWitt.

"With respect, sir, they may not have much time left. We haven't been able to make radio contact in days," Chase pressed. For the first time in a while, Jack agreed with him.

"We'll discuss it tomorrow." The finality in DeWitt's tone was clear.

As the others rose and followed Will, I helped Rebecca to stand.

"Actually, I'd like to discuss it now," said Chase. I braced against the frustration in his tone, aware of those around us who'd stopped to watch. We were hardly in the position to make demands. "And I want to know how you know about me, too," Chase finished.

Rebecca squeezed my elbow.

DeWitt chuckled dryly. "Why don't we take a walk? The three of us." He tilted his head in my direction.

"Where are you taking them?" Rebecca asked warily.

"Just for a walk," assured DeWitt. "They'll rejoin your people soon."

He turned without another word and headed to the long corridor that ran the length of the school.

Just a walk. I could manage that. Maybe he'd found a radio for us, although I wasn't sure why he wouldn't just come out and say so. From what we'd seen, neither DeWitt nor his people posed a threat to us, and this might be the perfect opportunity to figure out what exactly was going on.

A quick squeeze of Rebecca's hand, and Chase and I followed. Sean was scowling, watching the events unfold from his place on the opposite side of the table.

We came to the main hallway, lit by torches mounted to the walls at intervals, but instead of turning left toward the front of the building, DeWitt made a right. In silence, I followed him over the yellowed, peeling linoleum, waiting with growing anticipation for him to explain why he'd asked me to come along. The windows here had been blocked by planks of wood, but through the cracks I could see that dusk had come.

The hall curved slightly and we came upon two armed guards dressed in beige tunics like DeWitt, with loose pants. They gave him a formal nod, then stepped aside.

The north wing, I realized. Entry was forbidden without council approval, but I wasn't convinced it was just because the weapons were stored here, as DeWitt had claimed. The armed surveillance seemed a little excessive. I passed the guards, trying to ignore the familiar dread I felt around MM soldiers. These were the good guys, even if they did look similar.

"I'll ask you to keep what you see here confidential," said DeWitt, standing before an old classroom, also guarded by a man with a rifle.

We nodded.

He pushed through the door, and my mouth fell agape at the walls of radio equipment—it was tenfold what we'd had in Knoxville. Machines beeped and thrummed, attached by wires to what looked like car batteries, all bound together in the center of the room. Two women and three men wearing headphones sat in front of various machines, reading monitors and adjusting dials.

"What is . . ."

"Perfect timing." I was interrupted by one of the men, in his early thirties with a sharp nose and deeply set eyes. He ripped back his headphones. "I got him, sir. He's on another frequency this time. That makes four channels and counting."

DeWitt strode over to him quickly and pressed a button on the switchboard.

Static, and then Tucker's voice, muffled, despite their superior radio equipment.

"Mayday. Mayday. If you can hear this, clear the area. Roanoke, Virginia, is under FBR control. Do not attempt to evacuate to the safe house. It's gone. I repeat, the safe house is gone."

CHAPTER
8

I FELT the blood drain from my face. Beside me, Chase had grown still.

"The family in Knoxville, Chicago, and Virginia are gone," Tucker continued, and I twitched as he referenced the resistance under the One Whole Family banner used in MM propaganda. Even though the signal was weak his tension was obvious. "My team was hit this morning in Roanoke. We lost four. Half are injured, six are missing."

Static.

"You know this person," said DeWitt.

I nodded, frantically trying to process what Tucker had said. Who had been killed in the fight? The carriers? Truck from Chicago?

"Our radio was damaged," Chase said. "We've been in contact with them until today."

"Well he's telling everyone what happened," a tech said. "With the tower we have access to most underground frequencies, and he's working his way up the ladder."

I recalled the crooked pole emerging from behind the north wing.

"The MM can't hear him, can they?" I asked.

"No," said DeWitt. "He's still using an old frequency. One the Bureau doesn't monitor anymore."

"If you're still out there, we could really use some good news."

Now I had the distinct impression Tucker was talking just to me. The seconds ticked by. If Chase or I didn't respond soon, he was going to end the transmission.

"His name is Tucker Morris," I said. "He's looking for us."

DeWitt scowled at the receiver. Across the room, a woman with unruly auburn curls pushed a red pin into a map of the states. I tracked her hand to a location in western Virginia, and found another in Knoxville, and still another on the coast, in South Carolina. All places the MM had destroyed. Three more pins were scattered across the Midwest.

The static crackled over my nerves.

"We need to answer him." I said, hoping this was clearer.

DeWitt appraised me with caution, then tilted his head in consent. The tech who'd found the signal stood and directed me into his chair, then moved a small black microphone close to my mouth. Chase bent over my shoulder.

"Ready?" asked the tech.

When I nodded he flipped another switch. A small red light on the board turned to green.

Apprehension seized me. Answering a call on a CB radio in the wilderness surrounded by people I knew was a lot different than receiving a transmission in Three's operating room. Everyone was looking at me, and I was suddenly scared of saying the wrong thing.

"I can hear you," I said. "I'm here."

Static. And then, "About time."

A grin came, unbidden and unwelcome. This was Tucker I was talking to, not a friend.

"What happened? You said you'd be there."

"Our radio was damaged."

Pause. "Are you okay?"

I wasn't particularly comfortable with how worried he sounded. Chase huffed behind me, unwilling to believe the sentiment was genuine.

"You said you were hit. How are the drivers?"

Dread filled the moments that followed. Only the carriers knew where the other resistance pockets were—taking the posts' reports had been their job with Three. If they were gone, the other bases wouldn't receive warning about the safe house's destruction, and communication between those fighting the MM would effectively stop.

"The one with the bad teeth is MIA. He never came back. I think . . . I think they might have him."

I closed my eyes.

"The driver from Knoxville—he didn't make it. I told you Grandma's house was empty? He'd heard a tip of another place she'd relocated to so we went to check it out. It was like they knew we were coming. Me and a few other guys barely got out."

The carrier, Tubman, came to mind, with his ragged scar and kind smile, opening the garage door to the auto shop in Knoxville where he hid refugees in need of a safe house.

I fumbled for words. Tucker's raw confession had made me want to raise a shield between us. He must have sensed this, too, because before I could answer, he said, "How about you? Please tell me you found something. We could really use some good news."

DeWitt moved beside me, watching me closely.

"We did," I said. "Though not as many as we hoped for." I couldn't find it in my heart to have him relay the news to his team that so many had perished in the safe house. Not after all they'd been through.

Static. A short laugh. "I can't believe I'm saying this, but it's good to hear your voice."

Beside me, Chase stiffened.

As much as I hated to admit it, it was good to hear from Tucker, too. As crazy as it was, I was relieved he was alive. Still, his report was bleak. They'd been attacked. The resistance posts were being destroyed.

I looked to DeWitt, then to their map on the wall with the red pins. We needed to do something.

"Where are you?" Tucker asked.

Before I could answer, DeWitt flipped the switch. The green light turned red.

"Wait!" I tapped the microphone, then reached for his hand, still covering the switch. "Wait, we weren't done!"

"He'll attempt contact again tomorrow," said DeWitt. "After he reaches the next post."

I stood up, furious, the chair tipping behind me. "They might not make it until tomorrow! You heard him, they're in trouble. The post—"

"We're well aware of the issue," he said.

My fists tightened at my sides. "Then you'll send people to help them? Warn the other posts? You'll do *something*."

DeWitt's lips formed a thin line. "Do not forget that you're a guest in our home, Ms. Miller."

"The carrier he was talking about—if they captured him like Tucker thinks, he's as good as dead."

DeWitt made no response. The eyes of the others in the room bore holes straight through me. I became instantly aware that Chase and I were outnumbered.

"How?" I asked, trying to keep myself calm. "How do you know they'll go to the next post?"

"He'll follow the carrier's directives. That's protocol in the case something like this happens. Unless, of course, you have reason to believe he would do something different?"

I shook my head, aware he was implying Tucker would run, or worse, go back to the MM. Just a week ago I might have considered it, but now, after hearing the distress in his voice, it didn't seem possible.

"You were prepared for this?" I asked.

DeWitt inhaled. "We are prepared for many things."

"Ember." Chase was facing the opposite side of the room where a dozen pictures had been tacked to the wall.

I joined him, keeping my eye on DeWitt until the last possible moment. When I finally saw what Chase was staring at my hand rose to my mouth. I bit my knuckles to hold back the groan.

My mug shot was there, but only half was revealed, because overtop it lay another photo. A grainy black and white of the reception area at a hospital, just within the exit door, where two figures—a soldier and a Sister of Salvation—crouched over a body. The blood that spread from it was black, as if someone had spilled oil.

"You asked how I knew your name," said DeWitt. "Chase Jennings and Ember Miller, sighted in Chicago, at the Rehabilitation Center right there on Reformation Parkway. Bold, I think, to go back to the place where it all began for you, Jennings."

In a sudden burst of fury, Chase ripped the picture from the wall, balled it in his fist, and chucked it against the door. His shoulders were heaving, his face red. He strode out of the room into the hall, leaving me alone to face Three's leader.

DeWitt crossed his arms over his chest. After a moment he exhaled through his nostrils.

"It comes as a surprise the Bureau is looking for you?"

I shook my head, breathless. Tucker could have given me the head's up on one of his calls, but even if he knew what was he going to say? *Hey Ember, I saw your picture up on the side of a building again!* It was better he hadn't mentioned it.

A chair was nearby, and I gripped the back, watching my knuckles turn white. Believing that Harper would remain our secret had been wishful thinking. Of course the MM knew. Apparently *everyone* knew.

"It isn't what it looks like," I whispered, nodding to the picture slowly uncurling on the floor.

He placed a cautious hand on my shoulder.

"Believe me," he said. "That is something you do not have to explain here."

I nodded, thinking of the soldiers he'd killed in Virginia. Wondering what had actually transpired that day.

"I was surprised to see you with those from the safe house," he continued. "Last I heard you'd been captured in Greeneville."

"No," I said. "I was only captured once. Knoxville."

A muscle in DeWitt's neck jumped. "Interesting."

"There was another girl," I said, closing my eyes tightly. "She was with us. The MM shot her when we were in Greeneville. I heard they thought it was me."

I burned, hot and bright, just at the thought of the girl I'd met in Knoxville—the person I was sure was the sniper—and how the MM had framed me for her crimes, but the fire was extinguished as quickly as it had come. Cara had paid for her actions. She'd been killed by soldiers while out with Tucker. At least, that's what Tucker had said. It would never be easy taking his word for anything.

"What do you want from us?" I asked, looking around the roomful of equipment.

DeWitt turned to the pins pressed into the map.

"I want you to help me figure out who is giving away our locations to the FBR."

I unfolded my fingers slowly, forcing my damp palms to lay flat at my sides. "What makes you think we know anything about that?"

I followed DeWitt's gaze as it wandered across the wall. Runaways, mug shots, and even sketches were pinned up, a mosaic of faces, stats, and handwritten notes. It occurred to me that DeWitt suspected these people of ratting out the resistance.

That he suspected *us* of ratting out the resistance.

The room seemed to grow smaller.

"I'd like to trust you, Ember," he said.

I wasn't sure what to say; it wasn't like I trusted *him*. We'd only just met, and so far he seemed to know a lot more about me than I knew about him.

"Endurance is deep in the Red Zone. We don't have access to the mainframe here, so you'll have to forgive me if some of my information is outdated. We rely on the intelligence delivered from our informants in the interior, not all of which is delivered in a timely manner."

The carriers, I realized, who brought their messages to the safe house for Three.

"You escaped reform school and a base," DeWitt said. It may have been a simple statement of fact, but it felt like an accusation.

There was a photo high above the rest, a girl with dirty

blond hair who couldn't have been more than twelve. It was only her profile, but you could tell she was laughing. He removed the picture and folded it carefully into his hip pocket before I could get a closer look.

"I had help," I said.

"You know what they say, good help is hard to find."

I checked the exit; Endurance didn't feel so safe anymore. The urge to run was rearing up inside of me.

"You were in Chicago and Knoxville. Both of those places were destroyed by the Bureau."

"They were," I said.

"Destroyed," he repeated. "Like another of our long-standing resistance posts, as your friend just reported."

I jerked at the word *friend*. Tucker wasn't a friend. "I guess. That was the first I'd heard of Virginia."

Coming here had been stupid. I didn't know these people, and they didn't seem in any hurry to help us. I decided to cut to the point.

"You think I'm telling the FBR where to attack," I said.

DeWitt studied me for a long moment. "I think someone is."

I looked away, disgusted and disappointed.

"They killed my mother," I said. "They killed my friends in Knoxville, and all those people in the tunnels in Chicago and at the safe house. I would *never* tell them anything."

He considered this. "And the people that helped you, would they talk?"

Chase's face flashed to the forefront of my mind. Never. *Never* would he do such a thing. But there were others that had been with us, too. Sean. Billy. *Tucker.* Suspicion jabbed at me like needles in tender flesh.

They had suffered beside me. Even Tucker had nearly been killed. If he was a mole, they wouldn't have left him to die.

I shook my head. As much as I hated DeWitt's accusations, I understood them. In his place I might have suspected the same things.

"A team to warn the resistance posts that the safe house was gone," I said. "You yourself said that was protocol. When they left, only the carriers knew the locations of the bases."

He nodded, and then was quiet for some time.

"We'll send a team out to find your people first thing tomorrow," he finally said.

It didn't fix everything, but it was a start.

"When he calls back, will you find me?" I asked.

He nodded, a perplexed look on his face. It was like he knew what Tucker had done and couldn't figure out why I was so worried about him.

He wasn't the only one.

"Thank you," I said.

He didn't answer. He didn't even look at me. Instead, he stared at the radio, as if expecting another voice to come through.

Our conversation was clearly over.

CHASE was waiting outside the room, pacing in the hall. When he saw me he blew out a heavy breath, but we didn't speak because beside him was an armed guard, a short man with a pointed nose, who reminded me a little of what Rat might have looked like in twenty years. An image of the dead man's face, bloated and pale in the water, crept into my vision, and I stuffed it down, feeling my stomach turn.

We were led back through the cafeteria, and outside past the empty playground with its rusted slide and monkey bars on a crumbling cement path lit by a series of torches. Night had fallen, and darkness stretched its shadow out before us, giving the illusion that Endurance went on forever.

Down the path a plain cement building came into view. The entrance was hidden behind clotheslines crowded with the tunics and pants worn by the residents, all glowing a pale silver in the moonlight and fluttering gently in the breeze.

"Dorms," grunted the guard.

The muscles in my legs tightened. "How many people are in there?"

"Sleeps eighty. It'll sleep more tonight with you all."

All those people close together. More than fifty bodies within fifty yards. I shuddered to a stop, unable to go farther.

"Aren't you afraid the soldiers are going to find out about Endurance?" I whispered.

"No." The guard kept walking. "We got measures in place so that won't happen."

"Plants in the FBR, you mean," said Chase. The guard didn't disagree.

My anxiety rose another notch. "What about the bombs? They run by body heat. The FBR just needs to point one in this direction, and . . ."

"And nothin'," interrupted the guard. "We'd know if they planned to bomb us."

He turned when he realized we weren't following.

"And if they planned to bomb the safe house? Or Chicago? Would you know that?" Chase asked.

My blood ran cold, contrary to the balmy weather. After my discussion with Dr. DeWitt in the radio room, it seemed like a bad idea to accuse these people of knowing the MM's plans to kill innocents.

Our guide turned, and lifted his gaze skyward. "Look, sometimes we win, sometimes we don't. That's the way in war."

Part of me accepted this, but as we entered the dorms I couldn't shake the feeling that someone, somewhere was picking which tips to squash, and which to let slip by. That the safe house's destruction could have been stopped. That all those people could have been saved.

I DIDN'T know what to expect inside. The large room resembled one of the evacuation centers after the War, packed with row after row of bunk beds, nearly all filled with sleeping occupants. The mattresses, no more than thin pads, were draped with assorted blankets. The scuffed floor was littered with shoes and scored by pale red lines, like those in my high school gym. A few small groups whispered or played cards in the aisles. Dim flames flickered from candles lining the walls, but they did little to light the room.

Our people grouped together in the corner to my right. They slept close to one another, keeping a layer of separation between them and the residents. Only the kids mingled; I passed a dozen of varying ages passed out on an old wrestling mat as I made my way toward the back.

I'd nearly reached Billy, who was dead asleep and lying halfway off a cot, when a hand closed on my shoulder. Startled, I jumped, and turned to find Sean lifting his hands in surrender. He was wearing the same tan clothing as the others here wore.

"Just me." Concern shadowed his face. "What did DeWitt want?"

Confidential, DeWitt had said. I couldn't help but feel like this was a test. Chase and I had already decided not to tell Jack that Truck was missing. It wouldn't have done him any good to know, anyway.

I chewed my bottom lip; Chase was still buried in his thoughts, too consumed to answer.

"Just showing us around," I said.

Sean waited for more, and when I didn't offer any he frowned and pulled at the strings hanging from his shirt's collar.

"I saved you guys a bunk. It's above ours, so don't make me regret it. You can pick up your cult attire and extra blankets over there." He motioned toward an office, an offshoot from the main room where a stack of towels sat folded on the ledge of a half door. Chase went to pick up our supplies; though the idea of resting while Truck was missing, possibly captured, and half of our team was dead or injured, seemed selfish beyond belief.

"Cult attire looks good on you," I said.

"I know." He smirked. "They got all the material from an upholstery company down the road."

"You asked?"

He tied the collar strings in a neat bow. "Of course I asked."

Rebecca was already asleep, curled on her side on the bottom bunk when we arrived. Sean held the bed frame still while I climbed to the top, and leaned against the post while I settled.

"You're okay?" he asked.

"I'm okay." It was a testament to our friendship that he didn't ask more.

I pulled off my shoes, sighing with a sudden, drenching fatigue that overrode the lingering worries. Rolling onto my stomach, I looked down on Sean, less than a foot below me. He still leaned against the post, staring down at Rebecca in a way that made me feel like I was intruding on something private and important. I flipped over onto my back.

"Ember?" Sean asked. The rustling in the bunks around us had tapered to deep, hypnotizing breaths.

"Yeah?" I whispered back.

"Your feet stink."

I closed my eyes, a fleeting smile touching my lips.

"One day this is going to be over," he said softly. "Then things will finally be normal."

I wasn't sure if he was telling me or himself; I didn't even know what normal meant anymore. But after Chase returned and climbed up beside me, I wrapped myself as tightly as I could around him, and when my head came to rest on his heart I thought that whatever it was, it was worth fighting for. I just hoped this was the place to do it.

CHAPTER
9

WE were awoken before dawn by the ringing of a bell. Groggy, I dragged myself up, moving through a line to the women's showers outside the dorms. Then I finally changed into my upholstery "cult attire." Though it was scratchy, it was clean, and my skin felt shiny and new after so many days tromping through the sand and grass. When we were ready, Will led us to the back entrance of the lodge near the playground and cafeteria.

I could smell breakfast cooking—some kind of meat and more of the bread we'd had before—but the comforting scents couldn't take away the bad feeling rooting in my gut. The call with Tucker and the news he delivered gnawed at me. We needed to find out more—where he was headed, if they'd heard anything about Truck, and what DeWitt had meant when he said he wanted our help to catch the one ratting out the resistance bases. The other part was still sick about the photo from the rehab hospital, and wanted nothing more than to grab Chase and run.

"You look rested." DeWitt strode through the cafeteria door appearing the exact opposite of rested; his jaw was rough with stubble and dark rings bruised his eyes. I remembered the quick way he'd dismissed me from his office and was curious how he'd spent the last several hours.

Beside me, Chase crossed his arms over his chest, looking like someone from another time with his strange clothes and damp black hair shagging over his ears. The stoic expression on his face brought his uncle to mind, but when I glanced around, Jesse was nowhere to be found. I was just about to ask Chase about it when I heard Billy say, "Uh-oh."

I followed where he pointed, to the flock of people moving toward us through the trees a half mile away. As I watched they became too numerous to count—a hundred, then double that. Men and women, some as old as Dr. DeWitt and some younger than me. Their tunics were slightly darker, blending with the earth, but otherwise the only discernible difference between them and the other residents were the rifles, slung from straps across their chests. One figure stood out in the front—an older man with a patch over his eye who looked too frail to belong with the others. Though he walked more slowly than I imagined the rest could, no one passed him.

"Please tell me they're with you," said Sean.

Three's leader nodded behind him to the north wing. "Endurance has a brain." He pointed to the cafeteria. "A stomach." The dorms. "A heart." Then to the playground, where a group of children were playing tag. "And a soul. Our walls make up its bones, and our men make up its muscle."

"You've got an army?" Chase was impressed, and standing beside him, I couldn't help but feel it, too. A trained army, even a small one, could make a dent in the MM's momentum. Three had to be planning something important. My mind again turned to the fallen bases, and the attack on Tucker's team.

"*We've* got people willing to fight," corrected DeWitt. "Within these gates there is no I."

Doubt skittered through me. DeWitt had spoken of trust and discretion last night. Maybe we were all on the same team, but he was full of secrets.

The army approached, moving like cats: silent, with smooth, predatory strides. They merged with the other residents, and together observed us with interest.

Sweat dewed on my hairline.

"Endurance," DeWitt called out. "I give you our newest members. Survivors, like us all. I know you'll welcome them and teach them our ways." Silence reigned over the courtyard. DeWitt sighed, as though the sky itself were weighing on his shoulders. "They have confirmed, as we feared, the fall of the safe house." He waited as the murmurs rose, then faded. "Last night we intercepted a signal from a small team of rebels north of here. It is with a heavy heart that I inform you that Virginia has fallen. Reports of how substantial our loss is have yet to be determined. After Knoxville and Chicago, this makes four points hit in the last month."

The whispers began to fly. Jack and Billy were the first to suspect Tucker and the carriers. I could hear Sean reassuring Rebecca and some of the others that we were safe here. I forced my gaze forward.

"The council is determining an appropriate course of action. In the meantime, return to your posts and await orders."

With that, DeWitt placed his hand over his heart, like we used to do in school when we'd say the Pledge of Allegiance. All those before him did the same, even the children. Even Billy, who had about as much idea of what the gesture meant as I did.

Lines formed for breakfast, and as we went to them I caught sight of the guard who'd escorted Chase and me to the dorms last night. He stood two people behind us, and when I recognized him he quickly looked away.

"He's been tailing us all morning." Chase didn't look back. "Stayed outside the dorms all night, too."

"DeWitt doesn't trust us," I said under my breath. "He thinks we know something about the attacks on the resistance posts."

A scowl passed over his face before he flattened his expression.

"Because of Tucker," Chase surmised, biting down on the name. "Because he was broadcasting what happened, and looking for us."

Maybe I'd been uncertain about Tucker since he'd been kicked out of the FBR, but Chase would never trust him. And even if I trusted Tucker sometimes, I would never forgive him.

We took a step closer to the food.

"And because we were in Chicago and Knoxville when they were hit," I said.

Chase considered this, running his knuckles absently over his jaw.

"We have to prove we had nothing to do with it," said Chase. "I'd rather the MM want us dead than Three."

"Agreed." At least with the soldiers chasing us we could hide with the resistance. If the resistance was chasing us, nowhere was safe.

The guard behind us appeared in my peripheral vision, closer than before. Our conversation was no longer private.

"Where's your uncle?" I asked. "He wasn't here during Dr. DeWitt's announcement."

Chase stood tall, shielding his eyes from the sun as he searched. He nodded to my right, where Jesse appeared as if summoned.

"Nephew. And neighbor." Freshly shaven and with hair still damp, Jesse threw his arm over Chase's shoulders. I found myself mirroring Chase's scowl. With DeWitt on the hunt for traitors to the cause, Jesse should have been more careful to wake up on time.

"Bad news, kid," smirked Jesse. "Looks like you couldn't dodge the draft after all."

"He didn't dodge the first time," I said.

Jesse looked to Chase for confirmation, the skin around his eyes tightened with regret. He would have known that if he'd stuck around.

"What are you talking about?" Chase asked Jesse.

"The guy in charge—Doctor something," he began.

"DeWitt," I corrected quietly.

"Right. DeWitt." Jesse glanced away. "DeWitt's sending all able bodies down to join his little security detail."

I stood on my tiptoes and looked to where a group of our people crowded around the old man with the eye patch. Billy was the first in line. For some reason this worried me. It wasn't like he'd never done field work before—he'd left the Wayland Inn to find new recruits lots of times—but without Wallace watching over him, this seemed different.

I wasn't hungry anymore. Chase seemed to have lost his appetite as well, but he crammed down the meat patties and brown bread all the same.

"What do you know about Three?" Jesse asked Chase. He didn't look for my input, and given the way I'd reacted, I couldn't blame him.

"Not much." Chase pooled the crumbs in the center of his hand, then sifted them into his mouth.

"Nothing?" Jesse pressed, in a way that made me wonder what *he* had heard.

"There was a medic when I was in the service." Chase rubbed his thumb between his brows. "After fights he used to hold up his fingers and tell me three—"

"—is the only number you should remember?" Jesse snorted, and shook his head.

"Yeah." The corner of Chase's mouth quirked. "How'd you know?"

"Someone said the same to me once," he said. "Figured he was nuts."

They grinned at each other, as if relieved that they connected over something from their time apart.

"What exactly does the security team do?" I interrupted.

Jesse glanced down, as if he'd forgotten I was there. "Only one way to find out."

I didn't like it, but he was right. If Chase and I were going to prove we had nothing to do with the attacks on the resistance, we needed to gain Three's trust. I was just about to follow Chase toward the man with the eye patch when Will appeared at my side.

"The doc wants to see you," he told me.

For one strange, strained moment, he met Jesse's gaze, and then he looked down as if intimidated and hurried toward the cafeteria entrance to the lodge.

"Weird kid," commented Jesse. "Heard he's one of DeWitt's charity cases."

"What do you mean?" I asked.

"Sick folks hide out in the Red Zone," he said. "Sometimes

they abduct kids from near the border to do their dirty work. We ran into them a couple of times at the safe house—the Lost Boys, people called them. Bunch of little psychopaths, more like it."

"We met them," I said, thinking Jesse's assessment was pretty accurate. "Yesterday, before Dr. DeWitt's people showed up." I ran a hand over my bruised side, remembering the boy who'd kicked me there.

Jesse didn't look surprised. "Think DeWitt tries to take some in and rehabilitate them or something. Impossible to fix what's already broke though, if you ask me."

Chase shoved his hands in his pockets, and I could tell he was thinking about Harper, and the picture he'd torn off the wall in the north wing.

As the line reached its end, people began filtering to their assigned duties. I watched Sean help Rebecca toward the south wing, where we'd passed the classrooms, and felt the pull toward the opposite side, where Three's leader had summoned me.

Chase looked torn, and I tried to offer a reassuring smile. "I guess I'll see you later."

He nodded slowly, but his feet stuck to the ground. I didn't want to go either. Bad things happened when we split up. A memory of the last night before he'd been drafted into the FBR over a year ago came to the forefront of my mind. I shouldn't have let him go then, and I shouldn't be letting him go now.

"Find me if anything comes up." He glanced over my shoulder toward the lodge, reluctance in his eyes.

"I'll find you."

"Good god," said Jesse. "I just remembered why I never got married."

Chase smirked, then leaned down and planted a quick kiss

on my cheek. "Be careful," he whispered. I willed him to do the same as he turned and followed Jesse away.

"I WANT the location and status of your team." DeWitt loomed over my shoulder as I sat in my plastic bucket seat before the radio. The tech beside me was turning dials and pressing buttons on the black console. A crackle of static filled the small room.

On the opposite wall two other members were crammed side by side at a small table stacked with assorted papers, and I eavesdropped curiously as they muttered numbers aloud and recorded them on clipboards.

"Not a word about who you're with or where you are." De-Witt drew my attention back to the task at hand. "Obviously this Morris trusts you, but you may not be able to trust him anymore."

Anymore. As if I ever really did. "You think he's the one selling out the bases?"

DeWitt tilted his head. "Should I?"

I frowned, both at his suspicion and my doubt. A month ago I wouldn't have questioned it—Tucker was bad, end of story. But since then Tucker had proven he was on our side, making me question everything I knew about him.

I turned back toward the microphone. "He's with us."

I felt DeWitt's eyes on me, and when I looked up I saw that his expression had grown hard. Beside me, the tech shifted in his chair.

"Anything else I should know about him?"

He might as well have asked if Tucker had killed my mother, but maybe I was just being paranoid.

Be careful, Chase had said.

I reminded myself that DeWitt hadn't come into this position by chance. When he spoke, the entire compound had stopped to listen. That was a power I didn't want to fight against.

"No," I said.

I planted my feet on the floor, and scooted the chair to the microphone.

"I'm ready."

TUCKER didn't answer.

We attempted to make contact on the same frequency he'd used yesterday, but to no avail. Wherever he was headed, whatever danger he might have been in, he was unable to respond. As the hours passed, I became more and more convinced the something else had gone wrong.

By lunchtime it was clear we weren't going to make contact unless Tucker called first. DeWitt had disappeared late in the morning without explanation, and in his absence, I rose and wandered to the opposite side of the room where the operators were still recording numbers on a stack of paper.

A woman with a pencil between her teeth shoved back the dark bangs that stuck to her forehead with sweat. The heat coming off the radios in the room was tremendous, and it was beginning to make me drowsy.

I looked down at the notes she'd scribbled across the paper. There were two columns. On the left was a list of regions: 129, 257, 313, and so on. On the right, a census count—90, 568, and even in one region, 925.

Instantly, I was alert.

"Is that how many people are on our side, or theirs?" I asked.

The woman's head snapped up, her cap of greasy hair swinging and sticking momentarily to her cheek.

"I wish we had that many on our side," she said. "Rebels don't waste a lot of time counting their numbers."

I didn't need to ask why.

"You got the soldier counts from hacking into the mainframe?" I lowered my voice. "Can you check if someone's been captured? A carrier. He's missing."

"Does it look like we have mainframe access?" she said briskly.

"My friend Billy hacked into the mainframe in Knoxville."

She snorted. "That was Knoxville. This is No Man's Land. We haven't had Internet since the president shut down our satellites during the War—said it was too easy to organize terrorists that way, in case you're too young to remember. Now you need a hardline to crack into and we're too far out for that. Bureau's got bombs that run by body heat sensors, and we're still deciphering radio messages." She groaned and covered her face with her hands.

"Where'd you get those numbers then?"

"They're the last reports to come in from the safe house," she said.

"The carriers delivered messages from the posts to Three there," I said to myself. Sean had told me this once.

She nodded. "Hard to believe all these regions report to one base. Guess that's what happens when a war wipes out two-thirds of the country. Leaves everyone else a little thin."

Contemplating why Three was monitoring the soldiers present in each region filled me with a dark doubt. They couldn't possibly attack a base. There were only two hundred, maybe two hundred and fifty people in the army we'd seen this morning. Even if they recruited the help of the existing resistance posts, they wouldn't have the numbers to stand a chance. In Knoxville we'd had less than thirty people total. To attack the base would have been suicide.

A strong urge to find Chase shook through me. I was getting

a very bad feeling about the purpose of Three's "security" team.

"I don't know how we're supposed to pull this off when we don't even have current numbers," she muttered.

"Pull what off?"

She lowered her hands slowly. "Who are you again?" She reached suddenly for my shirt sleeve and gave it a tug. The collar untied, and my shoulder was exposed. I yanked it back up, retying the straps.

"What are you doing?" I asked.

Her brows lifted, and her mouth pursed. She flipped over the paper she'd been recording the census counts on, and I was surprised to see the bold, familiar type of a Statute circular staring back at me. There were at least a dozen sheets spread across the table.

"My mistake," she said.

It didn't seem like a mistake, but she clearly wasn't saying any more about it.

"That's the best use of the Statutes I've seen yet," I said cautiously. I'd seen them everywhere—stuck to the front doors of houses, old telephone poles, windows. Anywhere anyone might see them. But never used as scratch paper. The very idea seemed so defiant it brought a smile to my lips.

"We hijacked some trucks on their way from the printing plant awhile back." She jutted a thumb out the door without looking up. "They're down the hall."

Two soldiers, two halves of the same person really, came to mind. Marco and Polo, the night crew at the printing plant in Greeneville, where we'd taken refuge on our flight from Knoxville. I could still hear the deafening drone of the printing machines in the back room.

I wondered if those two had anything to do with some trucks being hijacked.

She held her hand over the stack of papers, clearly waiting for me to leave so she could continue.

I removed myself from the room and wandered down the hall until I found an open door. Inside the closet was a rack of office supplies, and boxes stacked upon boxes of Statute circulars.

I pulled one off the top open box, reading down the list I'd memorized long ago, feeling a familiar pang in my heart when I reached Article 5.

Children are considered valid citizens when conceived by a married man and wife. All other children are to be removed from the home and subjected to rehabilitative procedures.

"Looking for something?"

I spun to see the guard who'd been following us—the one who looked like Rat but older—standing in the doorway, and cringed, both inside and out. "Don't you have anything better to do than follow me around?"

The corner of his mouth quirked. "It appears not."

Resistance posts were being destroyed, our people—Tucker included—were possibly missing, and yet I was his assignment.

"I need to see my friends." I hoped this made it clear that I would be heading down through the tree line to find Chase.

"I'll take you." He turned, and I jogged after him to catch up, wondering how that had been so easy.

We passed the heavily guarded weapons depository and exited the north wing by way of an open foyer, but where I thought we would exit through the cafeteria the guard kept walking. He cut straight through to the south wing of the lodge, past the infant room with its colorful tattered squares of old carpet and handmade wooden toys. Inside I caught a glimpse of Sarah changing a diaper. Good practice for the months to come, although her hair was pulled loose on one side, and she didn't look particularly happy. I waved, and she called out a brief distracted hello.

"Where are we going?" I asked. Not out of the building to where the soldiers had emerged this morning, I was certain of that much.

"To see your people," he said.

We came to the end of the hallway, where two rooms split off in a T. From one side came the sharp smell of sage and other herbs I didn't recognize. From the other, a girl's high giggle.

I stuck my head in the doorway, surprised at the clean floor and sterile countertops. Clay jars filled the shelves, labeled with unfamiliar words like BETONY, AVENS, MILKWEED, and VALERIAN. A dozen cots were placed at even intervals, and on one of them sat Rebecca. Opposite her, on a round stool, DeWitt chuckled, a tool in his hand that looked like a petite hammer.

A strange mix of comfort and suspicion had me hurrying to Rebecca's side.

"Ember!" Rebecca beamed. I'd forgotten how beautiful she was when she smiled.

"What's going on?" My gaze raced over her, finding the sores on her arms bandaged with pale yellow cloth. A gray mud oozed down into the crook of her elbow. Her pants were pulled up above the knee; there were so many bruises you'd think her natural skin color was purple. I winced.

"Dr. DeWitt gave me some tea. It's good. You should have

some, too." She lifted a cup of what looked and smelled like dirty water, and when she giggled at my scrunched nose it occurred to me the concoction might be spiked.

"What did you give her?"

"Something for the pain," answered DeWitt. "Maypop root, to relax her muscles. Hopefully help her body heal naturally." He gave her a reassuring squeeze on the shoulder.

In my time with him, I'd yet to see DeWitt in this role, but watching him with Rebecca, it was clear he enjoyed taking care of people.

"He thinks I'm going to walk again!" Rebecca squeezed my hand and pulled me down beside her. "I mean, walk better. Without the crutches." She spilled some of the tea on the cot.

"Really?" I offered her a weak smile, reluctant to believe what I'd secretly closed off as an option. Was the doctor right? He didn't have any proper medical equipment that I could see.

"Slow down," said DeWitt with a kind smile. "I said there's a good chance you'll recover. But only if you take care of yourself. Relax. Eat right. Do the exercises we talked about."

"And rub moldy plants all over me every day," Rebecca added solemnly, then grinned at me. "Sean's going to flip his lid."

I was going to flip my lid. I didn't want to believe the impossible, but her joy was contagious. If this place could make her better, if DeWitt could help her, every ounce of pain we'd put her through for freedom had been worth it.

"I can't wait for you to tell him," I said. "Where is he?"

"He's a farmer now." She giggled. "Can you imagine? They've got him picking carrots I bet."

"How'd he pull that off?" All able-bodied fighters were being recruited to the army. I was sure they would have wanted him given that he was an actual soldier.

"He dislocated his shoulder," she said with a pouty frown.

"It must have happened when those boys ambushed us. He's so the suffer-in-silence type—I didn't even know about it until this morning when he had Dr. DeWitt reset it."

I'd seen Sean since the boys had attacked us. He hadn't been injured. I was almost positive this was a ploy to stay close to Rebecca. He'd promised he would never leave her again.

DeWitt was watching me out of the corner of my eye.

"He didn't want you to worry," I quickly told Rebecca. "I'm glad he finally got it looked at."

Some, but not all of the suspicion faded from the doctor's face. "Picking carrots is a noble job," he said. "It makes the horses very happy."

"Sir?" A radio tech appeared in the doorway, adjusting his glasses. His cheeks were stained red, and his hair, sweaty like mine, stuck straight out on the sides.

"Excuse me." DeWitt rose, and shook Rebecca's hand. "It was a pleasure, dear. We'll talk soon, all right?"

"Thanks, Dr. DeWitt."

My eyes tracked him to the door, where the calm, reassuring presence was stripped away as he listened to what the tech had to share. A moment later, they sped down the hallway, footsteps clicking.

"What happened?" Rebecca asked.

"I don't know." I stood, intent to follow, but before I could, Rebecca shoved something into the palm of my hand. Two unmarked squares in blue plastic wrapping. The same that had been in the jar on the counter. The same that were practically contraband in the civilian population without a prescription because they were the gateway to *immoral* behavior—the kind reserved only for married couples.

My face flooded with heat.

"They're condoms," she said.

"Rebecca, I know." My mom had traded for some at the soup kitchen to give me before Chase had been drafted, but we'd never gotten that far. I shoved them into my pocket; the sharp corners of the plastic stuck through the fabric into my thigh.

"They stole them from the FBR. Soldiers get them for free, you know. I figure you probably need them more than I do. For now, anyway." She snickered, but it was cut short when she saw my face. "Oh. I thought . . . I mean, wow. Really?"

"Shut up," I said. "I'm leaving."

"Wait." She snatched my hand and pulled me down beside her. "You're awfully squirmy."

"I'll see you later."

Her arms latched around my waist. "Stop it. I just want to say something real quick."

"Fine," I mumbled.

She took a deep breath, and I was reminded of the time my mom told me how babies are made. I didn't want to have the conversation when I was twelve; I sure didn't want to have it again now.

"I don't know a lot about this stuff, but from the sound of it I know more than you." She blushed, which made me feel a little better. "And I guess I just want to say that it's not bad like they said at the reformatory, not if you love the person. You're not dirty or anything if you want to. Although, some of the other girls, they didn't have someone like Sean their first time, and it *was* pretty bad for them." She met my eyes. "Anyway, if you have any questions or anything, you can ask me, okay?"

There were questions. Lots of questions. Questions I'd wondered about and questions I hadn't even considered until right then. About what I was supposed to do, and how much it would hurt, and how you knew when it was the right time if you already knew you were in love. All things that didn't really matter with everything else going on. I sighed, allowing her grip to turn into a hug. She was a good friend, and I was glad to have her back.

"Thanks," I said.

"Thank you," she replied. And I could see in her eyes that she meant for all of it: getting her out of the hospital and pushing her from town to town until we could finally come here.

I smiled, then pushed all thoughts of condoms, and Chase naked, and *me* naked in front of Chase from my mind. There were more pressing issues to deal with.

I walked evenly to the door so as not to scare her, but inside I was wary. Something urgent had pulled DeWitt away. Something bad.

As soon as I was out the door, I ran into my guard. But this time I didn't give him a chance to ask where I was headed. I raced back to the north wing, thoughts growing louder and louder in my mind.

Tucker called. They're in trouble. They've been hit again.

There were more people inside the radio room than before. Hastily, I reached the doorway, just as DeWitt was leaving. We collided, his expression furious and frightening. I could see then how this man could kill soldiers if prompted.

I glanced over his shoulder, eyes falling to the map on the far wall. It took only a moment to recognize that there was one more pin than yesterday—this one in Southern Ohio.

Another post had fallen.

"Wait—my friends," I said as DeWitt charged by. He didn't even notice me on his trek down the hall. The tech I'd sat beside earlier hunched over the radio, holding the round metal headphones to his ears as if the headband was useless. I tried to reach him but a guard shut the door in my face.

Within me, something dark flexed its claws. Another post had fallen. More good people were dead. I hated the MM. I hated them so much I could barely breathe.

I needed to find Chase. He needed to know what had happened. I couldn't hold this news alone; it was eating me from the inside out. But when I turned around, there was the guard.

"Going somewhere?" he asked.

CHAPTER

10

BARRED from finding Chase until the soldiers were done with their training, I was assigned to the kitchen, where I spent the remainder of the afternoon in the sweltering cafeteria. The north wing had grown eerily quiet, like a calm before the storm, and no one else came or went. According to my guard, whose name I had learned was Rocklin, DeWitt had requested I stay nearby in case Tucker tried to make contact. I didn't know where DeWitt himself had gone; after he'd left the north wing, I hadn't seen him. But I did as Rocklin ordered because if any new developments arose, I wanted to be close enough to hear them.

Panda, council member and kitchen commander, had tasked me to peel potatoes. By my guess there were probably about a thousand of them in the pile beside the stove. While I worked I watched him through my lashes. His head gleamed with perspiration, and his sleeves were rolled up to reveal names listed down his forearms. The muscles beneath flexed as he chopped cabbage.

I'd thought DeWitt might order a council meeting to discuss what had happened, but Panda hadn't been summoned. Each minute that passed wore down my patience. The questions replayed in my head over and over. If Tucker had been caught. If what remained of his team was being followed by the MM. If they were still on the mission, still trying to warn the other bases.

If Tucker was dead.

"What do your tattoos mean?" I asked Panda after I nicked my finger for the tenth time.

Panda didn't look up. "Will the answer help you peel potatoes?"

I tossed a potato into the dismal completed pile and reached for another. White, starchy residue coated my skin up to the elbows.

"They're my reminder," he said after a while. "I'm sure you've got your reasons for being here."

My chest constricted. There wasn't enough skin to fit my mother's name and those of all my friends lost at home, at the reformatory, in the resistance. I focused on peeling until Panda said it was time to serve dinner.

NIGHT came slowly, the color of the sky changing by the slightest degrees from red to purple to blue. I helped Will serve a hearty fish stew on the patio outside the cafeteria. He talked little once the fighters began to arrive through the curtain of trees. With his eyes as round as a puppy dog's, it was easy to see he wanted to be with them. I wondered why he wasn't—maybe that had been DeWitt's decree.

As I ladled the soup into bowls my thoughts drifted to my mother, of her days serving at the soup kitchen. It felt good to be doing something she'd done, even if half of that something was listening for gossip.

While searching for Chase I found Billy. He'd returned with Jack and some of the other safe house survivors, but lagged behind, not joining their conversation. The awkward hacker I'd known at the Wayland Inn had all but disappeared, and in his place was someone older and distant who oozed anger from every pore. He barely acknowledged me as he came through the line, and admittedly I didn't make much of an effort to draw him out. Even Sarah, who he'd seemed friendly with just yesterday, was ignored.

I grew weary as the darkness descended. I still hadn't seen Chase or his uncle, and DeWitt had yet to reappear. I listened to those who came through the line, but no one acknowledged their leader's absence. Talk was mostly of the arrival of a new shipment of weapons that had been hijacked somewhere near the Red Zone border on the outskirts of South Carolina.

Torches were lit around the cracked patio where the people of Endurance were finishing their meal. The tang of flames and earthy smell of wood made my nose crinkle as the smoke puffed into the night sky. I found Rebecca sitting with Sarah at one of the tables, and though I felt drawn to join them, my feet were leading me in the opposite direction, back toward where Chase had gone this morning.

"Where are you going?"

I cringed as Sean approached, right arm hanging in a sling against his chest.

"How's your shoulder?" I muttered.

He bit his lower lip, as if to hide a smirk. "It's incredibly uncomfortable, thank you for asking. Remind me not to ever pick a real fight with your boyfriend."

I closed my eyes and sighed, imagining how that scene had played out.

"I've got to go find Chase," I said.

"I'll go with you."

"No." I glanced back to Rebecca. "Stay here. I'll be back."

Sean placed himself in front of me, dipping some bread into a bowl tucked in his sling and stirring it around.

"They're watching us," he said. "That shifty kid that served the soup, he's been following me all day."

My gaze drifted over the tables in search of Will, but I was unable to find him. Everyone was distracted by the meal; it was the perfect time to take a walk. But before I could a tall, shadowed figure cut through the crowd, searching through the sea of faces until his eyes landed on me. My breath did a little hitch in my throat as it always did at Chase's slow smile, but automatically my gaze lowered. He wore the same hand-sewn outfit we all did, though I hadn't noticed this morning that the pants stopped short around his calves, revealing a band of skin between his boots and the hem.

I smirked, forgetting the rest of the world for a moment, and then covered my mouth with one hand.

"I think it's time you moved up to the big-boy pants," said Sean as Chase approached. He was met with a dangerous glare.

"Funny. That's the first time I've heard that today." Chase shook his head at me, then playfully pinched the ticklish spot on my side. "Not you, too."

"I think you look cute," I said.

"Cute," he repeated, as if I'd just called him something really terrible. He leaned down and kissed me—the kind of kiss that made the world tilt on its axis—and I gripped his shirt so I didn't fall over.

"Right," I heard Sean say somewhere beyond the rushing in my ears. "Thanks for making me a part of this."

Chase drew back slowly and I pulled away, unable to look directly at our friend. My lips still tingled. He seemed different today. Something about this place was changing him, maybe even healing him. He smiled more easily, and for the first time since Chicago I didn't sense that thoughts of Harper were waiting to drag him under. He needed a purpose, and Endurance was giving him that.

"You guys haven't seen my uncle, have you?" Chase asked.

I shook my head, thrust back into the present as quickly as I'd been flung out of it. At once I recalled everything that had happened while Chase and I had been apart. We needed to talk.

"I thought he joined up with you," said Sean.

"He did." Chase scratched the back of his head. "But he disappeared right after. Thought maybe he'd say good-bye first." He chuckled dryly, but it was obvious he didn't think the situation funny. I placed my hand in his and gave it a light squeeze.

Rebecca joined us, frowning.

"Something's happened." She nodded toward the concrete corner where Billy had staked his claim. A small group of people had gathered around them—mostly survivors, but others from Endurance as well.

We headed toward them, joined by others as we passed the rest of the serving tables. Soon the music faded, and those that had been dancing joined the pack.

Chase grabbed my hand and pulled me through to the front to where Jack sat on the bench of a picnic table, head in his hands. Billy was standing on the seat beside him adjusting the dials on an old radio he held against his chest.

"What's going on?" Chase asked.

"They'll play it again—it's run on two different channels already," said Billy, biting off the words. I remembered what the tech had said about boosting the signal with a tower and wondered for one alarming moment if Billy had connected with Tucker.

He clicked a switch at the top of the radio, eliciting a loud screech that made the back of my jaw light up. A second later the crackle of static, magnified off the patio, gave way to a familiar woman's voice.

". . . Reinhardt, who made his first public appearance this morning after surviving the attempt on his life in Region 414 last month, told reporters that measures have already been taken to crack down on domestic terrorism."

A short crackle came from the radio, and then another voice, this one male but softer, almost delicate, came through.

"The president has deemed Reformation to be the highest priority of our country, and I for one will not rest until that goal is achieved. Those who oppose progress shall be dealt with quickly, and without mercy."

Beside me, Rebecca gasped.

"The Chief of Reformation," she said. "He visited the hospital in Chicago once." Sean pulled her close under one arm.

"The chief reported that the individual responsible for the handmade bomb, delivered to him in person at a fundraising dinner, is still at large, but that all available resources will be dedicated to bringing him and his associates to justice. To demonstrate his seriousness, Chancellor Reinhardt has signed execution orders on fourteen suspects thought to be in collaboration with the rebellion, and released the name of one Thomas "the Truck" Rhodes, a known terrorist out of Chicago, who was executed this morning at the Charlotte Prison."

"No," I murmured. Part of me had accepted it would come to this, but had been denying it all the same. Hearing it out loud made it so much worse.

Jack rose, red in the face, and shoved away through the crowd. One of the other survivors followed him. I wanted to as well, but my boots were stuck in place.

I pictured the musclehead carrier with the missing tooth. I

remembered how he'd fought us just to see which side we were on, and driven us and the other survivors from Chicago's tunnel explosion to the coast. *My name's Truck*, came a weak voice in the back of my mind, *because I drive the truck.*

I looked at Chase, horrified. A muscle in his jaw ticked.

The Chief of Reformation's voice came on again.

"Despite our efforts to rehabilitate, these terrorists are determined to bring our country to ruin. They admit to being directly responsible for the deaths of good, honest people in Tennessee, in Kansas, Missouri, Indiana, and Virginia. Though they don't call themselves insurgents, make no mistake that they are terrorists, and before they can do the same damage as that of their predecessors, they will be stopped, expunged, as a demonstration of the power of Reformation. The safety of our people is too important to take any chances."

He was speaking to us. To Three. I could almost feel the MM's cold watch slide over Endurance.

The female reporter returned to the broadcast.

"Citizens are, as always, encouraged to contact the FBR with information on any suspicious activity, and reminded that assisting the noncompliant is in direct violation of the Moral Statutes. With more to come on this story, I'm Felicity Bridewell."

The line went dead.

I remembered where I'd heard her voice then: in a farmhouse in Virginia, where a couple had tried to turn us in as fugitives after she'd reported our flight. We'd barely escaped.

Nice to hear she was still the MM's mouthpiece.

"Maybe Reinhardt's bluffing," said Sean, but we all knew he wasn't. Truck was gone, and we didn't know who would be next.

"The chief's a dead man," said one of the fighters behind us.

"How many times you going to say that?" asked another. "Not like we haven't been trying."

At the Wayland Inn we'd heard a radio report that someone had nearly succeeded in assassinating the Chief of Reformation. We'd suspected Three's involvement, little that we knew about them. We'd been right.

"Shut it off."

We turned, finding Dr. DeWitt, chin lifted, gaze cold. Those around him cleared a space, as if at any moment he might erupt, like he presumably had when he'd killed those soldiers before going on the run.

"You shut it off." Billy swung the radio at the doctor, but Chase, between them, snagged it from the air. He pressed the top button, and the red light above the speaker went dark.

Truck was gone, not killed in an attack, but murdered by the FBR as a message to the resistance. Tucker could be next. A strange sense of numbness filled me as I considered the possibility of my mother's killer dying in the same manner that she had.

"Are you aware there are children around?" DeWitt said evenly.

Billy scoffed and tossed back his hair. "I'd heard worse by the time I was their age."

"Then it was a shame there was no one there to protect you," DeWitt said.

Billy stuffed his hands in his pockets, glancing away. There *had* been someone who'd looked out for Billy—Wallace. And now he was gone.

"What about the other thirteen?" said Chase, but we both knew that number meant nothing. The MM executed who they wanted, when they wanted. This was just the first time they chose to acknowledge it.

"We're dealing with it," said DeWitt.

"Doesn't look like it," muttered Billy. "If I hadn't lifted this radio none of us would even know this was happening."

To my left, Sarah hugged a bowl of soup tightly to her chest. We'd been pretending everything was fine while Felicity Bridewell had been broadcasting Truck's death across the country.

"Billy could find them," said Sean. "Get him on the mainframe. He can find anyone."

Billy puffed up.

"They can't access the mainframe here," I said, remembering what the woman in the north wing had said. We were out of range. All we could infiltrate were the radio signals. Since the safe house's destruction, we didn't even have the reports of the surviving carriers.

When DeWitt glanced at me, I remembered that no one from our party knew that Chase and I had been to the radio room and added, "I mean, that's what I heard from someone."

Billy turned on me. "So we're just going to sit here and do *nothing?*"

I lifted my hands in surrender, trying to tell him I was on the same side.

Truck was dead. The fact hit me again like a ton of bricks.

"You want to do something?" DeWitt's voice grew soft. "Come with me."

For a second I thought I saw a flicker of fear flash in Billy's eyes. I almost stopped him as he stalked past me to Three's leader.

"The rest of you, back to your posts," said DeWitt. He snatched the radio from Chase's hand and removed the batteries. "And the next man I catch stealing from our supply closet wins a permanent placement on latrine duty."

It was a punishment I'd heard before—Wallace had given it to Billy back at the Wayland Inn. I saw in the way Billy's shoulders hunched that he was remembering the same thing.

"Wait," I said. "The team you sent after our people, are they back yet?"

DeWitt paused, turning to face all those close by who were now awaiting his response.

"If they were, you would know," he said.

I stared at his back as he walked away. Waiting, trusting a man I barely knew to take care of something we should have been dealing with ourselves left me unsettled.

"Keep your ears open," Chase said. "I'll find you as soon as I can."

He left with the other fighters before I could tell him about the fallen post.

CHASE did not return to the dorms that evening, and neither did Billy nor Jesse. They might have been sent out to rescue the thirteen remaining prisoners, or back to the safe house wreckage to gather our injured. They might be doing a hundred different things helpful to the cause, while the rest of us were told there was nothing more we could do tonight.

The top bunk was no wider than a cot, but without Chase it seemed too big and empty. It was the first night I'd spent without him since I'd been in the holding cells in Knoxville, a reminder that just made things worse. When I grew tired of staring at the door, I stared at the ceiling. But one by one the candles went out, and the conversations went quiet.

The dreams were coming; I could feel their black, slippery fingers wrapping around the edges of my mind. Without Chase's arms around me, there'd be nothing to stop them. So I pinched myself awake.

My thoughts weren't much better.

I made myself sick wondering who of Tucker's team had

survived the attack on the post, and who had been tortured alongside Truck—or who was being tortured right now—but it was useless.

The thought of Tucker dying for the resistance had me tossing and turning.

In the bunk below me, Sean and Rebecca were talking in hushed tones. I hung my head over the side.

"What do you know about the Chief of Reformation?" I demanded.

Sean was lying on his back, Rebecca curled against his side. She didn't look up at me, but tightened her grip around Sean's waist.

"Chancellor Reinhardt," said Sean. "I know he's hard to get to. People have been trying to take him out since the Reformation. He keeps a security detail around him all the time."

I rested my cheek against the side rail, feeling the cool metal against my skin.

"He's evil. He used to call for patients at the hospital to be brought to the base." Rebecca paused. "When you came for me, I thought you might be with him. Before I saw that it was you, I mean." Her voice was barely above a breath.

The circus, Truck had called it in Chicago. Where they paraded the injured around to deter others from breaking the rules. A sour taste formed in the back of my mouth. That Rebecca had ever been subjected to that fear made me hate Chancellor Reinhardt even more.

"Do you think the prisoners are back in Chicago?" I asked. But they must not have heard me, because Sean had turned on his side and was whispering something I couldn't make out. I drew back, feeling distinctly like I was intruding on something private.

After a while I heard Rebecca giggle, a sound that pulled

me momentarily from my thoughts. Then her breath caught and hitched, and the mattress groaned as their weight shifted.

I covered my ears.

Time seemed to stall. Each minute felt like an hour. After a while even Rebecca and Sean grew quiet. Too restless to wait for news any longer, I decided to take my chances with Rocklin.

Carefully, I climbed down the ladder, placing my feet, still in their boots, on the floor. The creak of the frame made me cringe, but no one around me moved.

On the bottom bunk Rebecca slept with her head on Sean's shoulder, and I was reminded of a long time ago when she'd been the one sneaking out of the reformatory, and I'd been trying to follow.

Holding my breath, I tiptoed down the row, freezing every time someone shifted or murmured in their sleep. When I reached the door, I glanced out quickly, expecting to find Rocklin posted outside, but the entryway was clear. The torches on the path had been extinguished, and with only the moon to guide me, I sprinted around the back of the building. The trees were a quarter mile away, glowing a pale silver and swaying ever so slightly in the breeze. From beneath their curtain, a gravel road emerged, connecting to the cafeteria.

My heart was pounding. I didn't know where I was going, and if I did find the fighters, I didn't know how to find Chase among them.

A shadow crawled over the moon, and without further delay I carved through the untamed grass toward the trees. It would have been easier to take the road, but I didn't want to get caught—which was stupid, of course. It wasn't like I was doing anything wrong. They wouldn't stop me from seeing Chase.

I slowed, then stopped, and stared up at the sky.

Things were supposed to make sense once we got here.

We'd finally stopped running. This was a place where we were protected, where we could dig in and fight back. Instead I was dodging guards while people I'd fought beside died at the MM's hand.

I crossed the tree line; the branches formed a canopy overhead, and the dried leaves crunched beneath each step. The way opened suddenly into a clearing where the moonlight, unobstructed by the trees, highlighted small wooden crosses jutting up from the ground in neat lines.

I'd stumbled upon a cemetery. My skin began to crawl, and instinctively I took a few steps back.

Beyond the cemetery, down a long hill, flickered the flames from half a dozen bonfires. As I crept around the perimeter toward them, people became visible, moving to and from a row of storage units. To the right was a tall wooden fence, and as I squinted to where it disappeared into the dark distance I could barely make out what looked like a dozen FBR cruisers and several more military vans and trucks. Enough to transport a hundred soldiers or more.

I turned back to the storage units, surmising from the lack of other options that this was where the soldiers slept. There were enough people moving around that I thought I might be able to blend in without much notice. I was just about to exit the trees when a noise to my right made me freeze.

To my right was a rickety wooden toolshed slightly removed from the graveyard that I hadn't seen earlier. A guard stood outside, a rifle held ready across his chest. The twitch in his shoulder and nervous toss of his hair was too familiar. What Billy could possibly be doing out here in the middle of the night triggered my curiosity.

As I watched, another figure appeared in the doorway. The lean hips and straight shoulders identified him as male, but the fires were on the opposite side of the camp, and the shadows hid his face. He disappeared within, and then reappeared, and without a word to Billy headed straight toward me, cutting through the cemetery. He stopped at the last cross in the line and placed one hand gently on the wood.

I ducked as low as I could and held my breath. If I ran now I'd be seen.

A few seconds later another man came from the woods, moving quietly, but with purpose. More imposing with his height and muscular chest, he stopped at the edge of the woods, out of view from the shed. For a moment I felt a sharp need to call out a warning, but then the first man turned away from the grave marker and joined him, clearly having expected his arrival.

It was as good a time as any to make a quick exit, but something inside urged me to follow, and soon I was stooping behind a thicket of brush, ten feet away. The crosses watched over silently, the only witness to my eavesdropping.

"It's not going to jeopardize the mission. We've already verified what the girl said. A quick extraction, that's all we're talking about."

The slighter man had to be DeWitt; I recognized his voice but not the anxiety behind it. The second man responded with something I couldn't make out, though I strained my ears to catch it. As far as I could tell there were only two people, not the whole council that Three's leader had spoken of earlier.

I felt sure he was talking about sending a team out to rescue the prisoners. Still, I didn't know what other mission he spoke of, or what girl had given him information that would need to be verified. My mind raced through everything I'd told him, just in case.

"The injuries could be substantial," argued DeWitt.

I was reminded of our injured, left at the mini-mart miles up the coast. Hopefully they could hold on until we could reach them.

"There's still time. Please. I thought you of all people would understand." I held my breath as DeWitt's voice rose. A shadow paced in front of the door and I ducked lower, the sharp leaves of the bush cutting into my hands.

This wasn't the DeWitt I recognized from the radio room, or the one who had addressed his people this morning. Something had scared him. I wondered again who he was speaking to that had such control, and why anything he did required asking permission.

A second later a branch broke beneath my hand and both voices paused. Wincing, I crawled backward, behind a tree, but the two men were now coming my way. My heart was hammering. DeWitt already suspected me of having something to do with the fallen resistance posts. If he caught me sneaking around outside a meeting, he would never believe I was innocent.

"Did you hear that?" DeWitt asked.

I didn't wait another second. I turned and ran straight back to the dorms.

CHAPTER

11

EARLY morning found us packed inside the cafeteria. The council was convening before breakfast and we were summoned to hear an important announcement. After Tucker's last report, and the radio broadcast of Truck's death, I couldn't help but feel nervous waiting with the others. If ever Three would respond, the time was now.

I stood in the back near the exit beside Rebecca. Not everyone was accounted for; the children had been gathered and taken to the south wing, and Sean and some of the field workers had been summoned early to pack rations for some team heading to the interior. None of the fighters had come from the camps below. I kept my eyes pinned on the door, wanting to be the first to see Chase should he arrive.

The rain that had begun late in the night had yet to let up. It came in a constant sheet, dripping through the roof in a dozen different places. A familiar uneasiness spread through my muscles. Even with so many absent, this many people packed close together could not be safe.

Finally, Ms. Rita, Panda, and the man with the red hair who'd captured us in the grove arrived and sat behind a long table erected near the entrance to the kitchen. Dr. DeWitt followed closely behind them and even from across the room his exhaustion was apparent. He rubbed both hands over the stubble of his jaw and nodded to someone standing in the front.

"I feel bad for him," Rebecca whispered. "You know his family was killed by the MM."

"I know he supposedly killed a bunch of soldiers," I said.

Rebecca lowered her voice. "It was a routine inspection. Word is things got out of hand when the soldiers found the Article Violators hiding in their basement. The wife and daughter tried to run, and . . ."

"And . . ." I prompted, leaning close so that no one standing nearby could hear.

"They didn't make it. So the doctor, *you know*, finished it. Not without a fight though. That's how he got all the scars on his face."

Rumors usually only had bits of truth, if any at all, but what Rebecca had heard seemed possible.

I twisted my necklace around my finger, thinking of my own arrest. If Chase hadn't been there, I might not even still be alive. I closed the memories from my mind and scanned each of the other council members' faces and figures, trying to determine who DeWitt had met last night. None of them were right. The other person had obviously been male; Panda was too short, and the redhead was too thin. The only other person I knew was missing on the council was the old man with the eye patch, and he didn't fit either.

"All right," started DeWitt. He raised his hands and the room silenced. "In light of recent events, we're suspending all regular business for the present time."

I found myself looking for Billy, and wondering again what he'd been guarding by the cemetery last night.

"Another of our posts was attacked yesterday, making three in this week alone," continued DeWitt. "Prisoners were taken. Our sources tell us that in a little over two weeks, the Chief of Reformation plans to celebrate this series of victories with a party at the Charlotte base. It will be his first public appearance since his unfortunate recovery last month."

A grumble rose from the audience—it was a sick man who celebrated the deaths of others by throwing a party. As voices lifted in anger, a memory from the Wayland Inn came to the forefront of my mind: gathering around a radio while we learned of an assassination attempt on the Chief of Reformation's life. It had been the first time I'd heard about Three.

DeWitt raised his arms to silence the crowd.

"It will also be our first public appearance. As we speak, our teams are already being deployed to Charlotte, as well as other key FBR bases, to await instructions. The details of this mission will be kept highly confidential until our people reach their destination so as not to put anyone at unnecessary risk. In addition, we'll observe a radio silence effective immediately to limit the chances the FBR will receive any outgoing signals. Incoming transmissions will continue to be monitored."

The air in the room grew thick and heavy, and soon I realized I hadn't breathed in too long. I gasped shallowly, one thought alone burning into my mind.

Chase.

DeWitt was planning on sending him into a warzone. He might already be gone. I needed to find him. Find him and figure out what we would do next—run, or hide, or fight with the others. Whatever it was, we would do it together. I would not let him go again.

A cold hand gripped mine and I turned to meet Rebecca's bright blue eyes.

"It's going to be fine," she said. "It can't be as bad as it sounds."

The room had succumbed to whispers, but squeaking boots behind us rose over the sound.

"What'd I miss?" Sean shook the water out of his hair with one hand. His other arm was still strapped in a sling, reminding me of Chase's part in his assignment to the gardens.

"Tough crowd," he said when we didn't answer. "Great. Someone died, didn't they?"

I tried to force the implications of the council's orders from my mind, but I couldn't. People would die—Three's people. They'd be slaughtered; I'd seen the census numbers for the base yesterday in the radio room. Thousands against a couple of hundred. Though I wanted vengeance, an attack didn't make sense. There were simply too many of them and too few of us.

"Quiet!" called DeWitt. "We're taking volunteers—anyone nonessential to our daily operations here." He paused, and Ms. Rita put a hand on his shoulder. "This is the moment we've been waiting for. You chose this life. You know the reasons that led you down our path. We're asking you to remember those reasons now."

My gaze turned to Panda unconsciously, drifting down the names listed on his forearm.

"This is suicide," I said aloud. Those closest glared in my direction. I didn't care. Let them think what they wanted. The Three I'd heard spoken of in whispered rumors, both worshipped and feared by the resistance, was invincible. They made smart decisions. They weren't going to lead a revolution by becoming martyrs.

"We don't know the whole plan," said Rebecca. "Dr. DeWitt said the details are being kept a secret. Chase and his uncle probably know more."

Her words calmed me a little. She was right. DeWitt had alluded there was more to this mission than just the attack. I was already heading for the exit when Sean grabbed my forearm.

"Wait," he said. He removed a folded piece of paper from his pocket and shoved it into my hand. "Read it later."

I placed it into my pocket, barely giving it a second thought. The only thing on my mind was finding Chase. As long as he hadn't already left without me.

The mud splashed up my legs as I ran down the gravel road that disappeared into the woods. In the daylight, even with the drizzle, the fighters' beige tents could be seen peeking through the brush and spindly gray branches, heavy with drooping moss.

Chase had to be there. He couldn't have left without telling me. Even considering it made me sick.

As the road declined I glanced back and saw Rocklin in the distance emerging from the cafeteria with his hands on his hips. I didn't wait to see if he followed.

This time I stuck to the dirt road that cut through the trees, avoiding the cemetery and the shed where I'd seen Billy. All at once, the woods opened to reveal the camp I'd seen only from a distance the previous night. The rain pinged off the metal tops of the storage units. The fires were now extinguished, but now the fields that stretched between the road and the parking lot of stolen MM cars were alive with movement. The fighters—both men and women—were in a state of controlled chaos. Some were crowded at tables beneath the lean-tos, assembling weapons. Others were in lines for haircuts, given beneath a striped tent. Many of the women already wore Sisters of Salvation outfits, while the men were in various combinations of MM uniforms. Still others were dressed in street clothes. One guy jogged by in a navy flack jacket with his cropped Endurance pants beneath. He didn't seem to notice me.

It hit me then, in a way DeWitt's words couldn't. This was really happening. Three was preparing for war, and Chase was preparing with them.

A cold panic dripped down my spine. I took a deep breath and scanned the crowd for Chase, Billy, Jesse, anyone I might recognize, suddenly aware that I was an outsider here. Everyone seemed to have a job, a purpose, but even in the north wing, I was held at an arm's length and watched with suspicion. That wasn't the case here. Everyone was in a constant state of movement but me, like I was standing in the eye of a hurricane.

Near the weapons tent I caught a flash of short black hair a head above the rest. Without another thought I ran after him, sloshing through the puddles and slipping through the bodies that grew denser as we neared the heart of the camp.

He ducked behind a group of fake Sisters, and I circled around them, finally catching the back of his sleeve.

"Chase!"

But it was Jesse that turned around. He looked different with short hair. Younger, more serious. Just as dangerous—that sharp look was still in his dark eyes—but not as shifty as before. My gaze flicked to the tattoo on his neck.

"Sorry to disappoint, neighbor," he said with a fake smile.

"Where is he?" I asked.

Jesse scratched a hand through his short hair. "Last I saw he was getting a little taken off the top."

So he was still here. At least for now.

"I need to talk to him."

He held his arms out. "As you can see, we're all a little busy at the moment."

"Since when did you care so much about all this?" I nearly spit the words.

"All this . . ." He smiled like he didn't understand what I meant.

"The *cause*."

"Ah," he said. "I'm a fast learner."

A whistle cut through the rain, and the closest fighters immediately began heading to where the cars were parked, leaving Jesse and I standing alone.

"Dr. DeWitt told us what's happening." He blocked my view when I leaned around him. "Are they really sending Chase out?"

Jesse gave me a confused look. "They're sending everyone who isn't injured or essential to running this place. Or short." He measured my height with one hand. "The kids, for example. They'll stay behind."

I narrowed my gaze, swiping away the water that had gathered in my hair.

"Why?" I whispered, more to myself than to him. Rebecca had reminded me that those who went would receive more specific orders in the field, but the numbers I'd seen in the north wing were still embedded in my mind. Too many soldiers, not enough resistance.

"Because," said Jesse. "When a government becomes destructive, it is the right of the people to alter or abolish it, and to institute a new government."

I peeked out at him through the fingers that had covered my face. "Did you just make that up?" It didn't sound like anything he'd normally say. Not that I knew him well enough to know.

He laughed, and it struck me as odd that he spoke of such patriotism while in no apparent rush to join the others.

"Believe it or not, someone even older than me did. But that doesn't make it less true." He took a step back, turned away. "If

I see my nephew, I'll tell him you came by," he called over his shoulder as he walked away.

I stared at his back, aware of the encroaching footsteps that came up behind me. I knew who it would be, and wasn't in the mood to be babysat.

"The doc is looking for you," Rocklin said bluntly. "We got a message from your friend."

THE radio room in the north wing was still bustling with people when Rocklin and I arrived. This time the guards didn't block my way; they stood aside as if expecting me, and allowed me to enter the tight, dimly lit quarters. A wall of heat drew the sweat to my skin as I stepped over the threshold, and I found myself wishing for an open window.

"Hope your break was worth it." I spun around to face DeWitt, standing before the wall that had held the picture of Chase and I in the hospital. "You missed a call from your friend."

It took a beat to register what he meant. Tucker.

"He's still alive?"

The muscles beside DeWitt's mouth ticked, and his scarred jaw was gray with stubble. My throat worked to swallow. Besides learning that Chase had not been sent out for our injured, I had accomplished nothing, and now I'd missed something important. Something that affected more lives than just my own.

"Is he still . . ." I pointed to the radio and then realized I couldn't respond anyway. Besides receiving signals, Three was confined to air silence.

"No," said DeWitt. "He's gone now."

The disappointment weighed heavily on my shoulders.

"What did he say?"

DeWitt sighed and strode past me to the radio. He said

something to the operator, who flipped a few switches on the high right corner of the machine, and then removed his headphones.

"Lucky for you, we recorded it."

The transmission was not as clear as it had been before. Now it was glitchy and clicked on and off in intervals. But that didn't stop Tucker's voice, stretched thin with panic, from filling the room.

". . . if you're even still there . . . gone . . . all of them . . . just me left . . . if you're still . . . meet . . . at the beach. I'll be . . . soon as I can . . ." A crackling burst of static followed, and in it I realized I'd been holding my breath and quickly gulped down the air.

Then Tucker whispered, almost as a prayer, "Please be there."

The transmission went silent.

A stitch popped in the neck of my shirt. During the recording I'd gripped the hem and stretched it down my hips as far as it would go. I released it now, but my hands were still shaky. Old scars stood out on the backs of my knuckles, white on red blotchy skin.

Tucker was all that was left of the team we'd sent into the interior. It felt like he was coming back to find me, just as he had in Louisville after Cara's death. Just as he always would.

DeWitt broke the silence. "The beach—I assume he means the safe house?"

I backed into the wall and leaned against it, grateful it was sturdy while I was not.

"Yes," I managed. "That's where we split up."

"I don't suppose I have to tell you that he could be responsible for the FBR's attacks on our posts. That he could be baiting you into a trap."

He didn't have to tell me those things; I had already

considered them. But there was another possibility, too: that Tucker was honestly in danger and needed our help.

The pulse pounded in my ears.

"Someone's got to meet him," I said finally. "We need to find out what he knows about the resistance posts."

"And if he's been compromised?"

I breathed in slowly, let the air fill my lungs. "Someone's got to bring him in. Keep an eye on him if you don't trust him. Rocklin seems bored following me around."

DeWitt raised his brows, contemplating this.

"Send me," I heard myself say. "And Chase. He trusts us." If Chase was with me he wouldn't be back in the interior, hunted by soldiers.

"That may be difficult," said DeWitt, staring off at the map with the red pushpins, the fallen posts. I couldn't imagine why anyone would have a problem with this. We weren't crucial to Endurance's operations.

I pushed off the wall, meeting his eyes. "You want to send Chase to Charlotte."

DeWitt didn't answer.

"The MM's looking for him after what happened in the rehab hospital in Chicago." I paused to steady my voice. "I saw the census numbers yesterday. We don't have enough people to beat them."

"I know," said DeWitt softly.

"Then why?"

"Because half the country is too scared to stand up for themselves, and the other half is sleeping." He wandered around the room, distracted. "Do you know how many people have no idea the threat the FBR poses on their freedom? So they've had to cut back a little since the War, so they've moved to a smaller house, gotten a generator so they don't lose their power at curfew. They believe what the news tells them—that these at-tacks on our posts were for their own good. The FBR's gotten rid of more *insurgents*, more scum endangering their children's futures. They'll never see a city of starving people, living in tents. They'll never wait in a line for food or hide in a check point and wait for a carrier to take them somewhere safe." He stopped now, and slowly smashed his fist into the tabletop. "They will never watch someone they love murdered for help-ing their fellow man."

I could still hear my mother, arguing with the officers that took her away. *We're not animals,* she'd said. But they'd gotten rid of her like she was one.

It didn't seem possible that half the country had adjusted to the MM's demands, that they carried on as if nothing was wrong. It didn't seem possible that my mother and I had been doing exactly that just months ago. I pictured the neighbor-hood Tucker had told me about in his first radio transmission, the one that had boasted its compliance to the Statutes. These places did exist. They were why the MM could do what the MM did.

A horrible realization sunk into my bones.

"You're going to attack the MM knowing we'll lose."

"Nothing is certain," he said again. "We're going to set an example—show the Bureau what Three is capable of. We're going to wake up the country, and once they see the horrors of how their government will respond, they won't be able to stand by any longer."

"And the prisoners? The thirteen others that were with Truck?"

DeWitt hesitated. "We'll do what we can for them."

He might as well have said, *"They knew what they were get-ting into."* He would do nothing, and they would die.

My stomach turned. "There has to be another way."

His eyes flickered with desperation, and in that moment I knew he wanted another option, too, but then they hardened and went cold.

"You've got an idea, I'm willing to listen," he said. "In the meantime stay close. I've got to meet with the council."

IT was nearly dusk when Rocklin appeared at the kitchen door. I'd been scrubbing dishes since after lunch, and my hands were pruned and sore from the diluted lye soap. I removed them from the water and dried them on my pants, feeling the sharp corners of a plastic condom package in my left pocket, and the crinkle of paper in my right. Consumed by thoughts of Three's mission, Tucker's plight, and Chase down with the fighters, I'd forgotten about the gifts my friends had bestowed upon me. I still hadn't read the note Sean had given me this morning.

"Well?" I asked. I didn't expect an answer—DeWitt had said he would meet with the council, and Panda had yet to leave the kitchen.

"A team will be sent back to the safe house at dawn," said Rocklin.

My muscles tensed in anticipation. It would take hours to reach Tucker, and hours before we could return with the vital information he possessed. Another of our posts could fall in the time we wasted.

"We should leave now," I said.

Rocklin's nostrils flared. "You're not on the roster."

DeWitt still didn't trust me. He thought Tucker had been *compromised* and I would lead him and the MM straight back to Endurance. I didn't know how I was supposed to prove my loyalty to the cause on such a short leash.

"All right," I said. Rocklin left me staring at the door.

Rubbing the lines from between my brows I reached into my pocket and retrieved the crinkled note Sean had shoved my way earlier. I unfolded it carefully, blanching at the Statutes that were printed in bold type. Words on the other side of the paper had soaked through when I'd been outside in the rain and I flipped it over, skimming the grocery list of items in blank ink that bled across the page. Zucchini was first, followed by cabbage, kale, carrots, and a dozen other vegetables, along with their quantity by the crate.

I suspected Sean had given me the wrong note by mistake—this looked like the notes Panda had pegged on the wall of the kitchen that came from the gardens. But when I read it again, I saw that halfway down the page, between sweet potatoes and beets were two words, scratched in subtly different handwriting.

Barn, and *Tonight.*

I folded the note, a smile brushing my lips.

CHAPTER
12

I LAID in my bunk until dark, convinced that time had stopped while I waited to meet Chase. The dorms were less full than last night; many had volunteered to join the fight, and those that remained were restless.

The faces of those I'd come here with passed before me. I wondered if I would ever see them again. I could only imagine how Jack was feeling after hearing what had happened to Truck or what Wallace would think if he saw Billy now, hardened by grief. They'd both joined Three's army now; I almost pitied any MM soldiers that got in their way.

When the last candles finally flickered out and the last whispers faded, I climbed down the ladder again, but this time found Rebecca curled in a ball, alone. A solid, cold stone settled in the pit of my belly at Sean's absence. Too many friends were already unaccounted for.

I tiptoed around the bunks, past where Sarah slept on the mats near the children. I was almost to the exit when someone emerged from the supply room and took me off guard. I jumped to the side before we could collide.

Sean clutched his chest. When he recognized me, he tossed his head back.

"You scared the holy . . ."

"Where have you been?" I asked at the same time.

He muttered something about sneaking around a heart attack, but I had focused on the stack of blankets tucked under his sling and cut him off.

"What's all that for?"

His shoulders fell an inch, and I knew. He didn't even have to tell me.

"They're sending you after Tucker," I said.

Sean nodded, eyes narrowing. "Me, Jack. A few others."

I'd told DeWitt someone had to go, even volunteered myself. I hadn't thought he'd send Sean.

"What happened to your busted shoulder?" I asked. "I thought they made you a farmer because you couldn't fight."

"I've been assured there will be no heavy lifting." He shrugged, then winced and grabbed his injured shoulder with his other hand.

"You have to stay with Rebecca," I said. "You *promised*."

Immediately he shushed me and pulled me inside the supply room.

"You think I didn't try everything to make that possible?" he said, moving the blankets under his other arm. "You think I volunteered for this?"

No. I'd unintentionally done that for him.

"We'll switch. Chase and I will go instead."

He gave me a look like I was crazy. "If I didn't know better, I'd think you were itching to get back out there."

"I'm not," I said. "It's just that Tucker might have information about the fallen posts, or about the prisoners. Something that might help us."

"*Us*," said Sean, making a noise of disbelief. "Wow. They got to you fast. Next you'll be chanting at the full moon and shaving your head."

"What are you talking about?"

"This place," he said. "It's all smoke and mirrors."

I flinched. "What do you mean?"

"Don't," he said. "I'm not one of them, okay? You could have told me you talked to him. You actually can trust some people, you know."

As he adjusted the length of the sling, I shrunk into the floor.

"I know," I said in a small voice. "DeWitt asked me not to say anything." It was a stupid excuse. If our places were switched, Sean would have told me.

One of his brows arched, which was enough to call me out.

"He's not a bad guy," I said. "He runs this place all right, doesn't he? All these people wouldn't follow him otherwise. If anyone can stand up to the MM, it's Three."

"DeWitt's running this place like the FBR," he argued. "Training soldiers to kill the bad guys."

"It's a war," I said. "What else is he supposed to do?"

I was defending the same man who didn't even let me walk across the compound alone. I busied my hands straightening a stack of threadbare towels.

"He's helped Rebecca, hasn't he?" I felt certain about that at least.

"I never said he wasn't a good doctor."

"Then what are you saying?"

"I'm saying I need him to keep helping her, that's why I'm going." His voice had raised, and at my expression he lowered it. He stepped closer. "I'm saying *this* never stops. Soon they'll be bombing the cities and evacuating and it's chaos, all over again."

"It's different this time." Before it had been about the rich and everyone else. The insurgents, who tried to level the playing field and plunged the country into depression and madness. This was about surviving, about defending our rights as humans and taking back what was rightfully ours.

"Does it feel different?" he asked. "Because I'm not sure it does to Becca. Or those people starving in the Square in Knoxville. Or my brother, wherever he is." He shook his head. "It's the same. It's *always* the same. We're the good guys, they're the enemy."

I pressed the heels of my hands against my temples. "What are you talking about? Of course they're the enemy."

His blue eyes glinted in the dark. "You know, not that long ago you thought I was the enemy, too."

A shadow fell over the door, interrupting our argument. I recognized Rocklin's short stature immediately. As he moved closer his clothes glowed pale silver from the moonlight outside. I slipped deeper into the supply room, hiding behind the door.

"I'll take one of those," Rocklin said.

I watched Sean offer him one of the blankets. My mouth pulled tight in a grimace. With Rocklin guarding the door I'd never get past.

The old gym floor groaned when I shifted my weight. I fought the urge to backpedal and held absolutely motionless. Before me, Sean dug his heel into the floor, as if he'd been the one to make the noise.

"Hey, you think anyone would mind if I take an extra towel?" He stepped deeper into the supply room and I flattened myself as close as I could between the door and the wall. "My girlfriend used hers to dry off after the rain, and, well, you know. Girls." There was a soft thumping noise, followed by Sean's guilty, "Oops."

Towels spilled across the floor, stopping just before my feet.

Rocklin hesitated, then entered the supply room and began helping Sean pick up the mess.

Without wasting a moment I padded by, catching Sean's gaze just for a second as I passed. *You're welcome,* he seemed to say, and I nodded, and broke through the barrier into the cool night air.

The barn was at the front of Endurance, near the gardens and the fishing lake. I didn't go straight there, but made for a row of trees on the north side that would protect me from the accusing spotlight of the moon. The wet grass sloshed beneath my feet as I reached the high wooden fence that ran toward the length of the compound. Overhead, movement in the trees drew my attention—one of Three's guards like those outside the entrance. I ducked down low, catching my breath.

Even if I escaped Rocklin's watch, it didn't mean I could leave.

You can trust me, you know.

I did trust Sean. Outside of Chase and Rebecca, there was no one I trusted more.

Not that long ago you thought I was the enemy, too.

Things weren't black and white, but that didn't mean you couldn't pick a side.

I shook my head clear and raced along the vine-covered perimeter barricade until I reached the barn. Inside, the horses were restless, stamping their feet and snorting, but no human voices could be heard. I hoped I wasn't too late, that Chase hadn't thought I wouldn't come and returned to the camp. So much had happened since I'd seen him last. It felt like weeks had passed, not just two days.

A ladder stretching to the loft leaned against the siding. Thinking that I might have a better view of the surrounding area from higher ground, I clasped the splintered rungs and hauled myself up. Once I reached the top, I hopped through the opening and was surrounded by the sweet musty smell of hay and horses. The compartment was stacked with bales of straw, and there, already moving toward me, was Chase.

Before I could draw another breath, I was swept up in his arms. My feet lifted off the floor, my arms wound around his neck. He smelled like the rain and felt like home, and I held him just as tightly as he held me, relieved to finally be close to him again.

After too short a time he set me down, but his hands stayed on my waist and my fingers spread over his chest. The splinters of starlight that speared through the cracks in the ceiling softened the strong lines of his face, bringing out his smooth skin and dark, messy hair.

"I didn't think you were going to be able to shake your new friend," he said, referring to Rocklin. His lips quirked on one side.

"Sean helped," I said with a guilty pang. "Speaking of Sean, what did you do to his shoulder?"

His nose scrunched and he looked away. "I don't know what you're talking about."

"Never mind. I don't want to know," I said. "What about you? Are they watching?"

He shook his head. "Not since Jesse's been back."

I felt the scowl pull at my mouth. My conversation with Jesse at the camp reminded me of more pressing issues.

"Another post was attacked—"

"They're deploying teams—"

Simultaneously, we launched into our hurried reports, then stopped, and waited for the other to speak. When neither of us did, we both smiled.

As if by need his hand lifted, and his knuckles skimmed down my cheek. I closed my eyes, wanting to live forever in that moment but knowing it was impossible.

"Tucker sent another message."

His hand dropped.

"Okay." He sat on the hay bale and patted the space beside him. "Sounds like you better go first."

I told him everything. About the message from Tucker. About my request that Chase and I be the ones to bring him in for questioning, but that DeWitt had chosen Sean instead. About the census reports I'd seen the techs taking in the north wing, and how Three's mission to attack the Charlotte base was bound to fail because the numbers simply did not work out.

"Slow down," he said. I hadn't realized I'd been talking faster and faster, or that I'd risen and begun to pace until he grabbed my hands and stopped me. A light tug, and I was sitting beside him again, watching as he chewed his bottom lip and wound his fingers in and out of mine.

"It doesn't make sense. They wouldn't send everyone out if they didn't think we had a chance."

"I'm telling you, they are," I said, the anxiety crawling up my chest. "It's a suicide mission. DeWitt practically said it. The point is to show the people just what kind of retaliation the MM is capable of."

"But so many people know that already," he argued. "All those people in the Square in Knoxville. Everyone who doesn't pass a home inspection. People aren't stupid."

"I know," I said. "But they're scared, and they're not doing anything. They're just trying to survive day to day. Three wants to get the attention of everyone, even the compliant. They think it'll start some sort of large-scale uprising I guess."

Chase was silent for a long time. He lifted our clasped hands and brushed my fingers absently from side to side over his lips. I swallowed, feeling a flash of heat streak down my arm.

"The guy in charge down there—Patch—he hasn't said anything about that," he said finally.

"Well why would they?" I jerked my hand away, unable to concentrate while he was distracting me. "They wouldn't just tell you they're sending you out to die."

"I don't know," he said. "I think they might. Some of these people . . . the cause is all they have." He smoothed his furrowed brows and tucked a strand of hair behind my ear. It seemed impossible for him to go more than a few seconds without touching me. I hadn't realized it, but I'd already moved closer to him. Our knees brushed, and the toes of my boots came to rest on his.

"It's going to happen during the chief's celebration. We're supposed to wait for a sign," he said. "We'll know it when it happens. That's when we attack the base. Patch is talking like we have a good chance of making a mark."

It felt like bolts had straightened my spine. "What do you mean we?"

He glanced to the floor. When he spoke again his voice was lower, older, if that was possible. "We're always talking about doing something, aren't we? That it isn't fair how they keep taking everything away. Maybe this is how we get it back."

"Chase, you're not listening to me."

"I'm listening." He pulled out a fistful of hay from the bale beneath him and twisted it until the dry pieces popped and broke apart. "I know it sounds crazy, but I think I'm supposed to fight."

I shook my head. I wanted retribution, I wanted to fight back. But not like this. Not when we didn't even have a chance.

"I don't understand," I said. "You hate fighting." *You hate killing.*

"But maybe I keep going back to it for a reason." He scratched his head.

I'm a soldier, Tucker had told me once. *If I'm not out there, I'm not anything.* The likeness made my stomach hurt.

"Besides, Jesse says fighting's in our blood."

"Jesse . . ." I groaned. "Jesse's been here five minutes. Don't you think it's a little weird that he's all gung ho when just last week he was hiding out at a safe house?"

Chase frowned. "He was in the army, you know. The real army, before the FBR."

That wasn't enough to prove he was a hero in my book, but as always, going up against Chase's uncle got me nowhere. I floundered, looking for a way to make Chase see reason, but came up blank.

He gave a one-shouldered shrug, looking a little embarrassed. "He fought for something important once. He did great things."

I took a breath, held it a moment. "He did some things that weren't so great, too."

He nodded. "But the good things cancelled out the bad. Or, no . . ." He focused on a point on the floor and scratched the back of his head. "Nothing cancels out the bad. But doing enough good things can make the bad . . . less bad." He made a noise in the back of his throat. "Jesse's earned his rest in the Spirit World, that's all I'm trying to say."

The hay dust was suspended in the air between us, as if time had stopped.

"I don't know if the bad things ever go away," I said slowly.

"But if they could, I think your slate would be wiped clean. And if there is a Spirit World, I think you've earned your rest there, too."

He looked at me for a long time.

"Not yet," he finally said.

I looked at my hands that had turned into fists on my lap and watched as he took them and pulled gently, until I was curled up on his lap, my cheek against his neck.

"You're really going," I whispered. He kissed the top of my head. Everything inside of me felt stretched, like the handful of straw he'd twisted until it broke apart. "Then I'm coming with you," I said. It wasn't like I was going to meet Tucker, and anyway, Chase was more important. Even if I had to sneak out, I would be by his side.

He didn't say anything.

"This morning, when I heard they'd sent a team out to get our injured, I thought you were gone. I thought Three had sent you away. Those moments before I knew were some of the worst I've ever had." I sat up and faced him, running my thumbs down his jaw. "If you're going to fight, I'm going to fight. If you want to run, we'll run. But I'm not letting you leave without me."

I kissed him. I pressed all my fear and pride and love into that kiss, and when I pulled away his eyes were glassy with emotion and his breath came in one hard heave.

"Okay," he said. And then again. "Okay."

Then he kissed me back.

It was like every kiss we'd ever shared pressed into one, and because of that so different from anything I'd experienced before. The feelings seemed to collide inside of him, spark, and combust, and soon I was straddling his lap, gasping for breath while he poured every ounce of himself into each touch.

Tomorrow disappeared. *Everything* disappeared.

His fingers threaded through my hair and inched down my back, pressing us closer. I lifted my chin for air, and his mouth found my neck, leaving a trail of kisses down to my collarbone, where the Saint Michael pendant slid along the chain. The heat exploded within me, ricocheting out to my limbs, making every part of me come alive. My hands flew over his chest, his strong shoulders, around to his back and under his shirt to the rippled scar that wrapped around his side. I tugged the fabric over his head, needing to feel his skin. Needing to push us farther.

He stood, and for a moment I was weightless, my knees locked around his hips while he supported my back with one arm. And then the boards of the loft groaned softly as he kneeled and stuffed his shirt beneath us. He hovered over me, balancing his weight on his elbows, pausing for a moment to check my reaction.

I flattened my hand over his heart, feeling it beating hard. Feeling it as if it were mine, and knowing if he was gone, mine too would go silent. His chest rose and fell with each breath. He seemed to think I was pushing him back and added more distance between us, but I stopped him when I shimmied out of my shirt and tossed it aside.

I stared up at him.

He slowed then, and shifted to his side. His finger drew a line from my throat to my belly button and I wondered if he could feel the way my muscles jumped beneath his touch. I focused on his Adam's apple bobbing, aware of a new, demanding need taking over, overriding the fear and insecurities, blending us together, stripping us down to the truth: that there was nothing more than him and me, than warmth and trust and right now.

"Wait." I reached down into my pocket, and removed the

two plastic squares Rebecca had given me, reminding myself to thank her later. I shoved them into his hand.

He shook his head, as if trying to clear it.

"Where'd you get this? Never mind, it doesn't matter." He cleared his throat. His fingertips skimmed down my neck, to my bare shoulder, and down my arm to my wrist. "Are you sure?"

I knew he meant not just about this, but about my promise to stay with him, and I nodded, terrified, but in a good way, because he made me strong.

"Yes."

I watched as he placed a gentle, trembling hand in the curve of my waist.

He kissed me then, firmly, but slowly enough to break my heart. Our words turned to whispers, then to sighs, then to gasps. And as the moonlight shifted across the window, every worry of what tomorrow would bring, every worry that I didn't know what to do, melted away, until there was only us.

SOMETIME later we untangled our limbs and shyly sorted through our clothes. We took a long time to dress, as if dusting off our shirts and slowly tying our bootlaces meant that this thing—this really big, important thing that had happened between us—was over.

It was late; the moon had disappeared from the small window near the barn's ceiling and risen in the night sky. The heavy breathing of the horses in the stalls below filtered up through the boards. I stared at the ladder leading down to the ground, and thought of the dorms, of my bunk above Rebecca and Sean, who were preparing to say good-bye, and felt a sharp pain in my chest. I didn't want to go back.

Tomorrow Three would send us out to fight. I didn't know

what to expect, but I knew we would play our part. And hopefully, that would mean more than just these stolen moments.

Chase was seated on a bale of straw beside me, and I couldn't help but smile at the pieces of hay that stuck to him. I leaned forward, a little embarrassed, and shook out my hair, knowing it probably looked like a bird had made its nest there. He caught a piece in his hand, and as I sat up, he placed it back on my head.

"What are you doing?" I giggled. He put another piece back in my hair just as I removed the previous one.

"I like it." Another piece. "There," he said as if he'd completed a masterpiece. I went to jab him in the side, but his smile had softened. "You're the prettiest thing I've ever seen."

I swallowed, feeling my cheeks warm as all the other emotions rose up inside of me, love and fear and need and even sadness, because as much as this was the beginning of something, it was the end of something, too.

Beneath us, one of the horses stomped and snorted, and I glanced down, seeing the note he'd sent me that had fallen out of my pocket. I scooped it up.

"Sorry about that," he said. "Not a lot of options for scratch paper around here."

I nodded, thinking of the boxes of Statutes in the north wing, and the woman at the computer who'd told me they hijacked the distribution trucks on their way from the printer.

"Very clever," I said, unfolding it and staring at the words that had brought me here. *Barn Tonight*. I wondered if he would think I was silly if I kept it.

I flipped the sheet over again, preparing to fold it, but paused when I saw how the words written on the back had bled through the printed type when the sheet had gotten wet.

I thought of the Statutes posted on my door during the arrest. Posted on every door in the towns we'd passed through on our way here. Posted all over Knoxville and Louisville and every city in the country.

I thought of my mother and her magazines, the articles inside filled with *treason*.

And DeWitt: *The people are sleeping.* We needed a way to wake them up.

"What if Three doesn't have to fight the MM alone?" I asked.

Chase's brows arched. "What do you mean?"

"What if we could get the people to join with us?"

When a government becomes destructive, it is the right of the people to alter or abolish it, and to institute a new government. Jesse's words echoed in my mind.

"Then we'd have a revolution," he said.

I stood up, the note tight in my fist.

"Come on," I said. "We've got to find DeWitt."

CHAPTER
13

THE Lodge was quiet—eerie quiet. Like something might jump out of each shadow the flickering torchlight threw across the hallway. We bypassed the first two men guarding the north wing without any trouble, but once we got to the door of the radio room we came face-to-face with Rocklin. He crossed his arms over his narrow chest and leaned against the closed door.

"Why am I not surprised you'd show up here?" he asked.

"How strange," I said. "I was just about to say the same thing." I mimicked his posture, sick and tired of all the suspicion.

"Looks like great minds think alike," said Chase. "We need to talk to DeWitt."

I tried to smile nicely, but when I glanced over at Chase I saw there was still a piece of straw in his hair. I combed a hand through my own, hoping he might copy the move on himself, but instead he only gave me a strange look. The gesture was not lost on Rocklin, who snorted, and said, "Kind of late to be cleaning stalls."

I snatched the straw out of Chase's hair.

"DeWitt," I said. "Can you tell him we're here? Please."

"What makes you think he's here?"

The door opened inward, and Rocklin stumbled backward, catching himself on the frame just before he fell.

"Because I am. What's this about?" DeWitt appeared behind him. The room was dark but for a lantern resting on the table beside the radios, and the dim yellow light made his face appear gaunt, and the scars on his cheeks deeper.

None of the other techs were present.

"I . . . um . . ."

He didn't look pleased to see us. It hadn't occurred to me until just then that DeWitt might not hear me out.

"Sorry about the interruption, doctor," said Rocklin.

"What are you doing here?" said DeWitt, stepping into the hall. A muscle in his neck bulged. At the harshness in his tone, my gaze dropped behind him to a picture leaning against the lantern. I'd seen it my first time here—the profile of a young girl with dirty blond hair, laughing.

DeWitt returned to the room and snatched the photo off the table. He stuffed it in his pocket and grabbed the lantern. Then he cut between us and headed toward the main foyer.

"Wait," I said, racing to keep up. "We need to talk to you."

"I'm busy," snapped DeWitt. He glared over my head at Chase. "I don't care who you are."

A heavy feeling settled in the center of my chest—he must have heard something over the radio that had upset him. Another post had fallen. More of our people had been hurt. But if that was true, the other techs would have been called in.

"I have an idea," I said quickly. "I know how we can wake the people up."

He slowed. Stopped. Took a deep breath. "You've got one minute."

I uncrumpled the Statute circular I'd smashed in my fist.

"Look familiar?" When he only grunted, I hurried on.

"Everyone knows what the Statutes look like, but what if you could change what they said? If they looked the same, but said something different?" I scrambled for words, sensing his confusion. "Look, if someone changed the words on the flyers to something else—some kind of message—you could reach everyone. That message would be on the front of every business. Kids in school would read it. Half the houses in the country would have it posted on the front door."

"Change the words of the Moral Statutes?" DeWitt asked. "To what?"

"To what's really happening," Chase said.

"You could hide the truth right in plain sight," I said, thinking of the treason embedded in my mother's magazines. "Write about the arrests and executions of the Article violators, and the abuse at reform school, and the brainwashing of soldiers, and what happened to the safe house."

Chase grabbed my hand. His fingers locked between mine and squeezed, as if trying to hold me in place.

DeWitt mulled this over. I shoved the Statutes in front of Chase, feeling the plan grow wings inside of me.

"How often did you look at these—really look at them—when you were a soldier?" I asked.

He exhaled through his teeth. "Never. Not once, actually. In training we read from a handbook."

"Exactly. They're written for everyone else." I pulled my hand free from his. "There would be no reason to fight the bases alone. Once the people see the story, they'll fight with us. It could start a revolution, just like you said."

DeWitt ran his knuckles down his cheek. "If it's subtle enough, worked right into the text, the Bureau might not even notice," he said. "It could be distributed halfway across the country before they caught on."

"They'd deliver our message for us," I said. "There's still two weeks before the chief's party in Charlotte. If we could get it done before then, we'd have a better chance of taking the base, right?"

Excitement, but also something dark and terrible, swelled inside of me. If this worked, the FBR would be irate. Their vengeance would not be pretty.

DeWitt was quiet for several seconds. The light from the lantern threw lopsided circles across the ground as he twisted his wrist.

He nodded slowly.

"So how do you propose we hijack the message into the Statutes?" he asked.

For the first time since we'd arrived, Chase's mouth turned up in a slow, sly grin.

"We just so happen to know a couple of guys who might be able to help."

AN hour later Chase and I were sitting around a foldout table in the cafeteria. The council was summoned, and had been arguing since DeWitt had introduced my plan. They all agreed that hijacking the Statutes was a good, although risky, idea, but disagreed on what exactly the text would say.

"You need to focus on what happened at the safe house," said Ms. Rita, her hair hidden beneath a red scarf. "Go for sympathy, and then tell them the rallying point and time at the Charlotte base."

Patch, the old man who led the fighters, scoffed, tapping his cane against the metal edge of the table. "And if the Blues get the message before the people? Our operation's blown." He shook his head. "No, you have to keep it vague. Speak in general terms."

"Vague is not relatable," said DeWitt. "We need the civil-ians who read this to have something to hold on to. This happened to my cousin, my neighbor, my father. This could happen to me."

"Then you have to use names," said Panda, absently run-ning his fingers over the tattooed list on his opposite forearm. "Real stories, real names."

Chase and I glanced at each other. There were too many stories to count, too many people already lost. How could you choose?

"That list would be a thousand miles long," said Ms. Rita, speaking my thoughts.

There was a heap of Statutes on the table, and a pile of freshly sharpened pencils, but as of yet no one had taken any notes. I took one sheet and folded it in half. Then in half again. And again, and again, just to busy my hands.

"What about your friend with the spinal cord injury?" De-Witt turned to me; it was the first time since we'd arrived any of them had acknowledged us. "A girl who's beaten mercilessly at the reform school, and then purposefully kept out of treat-ment so she could be used to scare other girls into complying with the Statutes."

"Sweet God," murmured Ms. Rita.

I scrunched the thickly folded paper in my fists below the table. Yes, it was a horrifying story, but the last thing I wanted was to exploit my friend. Besides, even if she said yes, Sean would never go for it.

Before I could answer, Van Pelt, the caretaker of the fields, the red-haired man who'd captured us in the orchard, spoke up.

"We don't want this coming off as a sob story," he said. "It needs to inspire."

"Then you need a hero," said Chase. They all turned to

him, myself included. He straightened in his seat. "Someone people know and can look up to."

"That's you, doc." Panda slapped DeWitt on the back.

Three's leader rubbed his chin, lost in thought. "I'm hardly a hero. And I'm not sure my situation's the most relatable anyway. Most civilians aren't packing away refugees in their basement like we were."

He was looking right at me.

I swallowed.

"Right," I said. "The girl who was sent to reform school when her mom was arrested for noncompliance. Who escaped a Knoxville prison, joined the resistance, and supposedly became the sniper."

"There is a certain ring to it," said DeWitt.

Chase had paled. "You'd use her name."

"Yes," I said weakly. "You'd have to use my name. It's already out there—the MM's broadcasted it on and off since we escaped reform school." Part of me had known it would come to this when I'd come up with the plan. That didn't make it any easier to swallow though.

"People think you're dead," Chase argued. "When Cara died, your name died with her."

DeWitt flinched. "There's nothing like resurrecting a hero to get people's attention."

I turned to Chase, feeling a cool numbness override the fear. "The MM knows we're alive because of that stupid photo from the hospital. They're already looking for us. We might as well shove it in their face that I'm still alive despite everything they've done. At the same time we can tell the people what the FBR is really capable of."

"It's good," said Panda. "Look at her. She's the girl next door. Everyone either is her, or knows someone like her."

They looked at me like I was some kind of specimen to be studied, all the while considering if my past was traumatic enough, if I'd been innocent enough, if I was strong enough now. It didn't feel like they were talking about me as much as the me they needed me to be.

I fiddled with the Statutes, strewn across the table while they continued to talk about me like I wasn't there. My eyes landed on the number that had changed my life.

Article 5: Children are considered valid citizens when conceived by a married man and wife. All other children are to be removed from the home and subjected to rehabilitative procedures.

a) Unwed parents may be tried to determine legitimacy of children born out of wedlock. Evidence used in trial may include hospital records, birth certificates, identification cards and so forth.

a. (revised) Unwed parents may be tried to determine legitimacy of all children below the age of eighteen. Evidence used in trial may include hospital records, birth certificates, social security cards and so forth.

b) Those parents held in contempt of Section 2, Article 5 by the investigative board shall be sentenced appropriately.

c) Children's parental rights are absorbed by the state. Citizenship may be granted at the age of eighteen following completion of rehabilitation.

"I want it to tell what happened to my mother," I said, interrupting them. "Since this is my life and all, I think I should get a say in what it says."

The council stopped, stared at me.

"Of course," said Ms. Rita.

Chase's shoulders rounded. There were words inside of him struggling to get free. I could see his jaw working to hold them back.

"It's not enough time," said Patch. "Two weeks isn't enough time to distribute this message to a whole country."

"It just has to spark a flame," said Van Pelt. "Charlotte is just the beginning."

I hoped a spark was enough.

"You'd do this for us?" DeWitt asked me.

I put my hand on Chase's knee. Felt the muscles flex beneath, and then the warmth of his hand covering mine.

"No," I said. "I'll do it for my mom."

WE spent the next two hours going over any details we might be able to insert into the Statutes. I told DeWitt about my mother's arrest and Chase filled in the blanks. The words grew sticky and caught in my throat. It was like reliving the worst parts all over again.

And then, when we were done, we were excused so that the council could meet privately.

"Thank you for your story," DeWitt told me, as if I'd given it to him and it wasn't even mine anymore.

"You're kicking us out?" Chase asked. "Now?"

DeWitt led us to the cafeteria door.

"I can write it," I said. "It should be me. It's my life we're talking about."

"You've done your part," he said, making it clear his word was the last word. "It belongs to all of us now. Stay close. We'll call you soon."

I frowned, feeling somehow lighter without this burden, but infinitely more exposed.

Chase and I sat on the swings at the small playground just

outside the cafeteria, rocking gently forward and back. After a while, Will brought us some food, then disappeared back into the kitchen. We ate quietly, plates on our laps, and watched the light from the standing torches throw shapes against the concrete side of the building.

"The Expungement Initiative," I muttered. Chase had used the term earlier when describing what they'd done to my mother in the Lexington FBR base. It was a new protocol, approved by the Chief of Reformation, meant to make the Article violators disappear so the country could start fresh.

"I can't believe they named it," I said.

Chase leaned forward to put his plate on the ground.

"It's the government," he said, staring at the sand between his feet. "They have a name for everything. Even the things that don't really exist."

I pushed the rest of the food aside. An image of Tucker flashed in my mind. I didn't know if he'd made it to the safe house yet, but part of me was now glad I hadn't been sent to find him. The thought of seeing him now, with my mother's story fresh in my mind, made me sick.

"I hope this works," I said.

Chase didn't respond right away. "If it works, we'll never be able to go back."

I didn't know if he meant back home, or back outside of the Red Zone. It didn't much matter; either was a risk. I rested my head against the cool chain of the swing. "I know."

"What happens then?" He'd never asked me a question about the future before. I didn't know how to answer.

I pushed back on my heels and let the swing carry me forward. "Remember when we were little we'd see who could jump the farthest?"

He smiled. "I remember."

"You'd always let me win." I pumped my legs. "I bet I can jump farther now."

"That's what I'm afraid of," he said.

I didn't jump; I let the momentum carry me back to a stop. And then I walked out of the swing and sat on the crunchy sand against the jungle gym. He came and sat beside me, and I snuggled closer and laid my cheek on his chest.

"Sometimes I miss you when you're not even gone," he said.

I closed my eyes.

WE were woken some time later by Will's tentative footsteps on the playground sand. It was still dark outside, so not too much time could have passed. I wasn't sure when the kid slept; he always seemed to be lurking near the lodge. As he approached, he eyed Chase suspiciously.

"The doc wants to see you," he said. "He's with your dad." I rubbed my eyes and sat up.

Chase's brows scrunched. "My dad?"

"Yeah," said Will, spilling bread crumbs as he snatched my plate. He had a twitchy way of moving, always watching over his shoulder as if he suspected someone might be sneaking up on him. Throw some dirt on him and he easily could have been one of the Lost Boys who'd jumped us in the woods. "Who else's dad you think I'm talkin' about?" he said. "Big, tall, black hair. The hunter."

There was only one person here who could possibly be confused as Chase's father.

"You mean Jesse," I said. "Chase's uncle."

Will's mouth pulled to the side. "I 'spose."

"Why do you call him the hunter?" asked Chase. Jesse hadn't been assigned to any hunting party as far as I knew.

"I seen him before," said Will, checking behind him. "In the woods. He thinks I don't remember, but I remember."

It was possible he'd seen Jesse hunting from the safe house—Jesse had said they'd had run-ins with the Lost Boys before.

"You mean before DeWitt brought you here," Chase said.

"DeWitt didn't bring me nowhere." Will snatched his plate. "I go where I want."

"My mistake," said Chase.

At the sound of footsteps from inside the lodge, the boy paused, and lifted his nose like an animal who'd caught a scent.

"They're at the graveyard," said Will quickly. "It's—"

"I know where it is," I said, then wilted a little when Chase's brow cocked in my direction. I was surprised DeWitt had left the lodge without us knowing. We must have slept through it.

Before we could ask any more, Will sped away.

"Jumpy," said Chase.

"At least he's not trying to catch me in a net," I said, frowning as Will disappeared back inside the cafeteria. It *was* possible that he could have seen Chase's uncle in the woods. For an instant, I pictured Will throwing a net over the man twice his size and couldn't help but grin.

Chase smirked. "I guess some people can be rehabilitated after all."

"What can I say?" I said with a sigh. "I'm not Sister material."

"Definitely not."

I elbowed him in the side. "What's *that* supposed to mean?"

He laughed, then abruptly cleared his throat. The blood rushed to my skin. I could still feel his fingertips trailing down my arm, his grip, firm and warm behind my bent knee. The heat of his breath on my neck and the way we both fumbled, and trembled, and finally found each other.

I became acutely aware of my hands and how they dangled

awkwardly at my sides. I needed to do something with them. I settled on chewing my pinky nail.

"To the graveyard?" he asked.

"Right," I said. "Yes. Let's go."

CHAPTER

14

A NERVOUS energy sparked between us as we walked outside and entered the woods. This night had changed things; the usual butterflies I felt in his presence had tripled in size. My skin felt like it glowed when he looked at me, like I was the only girl in the whole world, and when he took my hand and his thumb ran up the side of my wrist I thought of one thing alone: I could not lose him. Not now. Not ever.

I wanted him to say something, anything, but he seemed to be waiting for me to do the same.

The sky was still dark, and the soft ground was blanketed with a wispy, gray mist. As the woods grew denser, I took the lead, having known the way to the cemetery. I started talking about Rebecca's rehab with Dr. DeWitt, searching for something to fill the silence, and when he didn't make a sound I glanced back to make sure he was still following.

His brows were drawn, his expression serious, and something small and silver flashed between his thumb and first finger.

I stopped. He nearly bumped into me, pulling up at the last minute. Chase Jennings was many things, but never distracted.

"Whatcha got there?" I asked. I knew what it was. His mother's ring. He kept it in his pocket. It was all he had left from the time before, and he carried it for luck, the same way I still wore the Saint Michael pendant on the chain around my neck.

I would have been lying if I said I didn't sometimes wonder what it would look like on my hand.

Slowly, his gaze traveled from his hand to my eyes, and my breath caught.

He swallowed.

A hundred thoughts crossed paths in my head, but before I could make any sense of them, someone approached from the shed. The dry leaves crackled beneath his boots.

"Who's there?" Billy's voice came through the trees.

Chase stuffed his hand back into his pocket. He had a panicked look on his face, like the time my mom caught him sneaking out my window after midnight, and I couldn't help but giggle. When he returned a shy grin, my heart tripped in my chest.

"It's me, Billy," I called. "It's Ember." It took a moment to tear my gaze away from Chase's.

We went to meet him. The woods thinned, revealing the neat rows of wooden crosses and the shed to our left. There was something wrong about that building, something creepy. I shivered. It reminded me of where they brought the girls who acted out at reform school.

Billy's steps had quickened when he recognized my voice, but when he came closer I could see he held a rifle against his chest like a shield.

"You guys aren't supposed to be out here," he said.

"What are *you* doing out here?" asked Chase, looking around.

He hesitated. "Keeping watch."

"Over what?" Chase asked.

Billy moved the gun over his shoulder, adjusting the strap across his chest. "Did you follow me or something?"

I took another step forward and Billy retreated into the shadows. It wasn't too late to see his eyes were red and swollen.

"Is everything okay?" I asked, fear tightening my chest. "What's going on?"

He didn't answer right away. "You don't have to keep worrying about me." But his voice wasn't as abrasive as it had been in the past.

"You're my friend," I said.

He picked at the weapon strap, keeping his eyes downcast.

"I gotta get out of here," he said. "If I could get on the mainframe, I could find out who Reinhardt's got in Charlotte."

Of course Billy would think Wallace was one of Chancellor Reinhardt's prisoners. He still thought his adopted father had survived the fire in Knoxville.

Another set of footsteps came from the shed, and this time DeWitt emerged through the trees. He didn't come toward us though; he made for the center of the cemetery, where he was joined by four other people coming from the road. A pear-shaped woman I recognized as Ms. Rita. A man with red hair— Van Pelt—and Panda, from the kitchen. Patch was there as well, a little behind the others, but ramrod straight. The entire council was here.

Will was wrong; Jesse was nowhere in sight. It hadn't made sense that he and DeWitt would be together anyway.

Billy lowered his head and hurried back to guard the door. I watched him go, wishing there was something I could do to help him.

Silently, Chase and I went to hear what the council had decided.

Dawn was coming, and though I rubbed my arms the chill would not leave my skin. I couldn't help but feel like something bad had happened, or was going to happen, but that couldn't be. No one was morbid enough to tell you bad news when you were standing among the dead.

When we reached them, I saw that DeWitt carried something under his arm. A stack of folded clothing—the navy jacket I'd recognize anywhere, and a long blue skirt made up the top and bottom. My eyes lowered to the two guns tucked in the front of his waistband.

"The printing plant in Greeneville is a minimum security facility, with just a skeleton staff after hours. Because of that we're only sending a small team." DeWitt passed Chase the clothing. "You're sure your contacts there will recognize you?"

"Yes," we both said. The thought of seeing Marco and Polo, the two soldiers who'd helped refugees make it to the safe house, lightened my mood. The last time I'd seen them, they'd let us steal an FBR cruiser so we could go back to Louisville.

"You'll have the staff reformat the Statutes to what the council has discussed, then deliver them to several key posts. Let them know that despite the fall of the safe house, Three still stands. Deliver the Statutes. And tell them we will be seeking vengeance for good lives lost." He paused as if he needed to catch his breath. "The carriers should be able to spread the word from there. Let them know our timetable. We need as many bodies on board before Charlotte as we can get."

Those bodies wouldn't be living if the MM destroyed those posts before we got there.

DeWitt nodded to Chase. "Your uncle's asked to be assigned to the mission."

It surprised me that Jesse already knew of it. They had put together this team so quickly.

"I want Billy to come, too," I interrupted. The council members stared at me. I guess people didn't question DeWitt's orders too much.

"He can break into the mainframe, find out what he can about the prisoners." The last time we were in Greeneville he'd hacked into Marco and Polo's computers to search for any new MM arrests from Knoxville. "Please," I added.

Patch scoffed. Panda was shaking his head at me.

"All right," said DeWitt. Panda froze.

The doctor focused on me.

"You remind me of my daughter," he said after a moment. "Maybe that's why I feel the need to tell you that this isn't going to be a walk in the park. Once people see you alive, see what you're doing with the Statutes, everything's going to change." He paused. "Consider staying behind. This mission can be run without you. We could send a decoy."

I couldn't believe what I was hearing. It was *my* idea, *my* name.

"First you don't trust me," I said. "Now you're trying to protect me?"

"You're a valuable asset," said DeWitt. "We'd like to eliminate risk."

So it wasn't about my safety, it was about my usefulness to Three. That's why Sean had been sent to get Tucker instead of me.

"Why don't you let me worry about that?" Chase's tone was cold.

I placed a hand on his chest, feeling the muscles flinch beneath.

"You're not sending someone out pretending to be me," I said, trying to keep an even tone. "We already did that in Knoxville."

Recognition flashed in DeWitt's eyes.

"I know Cara worked for you," I said, going on a hunch that

Cara's sniper attacks on the MM had truly been supported by Three, as I'd suspected. "And I know she died for you. I was there with her in Greeneville right before the MM took her. She gave everything to the cause. Nobody else is taking the fall in my name."

Twin red streaks blossomed on either side of DeWitt's jaw. My pulse quickened; I was playing with fire. Chase inched beside me.

"When do we leave?" he asked.

"Soon," said DeWitt. "There's just one small matter to attend to first."

I exhaled, but didn't feel relieved.

"Then do it already," said Panda.

"Do what?" asked Chase.

"We brought you here because this is where we honor the brave," said DeWitt. "Among those who gave all they had willingly." Three's leader watched me closely, gauging my response. The situation didn't sit right. The graves looked peaceful enough, blanketed with dried leaves, even bundled wildflowers in a couple of places, but that didn't mean someone's bones weren't under my feet.

"Show her," said Ms. Rita.

DeWitt untied the neck of his tunic and pulled it to the side, exposing one shoulder. Ms. Rita followed suit, then the others. There, on their left shoulders just below the collarbone, were three parallel scars, pale blue in the light of the moon. Scars I'd once seen on Cara the last time I'd seen her. They'd been what the woman in the radio room had been looking for when she'd told me about the soldier counts.

The breeze shifted then, and brought with it the heaviness of responsibility.

"You do this thing, you don't just do it for your mother," said DeWitt. "You do it for all the mothers. All the daughters and fathers and sons. Do you understand?"

I didn't. But I nodded anyway.

"We carry these marks as a symbol of our dedication to the cause." Patch's voice was strong despite his withered form.

"We carry them on our hearts as a mark of trust," said Ms. Rita. She turned to Panda.

"We carry them to remember those who have fallen," he said.

"We carry them so that no one can take them away," finished Van Pelt.

"We carry them," said DeWitt stepping closer, "because they remind us we are not alone." I glanced to the side, realizing the council members had formed a circle around us. Their right hands were resting over their hearts in the way I'd seen the people of Endurance do when we first arrived.

"Hold on," said Chase. I held out my hand to stop him. They were right; this was bigger than me, and the sooner I accepted that the better.

I wasn't afraid anymore—not of this place, not of the council members or their purpose.

Not even when DeWitt pulled the knife from his pocket.

"Are you ready?" he asked.

"Are you sure?" whispered Chase.

Nervously, I untied my collar, and tilted my head to the side as DeWitt brandished the knife against my heart.

"It only hurts for a moment," he said softly.

On the first cut I siphoned in a quick breath, locked my jaw, and stared at the closest cross.

On the second, I exhaled.

I never felt the third.

"Welcome to Three," said DeWitt.

THE cool night air made the mark sting, but I didn't care. For the first time since we'd arrived I felt like I actually belonged here.

DeWitt withdrew a bandage from his pocket. He removed the sticky backing and placed it gently over the wound. I followed the council members and tied the collar back in place; no one I knew to be a part of Three broadcasted their marks.

They looked to Chase, and Chase looked to me.

We'll never be able to go back, he'd said. These were our lives now.

But when I considered them marking him, I felt unsure of my choice. It was like standing on a cliff, inching closer to the edge.

A crash inside the shed distracted me, bringing a chill up my spine. DeWitt's head snapped in that direction, and soon he was running toward the sound.

"Billy," I whispered. Chase and I followed closely behind.

We reached the door and found Billy still outside. Physically, he looked fine; there was no blood, no broken bones. But his knuckles were flexed around the gun he pointed at the door.

Another crash came from inside, this time followed by a male's sharp cry of pain. DeWitt was struggling to open the deadbolt on the door with a key from around his neck.

"Who's in there?" Chase asked.

"Your uncle," muttered DeWitt. A second later he'd removed the lock, but Chase shoved him aside and plowed through the entrance. I followed him inside, blinking back the bright lantern light coming from three of the four walls.

To my left, hidden from view of the front door, was an animal cage, like that which would hold livestock, and curled across the bottom of it, too big to stretch out, was a man.

His face was bruised and swollen. His navy blue uniform jacket was stained with blood and sweat. Standing outside the cage, his hands entangled in the mesh, was Jesse. He had a pair of needle-nose pliers in his teeth.

"Oh," I said, siphoning in a breath.

Chase was staring at his uncle, the shock on his face hardening to rage.

"Rebel dogs," muttered the soldier. He grinned at me, teeth bloody. "You know what they call a female rebel dog?"

Jesse kicked the mesh, sending it rattling against the back wall. The man flipped over onto his other side. With him facing away I could breathe again.

"You keep prisoners here," I said, forcing myself to look away from the soldier.

This was a war. He was the enemy. Men like him were killing my friends.

Not that long ago you thought I was the enemy, too, Sean had said.

"How did you think we knew about the chief's party?" asked DeWitt quietly.

I turned and skipped the steps, landing on the ground. I couldn't be near him a second longer.

Chase followed me, one hand over his mouth.

"He's a man," I said, "not an animal."

Chase's eyes darkened. He lowered his hand. "I know that."

"They're holding him in a cage, Chase! That's what they do. That's not what we do!"

"I *know*," he said.

I pulled away from him, disgusted with what I'd seen, with

the marks still burning my chest. He stared into the night, fingers woven behind his neck.

"I'm sorry," I said. I felt sick. I was a part of this now, a part of all of it. Forever. The proof was right there on my skin.

But we still had to go. However bad Three was, the MM was worse.

I told myself this again and again.

Jesse stepped into the doorway, a dark shadow against the bright lights inside. He met Chase's accusing stare, the air between them growing heavy with challenge.

"If you want to know, just ask, Chase." It was the first time I'd heard Jesse use his first name. His voice was soft, careful, and seemed to hold DeWitt and Billy back from intervening.

"I don't," said Chase.

Jesse's head fell forward. Somewhere deep inside, I felt a slash of pity.

"I have to tell Rebecca we're leaving," I said. Sean may have already gone; I couldn't leave her alone without saying goodbye.

Chase led the way.

REBECCA was not in the kitchen or the south wing. Chase checked the dorms, but she wasn't there either. My search became frantic; if I didn't find her soon, I wouldn't be able to tell her we were going.

Finally, we made our way to the barn. The breezeway had recently been raked, and the stalls smelled of fresh hay. A few horses trotted close to the gates as we approached, looking for treats. They snorted and stomped their feet when I passed them by.

I spared a lingering glance up at the loft, then blushed when Chase caught me.

Outside, the slow *clomp-de-clomp* of hoof beats approached, and we turned toward the entry, where a girl's soothing voice carried into the barn.

"That's a good girl. A little closer to the fence. Good girl."

Chase and I shared a skeptical look, then stepped outside.

Rebecca was riding a horse. Our Rebecca, who could barely walk, had somehow managed to climb aboard a creature whose back was the height of my shoulders. Gently, the dark mare edged against the fence, and for a moment I thought Rebecca's leg was about to be crushed. Chase reached for the horse's bridle.

"I've got it," she said, waving him off. We watched as she maneuvered off the mare's back, and slowly, steadily, climbed down the fence to her waiting crutch. As she fitted it to her arm, she blew out a slow, painful breath, then smiled. The horse waited patiently, bobbing her head as if in approval.

"That was impressive," said Chase.

"I know." Rebecca smirked. "Doctor DeWitt says Junebug helps with my rehab."

I winced at DeWitt's name. His kindness to Rebecca made what I'd seen in the shed even harder to swallow.

"Where were you?" I asked.

She glanced over her shoulder. "The orchard."

"What?" The last time we were there we were attacked by a group of savage boys. "You went alone?"

"It's okay," she said. "I have Junebug. And this." She lifted a flap on the saddle bag, revealing a black handgun. "Sean gave it to me. There's a small stash of weapons at the front gate he wasn't supposed to know about. Hush, hush and all that."

I placed a tentative hand on the horse's neck, feeling the muscles flex beneath her soft coat. She swung her head toward me, one big brown eye staring me down, and nibbled at the loose fabric of my shirt.

"He said if something happens, I'm supposed to meet him at the orchard," she added. "He's a worry wart."

I looked to Chase, who shoved his hands in his pockets. When I turned back, tears had filled Rebecca's eyes, and I hugged her, harder than I meant to.

"Are you just here to check on me?" asked Rebecca, taking a deep breath. "Because Sean's coming back. He promised."

"We're leaving, too," I said quietly. I didn't let her go, even when her arms dropped from my shoulders. For the first time I truly considered we might not come back. If it wasn't going to be so dangerous, I would have taken her with us.

"Everyone's leaving," she said when I finally backed away. She turned back to Junebug, hiding her face. "Well, go then. I'm fine."

I waited a second, hating the hurt in her tone. Chase touched my arm. We needed to leave.

We'd made it to the end of the paddock fence before I heard her voice one last time.

"Be careful."

I didn't look back.

CHAPTER
15

THE day passed, but I only saw a narrow strip of it in the slash of yellow light painting the ceiling of the MM delivery truck. Hay-filled crates were packed against the rollaway door, creating the impression that the compartment was full. The back quarter was left open for Billy and me.

I wasn't sure if he was mad at me again, or just quiet. Either way, my mind was filled with thoughts of our mission. Worry of the danger we'd be in back in the interior, but also for those who would read the new Statutes and fight against the MM.

I didn't know if this would make a difference. I wanted it to, but at the same time, I didn't, because I didn't know if I was strong enough to carry the responsibility of innocent people risking their lives.

Maybe DeWitt felt this way when he sent people out. Maybe it was something you got used to. I didn't see how.

Chase and Jesse drove. There were only two seats in the cab, and if we were stopped by a border patrol it was better to have two ex-soldiers up front rather than a fourteen-year-old in a baggy MM uniform and a Sister of Salvation. If I had to guess, they still weren't speaking.

With each blind bump and turn we were tossed from side to

side, until finally, I pushed aside some of the boxes, spread out one of the packing blankets, and laid down on the floor. My thoughts turned to Sean—to the last words we'd shared—and to Rebecca, who'd been left alone to say good-bye to him. The air, already heavy with heat and tension, grew even more oppressive, and as I lay there, I wished I could ask if she thought I was doing the right thing with the Statutes.

It would have been nice to talk to her about what had happened with Chase, too.

I hoisted the borrowed wool skirt around my knees and opened the stuffy collar. Billy held out a few minutes longer, until he finally gave up and lowered beside me. For a long time we said nothing, just watched the light move across the ceiling. Then, without looking over, he said, "Sarah doesn't have a boyfriend."

It took a moment to realize he meant the same Sarah we'd found in Knoxville, who was still quite pregnant.

"Oh, no?" I asked.

"She hasn't said anything about me, has she?"

I hadn't had the chance to check in with her since we'd arrived at Endurance. "I saw her looking at you at dinner the other night."

I could feel him beam.

"I was thinking maybe after we get back I'd see if she wanted to hang out." It wasn't a question, but it sounded like one.

"You should bring her flowers. Steal some from the garden."

He snickered. "You're crazy for putting your name in those Statutes."

I breathed in slowly. "I know."

"It's what we said we'd do after we got to the safe house," he said. "Tell everyone what happened to them—your mom and Wallace."

The truck turned, and I bumped his arm as we slid six inches to the right.

"If you didn't know for sure she was dead, do you think you'd still be looking?"

His voice was different, not quite as hard. Like the old Billy. My friend.

"Yes," I said. "I would still be looking."

He reached over and grabbed my arm, latching us together. "I can't tell Wallace's story until I know for sure."

"I know." I rolled onto my side to face him. "Sarah, huh?"

He covered his eyes with his hands, but not his smile.

By the time we reached Greeneville, the light across the ceiling of the compartment had dimmed, and all but disappeared. Even with the scheduled detours that took us off the main highways, the trip had taken longer than I'd expected. By the time the truck eased to a stop and Chase's double knock came from the back, my patience had worn thin.

When the exit door rolled up, Chase was already reaching to help me down. Beside him stood a familiar soldier with a hooked nose and toothy smile.

"Marco!" Polo exclaimed. "Marco, look what the Red Zone dragged in!" He batted Chase's hand aside and instead helped me down himself. When my feet found the ground he lifted my knuckles to his lips and planted a wet, noisy kiss there.

"You're happy to see us," said Chase, stealing me away. "We get it."

Monstrous black machines with silver trays and black rubber belts that protruded like tongues stretched across the factory floor, sleeping and silent though still warm from recent use. Cardboard boxes of different sizes, some larger than me, were stacked against the side wall, and the room smelled musty, like old books that hadn't been opened in a long time.

A lanky man, with skin as dark as Polo's was light, stepped out from behind a machine on the opposite side of the loading dock. When he saw me a grin split his face from ear to ear.

"You missed us!" cried Marco. "You all missed us," he added as Billy hopped from the back of the truck.

"Hey, guys," said Billy.

Polo slapped him on the back. "Glad to see you didn't take the one-way train to Charlotte."

A lump formed in my throat. Marco muttered something that had Polo wincing.

"Sorry," he said. He reached a hand toward Jesse, who was checking the high back windows as if we'd been tailed. "Have we met before?"

Jesse shook his hand as he continued to assess the building.

"Doubt it," he said.

"Are you sure? Because I'm good with faces."

"He's terrible with faces," said Marco.

Polo gave him a pithy look. "I practically have a photographic memory."

"Just like I can practically read minds."

"Oh, yeah?" said Polo, gesturing rudely. "What am I thinking now?"

"Yet another reminder why I never settled down," grumbled Jesse.

"Speaking of photographs," said Polo cheerfully. "Saw a spooky one lately the Bureau was trying to pin on you two. In a hospital in Chicago, I think it said. You should see it. Didn't even look like you."

Chase and I glanced at each other.

"Hold the bus," said Polo. "That was you?" When neither of us answered, Polo slapped his partner in the chest. "Read their minds, Marco."

Marco grimaced. "Signs definitely point to yes, Polo."

"Are they always like this?" asked Jesse.

"Yes," said Billy and I together.

A noise came in the direction I knew to be the office, just beyond the factory doors. Before I could react, Jesse had already drawn his weapon and pointed it at the soldier who walked through. The trash bag in the soldier's grip fell to the floor with a dull thud.

"Whoa, easy big guy," said Polo. Marco had thrown his hands up in surrender, though he was not in the line of fire.

"That's a friend of ours. New Guy."

As Jesse lowered his weapon, Marco quickly beckoned the soldier forward. "Come on New Guy, don't be shy now."

The soldier was in his early twenties—younger than Marco and Polo—and wore his pants and sleeves a hair too short, making his limbs look long and skinny. As he approached, his pale skin took on a grayish tint, and his eyes grew round.

"Didn't mean to surprise you," said New Guy. He laughed weakly. "I cover the day shifts now. I was just heading out, actually."

"He's with you," Chase clarified.

"He's a good, old-fashioned double crosser," said Polo, slapping New Guy on the back. "Just like Marco and me. We needed to expand the operation to include non-vampire hours."

I forced a smile, though the introduction of a new player made me nervous.

"Marco and Polo," said Billy. "Turning the Bureau to rebels, one soldier at a time."

"That's it!" shouted Polo so loudly I jumped. "You're him!

Tattoo-on-the-neck guy from Chicago!" He pointed at the snake sneaking up under the collar of Jesse's borrowed uniform.

We looked at him blankly. All except Jesse, who had begun to glare.

"I knew I recognized you. You were at the protests!"

"Polo," said Marco with a frown. "We've talked about this . . ."

"You were talking about taking down the Bureau. You scared the hell out of me, man. I nearly ran before I signed the papers."

"I think you've got me mixed up with someone else," said Jesse.

"He mixes things up sometimes," said Marco.

"No, I'm telling you, I don't forget a face," Polo argued. "He was the one who said Restart was behind the bombs, and that they were blaming the insurgents so they could fly in and save the day."

Project Restart, President Scarboro's political platform. It was the big spending donors behind Restart that funded his ideas of bringing America back to old-fashioned values. The very ideas that helped spawn the Statutes and put the government in charge of policing morality.

Jesse considered this. "That does sound like me."

I couldn't tell if Jesse was admitting to Polo's claim or just avoiding the question. Either way, I unfolded the carefully worded message from the council and handed it to Marco.

"What's this?" he asked, his scowl pulling deeper the farther down the page he read.

"Are you writing your memoir?" asked Polo. "I've always wanted to do that."

"It's to put in the Statutes," I said.

Marco folded the paper gently. He looked to Polo and then back to me. "This isn't what we do."

"It is now," said Jesse. Polo frowned.

Marco looked worried. "We're happy to help fight the good fight and all . . ."

"They're orders from Three," said Chase.

Marco and Polo stopped fidgeting. They stared at us. It was so quiet you could hear the breeze outside rattle the rain gutters.

I opened the top button of my uniform and peeled aside the bandage.

"Whoa," said Polo. "They're in deep, Marco."

"Yes, Polo." Marco swallowed, his Adam's apple bobbing. "And that means we're in deep, too."

Polo took a step closer to examine the marks. "Maybe pull that open a little more?" He demonstrated on his own collar, showing off a significant amount of skin.

"All right," said Chase, pulling me closer to him. "They get the point." I rebuttoned my shirt, laughing under my breath.

"I guess we'll get started," said Marco, looking not very enthusiastic. "I suppose you'll want to take your delivery and move on."

"What delivery?" asked Chase with a frown.

Polo did stop then. Silently, the three soldiers led us to the supply room, to the back corner where a trap door I hadn't seen before was fitted into the corner of the floor. Polo crouched and knocked on the wood three times, then with a heave, Marco pulled the latch back.

A dozen faces stared up at us from the basement.

"They've had nowhere to go since the train to the safe house stopped," said Polo. "You're here to take them, right?"

"What are we supposed to do with them?" I huddled closer to Chase and his uncle, creating a shield against the almost twenty refugees that stared at us from outside the supply room door. Most of them were probably draft dodgers, but there were families, too, some with young children, and two women holding hands, and a man laying a mat out on the floor to kneel and pray in a language I didn't know.

"They aren't on my to-do list," said Jesse. I was grateful we were the only ones within earshot. Behind him, the printing press was up and running. An hour ago I'd delivered the carefully worded message to Marco, who reformatted the silver lettering by hand, and brought the machines to life with the flip of a switch and an anxious warning: "I'd disappear after this one if I were you. For good this time."

His words had made me cold, and before I thought too much about them I'd sought out Chase and Jesse.

"We can't leave them," I said. "We have to bring them back to Endurance."

Chase's thumb dragged absently over his lip. Behind him, Marco and Polo were doling out rations to those who'd been delivered by four different carriers from four different states, who'd heard of the safe house's fall too late in their journey. Their silent pleas for help weighed heavy on my shoulders.

"Sure, let's take them with us. Show them the sights," said Jesse. "We've still got work to do, neighbor."

Chase gave him a warning glance.

"Em's right," he said. "We can't leave them here. If Marco and Polo get caught, this whole operation's blown." My mind turned to the new guy who'd gone home shortly after we'd arrived. I hoped he understood the risks, and responsibilities, of these secrets.

My gaze turned to Billy, currently behind the computer in the office searching for the names of the rebels captured by the Chief of Reformation.

"There may be another option," said Jesse. "A settlement near here. In the mountains," he added after a moment.

"The Appalachians?" said Chase.

"The Smokies," clarified Jesse.

"A settlement?" I asked. "Another safe house?" Rumors Jesse had heard had taken us to Endurance. He'd managed to gather a lot of information over the years.

Jesse scratched his dirty nails over his chin.

"What?" asked Chase suspiciously.

"I was there for a while before going to the coast," said Jesse. "Didn't end too well."

I narrowed my gaze. "It didn't end too well for them or it didn't end too well for you?"

He smirked. "Let's say neither party benefitted from my presence."

Chase rubbed his jaw. "He got kicked out is what he means." He didn't seem too surprised.

"A disagreement," said Jesse. "Long time ago. I doubt they even remember me after all these years."

Somehow I wasn't entirely convinced that was true.

"Marco and Polo haven't mentioned it," I said. "Maybe it's been found out."

Jesse shook his head. "The carriers don't typically go there." At my look he added, "They're a little antisocial."

I didn't like it, but wasn't seeing a lot of other options. We couldn't leave these people here, and if we were going to go to the existing posts to spread the word about the Statutes, we would need to be light on our feet.

"You remember the way?" Chase asked.

Jesse nodded reluctantly.

"Excuse me."

I turned to find a girl with a messy blond braid, dressed in the borrowed clothing provided from Greeneville's stash. Her face betrayed her youth; she was my height but couldn't have been more than twelve or thirteen. At the sudden attention her round cheeks darkened and she looked to her hands, where she clutched a piece of paper.

"You're Ember, right?"

I nodded. There was no use hiding it now. Behind me, I heard Chase and Jesse step away, giving us a little privacy.

"Is everything okay?" I asked, immediately regretting the question. Of course things weren't okay; that was why she was here. In confirmation of my thoughts her hazel eyes welled with tears.

I placed a hand on her forearm, unsure what else to do.

"My dad sent me here," she said. "He had to take another ride to the safe house, our ride was too full. Now they're saying it's gone. Is it gone?"

I exhaled. "Yes." There was no point in lying; she would hear it sooner or later.

A sudden bravery took her, and she wiped away her tears with the back of one hand. "I thought so." She seemed to remember the paper she was holding then and shoved it into my grasp. "I'm Kaylee. We talked about you where I'm from."

I looked at her, confused. "Where is that?"

"Outside Nashville. We said if we ever got busted, we'd escape reform school, too."

I shifted. "Who's we?"

"Just some of the girls at school," she said, as if it wasn't strange for people I'd never met to be discussing my life. "I know I don't look it, but I'm pretty good in a fight. My dad taught me how to shoot."

"Hope he taught you how to run, too," I said before I caught myself.

Her hands balled into fists. "He did. But sometimes you can't get away." The hard sound of her voice brought a wave of pity through me. "He's got an Article 5, too. My mom split when I was a kid."

You still are a kid, I wanted to say.

"Kaylee," called one of the women from the group. She held a bottle of water in each hand and tried to hide her worried look.

The girl slumped, like a child who'd been reprimanded.

"I can fight, that's all I wanted to say," said Kaylee before walking away toward the woman.

I unfolded the paper in my hand, seeing the neatly printed words of the Statute circular. I knew what it was supposed to say, but still my heart began to pound. It looked like any other that I'd seen—the format was the same, nothing looked out of sorts. But as I read more carefully, the change became glaringly obvious. Articles 1 through 4 had not been tampered with, but after Article 5 the following message was printed:

You've wondered what happens to the noncompliant—to every neighbor or family member the FBR has taken. Truth: they are being tortured, brainwashed, and murdered by the soldiers that are supposed to keep you safe.
a) When ARTICLE 5 was revised, Ember Miller was removed from her home and school. She was placed in rehabilitation where she was beaten and tortured for her mother's noncompliance.

a) (revised) Ember's mother was arrested by FBR soldiers and murdered for her "crimes" as part of the government's new Expungement Initiative to cleanse the country of immoral behavior.

b) Every day families are ripped apart by the FBR. Yours will be next unless you help stop it.

c) The time for hiding is over. Protect your family and your freedom. Join Ember when the first base falls and FIGHT.

"Oh," I said aloud.

A darkness made my insides grow slick, like the wings of the birds we'd found on the beach, drenched in oil. It spoke of validation and vengeance, and then with Sean's words: *This never stops. It will be chaos all over again.*

There was no turning back now. I'd known that before, but holding the Statutes in my hands, hearing that my name was being spread around the country in a blatant cry of treason, gave me the sudden sensation of drowning. Three, the Statutes, what it would mean when people read them beat at me, wave after wave, until my hands were shaking and I could barely breathe.

As evenly as I could, I walked to the side door and pushed outside into the night.

It was quiet now, and from this side exit I had a clear view of the woods behind the brick building. I crossed the asphalt track that surrounded the brick building, careful to keep to the shadows, and approached the chain-link fence. It was tall, twice Chase's height, and topped by a spiral of barbed wire, and for the first time since we'd arrived I felt like a prisoner.

The door opened and closed behind me, and Chase came beside me, staring out into the dark forest, breathing in the pine that came on the wind. He didn't speak, but his presence was enough to tear down the last layer of reserve.

I sunk to the ground and turned away from the freedom of the Red Zone, just beyond the fence.

"What have I done?"

"You told the truth." He knelt before me.

"The truth?" I asked, holding up the Statutes. "I'm asking these people to fight. To die, maybe."

He rocked back on his heels, staring at my hands, small in his.

"You're more than you," he said. "You're them. If people fight, it's because your story could just as easily be theirs."

I thought of Kaylee inside, a young girl with the same brand I carried, willing to stand up to the MM.

"How does this story end?" I asked.

He glanced down, then reached for my forearm to help pull me to a stand. He reached into his pocket and withdrew something small, hidden in his fist. He locked it into the palm of my hand and closed my fingers around it, squeezing tightly.

Small and round. A perfect circle, never ending.

"It ends with our someday," he said.

I blinked rapidly, stuffing the tears back down, and touched his face. He turned his cheek into my hand and kissed my thumb, and then he removed my necklace and placed the ring on the chain beside the Saint Michael pendant.

Someday, I thought. When we were so far outside this fence we wouldn't even bother looking back.

"Someday," I promised. His arms surrounded my waist, and we kissed in the silence, with only the floodlights high atop the chain-link fence to bear witness.

BY the time we returned inside, several of the refugees were loading the hijacked Statutes into boxes under Marco and Polo's direction. I went to join them but was stopped by raised voices outside the office. Chase and I hurried over, finding Jesse and Billy arguing.

"It's less than half a day away!" Billy shouted. "Half of Endurance is going there any—"

"Enough," barked Jesse. He leaned over Billy, casting a wide shadow over him, and lowered his voice. "You could no more easily break into the Charlotte prison than break out of it. The place is impenetrable. Trust me."

If I didn't know better, I would say that Jesse had tried.

"What's going on?" Chase asked.

"Last week there was a prisoner transfer to the Charlotte base. Some from Virginia, a few from up north. One from Knoxville." Billy stared into my eyes, willing me to understand. "All of them were flagged as high priority and marked for completion."

The chill of their impending deaths shivered through me.

"Did it say their names?" asked Chase.

"No," answered Jesse for him.

"It's Wallace," said Billy. "Who else from Knoxville would they keep alive this long?"

A glimmer of black hope lit inside of me. A man with shoulder-length hair, peppered around the temples, and a sharp, twisting tattoo climbing his wrist came into view.

You figure out what matters, he'd told me once. *And you do something about it.*

"Wallace," repeated Jesse. "Franklin Wallace from the Knoxville post."

"Who'd you think I was talking about?" shot Billy.

Jesse wove his fingers behind his head and turned his gaze toward the ceiling.

"You knew him?" Chase asked.

For several seconds Jesse was silent, but his shoulders had

begun to sag and it was obvious there was more than just recognition at play.

"I've heard of him," he said. "A good man."

"Which is why we've got to get him out before they *kill* him," said Billy.

"We don't even know he's alive," I said gently.

"Let's say he is," said Jesse. "Would he leave the others behind? Could he walk away knowing others had been sentenced to die?"

Now I was certain that Jesse knew Wallace. There was no way Wallace would leave his brothers—family had always been what he'd preached at the Wayland Inn. But Jesse's words reminded me of being trapped in the Knoxville holding cells, and all the men I'd left behind to save Chase and myself.

"He would for me," said Billy obstinately.

Jesse scoffed. "Then he's not worth saving."

Beside me, Chase's posture grew rigid. He stared at Jesse as if waiting for him to say something more, but Jesse met his gaze evenly and added nothing.

"We can't take these people with us," I said. "And we can't leave them here." Billy looked as if I'd betrayed him.

"We're wasting time!" he pleaded.

Jesse was right; this was a mission that required planning. I'd heard of the Charlotte prison during my time in the Knoxville holding cells—it would be no easy feat to break into. Even with Three's forces gathering outside the gates, there were no guarantees we could save anybody without getting caught in the crossfire.

"Three will save the prisoners," I said, hoping it was true.

A commotion from the main floor distracted us from the conversation. The refugees were charging away from the back exit.

"Hurry!" shouted Marco.

Polo ushered them through the supply room door where one by one they disappeared.

Chase and Jesse ran onto the floor, weapons drawn. I caught sight of the girl—Kaylee—the last in line to reach the room. She glanced back over her shoulder, eyes wide, as the garage door at the back of the loading dock began to rise.

"Hide," whispered Marco.

I dove beneath the nearest printing press, feeling the heat radiating off it in waves. Across the floor, Chase crammed behind a tall stack of boxes near the emergency exit. Jesse followed Kaylee into the supply room and rammed the door closed just as the garage lifted fully.

The noise of the machines clanged into sudden silence, replaced by the growl of the delivery truck as it backed into place beside the parked car we had brought. From my viewpoint, I could see the glossy black boots of a soldier emerge from the passenger side of the cab and step to the ground.

The boxes of hijacked Statutes waited at the edge of the loading dock, boxed and ready, though there were still stacks that were unpackaged sitting on the black belt above me.

I held my breath until my lungs burned, knowing I could not make a sound.

"Kind of late for a delivery," I heard Polo say.

Another man—the driver—came around the hood of the car to join the first. I could only see four pairs of boots and their pants from the knees down.

"We're on doubles, they didn't tell you?" The new soldier yawned loudly for effect.

"Always the last to know," said Marco.

"Chief's throwing a party on account of all those rat nests we took out last week," said the driver. "Everyone in the region's been invited. Didn't you get leave approved from command?"

"Oh, *that* party," said Polo. "We get invited to so many . . ."

"We'll be there," said Marco. "Um . . . where exactly was it again?"

"Charlotte," said the driver. The second laughed, obviously realizing Marco and Polo had not received an invitation. "That's our last stop on this run."

"Charlotte?" asked Polo. "Why are you taking Statutes to the base?"

My stomach twisted.

"We're not," said the passenger. "We're half full with booze for the party. We'll drop these off at the distribution center in Asheville then head over to the base. Trying to get our run in before the bender." He snickered.

"In that case let's get you loaded so you can get out of here," said Marco.

The back of the truck was opened.

"You got company?" asked the passenger.

"No," said Polo quickly. "Why?"

"The other truck."

"Down for repairs," Marco explained. "Transmission went out on the road and they towed it here. Said they'd pick it up last week, but . . ."

"Huh," said the driver. "Thought maybe it was your rebels again." The other soldier laughed as they began throwing boxes haphazardly into the back.

"What rebels?" Polo's voice had dropped. I glanced to the side, catching Chase's dark gaze just for a moment before looking back to the truck.

"Your cruiser," said the driver. "Everyone heard how someone stole it from the lot."

We'd taken it—Chase, Sean, and I—to get back to Louisville the last time we were here. Marco and Polo had reported the car stolen when we didn't return.

"Can't even keep your hands on a two-ton piece of metal," jibed the passenger.

"Everyone knows?" said Polo. "Well, that's embarrassing."

"Probably why you missed your invite to the party," said the driver.

Marco and Polo laughed weakly.

They exchanged a few more words as they loaded the back of the truck with the hijacked Statutes. I felt sick. If they looked at what they were doing—if they stopped for one second to actually read what they were packing up—we were all dead.

But they didn't. It was business as usual, and soon they were slamming the door closed and saying their good-byes.

I could hardly believe it; we were going to get out of this. But just as my muscles began to release, one last pair of boots went sprinting silently for the back of the truck. The door was rolled up, just a few inches, enough for a flash of navy blue to roll over the tailgate into the main compartment.

"No!" I whispered. My fingers dug into the cool cement floor.

By the time the soldier had returned with the key to lock the back, the gate was in place, as if it had not been moved. The two soldiers continued their routine, said their good-byes, and started the truck. A minute later they pulled out of the loading dock into the night, taking Billy with them.

"WE can't leave him!" I argued to a stone-faced Jesse.

"We didn't leave him anywhere," he said. "He made his decision, now he's got to play it out."

Chase swore quietly.

"You heard what the soldier said," Jesse added. "They're on doubles. How long before another truck comes through here?"

"You've got to get them out," interrupted Marco, coming toward us from the supply room where Polo was still trying to calm the refugees. "We've got one scheduled visit a week on the night shift. Now who knows when they'll be dropping in. If we don't get these people out of here, we're closing up shop. I mean it." The fear thinned his voice until it almost broke.

They were right. All we could do for Billy now was hope Three's army would be able to help him in Charlotte. If he was caught, he was as good as dead.

"Then let's get out of here already," I said grimly.

CHAPTER
16

THIS time I rode in the front of the truck, seated on a folded blanket in the narrow space behind Chase's seat. There was no longer enough room in the back; the space was packed with the twenty-one refugees and boxes of hijacked Statute circulars that we would use to show the resistance posts once we found them. The thousands of flyers running through Marco and Polo's printing press would be taken and distributed by the MM. At least until someone in a blue uniform actually read them.

I hoped Marco and Polo had a good exit strategy before the MM figured out what they'd done.

Night shifted to dawn. The gears of the truck grinding loudly beneath the sticky floor mats were not enough to stave off thoughts of Billy on his way to the prison base, or Sean and Jack in search of Tucker. I didn't like us all being split up like this, not knowing when, or even if, we would see each other again.

I reached between the passenger seat and the door until I found Chase's hip. His hand closed around mine and squeezed. It was enough to say he was thinking the same.

We stopped twice during the day to give everyone a break. Once at an old rest stop off the highway with wooden benches under gazebos, and posters featuring information about the over one hundred species of trees found in the Great Smoky Mountains. The second right off a deserted road, where the smell of moss and damp leaves was so thick you could taste the earthiness on your tongue.

Our drive became increasingly more difficult in the delivery truck. We had to slow in the afternoon on account of all the fallen branches and debris in our path. Chase and I took to walking ahead, clearing the road by hand as we climbed the curvy incline.

"I sure hope he knows where he's going," I said between breaths, the sweat running down my face. I'd tied the heavy skirt around my thighs and caught Chase looking, not for the first time since I'd done so.

"Jesse never lies," answered Chase, returning to the task. "He may not always tell the whole story, but the parts he does tell are true."

"Kind of the same as lying," I muttered, thinking of the prisoner at the cemetery.

Chase gave a half smile, then pointed ahead to where a dirt road forked into our path. A closer inspection revealed tire tracks in the mud that hadn't yet been washed away by rain.

It looked like Jesse was right after all.

IT was late afternoon as we clunked along through the low clouds into the mist. My pity for those stuck in the back was about to get the better of me when Jesse hit a sharp bump, and the truck began to rock unsteadily. I gripped the seat in front of me for support and felt the air hiss from my lungs just as it began to hiss from the front tire.

"Damn," said Jesse. He opened the door.

There was a movement in the trees behind him, a flash of

gray in the bright emerald hues. It could have been nothing, but the tingling in my hands told me differently.

"Ten o'clock," said Chase. And then a moment later. "Another at two o'clock."

I forced my breath to steady. Soldiers would have set up a road block, but there were other things that lurked off the map—the Lost Boys on the coast had proven that.

"Leave your weapons on the dash," instructed Jesse. "Everything you've got."

The metal gun clattered against the plastic partition as Chase did as he was told. He reached into his boot and removed a knife. I had a gun, too, one I'd placed beneath the seat in front of me and hadn't realized I'd reached for. I leaned between the front seats and put it beside Chase's, hoping Jesse knew what he was doing.

Jesse stepped slowly out of the cab, hands raised.

"We aren't here to stir trouble," he said. His uniform jacket was still in the car, and his undershirt, damp with sweat, stuck to the caramel skin of his back in a V shape. "There are two more in the cab, and a whole mess in the back."

A beat of silence, and then four figures, two on each side, emerged from the woods. They were armed with rifles and wearing tattered old-school military fatigues, camouflaged with browns and greens and gray. Their faces were painted in the same colors, making it hard, but not impossible to distinguish that the two on my right were women. I jumped as the back door slid open. There were more of them, now verifying Jesse's claim.

The closest man walked up to Jesse and patted him down. When it was clear he was unarmed, he withdrew, the whites of his eyes standing out in sharp contrast to his dark face paint.

Jesse saluted him, the way I'd once seen the army soldiers do during the national anthem at a minor league baseball game I'd gone to with Chase's family. With his chest puffed out and his shoulders thrown back he looked like a different man.

"Sergeant Major Waite," said Jesse. "I was with the thirty-first cavalry division in Operation Unchained."

Chase had said that Jesse had served in the army before the War—I remembered a photo that had hung in the hallway of his home when we'd been little: Jesse—much younger, though just as serious—in a dress uniform seated before the American flag.

The man before him hesitated, then released his weapon to its shoulder strap, and returned the salute.

"Lance Corporal Blackstone," he answered. A smile split his face, revealing white teeth. "U.S. Marines." Jesse gave a short groan as if this were funny.

Captain Blackstone lifted a radio from his belt and stepped away from the truck. The others didn't move. I found myself watching the women—one had spiked hair, the other a slicked-back ponytail. In uniform they looked absolutely fierce.

Not more than a few minutes passed before a Jeep came careening down the road and slammed to a stop before us. A man in his mid-forties with a black goatee grabbed the overhead bar and swung out, shoved past Lance Corporal Blackstone, and came toe to toe with Jesse. He was easily six inches shorter and swimming in his faded red sweatshirt.

"No," he said emphatically. "Not this one. Not after last time."

"Uh-oh," I whispered. Chase stepped out of the cab but was yarded by the two women. I scrambled out over the seat to get outside.

"Max," said Jesse between his teeth. "Nice to see you."

"Don't get smart, Waite," said Max. "Thought we made it clear you were done here."

Jesse's shoulders slouched as his hands came to rest in his pockets. "Is that what we said?"

"Go," barked Max. "Turn this rig around."

"Not a lot of room . . ."

"Then back it down the hill," said Max clearly. "Blackstone? Help Sergeant Waite—"

"And my tire's blown out. Don't know if you saw that."

I looked down, now noticing the strip of nails half-buried beneath the dirt.

"We'll get that fixed right up for you," said Max, his grin as genuine as an MM officer's.

"Sir," said Chase. "I don't know what he's done—I'm sure it wasn't good—but we've got twenty people in the back in need of refuge."

Max turned, as if noticing us for the first time.

"And you are?" he asked.

Chase stood tall, but didn't salute as Jesse had.

"Chase Jennings," he said.

"Careful," said Jesse. "He might bite. He *is* related to me after all."

"Ember Miller," I said, giving Jesse a look.

Max scoffed. "Of course you are."

"Sir," came a voice from behind the truck. Another man in fatigues came around the compartment, followed first by Kaylee, pale and drenched with sweat, and then half a dozen others.

"We come in peace," said Jesse, half-kidding.

Max turned back, laughing suddenly. An instant later the sound silenced, replaced by a sneer.

"Perfect," he said, muttering something else unintelligible as his skin turned blotchy red. He stalked back to the Jeep, the engine still thrumming.

"Blackstone, clear the truck and take these people up the hill." He hit the gas hard, spraying us with mud as he spun the car and sped back up the mountain pass.

An hour later we were searched, disarmed, and informed in no uncertain terms that we were not to tell another living soul what we found here. Their demands raised my curiosity, but as we walked into camp I couldn't help but feel a little disappointment. This was not the sprawling campus of Endurance with its gardens and livestock. There were a few horses watching us with interest from a round pen beside a small stable, but otherwise the compound looked more like a quiet mountain resort. The single lane beside a river was lined with small log cabins, many of which had tendrils of smoke spiraling from their chimneys. There was no fortified wall, no team looking down their rifles at us from the trees. Still, it had an air of secrecy about it, like the whole place might disappear if you blinked too long. I wondered what was here that they were so intent on protecting.

We were given the option to clean up or go to the "cookhouse" for food. As hungry as I was, I couldn't relax until I scraped some of the sweat off. Some of the other girls, Kaylee included, lined up behind me, and with a quick nod to Chase I was first to follow the soldiers up a path beside the river. Through the mist the crash of water could be heard, like a fall was somewhere near, and as we drew closer, the path opened to a swimming hole.

Now that we'd delivered the refugees we'd have to move out, but I would have been lying if I'd said the bath didn't make me feel better about what we were about to do.

. . .

LATER, I hiked down the main road of the camp toward the fires that were already lit outside the cookhouse. There were more people milling around now—they seemed to come out of the woodwork, out of the very mountains. Men and women. Dogs, barking and chasing after the children who threw sticks for them. None dressed in uniforms we'd seen before, but that didn't mean they weren't soldiers. There was an air of dignity about the adults. Of pride, despite the fact that they looked like they'd gotten their clothes from the same donation bins I used to. They smiled and waved, said hellos and shook my hand. It was so welcoming, I nearly forgot about all the soldiers protecting this place. Where Endurance had felt like a resistance post, this felt more like home. The camp turned lively with conversation, and though I knew we had to move on, part of me wanted to stay.

I searched for Chase and Jesse, and was informed by the female soldier with the ponytail—now wearing jeans and a patched thermal shirt—that they were with Corporal Blackstone patching the tire. Dusk was coming, shadowing the paths, and instead of wandering through the woods I discovered the cookhouse, a cabin with sweeping, vaulted ceilings, and grabbed a plate of food, pocketing a little extra bread in case we went without for some time. Taking my plate, I went outside, marveling at the families who sat on picnic-style blankets or logs circled around a fire.

I wanted to sit with them, but felt strangely separate at the same time, like it was my first day at school and I couldn't find my friends. My Sisters of Salvation uniform was drying—I'd washed it at the swimming hole—and my clothes were borrowed. They hung off my shoulders and hips like I was a kid playing dress up.

Beside the cookhouse was a small cabin, and on the front

porch sat a man reading a book and minding his own business. A woman on the ground was leaning against the railing, looking out over the group, but when I approached, she caught my eye.

"Do you mind if I sit here?" I asked when I reached the bottom steps. She tucked her black hair behind one ear and glanced over her shoulder at the man, clearly waiting for him to respond.

He lifted his chin, and though I couldn't place it, there was definitely something familiar about him. His skin was browned by the sun, his hair short and gray like the smoke that rose from the fires. Wrinkles popped up beside his eyes as he smiled.

"I do," he said in a kind way, but with a voice that demanded attention. He stood to remove a stack of books from the wooden rocking chair beside him. "I'd mind less if you joined me."

He seemed friendly enough, so I climbed the steps past the woman and took my place beside him. From this point I still had a clear view of the road, the cookhouse, and the paths leading into camp. I would be able to see Chase and Jesse as soon as they arrived. The woman returned to her spot leaning against the porch, and though another man came to talk to her, I could tell she was keeping her eye on me. I wondered if the man was the leader of this post; he had to be someone important to have a guard.

We sat in the quiet, the porch creaking as we rocked, the crickets chirping from their secret perches. I kept eyeing his stack of books, now at his feet. There were titles there I'd never seen, and some I hadn't seen in years. All contraband from what I could recall.

"You like to read?" he asked.

I glanced back at the fire. "I used to."

"I like a good story," he said. After a moment he rose, a sneaky twinkle in his eye. "Come take a look at this."

I balanced the plate on the banister, glancing back down the path, but the man didn't go far. He opened the front door of the cabin to reveal a dozen bookcases, all lined with paperbacks, hardcovers, pamphlets, and magazines. My mouth dropped open in awe as I stepped over the threshold.

"Not bad, huh?"

I shook my head, unable to speak. I hadn't seen this many books in one place since before the War. Unable to help myself, I touched the nearest stack, feeling the worn covers and waterlogged pages before drawing back to wipe my hands on my pant leg.

"Where'd you get all these?" I managed.

"Here and there," he said. "When the teams make supply runs into town sometimes they bring me back one or two if they come across them."

"You must rank pretty high," I said, and he laughed. I removed a children's book with flimsy gold binding. A blue train was painted on the cover. "My mom used to read this to me when I was little."

"My son's favorite," he said. "I can't tell you how many times he brought it to bed with him. He'd memorized the words before he could read. Could play back every word."

"Did he make it?" The nostalgia between us turned heavy. I didn't know why I asked that. I didn't even know this man.

"I haven't seen him in years," said the man. "He's with his mother, and though I hate to admit it, they're in a far better place right now."

My mouth formed a small *o*, and a wave of pity passed over me. I hoped my mother was in a better place, too.

He smiled. "Mexico."

"Mexico," I said slowly, and this time when he laughed, he placed his hand on my arm.

"Sure," he said. "That big country across the border."

"The U.S. border," I clarified. Surely this man was not in his right mind. I gave him my most polite, whatever-you-say smile.

"Kids these days," he said with a sigh. "Thought you said you liked to read."

"I know what Mexico is," I said, keeping my voice light. "It's just . . . they closed their borders during the War. They built a fence to keep us out. They sent an army to defend it." I remembered the images from the news: people trying to climb the wall during the worst of the riots, setting homemade bombs to break through the weak spots. The Mexican Militia rounding them up and dumping them back in Texas and California. They didn't want anything to do with America, fearing the same rise of insurgents in their own overcrowded country.

He winced. "I recall all too well." We rounded the corner and paused in front of a series of wrinkled maps tacked to the wall, some of different continents, some of the Great Smoky Mountains.

One looked very similar to the map in the radio room in Endurance, stuck with red and green pins, but not just on the eastern side of the country, on the western half as well.

"Things change," he said.

One of the maps highlighted the countries of the world in faded colors and he tapped Mexico, then let his hand linger over the spot. His gaze grew distant.

He couldn't have been telling the truth—no country took U.S. citizens, especially after President Scarboro had made it illegal to jump the borders. The War had plunged the world into a depression, and when Scarboro had made economic independence a cornerstone of Reformation, it had finally abandoned us to rebuild on our own.

My gaze continued down the wall to a stack of flat wooden crates.

"You want to take a look?" he said with a twinkle in his eye.

I followed him to the boxes, where he pulled back the top lid. "Do you know what this is?"

My mouth fell open. Inside was a glass case, nestled in straw, and inside it was an old document, yellowed with age.

"IN CONGRESS, July 4, 1776" was written across the top. And just underneath: "The unanimous Declaration of the thirteen united States of America."

"It's the Declaration of Independence," I said. "Is this real? I thought Scarboro had it put in the archives during the Reformation Act."

"He did," said the man with a troubled look. "Ah, the archives. The greatest collection of noncompliant literature since the Vatican. I'm glad to see you recognize it."

"I haven't even seen a picture of it since I was a kid," I said. "How'd you get it?"

"My people managed to get a few things out before I was kicked out of town."

I wasn't sure what he meant by that. My gaze traveled down the page, stopping on the following words:

That whenever any Form of Government becomes destructive of these ends, it is the Right of the People to alter or to abolish it, and to institute new Government, laying its foundation on such principles and organizing its powers in such form, as to them shall seem most likely to effect their Safety and Happiness.

Jesse had told me something just like that in Endurance. "Who are you?" I asked.

The front door opened before he could answer, and noise outside drew my attention. Laughter filtered in through the blue night. Laughter and cheering, and something else.

Singing.

Two figures stood in the doorway—the angry man with the goatee, Max, who based on his expression was still less than amused by our presence, and Jesse, who blinked when he found me. He saluted again, this time at the old librarian. This place had certainly changed his demeanor.

"Sergeant Major Waite," introduced Max, but from the twitch in the librarian's eye I wasn't so sure he didn't recognize Chase's uncle.

"Sorry to bother you, sir," said Jesse. He stood straighter than I'd ever seen, like he wasn't even capable of the sarcasm I was so used to hearing come out of his mouth.

I smoothed out my sweatshirt, realizing I'd underestimated this man's importance to the compound. The librarian only waved his hand.

"Please," he said, dismissing Jesse's show of respect. "Those times are long past."

"Not for me," said Jesse.

The man nodded somberly, then saluted him back. "Thank you, soldier."

It finally occurred to me where I'd seen him before. Years ago, before the War, on the cover of one of my mother's magazines.

"Oh," I said, my eyes growing wide. A second later Jesse had reached for my arm and was escorting me from the building.

"Was that . . ."

"Yes," said Jesse. "It was."

The president before Scarboro. The man who'd lost in his

reelection, blamed for the insurgents' attacks on the major cities. The one who took the fall only to have Project Restart pick up the broken pieces.

"I didn't know. I'm such an idiot," I said, wondering if I should have told him about the hijacked Statutes and the fallen bases, and everything else I'd heard in the radio room in Endurance. I was suddenly unsure what I was supposed to share.

"Wait here," said Jesse bluntly, leaving me on the porch. The door closed in my face.

"Is it true? Is he really here?"

I turned to find Chase climbing the stairs, speculation quirking his brows.

"I think so," I said. "I was just kicked out. I guess Jesse's making a report."

"Or an apology," said Chase. This hadn't occurred to me. At my expectant look, Chase added, "I overhead Max telling Corporal Blackstone that the last time Jesse was here he went down the hill on a routine supply run and came back with ten soldiers on his tail. It took some effort to"—he hesitated, frowned—"cover things up."

"What did he do?"

"Hard to say," said Chase. "Riling people up is what it sounds like."

I remembered Polo saying that he knew Jesse from a demonstration outside the draft board. If that was truth, he'd been in the game a long time.

Inside, Max was saying something I couldn't make out.

"We have the same goal, sir." At Jesse's voice, Chase and I both turned our gazes to the door, as if it might spontaneously open again.

"Yes, but we're going about it in vastly different ways," said the president. "I won't be boosted back into office by an organization that condones assassination attempts and guerrilla warfare. The people have that now. They deserve better."

Chase and I glanced at each other. DeWitt hadn't told us that Three was supporting the president; he must have conveyed this message to Jesse privately.

"This plan with the Statutes," said Jesse. "It's different from what's been done in the past."

"I'm listening."

I felt my heart rate kick up a notch. The former president of the United States was about to hear a plan I'd come up with. I didn't know if I wanted to scream in excitement or throw up.

Inside, the conversation had gone quiet. Either the president was taking a long time to read and think about the plan, or they'd moved out of earshot.

I pushed my hands in my pockets, disappointed not to hear his reaction.

"Have you heard about Three supporting this president?" I asked. I hadn't much thought of what would happen if the MM was knocked out of power.

Chase shook his head. "Sounds like he's not a big fan."

I rubbed the three marks on my chest. "I don't know that he's got a lot of choice if he wants back in office. I don't see anyone else opposing the MM."

"We have our methods," said Corporal Blackstone, emerging from around the corner of the deck. He was still wearing fatigues, though his skin had been wiped clean of camouflage paint. His face looked stretched, with large eyes, thick brows, and a flat nose.

Chase cleared his throat. "While you were gone, Corporal Blackstone was telling me how Restart paid off the insurgents," said Chase.

"Didn't just pay them off," said Blackstone, his heavy jaw flexing with each word. "Formed them. Recruited them. And then paid off their families. We have proof—witnesses. Willing to share what they know." He glanced down to the campfires and I wondered if some of these individuals were here now. "Chancellor Reinhardt was behind the attacks. He set 'em up so Scarboro could pick up the pieces."

I'd heard talk of this before from Marco and Polo, but that didn't make the conspiracy any less appalling. I cringed, thinking of Reinhardt's creepy voice coming through the radio as he talked about the executions of the terrorists. The man was clearly capable of damage and unafraid of any consequences.

"When the time comes, we'll be ready," said Corporal Blackstone. He tapped his breast pocket, where for the first time I noticed a folded piece of paper emerging from it. The Moral Statutes—probably the ones we'd hijacked.

I swallowed.

"The president will be reinstated. The Bureau will be charged for their crimes. We'll have freedom once again." It occurred to me Blackstone was not referring to Scarboro. "In the meantime," he finished, "your truck will be topped off and good to go by morning."

"Thank you, sir," said Chase, shaking his hand.

"Tomorrow?" I asked. "Shouldn't we try to get out tonight?"

Chase motioned toward the food, a look of longing in his eyes. He had skipped eating in order to check on the truck and had yet to clean up. "They have rules about coming and going," he said. "They have rules about who you talk to and what you say and how to assure you aren't followed back. They have *rules*."

"Ah," I said. "Understandable, considering their guest list."

He snorted.

I wondered how Sean was faring—if he'd found Tucker yet. If he'd wrung Jack's neck yet; the last time I remembered them doing anything together, Sean was punching him in the face outside the swamp before we'd been ambushed by the survivors. He was going to freak out when I told him we had stayed the night in the Smoky Mountains, guests of the veterans of the dispersed military branches and the old president himself. It seemed too unreal to be true.

As Chase went to get a bowl of stew and canned mixed vegetables, I was distracted by something I hadn't heard in years. Music. Not the preapproved church music piped in through the speakers at Sunday services, but not quite like the kind my mother used to play on the stereo when I was little, either. This was fresher, brighter. Alive. It began with the soft, high wail of a violin, then came the thump of a drum, followed by a brassy horn I couldn't pinpoint, blending together as if they'd come from a singular source. It pulled at something inside of me, but at the same time raised the hairs on my skin, because beautiful things were always dangerous.

The musicians had congregated behind the largest of the campfires, and on the ground before them sat several children, entranced. As I watched, a few other people joined them, and soon they'd clasped hands and formed a ring around two men. For an instant, I thought they were fighting, until I saw one leap to the side and burst into an intricate pattern of kicks and stomps then challenge the other to follow. The other took the center of the circle, cheered on by those around him, and doubled the speed of the dance. Soon I found myself edging closer, gravitating toward the show.

They laughed as if our posts had not fallen. As if our people—good people—weren't missing or stranded. As if there was no reason to be afraid. And I watched because I wanted to believe them.

A breath of air came from the direction of the trees, blowing the damp hair away from my face. It brought with it a sense of calm, like when I'd hear my mother singing in the kitchen, or when she'd wait on the porch for me when I walked home from school.

Chase came beside me, standing quietly. We both watched the musicians, who'd slowed their song to a haunting melody. A woman began to sing, her voice lifting above the conversations and clatter of dishes. A song without words.

"It's beautiful," I said, rubbing the goose bumps that had streaked down my arms. For some reason the song reminded me again of Truck, killed by Reinhardt. And Sean, and Billy, and finally, my mother. "Is it strange to be having a party when people are out there dying?"

Chase moved the food around on his plate, not yet having taken a bite.

"I don't know," he said. "After the War at some of the camps around the city people would play music like this. They had weddings, too. Everyone was invited, even if you didn't know the person. Sometimes the people that got married didn't even know each other."

He glanced below my chin, to the necklace that carried his mother's ring. My someday promise.

"Why do it then?" I asked.

"You'd be surprised what you'll do when you think there's no tomorrow," said Chase. "Everything feels more intense. Everything you ever wanted to do, you've got to do it right now. You might not have another chance."

I looked out over the dancers, the children, delighted by the festivities. Was that what this was? A last attempt to enjoy life before the end? I closed my eyes, part of me wishing I could join them. I didn't know the steps, but maybe it didn't matter. Maybe all that mattered was wanting to.

Two girls led Kaylee into the circle. Her hair was braided back in pigtails, making her look younger than she had when she'd talked to me about her father in Greeneville. The two girls spun in a circle, and then she followed, until they fell into a heap of limbs and laughter.

Chase smiled, the kind of smile that made my heart leap just to see it. I was suddenly warm and light, and I reached out to touch his cheek, my fingers skimming down to his chin. There was nowhere I'd rather be than with him, right now.

"I've never been to a dance," I confessed. "Mom and I used to in the house sometimes. And Beth—we played around when I was little."

He tilted his head toward the music. "Are you asking me to dance?"

"No," I said quickly, pinning my hands at my side. "I don't know how."

But yes. I wanted to dance just as much as I was afraid of looking foolish.

Before he could say anything more about it I walked to another fire and found us a place on the ground where he could eat. We made small talk with the people around the circle, and I wasn't surprised to learn that a great many more than I'd anticipated had once served our country.

It was in one of these conversations that I learned of another sniper shooting. The female soldier with the short hair was the one to break the news.

"They haven't caught the sniper from what I've heard," she said, leaning back against a felled trunk and tossing twigs into the fire. The flames seemed to brighten in contrast with the growing darkness, and the scent of smoke was sharp in my nose and eyes.

"What happened to the one they caught in Greeneville?" I asked, careful not to reveal too much about Cara.

"I don't know," she said. "All I know is there was another shooting, same style, three days back. Near the Red Zone border. One of the Carolinas, I think."

I wondered if someone had taken up Cara's cause. It could have been anyone. A copycat, or a disgruntled civilian. Or it could have been someone working for Three. Teams had gone in and out of Endurance while we were there—I wondered if they'd had anything to do with it.

It occurred to me that this may have contributed to Reinhardt's public announcement and Truck's execution.

"Do you know anything about Mexico?" I asked.

"Big country below the border," she said. "Used to have great food. Spicy, though."

"Not exactly what I meant," I said.

She tilted her head. "I know most of the big shots took the boat there when Reinhardt started hunting folks down."

"So there is a boat."

She snorted. "Course there's a boat. What are you supposed to do, swim from Tampa?"

"I guess not," I said, trying to picture the state of Florida on the old president's map—an evacuated zone since its fall in the War.

She grinned at me then. "Keeping your options open, huh?"

I didn't answer, but she nodded anyway.

"Smart," she said. "I would too if my name was all over those Statutes."

Word had spread quickly. I shivered, but the fear was too

deep to shake off. It was like before, in Knoxville, when people recognized me as the sniper, but worse because now I was asking them to fight, even risk dying, to bring down the MM.

I realized that Jesse had sat down on a log across the fire, and had drawn the attention of most of the others, Chase included. He was midway through a story when I tuned in, and as he spoke I couldn't help but become entranced, all questions of what had occurred in the library drifting away.

"When the old man saw that his grandson had stolen his mother's basket he told him of the two wolves battling inside of him," said Jesse, his voice deeper somehow. Wiser. "The first wolf feeds on anger and fear. Weakness and lies. He is thin with sickness and doubt, but fights with sharp teeth and long claws. The other is clean and good. He is bravery and kindness and truth, and his coat is always stained with the blood of the wounds given by his brother.

"This frightened the boy, who asked his grandfather which wolf would eventually destroy the other."

Jesse lifted his chin and looked directly at Chase. "Which wolf wins, nephew?"

All eyes turned to face us.

Chase cleared his throat.

"The one you feed," he said.

A reflective quiet fell over the circle, the crackling and pop of wood Jesse's only applause. Since seeing him with the president, my opinion of him had grown softer. I hadn't forgiven him for abandoning his nephew, but I could see now why Chase had.

I rose and offered Chase my hand.

"Come dance with me," I said.

With a laugh he reached for me, and I had to lean all my weight back in order to pull him up.

"No one's dancing anymore," he said, a small dimple forming on one cheek. It was true; the musicians were facing each other now, speaking a language I didn't know.

"Come dance with me," I said again. I'd come to understand something while Jesse was talking. There was more to me than what I'd become, a part only Chase could access. And if I didn't feed it, it would die.

With both of my hands surrounding his, I led him over to the space before the musicians. People cheered for us but I barely heard them. The old president smiled my way but I wasn't embarrassed. Chase's fingers spread around my waist and dragged my hips close, and his back rounded beneath my grasp. He took the lead, rocking gently from side to side, leading me, guiding me. Reminding me.

"There you are," he whispered in my ear. "I found you."

We danced until the last musician packed up his instrument and disappeared into the woods. And then I led Chase up past the falls, to the place where he could finally take a bath.

CHAPTER
17

THE next morning we left before dawn in a truck with a newly patched tire. The previous night we'd revised our trip, accounting for this unexpected stop, and mapped out the rest of our journey based on the locations of the posts DeWitt had given us. Our next stop was in central Tennessee. The refugees stayed behind with the others, and as we descended from the mountains, I watched the compound blend with the low-hanging clouds and couldn't help but think there was a storm coming.

Outside Tennessee I returned to the back of the truck, surrounded by my Statutes. We'd left some behind at the president's camp for the soldiers to spread around the nearby towns, but the bulk would be distributed by the MM. I wondered how many had already been stuck to houses, schools, and shops around the Midwest.

The truck was stopped once at a road block; I heard the voices of the soldiers outside questioning our purpose. Not more than five minutes passed before we moved on, but I don't think I truly breathed until we were back to driving at a steady pace.

DeWitt had given us the location of a contact in Chattanooga, and we parked on the second floor of an old aquarium parking garage to wait.

An hour passed before they arrived. Three women, all dressed in Sisters of Salvation uniforms. The oldest had to be in her seventies; her silver hair was pinned back, and her skirt was pulled up just below her bra. The youngest would have been my mother's age. She was pretty, but had a sour look on her face, and tried to hide the gun in her waistband with an oversized blouse. The third looked too polished to be a Sister; her raven hair hung in short, neat curls around her high cheekbones. She held a notepad and a pencil in one hand, and made me nervous.

"Three of you," said the old woman. "Three of us. Quite a coincidence."

"There's no coincidence," said Jesse, and I winced, thinking that Billy would have made four. The woman nodded.

"You'll forgive us for not bringing you home to the roost," said the old woman, holding Chase's hand while she spoke. "Given the circumstances with the other posts, we'd rather not risk discovery." Her voice was brittle, but her back was ramrod straight.

"We understand," said Chase.

The woman with the notepad raised her brows at me. "I have to admit, I never thought I'd see you two alive." There was something familiar about her voice, the way she articulated every single word. The muscles in my shoulders tensed.

"Faye," warned the sour-faced woman.

"You have powerful friends," she said, tapping her pencil on the paper.

"I'm sorry, who are you?" I asked.

"Faye Brown," she answered with a little smirk.

"AKA Felicity Bridewell," said Sour Face.

"The reporter," I recognized, and felt my lips draw back. "You reported on Truck's execution."

"And my AWOL," said Chase. "You almost got us arrested."

The farmhouse with the barred windows. The stolen bike. Our escape in the middle of the night. The memories were all too clear.

"No," she said. "*You* almost got you arrested. I just made you famous for it."

I took a step closer. "What are you doing here?" I looked to the old woman. "What's she doing here?" It occurred to me too late that this might be a bust. I stopped short and glanced back at the truck.

"Didn't know you'd have such high-priority visitors, did you Jane?" Felicity—or Faye, whatever her name was—asked the old woman.

"Felicity's with us." Jane frowned. "She's also employed by the FBR as a newscaster."

She may have been working both sides, but that didn't ease my mind as it had with Marco and Polo. She'd done a lot of damage with her words.

"While we're making introductions, this is Ember Miller and Chase Jennings," Felicity announced. "AWOL and . . ." She tapped her lip with the pencil. "Reform school runaway turned sniper, am I right? You two are still big news in this region. Congratulations."

"Let's go," I said.

"Haven't been in the game too long, have you?" she surmised, writing something on her notepad. Before thinking twice I'd slapped it out of her hand. The pencil rolled across the ground and she stopped it with her foot and bent slowly to retrieve it. Behind me, Jesse chuckled.

"We were nearly killed because of your reports," I snapped.

"Look," she said. "I just read what comes across my desk. It's nothing personal."

"Maybe you could report something worthwhile," I said. "What the Bureau's doing to the Article violators, or their own soldiers that go AWOL. Those would be real stories."

"I'd be dead in five minutes," she retorted. "And then who would give you your precious intel?"

"Ease up," said Jane to the reporter. She looked to me with apology in her eyes. "Faye's provided your organization with a lot of Bureau secrets over the years."

"By way of Truck," said Sour Face. "God rest his soul."

Felicity dropped her injured expression at the mention of his name.

"Look," she said, her tone not quite so biting. "I'm one of a handful of female reporters left in the country. The *entire* country. The FBR is not exactly the most inclusive workplace for women." She inhaled through her nostrils. "I'm only there because they need to appeal to the illusion that they're still looking out for everyone's best interests. Felicity Bridewell: the token girl. If they knew I was here, I'd be no better off than you two."

"That's very sweet of you," I said.

"Heard anything interesting lately?" Jesse asked Felicity.

"That depends," she answered, chin lifted. "You don't get yours until I get mine. That's the way I work."

Jesse smirked. "I bet it is."

"What do you want?" asked Chase. She turned to him, but wilted under his intimidating glare.

"A ride to the safe house," she said. "Since his assassination attempt, Chancellor Reinhardt's been on a witch hunt. Anyone with field connections is being brought in for *questioning*."

She air-quoted the word. "Things are getting a little too hot here for my taste."

"A ride to the safe house," I said. "I'm sure we can arrange that."

She narrowed her gaze. "And yet somehow I'm not convinced."

"It's gone," said Chase bluntly.

"Gone?" said Sour Face. "What do you mean *gone*?"

Jane crossed herself and muttered a quiet prayer.

Felicity paled, but gained composure quickly. "What happened to it?"

"The FBR flattened it. I guess that didn't come across your desk," said Chase.

The look on her face indicated that it had not.

"Where am I supposed to go now?" she asked, more annoyed than afraid. Even if the soldiers at the old president's hideout hadn't explicitly told us not to direct anyone else that way, I wasn't sure I would tell this woman about it.

I crossed my arms over my chest. "The same place any of us are supposed to go."

"Well that's reassuring," she said.

"You'll lay low with us until this clears," said Jane.

Felicity's mouth had pulled tight, and she gave one curt nod. "There's an informant that's been turned by the FBR. He's feeding the locations of the posts to the FBR. He's got some sort of deal worked out with Reinhardt."

"What kind of deal?" asked Jesse.

"I don't know," said Felicity. "No one knows his name or location. He talks directly with the chief on a private radio frequency."

"No one has seen him?" asked Chase.

"No one I know," she said.

This wasn't new news; we knew someone was selling out the resistance. The only thing that had changed was that we now knew whoever it was had connections with Reinhardt.

"That's all I've got," said Felicity. She paused, and then looked at Jesse. "I hope Three's planning on making the Bureau pay for this."

I didn't like the woman, but on some level I understood her. She was risking a lot with no way out.

As the sun peeked through the concrete pylons, we told them that Three planned to attack Reinhardt's party in Charlotte. I removed a Statute from the boxes designated for this post that Jesse had begun to unload and gave it to Jane.

"Three can't fight the FBR alone," I said. "We need help. If everyone stood together, they'd have to listen."

Jane rubbed the heel of her hand over her collarbone.

"This town is afraid," she said. "Last year the Blues came through on one of their census runs and tore this place apart. There's not many still here that would even consider fighting back."

"Maybe they just need a little motivation," suggested Jesse. My mind flashed to the cemetery and the soldier in the cage, and I wondered morbidly if he'd helped provide some motivation there, too.

Felicity's brows lifted, and I wasn't the only one who saw her gaze drift down to his grinning mouth.

"We'll do what we can with these Statutes," said Sour Face. "There's another printing press in Dalton. We've got a source inside that might be willing to double your efforts. I suggest you make that your next stop."

My heart lifted. "Thank you."

"Don't thank me yet," she said.

THAT night we stayed at a checkpoint within the city. An old abandoned apartment in a rough neighborhood, where the growls of stray dogs and the drunken laughter from the drug houses penetrated the plastic covering the windows. In the living room was a metal trash can where a fire had been lit, and Chase and I gathered around it, neither of us mentioning the difference between this night and the last.

Jesse came into the room after dark, pulling the hood of a sweatshirt over his head.

"I'm going out," he said.

"Where?" I asked.

"Uh . . ." Jesse smirked. "To visit a friend."

"A friend you made earlier today?" asked Chase flatly, and I remembered the way Felicity had looked at him in the garage.

"We should stay together," I said.

"You're welcome to come," offered Jesse, spreading his arms wide. When I rolled my eyes, he shrugged. "Your call, neighbor. I'll be back before dawn."

"Fine," I said.

Chase and I sat and ate with a few more people awaiting a transport that might never come. After dark I told them about reform school, and then Chase and I recounted the story of our escape from the Knoxville base. It sounded different than it ever had before that night. There was a layer of separation that hadn't been there before, as if we were talking about two other people entirely.

I fell asleep leaning against the wall, on a crinkly trash bag that separated my thin layer of clothes from the dirty, shredded carpet. I didn't stay out long. Sometime in the middle of the night I woke to find Jesse kneeling before a still sleeping Chase. As I watched, Jesse adjusted the tattered blanket that had fallen off his nephew's shoulder. His lips were moving, but no sound came out. Then his head bowed, and he scraped a hand over his skull.

I didn't know what he was doing, but it seemed kind, and for some reason that made me nervous.

"How was your date?" I whispered. Chase stretched his long arms overhead.

Jesse's head lifted.

"It's time to go," he said.

We followed him around the block to where a large city trash truck was parked. It stunk, even from a distance, and when I saw the man outside leaning against the door, I stopped.

"Where's the truck?" asked Chase.

"Traded it to the ladies," said Jesse. "Meet August. He's our new set of wheels."

August smiled, revealing a couple of crooked teeth. He was average height, not heavy, but not too lean. His hair was thin up top and he stood a little hunched over. It occurred to me that he had no distinguishing features; I'd probably never give him a second look if I didn't know him.

"You're a carrier?" I asked. He nodded. A closer view revealed his gray city worker's uniform. "And the Statutes?" The women in Chattanooga had only taken a third of the boxes.

"Already loaded up." August motioned to a ladder alongside the green metal Dumpster. "You'll have more air in the bucket at the top. Sorry about the smell, but at least I don't get searched a lot."

My stomach churned.

"You've been busy," I told Jesse. He looked surprised that I had expected any differently.

Chase snorted.

The three of us climbed into the bucket and laid across the

dirty steel. It didn't even smell that bad once we started moving, and we had a great view of the sunrise.

We stayed in Dalton, Georgia, for no longer than it took to pass along the Statutes. The man who worked there said he knew some other printers in the North who would also be willing to support the cause, and would pass along the message as soon as he could. I couldn't help but feel the glimmer of excitement growing within me. This was actually working.

We stopped to stretch our legs and practice fighting. Chase was perfectly willing to spar, especially when we ended up tangled on the ground, but was more wary of helping me work the handgun, another side effect of Harper's death. Jesse took over, teaching me to take it apart, clean the small pieces, and put it back together. By the end of our first session I could load a cartridge and switch off the safety gage by feel. It wasn't a skill I was particularly glad to have, but it was a necessary one, all the same.

Calhoun. Rome. A roadblock sent us on a detour through Fort Payne, and we spent the night in Gadsden with some Sisters running a safe house for reform school runaways. By then word of our trip had gotten out and we met carriers who drove as far as Columbus, Ohio, and Northern Texas, all willing to spread the word about the Statutes.

Taking the back roads took time, and ten days after we'd left Endurance, we reached Birmingham. Like most of the others, they were cagey, but when they'd heard our report, and seen that we'd come to deliver the Statutes personally, they held a potluck dinner at the refectory of an old church. Some of the men even cleaned out the bucket atop of the trash truck for us.

We reached the outskirts of Atlanta at dusk the next day, and spent the night under the stars at an old rest stop. The next morning we entered the city, Chase and Jesse dressed as soldiers, me in my Sisters of Salvation uniform. Despite the MM's heavy presence there, our spirits were high. The carrier, August, drove us right downtown, where we were released outside an old theater near a large factory. It must have been doing well enough; half a dozen civilian cars were pulling into its parking lot. We tried to play it cool, but so many potential witnesses made me nervous.

We entered through the back doors and found ourselves on a wooden stage, a heavy burgundy curtain marred by moth holes sweeping at an angle from the ceiling. The auditorium was silent, rows of dusty red velvet seats empty and broken, and the air was cold and stale. I shivered. It felt like we were preparing to give a performance to ghosts.

Hard-soled boots clicked across the stage, and the curtain was pulled back to reveal a man in clean slacks and a button-down shirt with a snow-white, handlebar moustache. I stood back reluctantly; he didn't look like resistance.

"It's been awhile since we've seen you, August," said the man to the carrier as they shook hands. He had a thick, buttery accent.

"Stopped up," said August bluntly. "These folks, they'll tell you more."

None of us spoke.

The man smiled. "Let me guess, I'm not what you expected?"

"Not exactly," said Chase.

"Well set your mind at ease, son," said the man. "I dress this way to keep my day job. I keep my day job because it helps feed the folks of this city."

"And your work, what would that be?" asked Jesse.

"Food," said the man. "Boxed food. Atlanta's home to Horizons national distribution warehouse."

This made me feel minutely better.

"Awfully trusting to come alone, unarmed," said Jesse.

The man smiled again, his blue eyes twinkling. "Now what makes you think I'd do a thing like that?"

He snapped his fingers over his head, and suddenly three more men stepped out from behind the curtain, all with guns in their hands. Chase turned, and when I followed, another four were behind us. There was even a woman in a theater box lifting a hand from her rifle to send us a friendly wave.

For some reason, this calmed my nerves considerably.

Chase and I fell into our report while Jesse continued to assess our guards.

"You people responsible for that new sniper shooting?"

"The one near the Red Zone?" I asked, remembering what the woman had told me in the Smokys.

"Sure, that one. And the one last week in Chattanooga. Shot up four soldiers on a patrol. Report said there was a big one, two, *three* carved into the cruiser's hood." He held up his fingers to accentuate the point. "Reinhardt put down four more of his prisoners in retaliation according to the radio last night. Poor souls." He smoothed down his moustache with one hand.

I froze. "We were just there and didn't hear anything . . ."

Beside me Chase had stilled. Jesse found something fascinating to stare at on the ceiling.

"Excuse me a moment," Moustache said when one of the guards behind him turned up the volume on his radio. As he turned back to convene with the three men behind him, Chase closed our small circle, boxing out August the carrier.

"Was that you?" The lines of Chase's neck were pulled taut.

Jesse picked at something in his teeth.

He was going to act as if it were nothing. As if he hadn't

potentially compromised our mission and taunted the MM to come and find us.

"The prisoners," I said. "Reinhardt killed more of our people because of you."

"Once they hit that prison they were already lost," said Jesse.

Not according to Billy, who might now have been among them.

"You should have told us," said Chase.

"You should have told those women," I said, the fury overridden by a sudden dose of fear. "What do you think the MM is going to do to their people now?"

"I did tell those women. Well, the one at least. *Felicity*." Jesse sounded out the name and flashed a dangerous smile. "I have a better question. What do you think the civilians in town will do with that push?"

"That's what the Statutes were for!" I shook my head, swallowing the growl.

Jesse leaned down until we were the same height.

"Are you sure you're cut out for this, neighbor?" he asked. "War is ugly. Sometimes you've got to do things you don't like and hope they're better for everyone in the long run."

"Like keep a man in a cage?" asked Chase.

Jesse lifted his chin. The tension hummed between them.

"Better if you don't think of them as men," he said finally.

Chase scoffed and turned away.

"Easier, you mean," I whispered. It would have been easier to live with Harper's death had he not been flesh and blood. Easier, but not right.

The three cuts on my chest stung.

"Might want to take a listen, friends," called Moustache.

He motioned us over to where the other guards were now gathering.

A radio report was playing on the handheld, and the voice I recognized all too well.

"In what the chief has called a momentous victory in the fight against terrorism, Doctor Aiden DeWitt was captured this morning during an FBR raid. DeWitt, leader of the rebel organization known as Three, has confessed to the sniper shootings throughout Virginia and Tennessee in the last three months, including the attack on the FBR draft in Knoxville. His sentencing, as determined by the Chief of Reformation, has yet to be decided. With more to come on this story, this is Felicity Bridewell."

My gut plummeted through the floor.

DeWitt had been captured. The report didn't say where, or if they'd found Endurance, but the cold snaking through my veins said that Rebecca, Will, the children, and the rest who remained in Endurance were in trouble.

A scene played out before my eyes, of Sean and Jack reaching the safe house wreckage, finding Tucker, and bringing him back to Endurance. Of the MM following them, attacking, taking DeWitt.

Rebecca wouldn't even be able to run.

Chase was watching me, the same horror I felt mirrored on his face.

One of the guards with Moustache suddenly bolted toward the front of the stage, his previously silent shoes now slapping up the center aisle. He disappeared behind the auditorium door, leaving a strained silence behind him.

For several seconds no one moved. Then two shots rang out, magnified off the theater's high ceiling. My heart slammed into my throat. I backed against the nearest wall, my gun drawn. Chase and August hid behind the curtain.

"Soldiers?" Chase whispered to August.

"It's time to go," said August. "Someone was followed."

Jesse crouched on the opposite side of the stage behind a false wall painted with orange and red flames. If it was us, the MM could have found the trash truck, still packed with boxes of hijacked Statutes.

Moustache crawled toward us. He slapped a set of keys into Chase's outstretched hand.

"Silver sedan around the southeast corner of the building," he said. "It's time you three hit the road."

"The Statutes," I hissed.

"We'll take care of it, just go!"

He led us to another exit, this one emerging below the sidewalk, where Jesse joined us. Carefully we surveyed the street, and finding it empty, climbed the steps and made a dash for the nearest cover—an old bus stop awning. Chase led the way and Jesse took the rear, smashing me between their backs when we came to a sudden stop.

"See anything?" As soon as Chase asked, a volley of shots came from the front of the building, followed by a man's sharp cry of pain. I clenched my teeth.

We should have helped, but we couldn't risk capture, not with the Statutes out in circulation and not if DeWitt was really gone. We needed to get back to Endurance to find out what had happened.

"There's the car," said Chase, pointing across the street with his weapon. He removed the keys from his pocket and rolled back his shoulders, ready to run.

"We've got you covered," said Jesse.

"Go," I said. "Now!"

Chase took off toward the car, just as another shot rang out. I glanced around the metal siding of the bus stop and searched for any signs of movement.

Seconds after Chase made it to the car, the engine sputtered, then revved. An eerie silence punctuated the firefight at the front of the building, and in it I knew they were coming for us. The seconds ticked down.

I ran for the car, sliding into the backseat, Jesse just after me. Chase hit the gas and the tires squealed against the pavement. We stayed low, out of view from the windows.

As soon as he was out of range Chase slowed our speed, trying to make us appear inconspicuous, like the other cars passing through this part of the city. After a while I peeled my cheek off the leather seat and chanced a quick look around. We hadn't been followed. Yet.

"We have to go back to Endurance," I said.

"If DeWitt's gone, Endurance is gone," said Jesse. He stared out the side window, a blank expression on his face.

"He could have been captured somewhere else," said Chase. "They told us Endurance was protected. Off the MM's radar."

I hoped he was right.

CHAPTER
18

BY late afternoon we'd crossed into the Red Zone by way of an obscure dirt road that cut through the woods. Jesse had learned of the route from DeWitt before we'd left, and it was a good thing he had, because the radio in the sedan's glove compartment picked up a signal that indicated the MM had increased their border patrol. It left me with a bad feeling that they'd already reached Endurance.

We parked under a highway two miles away and hiked in through a cement ditch that led to a junkyard behind the compound. The gate we'd left through three days earlier was open, and as far as I could tell there weren't any guards lurking in the old oak trees that ran along the sides of the barricade.

"What are the chances everyone went to Charlotte?" I asked.

Slim. Chase had already told me on our drive here that the last shift of fighters would have left yesterday, but that a core group would be left behind to guard the compound. There were children here, and too many secrets.

At least there had been.

"Come on," I said.

The sky was clear and quiet, and the air smelled vaguely

metallic, like blood and electricity. We stayed low and kept together, and crept closer.

Just outside the gate we paused, hiding behind the rusted body of a van that had been propped up on cinder blocks. Chase threw a rock over the hood, and it skidded through the open gate before coming to a stop.

Nothing happened.

"Evacuated?" asked Chase.

"Maybe they're up at the lodge," I said.

"I'll go take a look," said Jesse. He jogged toward the open entrance while Chase and I kept our eyes open and mouths closed, struggling to hear if anyone was coming.

I slipped the ring Chase had given me over my finger and then slid it back off. It didn't feel right to wear it yet, not when that *someday* we'd talked about wasn't today. In the meantime I would keep it safe, and hold on to a future where things were different. *Normal*, like Sean had said.

Chase was watching me; I felt his gaze before I looked up. He had a streak of dirt down the side of his cheek, and I wiped it away slowly with my thumb. His breath quickened. I had the urge to lean closer, to bring my fingertips to his lips and feel the soft curve of them, but instead I lowered my hand and listened.

Long minutes passed, and when Jesse didn't return, Chase stretched his legs.

"It's been too long," he said.

I nodded. If this was a trap, it was an awfully quiet one. Jesse was probably still searching, or had already found the others, but that didn't mean we could take any chances.

"Stay out of the open," I said. "We'll go around the woods through the cemetery. Keep the wall on our side." It was longer than taking the road that cut straight through the middle of the compound, but it wasn't worth the risk of exposure.

The corner of his mouth quirked. "Yes, ma'am."

"What?" Silently, I cursed the heavy Sisters of Salvation skirt I still wore and tied the excess in a knot around my thighs.

"Nothing." He grinned fully as he checked the chamber of his gun. "I'd take orders from you anytime."

The laugh bubbled out of my throat. I covered my mouth to lock it down, but that didn't stop the tingling in my belly.

"I'll take point." His dark, amused eyes met mine. "If that's okay with you."

"By all means." I gestured for him to lead the way.

Before he stood fully he ran the back of his finger up my calf. The heat raced through my veins.

"You might run faster if you lose the skirt."

Before I could respond, he was off, running for the gate with his gun pointed at the ground. I raced after him thinking he was probably right; it would have been a lot easier to move without this stupid uniform.

The back fields where the army had trained were empty— the fire pits had been covered as if they'd never been lit, and the storage sheds were cleaned out. In the parking lot only a large yellow bulldozer, a car, and a white moving truck remained. None of them bore MM emblems.

Jesse was nowhere to be seen.

Without speaking, we moved on, staying close to the barricade as we entered the woods. We came to the cemetery and found the shed unguarded and the door open. I cringed, remembering how we'd found Jesse inside with the caged soldier. We searched it quickly, finding not only the cage empty, but the entire room stripped. The bright lights that had hung on the ceiling were gone. It looked like it hadn't been occupied in years.

We moved faster now, climbing the hill along the perimeter. My heart was pumping by the time the trees began to clear, and the sweat was flowing freely down my brow. Finally, the dorms came into view, but only one person could be seen. A man, standing outside the back entrance of the lodge's cafeteria.

Jesse.

The panic swelled and broke inside of me. I abandoned the fence and forced myself to walk toward him, coming to a stop beside the swing set. It was broken now, the chains lying across the ground like dead snakes.

What I'd come to recognize as Endurance looked nothing like the fully functioning compound I'd left just days before. Outside, the lodge was in ruins. The north wing had been demolished; all that remained was a heap of concrete and broken wood. Though the smoke had died away, the air still smelled charred and acidic, as if there'd recently been a mechanical fire. Over the wreckage I saw that the barn had been torn down, and the gardens, once a jungle of green living things, had been torn up by a car's tires.

The breath scored my throat, coming faster and faster. The safe house had been destroyed. The posts were falling, one by one. And now Endurance had been demolished, too.

"We're too late," I said. And then again. "We're too late."

Our friends were gone.

Jesse was staring straight ahead, a blank look on his face.

"It's been days," he said. "This didn't happen this morning."

He was right. The dust had settled and the fires had died. Endurance had fallen days ago.

"Em," said Chase. His shoulders were rising and falling; the collar of his shirt clung to his skin. "The orchard."

Rebecca. Sean had told her to go to the orchard if something happened. My legs were already shaking from the run across campus, but I pushed them on again. This time I tucked the gun into my waistband and ran full out, hearing the blood rushing through my eardrums. Chase pulled ahead, which drove me on harder, until my heart felt like it might burst in my chest.

We ran through down the narrow path lined by junk as if we could outrun any danger that might be watching, but when we turned into the orchard the rows of trees were still and quiet.

Just as I opened my mouth to call for Rebecca, a shot cracked through the air. Dirt sprayed up from the ground at Chase's feet and he threw himself backward, stumbling before he slammed into me. I grabbed his navy uniform jacket and pushed him up.

My first thought was of the Lost Boys, and when I heard the hoof beats behind us, I braced to defend myself.

"Get out!" The command was shrill, the girl's voice familiar. A coffee-colored horse with four white socks came barreling through the trees and pulled up short before us, snorting and pawing at the ground. Astride her was a skinny girl with a dirty face and a matted cap of golden hair. The fierce look on her face said she wasn't afraid to use the gun she pointed straight at us.

"Get out or I swear to God, I'll . . ."

"Rebecca!" I lurched forward as Rebecca dropped the weapon on the ground. She leaned forward on Junebug's neck and scrambled off, clinging to the saddle for support. I'd already reached her by then and knocked her all the way to the ground. We landed in a heap, tears smearing the sweat and dirt on each other's faces.

"You're alive!" She sobbed. And then she was punching me in the shoulder. "I thought you were dead!"

"You thought *I* was dead?" I half laughed, half hiccupped, and wiped my cheeks with the back of my hand. "What happened? Where are the others? Where is Sean?"

She glanced over my shoulder and when I looked back I found Chase, reaching to help us both up. She slapped both hands on his chest, wobbling forward. He caught her before she fell while I pulled her crutch off the back of the saddle where it had been fastened. Junebug, no longer fearsome, nipped at my blouse.

"You almost got yourself shot wearing that stupid jacket," Rebecca was telling Chase. "I thought you were a soldier!"

"I got that," said Chase. He grinned at her and she gave up and hugged him.

I went to pick up the gun and only then realized we weren't alone. Will had emerged from the grove behind us, along with Sarah. As the seconds passed, several of the children followed. They looked tired, frightened, and more than a little shocked. I could see more of them lurking back in the trees, along with a few of the women I recognized from the safe house survivors.

"Is this all that made it out?" Chase asked bleakly.

Rebecca adjusted her arm in the crutch and tucked the gun back in Junebug's saddlebag. "We evacuated when we heard the soldiers were coming."

"So much for being off the MM's radar," I mumbled.

She nodded grimly. "That's when the doctor tore the place down."

Chase had been counting the others, but at this he promptly turned back around. "DeWitt tore Endurance down?"

"With a tractor," piped in Will. "Him and the other council members. They wrecked the whole place."

I remembered seeing the bulldozer in the parking lot by the other cars.

"Why?" I asked.

"So the Bureau wouldn't find anything worthwhile when they showed up." Jesse had arrived, his shoulders laced back and a lethal look in his eyes. I found myself taking a step away.

"We were going to take the cars when they showed up," Rebecca continued. "It was getting dark. Ms. Rita and the other council members took off to lead them off course. I don't know if they made it. I don't think they did." Her voice had lowered to a whisper. "Rocklin and a few more that didn't go to Charlotte stayed with the doctor. The soldiers came in through the back gates. They took them—all of them, women and some of the kids, too—in a blue bus with the windows blacked out. I didn't know what else to do. We gathered who we could, snuck out the front, and came here."

"You did good," said Chase, his arm still around her waist for support.

"I been looking out for us," said Will. He was looking at Jesse, who gave him a brief nod.

"The soldiers are gone now," I said. "We just came from there and didn't see anyone."

"Ember," she said, her voice wavering for the first time. "Sean never came back."

Beside me, Chase exhaled. "He's been gone almost two weeks. He could still be waiting for Tucker. With the radio silence . . ."

"Tucker called on the radio," she said, leaning in close. "Just before we evacuated we got a message from him. He'd reached the meeting point but no one was there. Not even the people we left with the medic at the mini-mart."

My pulse began to pick up speed again. "Did DeWitt say anything else? Did he send anyone after him?"

"The soldiers were already closing in," said Rebecca. "There was no one to send."

Frantically I tried to piece it all together. DeWitt had been captured, just as Felicity Bridewell had reported. He'd torn apart Endurance himself to hide what we'd done here. Now Tucker had arrived at the safe house wreckage but Sean and Jack were missing. We had to find him, find out what he knew, and somehow find Sean as well.

"What do we do now?" Sarah asked. Her face had rounded since we'd arrived, and apart from a scar through her right eyebrow, barely showed any signs of the beating she'd taken in Knoxville. My gaze automatically fell to her belly. She was getting bigger. I didn't know how far along she was, but soon she would have to find a stable place to have the baby.

"There's a place I heard about," I said. "I'm not positive it's a sure thing."

Chase's hand came to rest on my lower back. I took a deep breath.

"I think there's a boat from Tampa that goes to Mexico."

I felt the weight of Jesse's stare and wished I felt more confident about this option.

"How are we supposed to get there?" There was desperation in her wide brown eyes.

"We can take the cars," said Chase. "But it's probably better to lay low for a while. Stay off the roads."

A day might give us enough time to find Sean, Jack, and Tucker. If Rebecca and the others could hold out a little longer we could be back to take them to Tampa ourselves.

Chase's thumb rose up my spine, telling me he was thinking the same thing I was.

Sarah's gaze passed from Chase to Jesse, and her lower lip began to quiver. "Did Billy make it?"

I tried to offer a reassuring smile. "He went to Charlotte to join the others." I wasn't sure what else to say.

She lifted her chin and tucked her hair behind her ears. "That's very brave. I wish I'd gotten to say good-bye. He was . . ." She smiled. "He was cute, you know?"

I bit my lip. "He thought the same about you."

She lit up. I hoped someday Billy would get to see that look.

WE agreed to stay the night and leave at dawn for the safe house wreckage. Chase and Jesse did a thorough perimeter sweep, and then returned to Endurance to scavenge for food and supplies. I stayed behind with Rebecca, leaning against the trunk of an orange tree while the children and Sarah laid on the grass at our feet. Both of us kept our guns on the ground beside us, listening to the crickets chirp. After a while it started to get cold, and she scooted closer, until our hips were touching. She linked her arm around mine.

"The first time I kissed Sean was in the shower at the reformatory." She giggled.

I leaned away to look at her and found her biting her lower lip. Now I laughed. "That's . . . bold."

"Oh, please," she said. "It wasn't like that."

"Then what *was* it like?"

She snuggled deeper into my side. "He'd been stationed there for a month. He was different than the others. You could tell he was putting on a show—he wasn't as good at disguising it in the beginning. Once I even caught him laughing at something the headmistress said."

Sean had always made a point of agreeing with everything

the headmistress said. It was how he stayed under the radar and kept his relationship with Rebecca a secret.

"I bet that went over well."

"He hid it in a coughing fit." She smiled. "And that's when I knew I had to talk to him."

A noise crackled across the way, but it was just Will circling our position in search of trespassers. If anyone had an eye out for the Lost Boys, it would be him.

We settled back against the tree.

"I stuck a note in his pocket at line formation one morning," she said. "It said, 'Meet me in the showers at midnight.'"

"That *is* bold," I said.

"Okay, maybe." She snorted. "He read it and threw it away. Right in front of me. So rude. Anyway, I was sure he was going to turn me in, but nothing happened all afternoon. And I mean *nothing*. He didn't even look at me."

Of course he hadn't. If he'd been caught ogling her he would have been busted.

"*So*," I prompted.

"So I waited until midnight and snuck down the hall to the bathrooms. I thought for sure he wasn't going to show, but there he was, hiding out in one of the stalls. Later he told me he'd been there since right after curfew in case I came early. Apparently he felt like a real creeper."

"And you walked right in and kissed him," I said, marveling at her audacity.

"No," she said, aghast. "I introduced myself first."

Some of the closest kids stirred as we fell into stifled laughter.

Chase and Jesse returned, but didn't approach us right away. Chase motioned that they were going to do another walk of the perimeter and I nodded. He left a handful of supplies on the ground a few feet away. Some clothing, it looked like, and some food.

I watched him disappear into the darkness, wondering what I would do if we were separated.

"Sorry they destroyed the barn," Rebecca said.

"Hmm?" I tore my eyes away from the last place I'd been able to see him.

"I know that place had sentimental value for you." She stretched out her legs.

"Rebecca!" She shushed me with a sneaky grin.

"Sean told me before he left you two had a midnight rendezvous there. How very romantic."

I covered my eyes with the heels of my hands, remembering with a streak of heat the hay in my hair, and the specs of dust lit by the moon through the high loft window.

"It may have been romantic." I paused. "Thanks, by the way. For your, um . . . thoughtful gift."

She was wiggling now, unable to hold the glee inside of her.

"Stop," I groaned. "Please? Pretty please?"

She finally settled down and rolled onto her side. "I knew it when I saw you two together. You're different, you know; the way you look at each other."

"Different how?"

She combed her hair back over one ear. "I don't know. Like you have a secret no one else knows."

I liked that. A secret no one else knew.

For a few seconds the fear of what had happened to Sean had faded. The hole of his absence was filled with warm memories. It was like we were living in another time. But when it came back, it hurt twice as much.

"I almost left the kids," she confessed. "All I could think was I had to get out of there. I couldn't get caught again."

I squeezed her hand. "Most people would have left them."

"We were supposed to meet here. Why hasn't he come back?"

"We'll find him."

But I didn't feel so confident. The MM could have him. His car could have broken down or been held back by debris in the road. A throbbing began at the base of my skull. Sean had left Rebecca's side, broken his promise not to leave her, to keep her safe. We had to find him.

"I can't go with you, can I?" she said.

I knew this had been coming. If we were going to reach Tucker and search for Sean, we needed to be light and move fast. Even with Rebecca's advancements, we couldn't chance her safety, or her slowing us down.

"I'm sorry," I said.

She brushed away a tear impatiently.

"Stupid, stupid legs," she said.

I put my arm over her shoulders, not knowing what else to do.

"Bring him back," she said finally. "And both of you come back, too."

CHAPTER

19

THE trip to the mini-mart would take nine hours, depending on the amount of wreckage on the highways and streets. We took the moving truck, leaving the sedan from Atlanta with the fuel gage on empty. I traded my Sisters of Salvation uniform for a pair of cropped pants and a hand-sewn tunic Chase had found, and left Rebecca with a quick, wordless hug.

I made a silent promise to myself that it would not be the last time I saw her.

Jesse drove while Chase took shotgun. I sat between them on the bench seat thinking of Tucker. It was strange and unsettling, but I found I wanted to see him again. I wanted to find out what had happened on his mission, and if he knew any more about DeWitt or the Chief of Reformation's party, now only two days away. As we reached the highway, I flattened my hands over my thighs and turned my thoughts to Sean. I pictured him and Jack stranded on the side of the road beside a broken down car and hoped their delay was that simple.

The world passed by out of the side window. The sun grew hot, and the wind whipped my hair around my face. My worry edged into fear; the Red Zone was huge, the entire East Coast, and Sean could be anywhere within it. I imagined having to tell Rebecca we couldn't find him, felt the hole punch through me as if she'd been the one telling me that Chase was lost.

Twice in the first hour we had to leave the main road because of abandoned cars and debris, and return to surface streets. Sean and Jack were nowhere to be seen.

I felt something brush against the back of my hand, and when I looked down, saw Chase's knuckles. He stared straight ahead, so I did, too, but his fingertips continued to trace lines over the back of my hand, then around my wrist. It gave me hope.

In the afternoon, Jesse switched the radio to a frequency the injured had used to contact us when we were on our search for the survivors. We were within range now, and if their batteries were by some chance still working, we should have been able to pick up a signal.

No one was broadcasting.

The clouds stretched thin and high across a pale sky as we reached the outskirts of where the safe house had been. We parked several miles back, where a pile of rubble blocked the road. I searched for evidence of another car but was no longer surprised when I didn't see one. Wherever Sean was, it was not here.

I slung a pack of medical supplies from the truck's cab over my back. Chase took point, his gun held high and ready, while Jesse covered our backs. No one knew what to expect as we hiked through the high grass between the beach and what was left of the town, but we prepared for the worst.

It didn't help that I had the skin-crawling sensation of someone's eyes on my back.

"Here," Chase said quietly as a stop sign on the main road came into view. Once we reached the street I recognized the area. Two half-burned houses, their remains still black and raw, butted up against an old shipyard where half a dozen boats were turned on their sides. Three blocks down was the mini-mart where the injured had taken refuge, and as we made our way toward it I counted how many places there were to hide.

The intersection before the mini-mart was empty. The gas pumps still stood, but their hoses were ripped away. In the sun outside the entrance a man in street clothes was seated on a metal chair. He was slumped forward, asleep, his hands on his lap, his chin on his chest.

His hair was blond and messy.

"Tucker." I started forward, but Jesse snagged my forearm.

Muscles tense, I crouched beside him behind an overturned sailboat, twenty feet away. Chase crept forward, disappearing behind the shop on the opposite side of the street.

"Listen," Jesse whispered.

Silence. Nothing but the birds and the crash of the waves at the beach. My blood began to buzz. No shadows moved behind the broken windows. Those that had stayed behind with the medic were hurt, and I had supplies on my back that could help.

"Stay here." Stealthily, Jesse bled into the surrounding landscape, making his way around the building.

I kept my eyes on Tucker, finding it odd that he sat in the sun when the metal awning provided shade just a few feet to his right. He seemed to sense that I was watching him because a second later he shook himself awake and rolled his head in a slow circle. Even from a distance I could see the red welts on his face, and the brown spattering of dried blood across his chest.

Someone had done a number on him.

I lowered the pack of medical supplies to the ground beside me while I waited. Across the street Chase stepped out into the open. I caught a glimpse of Jesse's white undershirt moving through the thick emerald shrubbery behind the overturned trash cans in the back. He waved to Chase.

I left the pack and hurried toward Tucker, the gun I carried heavy in the back of my waistband. In the open, the sun was hot, and I couldn't imagine how Tucker had been able to stand it.

I had only reached the first set of gas pumps when he saw me. He did a double take, and I cringed at the deep cut across his jaw. Then, so subtly I almost missed it, his gaze lifted.

"You shouldn't have come," he whispered.

The next moments seemed to pause, and then lurch forward at twice the speed.

I followed Tucker's gaze, and saw the flash of a navy dart across the roof. Seconds after a clatter on the metal came a loud *crack,* but I didn't stop to see where the shot had been aimed because I was running for the closest cover, the mini-mart.

Another shot, and then another. I crashed into Tucker, and knocked him into the side of the building. We fell hard, a mess of arms, legs, and the hard metal angles of the chair.

"Help me up!" he shouted.

I was already scrambling toward the entrance on my hands and knees. A quick look over my shoulder revealed that he had yet to rise, and was thrashing around like a fish out of water. It was only then I saw that his hands were bound in front of him, and his waist and legs were fastened to the chair.

What remained of the glass double doors behind me shattered as a bullet screamed by my left ear. My ears rang, my heart hammered against my rib cage. I drew myself as close as I could to the building, feeling the shards of glass slash my thighs, and reached for the gun.

The trigger stuck.

An instant of frozen panic.

I released the safety, cocked the slide, and fired up at the roof.

Once, twice. The kickback sent reverberations up my arms. I locked my elbows and fired again, straight into the metal overhead, watching the holes puncture through it like it was tin foil. There was a stunted cry, and then a crash as the awning gave way near my last shot, and a man fell through, landing ten feet away. There was blood on his face. It soaked through his open uniform jacket. He gripped his leg, screaming. It bent forward at the knee to the same degree that the other bent back.

I shoved myself up. In a surge of strength I grabbed Tucker's shoulders and began to drag him backward through the front doors of the mini-mart. He twisted, trying to help me, and threw the chair onto its side.

My back strained. The muscles of my legs quaked. With a cry, I jerked us both through the entrance, landing on a warm, dusty floor.

Immediately I searched for more soldiers, any signs of movement. It wasn't until that moment that I saw what filled the mini-mart.

Bodies. A dozen of them. Tossed over each other like dirty laundry. I smelled it then, the rotting flesh, the sharp tang of blood. Flies buzzed through the air, a thick black cloud over them.

The medic from Chicago leaned against an empty rack, his face white with death, a hole in the center of his forehead.

I stared at the gun in my hands needing something, anything, solid to hold on to. My vision shook, or maybe it was my grasp. Maybe it was my whole body.

We were too late. The MM had set an ambush and used Tucker as the bait. And DeWitt, who'd led us to believe he'd sent a team to help, had done nothing.

There was no time to think about it now.

I crouched behind the counter, locking my jaw as I removed

an icicle-shaped piece of glass an inch wide from my side. My mouth opened in a silent scream, but though the beige tunic blossomed red, the pain numbed instantly. I pressed down on it to slow the bleeding.

"Chase," I said between my teeth. "Do you see him?"

Tucker had managed to free his waist from the chair, though his ankles and wrists were still bound.

"Find something sharp!" he ordered.

I grabbed the closest thing I could, the piece of glass that had been embedded in my skin, and crawled over to him, keeping as low as I could. I sawed at the tight ropes around his hands.

"Don't move!" I snapped at him when he strained against the ties.

"Hurry, hurry, hurry," he chanted.

The shots continued outside, and when I heard a grunt, and a drawn-out groan of pain, I dropped the glass and shoved past him, ducking low to see who had been hit.

A soldier kneeled out in the middle of the street. He lifted the rifle to his shoulder too slowly, and in the time before he fired he was hit three times across the chest. He fell back, motionless. I didn't see the shooter until Jesse streaked by toward the cover of the shipyard.

Another window shattered. Tucker, hands now released, grabbed my arm and ripped me back. He returned to frantically trying to cut the rope around his ankles.

"They followed me," he said. "I didn't know. I swear." His eyes, green and glassy, met mine. "I didn't think you'd come."

I believed him.

A groan behind me drew my attention, and both Tucker and I froze. Still with the gun aimed on the door I crawled backward, keeping my head low.

The first thing I saw was Jack, or what had once been Jack,

his long body splayed out across the floor as if he'd been tossed there. Under his legs was someone else. Someone whose pale face was turned to the side, revealing a head of light brown hair, matted with blood.

"Sean?" I kept my eyes on the door but crouched low, close to his face. I gave his arm a firm shake and he groaned again. He'd been shot low in the shoulder, but from the looks of his shirt had bled significantly.

A bullet zipped overhead, implanting in the back wall. Tucker swore.

With one arm I shoved Jack's legs off of Sean's, and pinched him as hard as I could beneath one knee.

He gasped, coughed weakly. The tears burned my eyes. I was so overcome with relief I nearly broke down.

"Sean!" My voice cracked. "Get up right now!"

"Ember?"

"*Up!*" I ordered. He struggled to get to his elbows. His eyes found Jack and wandered around the rest of the room before falling out of focus.

"Three," he said faintly. "They know where the doctor is. We've got to get back. Becca's . . ."

The screech of metal behind me, and someone burst through the back door.

I jerked my gun around, and felt the sob strangle my breath when I saw Chase.

"Ember!"

"Here," I said. He dodged between the bodies, eyes going wide with horror before stooping beside me.

"DeWitt didn't send anyone," I said.

"You sure about that?" His voice was cold, and his intention made my blood run cold. This couldn't have been Three's work. This had to be the MM.

"Good. You brought backup," mumbled Sean. His eyes began to roll back.

I pinched him again, this time in the crook of his elbow.

"Ow!" Sean shook his head.

"Jesse?" Chase asked me.

"Last I saw he was running for the shipyard."

His lip curled back as he saw the way my shirt was sticking to my side. "You're hit."

"Just glass," I told him. "I'm fine."

He looked as though he didn't believe me, but nodded anyway. "I'll clear the back for you. It's a straight shot into the woods; we'll meet back at the car."

"You hear that Sean? We're running," I said. "Get ready."

He groaned as Chase hoisted him to his feet.

"Wait," I heard Tucker say from the other side of the counter. "Wait, I'm almost . . . wait, okay?"

Chase flinched, his eyes cold and hard.

"We can't leave him," I said.

"Once you're clear, I'll come back for him."

"Chase . . ."

His hand cupped the back of my neck and drew me forward, smashing his lips against my brow. He was gone too soon; when I opened my eyes it was to see his back as he dodged toward the exit.

I ducked under Sean's arm and we hobbled after Chase. When we were in the doorframe, I wiped the sweat off my hand and replaced the gun, then made sure my friend was tight against my side.

"Ready?" Chase asked.

I glanced to Sean. He inhaled through his nostrils, face beginning to flush in patches.

"Now or never," he said.

I nodded.

Chase stepped out on the crumbling concrete step and aimed directly into the woods. Shots came from the roof, and then someone called, "Hey! They're back here!"

Without hesitation, Chase ran to the side, spun, and fired up at the roof. Sean and I sprinted toward the tree line. We hit the bushes with a crash, barely staying upright. I told my feet to keep moving, and they pedaled on, tearing through the vines and flimsy roots. Sean stumbled, then regained his footing, shoving forward.

I grabbed his arm. "Keep going," I said. "There's a truck three miles south where the road ends. I'll meet you there."

He looked like he would object, but when I pushed him, he turned and stumbled away.

"Come on, Chase," I whispered. Gripping the gun I ducked behind an overturned refrigerator someone had left out here years ago. Chase was back inside the building now; I could see his shadow move across the room.

Ten seconds, I told myself. I would give him ten seconds to get out, then I was going back after him.

Nine.

Eight.

Seven.

Six.

Chase sprinted through the exit, head down. Someone rounded the side of the building and began firing, and Chase dropped, rolling across the ground.

I jumped to my feet. Just before I crossed into the open, Tucker broke through the door and ran to Chase. He bent and grabbed his shirt, pulling him up.

Another shot, only this one from around the side of the building. Automatically, I ducked low, but my mouth fell open in shock when I saw Jesse firing toward Chase and Tucker.

No! I wanted to scream, but I couldn't find my voice. Jesse was making a mistake. Tucker was with us, he'd been imprisoned.

Tucker fell to his side with a blunted cry. He gripped his thigh and drew his knee to his chest.

Jesse disappeared around the side of the building again.

Chase looked down at Tucker for one instant, but that was all it took.

"Freeze!" shouted a soldier from the opposite side of the building. "Drop your weapon!"

I raised my gun, willing my arms to stop shaking. A noise in the bushes behind me startled me, and I glanced back, but saw nothing. When I turned back around, Chase had lowered his gun, and dropped it on the ground. Two soldiers faced him now, and another emerged from where Jesse had been hiding just seconds ago. The guard on the roof aimed down his sights at both he and Tucker.

Chase raised his hands in surrender.

A soldier approached and kicked Chase's gun across the dirt in my direction.

"Lucky I don't kill you right now," he spat. "On the ground. Hands behind your head. The chief's got some questions for you."

The chief was in Charlotte for the celebration. They meant for Chase to join the other prisoners there.

I lifted my gun again, blinking through the sweat dripping in my eyes, ignoring the whispering in the grass behind me.

I aimed.

I never saw the rope slip around my neck.

CHAPTER
20

THE boat rocked gently from side to side. *The water below was silent, slick and black as oil, coating the metal siding and dripping over the rim with the sway. Overhead, the sun beat down, cold and unmerciful. I shivered.*

Chase stood on the shore ten feet away. He dragged his toe in the water, jolting back when it burned the bottom of his boot with a harsh hiss. I searched the hull desperately for a paddle, but found only splintered pieces of wood.

"It's broken," I called, holding them up. The waves dragged me away, inch by inch. They thrashed harder, and I gripped the wooden bench I sat upon, fearful the boat would capsize.

I couldn't fix this. I couldn't get home.

He was no more than a tiny speck now, on a shore far away, and his voice came to me as a whisper.

"I'll find you," he said. "And I'll bring you back."

A LOW groan came from my raw throat, magnifying the pounding in my head. I blinked, but was confused by the sight that greeted me: thick ropes, branches and leaves, and through them, the clear night sky.

Side to side I swayed, as if I was lying in a hammock.

Not a hammock—a net, strapped to a tree. I tried to twist, but my legs were tangled up, and I only managed to tighten the ropes around my knees. The ground below was six feet away, and as I stared at it my temple throbbed, and the patches of grass wavered in my vision.

I grasped my neck, feeling the heat from the rope that had cut off my air supply, and the spike of panic when I realized my necklace was no longer around my neck.

The memories cropped up, fuzzy at first, then sharper, driving my pulse like the beat of a drum. Tucker outside the mini-mart. The bodies within. The soldiers surrounding us. Sean—had he made it?

Chase.

My heart clenched so hard I grit my teeth so I didn't cry out.

He'd been taken. Tucker as well, and maybe even Jesse.

I'd been taken. Though . . . not by the same people.

Voices came from my right, and I pretended to be unconscious as several sets of footsteps crunched over the dead leaves.

"Watch this," said a boy excitedly. I held still but tracked them through my lashes as they approached. I recognized the speaker; I'd met him in the grove weeks ago, before we'd been brought to Endurance, where he'd told me to shut up and kicked me in the side. A dirty blanket was wrapped around his shoulders, but the mean, hungry look on his bony face was still the same.

He grabbed my ankles and spun me in a circle. I went faster and faster until my stomach heaved and I had to swallow the bile. The net dug into my arms and my chest and my face. And then I paused, and the boy hollered in glee as I began to unwind, whipping around with greater speed than before. The branch above groaned and I braced for the fall that never came.

"What're you gonna do with her?" asked another.

"Don't know," the boy answered. "Maybe we'll cut off her fingers an' feed 'em to the dog."

Chills raced over my skin.

"Shuddup." This voice was farther removed from the others, and higher pitched. When I followed the sound I recognized the younger one that I'd been foolish enough to follow in the grove. He was still shirtless despite the cold, and covered in mud.

"What's that, dog?"

The boy who'd spun me disappeared from my view and I heard the familiar thump of a solid hit, and a high whine that followed.

"Bad dog! Bad dog doesn't get a bone!" shouted the boy. Several others laughed. While they were distracted I freed my arms completely, feeling for any break in the net. The branch above me groaned again.

I glanced at the boys, my body still. There were more of them now, maybe fifteen, standing by a large campfire, surrounding a child who crawled around on his hands and knees. Every few seconds someone kicked him. He began to bark and howl, and they clapped their hands and laughed.

I went to work on the net again, but the boys suddenly grew quiet. From behind them came the sound of scraping metal, and I squinted through the darkness to where a series of torches sticking out of the ground surrounded an old trailer home. A fat man wearing only a stained undershirt stumbled down the steps and belched loudly. Several of the boys laughed.

"Quit all that racket!" he yelled. They silenced.

He walked among them, pushing a few out of his way. "Charlie, I think I owe you somethin', don't I?"

The mean boy stepped forward timidly, hands clasped down low in front of him. With more dexterity than I would've thought possible, the man swung his fist toward Charlie's face, but stopped an inch away. Charlie flinched, and when the man began to laugh, smiled weakly.

"Naw, I owe you better'n that. I take care of my boys, don't I?"

"Yes, sir," said several of them.

"What's that?"

"Yes, sir!" they chimed together.

"Ungrateful bastards," muttered the man. Finally I found a weak link in the net and succeeded in ripping a hole large enough to shove my wrist through. Frantically, I began pulling at the ropes, but a flash of pain in my side made me grit my teeth and hold perfectly still while it passed. The glass puncture from the mini-mart had reopened. When it was manageable again I resumed my attack on the net.

"Charlie got me a little prize today, and for that, he gets a little prize of his own, don't he?"

Charlie unclasped his hands, and looked up at the man with interest.

The man reached into his pocket and removed a handgun. I froze. It was *my* gun.

He placed it in Charlie's hands.

"Thanks, sir!" The others gathered close around him as the man began to stumble in my direction. He belched again as he came close, and then smiled, revealing a mouthful of crooked, rotting teeth. His breath was enough to make my stomach heave again. The smell of alcohol wafted off of him.

"Pretty little thing," he whispered. I watched him, holding my breath. He stuck a finger through the net and poked me in the side. I couldn't help wincing; his finger pressed right against the cut the glass had made.

"Tickle, tickle, tu-tu!" He giggled. The net began to sway again.

I fought the urge to scream.

"Now why were you all alone out there?" he mused. "I know you must have friends."

I sensed he wasn't asking me. The boys had gathered in a half circle behind him.

"She had friends," said Charlie. "But some Blues came and snatched 'em up."

"They see you?" asked the man.

"Nah," said Charlie. "They might've though, what with that dog making all kinds of noise. Nearly got us found out." He kicked the ground, spraying dirt on the youngest boy. "He's always trying to blow it for us. Can't keep his yap shut."

The boys silenced as the man turned around. He clucked and shook his head from side to side. "You gonna handle this, Charlie?"

Charlie looked confused. "Sure. Sure, I'm gonna."

"Well?" said the man expectantly when Charlie didn't move. "When a dog gets unruly, you got to put him down."

I couldn't believe what I was hearing. As I waited, the small boy began to weep. He fell to his hands and knees and managed a weak bark. He crawled up to Charlie's leg and pawed at his knees.

"Ruff," he said between sobs. "Ruff, ruff, right, Charlie?"

Charlie, scrawny armed and trembling, held out the gun.

"Stop it," I said, unable to hold my silence any longer. "I let my friends go, not the kid."

"My pretty bird sings!" The man clapped his hands together, then paused and frowned, his neck doubling as he pulled his chin down. "I'll hear you sing some more later, I think. First, someone needs a lesson." He made a pouty face and pretended to sniffle.

He grabbed the back of the dog boy's shirt and hoisted him up, then began to drag him toward the trailer.

"Stop!" I struggled against the net, ripping a larger hole. My whole arm was free now.

"Charlie, she's gettin' free!" whispered one of the boys.

Charlie watched the door to the trailer slam shut, and then stalked toward me.

"You have to stop that man," I told him desperately. "Let me go, I'll do it."

Charlie's face contorted into a twisted smile. He reached in his pocket and removed my silver necklace, and then swung it like a pendulum in front of my face. The Saint Michael pendant, along with Chase's mother's ring, were still hanging from the end.

"You want this?"

I couldn't help it; I reached through the hole and tried to snag it. Charlie pulled the necklace away at the last second, laughing. He tried it again, only this time I glared at him, losing his gaze only briefly as the net made a slow turn.

From within the trailer, a shot rang out. I stared at it in horror, as if I might be able to see through the walls, see what the man had done.

"Soldiers!" called a male voice from beyond the brush encircling the campfire. This voice was older than the others, vaguely familiar, though distorted by the forest, and I searched madly for some sign of origin.

For a moment no one moved. Then Charlie dropped my necklace, and the gun, and he and the boys scattered into the darkness. I threw every bit of strength into peeling back the

net, but it spun and swayed, making the task more chal-
lenging.

The door to the trailer never opened.

A shadowed figure raced from behind the trees and I
bucked against his sudden hold on the net.

"Hold still," Sean said between his teeth. Never in my life
had I been so happy to see him.

The net ripped, and I fell halfway out, suspended upside
down. He tried to catch me, but his arm was weak and couldn't
support my weight. A flash of a knife, and another rip, and I
fell flat on my back, the wind knocked out of me.

"Come on!" He dragged me to my feet. "I wasn't kidding—
there's soldiers fifty yards behind us!"

"Wait!" I felt my way across the ground as another burst of
shots echoed in the woods behind the trailer. Finally, my fingers grasped the metal chain, and I snatched it up, running
after Sean into the darkness.

He hesitated twenty steps in, and I smacked into his back.
Without so much as a glance at me he cocked his head to the
side as if looking for something.

"Soldiers?" I whispered. As if in answer, another round of
gunfire erupted from behind us. Several male voices began to
yell all at once.

"This way." He sprinted to the right, and I tore after him.
We ran until we reached a small dirt road, and then kept to a
ditch, sloshing through the muck toward a series of houses. I
didn't hear Sean's labored breathing, or the grunt of pain that
came every few steps, until we slowed.

A small delivery truck came into view, parked in the high
grass between two houses. Only then did we speak.

"Where's Chase?" I gasped, a new panic enveloping my
senses.

White stars were twinkling in my vision and I blinked them away. I was so thirsty and tired since we'd stopped.

Sean didn't answer. He swung open the passenger door and fell back against the seat. His shirt, though still drenched with blood, was bulky around the shoulder, and as he drew back the collar I saw that it had been bandaged with the supplies we'd brought from Endurance.

"Did you get her?" came a low voice through the darkness.

I turned to find Jesse stepping from the shadows into the weak ring of light cast from the overhead lamp in the cabin of the truck. A small boy was thrown over his shoulder, carried like he weighed no more than a sack of flour. It was the boy they'd called a dog, and he stared straight ahead blankly as Jesse set him down. It took a moment to connect the slash of blood on Jesse's shirt with the boy's presence.

That was why the trailer door had not reopened.

Jesse and the boy were not alone. Several other boys followed him. A half dozen, a dozen. Almost all that I'd seen, including the little psychopath with the gun, Charlie. He didn't look so tough with his dirty cheeks tear-stained.

"The hunter," I heard one whisper. "The one that took Will."

"He came back for us," said another.

Jesse had done this before. That meant he'd been to Endurance before. My head felt muddled. I couldn't make sense of it right now.

"Get in the back of the truck, all of you," Jesse ordered.

"Where you takin' us?" asked Charlie.

Jesse faced me, not those behind him. It was only Sean and I who saw his mouth tighten and his gaze fall.

"Somewhere safe, kid," he said.

Another wave of dizziness took me and I gripped the open

car door for support. It was because of all the running, I told myself. Lack of food and water.

Sean stood and gripped my forearm.

"We've got soldiers on our tail," he told Jesse.

"They took Chase," I said. "Why didn't you go after Chase?"

Jesse's eye twitched as he looked down over me.

"You're bleeding, neighbor."

He nodded at my waist, and when I looked down I saw that the glass puncture wound from the mini-mart was bleeding again. The patch of rose red on my shirt had blossomed to half of my torso.

"Ember . . ." Sean pulled me back, toward the car, but I stumbled into his arms. "Hang on," he said. My cheek rested against the bandages on his shoulder.

"You shouldn't have left him," I whispered.

I didn't remember much after that.

WHEN I woke again I was lying on a couch, blinking up at the yellow water rings on a white ceiling. It was late afternoon, or maybe early morning based on the red light seeping across the floor.

I tried to sit up, but was stopped by a shooting pain that emanated from the right side of my waist. When I pulled up the hem of my clean shirt I found a swell of bandages tied to my skin by long strips of cloth. My wound had been cleaned.

I took in my surroundings, recognizing the antique coffee table beneath the box of medical supplies, and the wilted magazines, now stacked on the carpet beside one of the legs.

The house with the supplies. The address: 3. The bodies on the bed.

The mini-mart where Chase had been taken was now miles and miles away.

I wasn't alone; against the wall on a blanket lay a girl. I shimmied up to my elbows. The rest of the room was empty, though the floor was covered with muddy footprints, some tinged with red.

I swung my legs to the floor, stretching a little from side to side to test my range of motion. It pinched, and stole my breath.

Dark fingers of dread curled around my chest. How long had I been here?

The girl on the floor lifted her hands to her face, fingers probing through a crop of dark hair. She had blond roots, so it must have been dyed.

I looked closer; there were red welts around her neck and unconsciously my own hand went to my throat, finding only rough skin where the rope had previously burned. My necklace hung loosely there, the ring and the pendant resting just over the notch in my collarbone where a round burn had been left from the Knoxville fire.

The girl groaned quietly. One shoulder was bandaged, and her leg had been splinted. Whatever had happened to her, it hadn't been easy.

Then she removed the hands from her face, and my mouth fell open in surprise.

"Cara?"

Her gaze flicked my way, a little dazed. "Hey, sister." I noticed then that there was a bottle of pills by her shoulder on the floor. She grabbed it and without sitting up threw back a mouthful. At the sound of her dry swallow, I cringed.

Cara was alive. Cara, who'd let the country think *I* was the sniper, not her. Who'd been murdered by the FBR in Greeneville while out with Tucker.

"I thought you were dead." As the shock passed, my hands

curled to fists. If she wasn't so injured, I might have strangled her.

"I thought so, too."

She looked smaller than before. Not necessarily thinner—though her cheeks did look hollow—but more delicate. Never did I think I would see her so broken. She looked like a different person completely.

"What happened to you?"

She lifted her eyes to the ceiling. "I got caught."

I scoffed. That much was obvious.

"How'd you get here?"

Her brows scrunched. "I don't know." She hesitated. "They let me go. Some Sisters fixed me up and gave me some meds and a ride to the Red Zone. I walked from there."

"Your leg . . ."

"Hurts," she finished.

I didn't understand how the MM had released her. I hadn't heard of them releasing anyone.

"What is this place?" I asked.

"A safe house of sorts," she said. "A hiding place. Hasn't been used in years. The old couple that ran the place kicked the bucket I guess."

I cringed, remembering the bodies covered with roaches.

"Why didn't you tell me you were the sniper?"

She pulled open her collar, tapped the same scar on her collarbone that now scabbed over mine. "The cause comes first. It always comes first." Her weak laugh was laced with cynicism.

"It was my name, Cara. You killed people in my name." My voice, raised in anger, scratched my parched throat.

"Isn't that what you wanted? Revenge? Well, you got it. At least, everyone thought you did." She coughed once, then shuddered. "Don't tell me you're already jaded. No one has to know it was me. You got all the credit, sister."

"I didn't want the credit."

Cara closed her eyes. "You may not have, but Ember Miller did."

I opened my mouth to object, but realized with a flutter of panic that it was no use. Cara was right. Just as I'd once seen two people in Chase—the soldier and the boy I loved—she now saw two people in me. The sniper, who thirsted for revenge, who called the people to fight through the Statutes, and the real me. The girl behind the curtain.

The girl who nobody really knew but Chase.

If I didn't find him, I would be lost.

"DeWitt said it was him anyway," I remembered. "We heard it on the radio. He was captured, and told the MM he was the sniper."

She lowered the bottle and stared at the ceiling.

"Endurance endures no more," she said. "I guess he got me out after all."

Her words triggered a memory. The night I'd snuck out in search of Chase, and instead overheard Dr. DeWitt talking to someone at the cemetery.

"It's not going to jeopardize the mission. We've already verified what the girl said. A quick extraction, that's all we're talking about."

Had DeWitt been talking about Cara?

"You think DeWitt arranged for you to be let go?" I asked.

"We're not so different, you know," she said quietly, avoiding my question. "They took my mom, too. For harboring the enemy."

She propped herself against the wall, expression pained. Her jaw was swollen, a collage of brown and purple, and her bottom lip was cracked and bloody. She shook the bottle of pills, the excess making a rattling sound. The strained lines beside her eyes relaxed. I wondered how many she'd taken.

I tried to clear my head. Sean had said the soldiers had followed us from the mini-mart to the Lost Boys—it would only be a matter of time before they tracked us to this house.

"We need to get out of here," I said.

Something caught Cara's attention over my shoulder and I turned to find Sean coming down the hall where the bodies had been. He reached me in three long strides, a look of urgency on his face.

"You're awake. *Finally.*"

He sat beside me on the couch and gave me a hug so hard we both winced. I glanced over his shoulder to the window, where outside the morning sky was turning gray from the clouds rolling in off the ocean. "How long have I been out?"

"Seven hours," he answered, pulling back. "Not that I've been counting. Jesse brought us here. All of us. Those boys, too."

"Help me up." Chase had been with the MM for seven hours. I couldn't think of what had happened to him during that time. I wouldn't think of it.

"Jesse told me about Endurance," Sean said, lowering his voice. "He said you found Becca in the grove with the others. I've got to go find her."

He looked more serious than I'd ever seen him.

"They took Chase," I said.

"I know." For a second he didn't say anything, and then he grabbed my shoulders. "He's my friend, too, Ember, but you can't stay here. You have to come."

"I have to find him." He made a noise of frustration, but I could see in his eyes he'd expected this answer.

"You'd better hurry," said Cara.

Something about her tone made my blood turn cold.

"Why?" She hesitated, and I kneeled beside her. "*Why,* Cara?"

She took another swig of pills and in a flash of fury I slapped it from her hand. What few remained spilled across the dusty carpet.

"The walls are about to come tumbling down."

I rose slowly.

"We're going to bomb Charlotte," she said. "Just the way they bombed us in Chicago. Just like they did with the safe house."

CHAPTER
21

IT took a moment for her words to sink in, to push past the buzzing in my brain.

"We have bombs?" Sean asked.

"*They* have bombs," she said. "Long distance explosive devices. *We* have access to their control panels."

And access to the census reports for each base, as I'd seen documented in the radio room. We knew how many soldiers in each region would be attending to Charlotte for the chief's party. The amount of damage we could do took my breath away.

"Three has people working in the FBR," I said, remembering what Rocklin had told Chase and I our first night there. "It's how they assured that Endurance wouldn't get bombed like the safe house or Chicago."

Some good that did. They found Three's base anyway.

"That doesn't make sense," said Sean, crossing his arms over his chest. "If that were true they wouldn't have let the safe house get hit."

"We had no choice."

Sean and I turned to find Jesse, his face and clothing smeared with grime, striding through the door. He wiped his palms on his pant legs as he crossed the room to where Cara lay.

"Hey, Jesse," she said, eyelids heavy.

They knew each other. How, I had no idea.

"What does that mean, *no choice?*" asked Sean.

When Jesse didn't answer, Sean blocked his path, standing between him and Cara. Next to Sean, it was clear how much taller and physically imposing Jesse was. The tattoo on his neck glistened under a fine layer of sweat. For a moment I thought he might fight Sean—his bloodshot eyes flashed with something feral and dangerous—but when Sean lifted his chin in challenge, Jesse rocked back on his heels and put his hands on his hips.

"The location of the safe house had already been compromised. Our men on the inside had no choice but to follow the Bureau's orders and take it down."

"What are you talking about, *our* men?" I gripped my side, feeling weak, as another piece fell into place. "You knew they'd bomb the safe house. That's why you weren't there."

He didn't answer. He didn't even look at me.

"All those people died," said Sean. "You're saying that Three killed them?" He sent a dark glance my way, confirming that every suspicion he'd had about this place had been true. The triple scar on my chest tingled uncomfortably.

"Three didn't kill them, the Bureau did," said Jesse, passing Sean to reach Cara.

The Bureau may have killed them, but Three let it happen.

"They could have at least warned them. They could have tried to evacuate."

Jesse twitched. "I tried to warn them. I wasn't fast enough."

He'd told us he'd been in the woods. Sarah had been by the beach. He'd saved her, she'd said.

"How long have you been with Three?" I asked. The location of the president's hideout in the mountains. The men

Jesse had killed in Chattanooga. The soldier in the cage at the cemetery. He'd known all along Endurance would be there, that they'd bring us in without question.

Cara snorted. "Oh, I'd say awhile, huh, Jesse?"

He kneeled beside her, picked up the nearly empty pill bottle and with a grim look stuck it in his pocket. "There are choices we have to make that aren't easy. Save the safe house, or save the mission. Either way we lose good people."

"You could have stopped it," Sean said.

"And lost the chance to strike back," countered Jesse. "Right now our people are outside of Charlotte, waiting for it to fall. Ready to claim our victory."

This had been the plan all along, the orders that the fighters would receive once they arrived. Without knowing it, I'd called the people to join them.

"Chase could be in Charlotte." My knees grew weak, and I leaned against the side of the couch for support. "*Your nephew* could be in Charlotte."

Jesse stood rigid, filling the whole room.

"Yes," he said.

"You're going to stop it, then. You're going to get him out."

"It's too late."

I did not believe that. I would not believe it. But the evidence was thick and heavy and filled me with dread.

"You're bombing it tonight. For the chief's party." To kill one man they would risk hundreds more.

Jesse's jaw twitched.

"We all make sacrifices," he said.

A veil of red passed before my eyes. I thought of how he'd taken Chase away when I was twelve, how he'd left him when he was sixteen in Chicago to fend for himself. I hated Jesse then. I hated him for not even trying.

I'd wanted to believe in Three so much I'd neglected to see it for what it really was. Just another group of insurgents trying to tear apart the system. They didn't care about the truth—that our injured had been murdered, that the prisoners were dying each day, that Chase was gone and Tucker had been used as bait—they only cared about the outcome.

Jesse had scooped Cara up in his arms and was making for the entryway. He twisted, reaching for the handle to open the door without bumping her splinted leg.

"We're leaving," he said, carrying her to the porch and down the steps to where the Lost Boys waited on the patchy front lawn.

I followed him outside, Sean on my heels. The standalone garage where Rebecca and I had fought off the pack of dogs was behind the parked white moving truck. The sun hid behind the thick thunderclouds, but was climbing, counting down the minutes to the Chief of Reformation's party.

"Where?" I called.

"Tampa," he answered bluntly. The nasty boy, Charlie, rose, and helped him lift the back gate of the moving truck. Gently, Jesse settled Cara on the flatbed.

My nerves cracked like a whip. I was not going to Tampa. I was going to Charlotte. I needed to get to Chase before the bombs hit, and the only way I knew to do that was to sneak in.

"I need this truck," I said. I glanced at Sean. *"I'm sorry,"* I mouthed. He needed it, too, to get back to Rebecca.

"Don't test me, neighbor." Jesse didn't turn around.

My gun was missing, and before Sean could stop me I'd snatched his from behind his back. I released the safety but kept it lowered. Jesse, hearing the noise, turned slowly.

"Don't test *me*," I said, trying to stop my hands from shaking. "I'm taking this truck."

"Put down the gun," said Jesse.

"Give me the keys." It occurred to me that I didn't know how to get to Greeneville. I didn't even know how to drive. It didn't matter. I'd figure it out. Fast.

I glanced to my right, to Sean, his stare shifting between me and Jesse. The eyes of the children had all turned my direction, and I couldn't help but feel a little bad for that.

"You're not going to shoot anyone," said Cara from inside the truck.

I lifted the gun and fired into the air. The adrenaline kicked down my arm.

"She's gonna shoot someone," said Charlie.

"The keys!"

Jesse reached into his pocket, teeth bared.

"I knew you'd be a pain in the ass." He tossed me a silver key ring.

I heard footsteps on my right, and felt Sean stand beside me.

"Get out of here," he said quietly. "Do what you've got to do."

"What's your plan?" Jesse asked him. "How are you going to get back to your girl?"

"The Horizons truck in the garage," said Sean. I'd forgotten about that—we'd pulled supplies out of the back the first time we'd been here.

"The tires are flat," said Jesse.

"A lot of kids here," he said. "I'm sure we can find a few spares."

"You just need to make it to Endurance," I said. "There's one more car left in the lot." It would be a tight fit with all the kids, but I had confidence Sean would make it work.

He nodded.

"Hey, sister," called Cara weakly. I glanced over at her, half expecting her to have a gun pointed in my direction, too. Instead, she wore a lopsided grin. "If you're breaking into a base, make sure you dress the part." She winked.

Clearly she'd had too much pain medicine.

Jesse made a move toward me, but Sean blocked his way. "Uh-uh," he said with a firm shake of his head. Jesse could have flattened Sean if he'd wanted to, but something had him falling back. He swore, and then reached into the truck to help Cara out.

"Think about this," Jesse said. "The first bomb hits Charlotte at midnight. The rest follow every fifteen minutes. Chicago, Atlanta, Knoxville, and Lexington."

Every major base between here and the middle of the country.

The breath trembled in my lungs. After the bombing, Three would attack Charlotte. If the Statutes I'd put my name on worked, the same thing would happen across the country.

"You're sure?" whispered Sean over his shoulder.

"I'm sure," I said.

"Then get going." He nudged me toward the door. I saw in his face he wasn't coming. Better that way. He needed to find Rebecca.

I looked into his bright blue eyes, flooded with memories of him helping me escape from the reformatory. Here he was, doing it again. Being the friend I needed him to be.

I gave him a quick hug, our only good-bye.

"Tampa," he said. "I'll see you there."

I nodded, throat hot. I jumped in the front seat, slammed the door shut, and pushed the key into the ignition. Driving couldn't be so hard; I'd seen Chase do it tons of times.

I pressed the gas and the engine revved, dust spraying out behind the car. I dropped the gun and white-knuckled the wheel. Normally this was the part where we were supposed to go forward. Gently, I tapped the gas again, to the same effect.

"Come on," I coaxed the car, bouncing in the seat.

Sean jerked open my door. He reached down to the floor, grabbed my ankle, and shoved my foot on the pedal to the right.

"Brake," he said. He pointed to the other. "Gas." Then he leaned across my body, grabbed the shifter emerging from the wheel and adjusted it down a notch. A light on the console beside the speedometer switched from *P* to *D*.

I couldn't believe I hadn't remembered that part.

"Drive," he said. He stepped back and shut the door.

I pressed down hard on the gas. Something slammed behind me—probably the back gate closing. The last view I had in the mirror as I tore down the street was Sean surrounded by the boys, watching me go.

I JERKED to a stop in the middle of an empty road. The freeway onramp was to my right, but there was another road that wound around the left. North was the direction I needed to go to get to Charlotte, but I didn't have time to backtrack if I was wrong.

Eighteen hours. I had less than a day to find where the MM had taken Chase and to figure out a way to get him out. Dark thoughts shimmered on the edge of my focus. A voice that said he was already dead, that he'd died in pain, alone, while I'd been miles away, unconscious. And that if he was dead, every soldier that died when the bases fell would not be enough to fill the hole left inside of me.

I pulled out the map from the sun visor and spread it across my lap, but my hands were shaking so hard I ripped it down the center.

"No!" My throat was tied in knots.

I wouldn't cry. I would not.

A knock at the passenger window made me scream. I leaped out of the seat and scrambled for the gun, but instead knocked it to the floor.

Jesse stood outside, arms crossed over his chest, mouth pulled into a thin, tight line.

"What's the plan, neighbor?"

I couldn't believe it. A stowaway.

"What are you doing here?" I asked, venom on my tongue.

Slowly, he lifted his hands, and then opened the passenger door and sat down. He stared straight ahead through the window.

"My nephew—he told me to look out for you if something happened to him."

I closed my eyes.

"I guess I don't have to tell you I owe him one."

I flexed my legs. "I guess not."

"And if he got caught, I had to stop you from going after him."

I imagined Chase asking Jesse to make this promise and my heart cracked open.

"You can't stop me," I said. "I'm going to find him."

"I know." He smiled, and his eyes were glistening. "I had to try."

A silent moment passed.

"You're sort of like her, you know," he said. "My sister. She was hard-headed, too. You should have seen our dad when she told him who she was marrying." He whistled, shaking his head.

I'd never given much thought to Chase's mixed heritage. His parents were always so warm and nonjudgmental, and I resented that they would have to fight that battle. Either way, talking about Chase's mother made me uncomfortable, like Jesse and I had too much in common.

We sat in silence for a moment.

"Chase taught me how to shoot," I said. "Not to drive."

He laughed, and slapped a hand on his chest.

"Where we headed?"

"Charlotte," I told him. "Unless you have a better idea."

"You want to join Three outside the base, or just drive in through the front gates?"

I turned away, staring out the window. "I need to get into the prison." There wasn't time to gather with the other fighters, and anyway, they wouldn't let me get close to the base before it blew. "Once Chase got himself arrested to find me in the Knoxville holding cells."

"Well, that was stupid," he said.

My hands began to shake again. I needed to get in and out of the base before midnight. I wished Billy was here—he would have at least been able to hack into the mainframe and tell me for sure if Charlotte had taken a new prisoner.

But Billy had jumped aboard an MM delivery truck, bound for Charlotte.

"Greeneville," I said, the idea lighting inside of me. "Marco and Polo have an FBR delivery truck."

A slow, dangerous smile spread over Jesse's face. He got out of the front seat and stepped outside. I scooted over as he rounded the front of the car, folding the map as he opened the door and climbed into the front seat.

Jesse was a lot faster driver than I was.

. . .

THE thick clouds patched together as we neared the line where the Red Zone gave way to occupied area. In the early afternoon Jesse left the highway, because the MM had set up checkpoints at all major crossings to block civilians from heading into the restricted areas. Because of this, we ended up in a small suburban community, weaving through abandoned cars and debris blown by the weather, at a pace slow enough to make my skin crawl.

I kept my eyes pinned on the road highlighted in the headlights. A rickety wooden bridge was coming up, and beyond it the trees grew thick, a wall of green and gray shale.

"Why didn't you tell us you were with Three?"

He slowed as he steered around an overturned trash can in the road. "Never came up."

I shifted to face him fully. "Oh, I can think of a few times you could have said something."

He chuckled. "You never asked."

I groaned. "You couldn't answer a straight question if your life depended on it."

"My life, neighbor, often depends on not answering straight questions."

He pointed ahead, to a thick cropping of pine trees, the slender gray trunks of which were skirted by emerald holly shrubs. "We'll turn off the road past the bridge and park back a ways. The outer fence of the printing plant backs up against those woods."

Though I didn't say so, I was secretly glad he'd come. Last time we'd come here, I'd arrived in the back of a delivery truck. Sneaking in the back was a whole different game.

I kicked at the floor mat, and glanced back automatically to assure we weren't being followed. It was clear I'd have to try a different tactic. "The Lost Boys call you the hunter, you know."

He squinted, watching the road.

"How many have you brought to Endurance besides Will?"

"Not as many as I should have. I thought . . ." He sighed. "I thought that guy in the trailer was looking out for them. I should have paid more attention."

Jesse scratched at the stubble on his chin, silent for some time.

"I wasn't meant to be a dad," he said finally. "What happened with my nephew—with *Chase*." He hesitated. "It wasn't supposed to happen. I never wanted him."

I didn't know how to respond; the raw confession had surprised me.

"Maybe before," he said quietly, almost as if he wasn't talking to me at all. "I was a soldier once—not in the Bureau. Before the War. Before the insurgents. U.S. Army, Sergeant Major Waite." He sat a little straighter in his seat. "We fought enemies from the outside, not the inside. But no one noticed. They just went on like life was normal, like men and women weren't dying so they could watch TV and go to bed without a gun under their pillow. No one here even knew there was a threat—not until the insurgents brought the fight home, and Reinhardt and his tool Scarboro made their move."

The president's platform—one whole country, one whole family—had been just what the country was looking for after the chaos began. It didn't matter that the government they proposed would sink its teeth into our everyday freedoms, just as long as the bombs stopped falling.

Again, I considered what it might be like if the old president resumed his post. If the people had a vote again. But a system backed by Three, who was preparing to bomb the bases—kill their own just to take out more soldiers—seemed just as corrupt as a system backed by Restart.

"Some of us saw what they were doing," continued Jesse. "Me and Frank and Aiden—he was an army doc back then."

Doctor Aiden DeWitt. I felt myself leaning toward him, drawn in by the story. Fat droplets of rain began to splatter against the windshield.

"Frank?" I asked, and then shook my head, piecing together what Jesse had said in Greeneville to Billy. "Frank Wallace. From Knoxville."

Jesse nodded. "Frank and Aiden took the high road—tried to fight from within the system. I told them that wouldn't do anything. Frank ended up shooting his partner and Aiden lost his girls." He shook his head. "When Restart formed the Bureau, I joined the protests. They stripped me of my rank and threw me in jail."

I'd always assumed Jesse had been in jail for robbery or assault, something bad. Not this. Not the same thing I was doing now with the Statutes.

"They never took their eye off me. The Bureau, they were always watching. I kept quiet after my sister died and I got Chase. I tried to do what Aiden did—play the family man. I did all right for a while. But they kept watching. Once the bombs started falling, Restart needed names—people to blame. Who better than a guy they already had on record?" He laughed bitterly. "I tried to get the kid out once the fighting came to Chicago. I swear. I tried to keep him safe like his mother would have wanted. But they found me. The only way Chase had a chance was on his own."

"How come you never told him?" I asked. "He thinks you cut him loose because you couldn't take care of him."

Jesse started, as though he hadn't expected me to be listening.

"I couldn't," he said. "That's the truth."

"It's *part* of the truth," I stressed, unsure what to think of this man now that I'd heard his story.

"I didn't want this life for him. I wanted him out of the way."

"So you found him in Chicago and told him about the safe house."

"I thought I was too late," he said, regret hanging heavy over his shoulders. "The Bureau had already gotten him."

"You weren't too late," I said. "You helped save him. Just like you helped save those Lost Boys." I wondered if they were penance for the nephew Jesse had left behind.

Jesse slammed on the brakes then, and I braced against the dash a moment before I hit it. We'd reached the bridge. I hadn't noticed we'd gotten so close. Twenty feet below rushed the muddy water of an overflowed creek.

Across the bridge were three Bureau cars, blocking the way. My heart slowed, but began to pound twice as hard. With damp hands I reached for the gun I'd placed between us on the center console.

"I believe it's time we split up, neighbor."

The rain pounded against the windshield, too hard and fast for the truck's shredded wipers to keep up.

Our options were limited: we couldn't outrun them, not in an old beat-up moving truck while they were in cruisers, and not on streets marred by potholes and debris. If we ran, they'd hunt us, and we'd never make it to the printing plant. As I watched, one soldier got out of the driver's side door, talking into a handheld radio.

"The warehouse is five miles northwest—through the trees. Look for the lights." Jesse reached across my lap and opened the door. "Get out."

"They've seen us!"

"I'll cover you."

I stared at him in horror.

"My nephew did good when he chose you."

With that he pushed me out of the seat. I scrambled to stay upright, crouching in the shrubs beside the road. Now my pulse was flying, and the rain that fell sizzled against my hot skin.

A second later Jesse gunned the engine, aiming straight toward the cruisers.

CHAPTER
22

THE truck hit the bridge with a squeal, and even through the rain I could hear the shouts of surprise from the other side. Thirty feet below roared the swollen creek, brown and frothy, like the chocolate milk I used to drink as a child. The fastest path was straight down the hill, but the way was steep and treacherous.

Without looking back, I aimed for the water, legs churning to keep up with the barreling pace of my body. The loose gravel gave way beneath my boots and soon I was rolling, crashing through the prickly shrubs and sharp rocks that tore at my clothes and my skin. The gun was torn from my grasp.

With a splash I hit the bottom, gagging on a mouthful of silt. My empty, reaching hands found the bottom and pushed up, and as my head bobbed above the waterline I heard it, metal slamming against metal.

My view was blocked by the underside of the bridge but the shots could still be heard, firing fast, mixed with male voices raised in confusion. I planted my feet; the current was fast but not deep. I dragged my waterlogged body beneath the bridge just as the shots began to rain down.

"One of them's getting away!" shouted one of the soldiers.

I dove, the chaos above suddenly muffled by murky liquid. My boots were heavy, my clothing slowed me down, but I kicked hard, driving myself to the bottom. The flashlight beams from above carved darting rays into the gold-flecked water I swam through. The surface was dappled by the rain and punctured by bullets, tiny streams of bubbles streaking behind them. I passed beneath the shadow of the bridge to the opposite side.

My lungs felt like they might explode but I didn't dare lift my head. From behind came a splash, and I looked back, unable to stop my mouth from opening to scream. I swallowed water, choking, panicking. A soldier had fallen in, a man whose eyes were still wide open in shock. His blue uniform and flaxen hair floated weightlessly around him as the water turned dark with his blood. I kicked deeper. He passed over me as if flying, a black shadow in the gloom.

At the last second I reached up and grabbed a handful of his jacket, and then I swam with every bit of strength I had left, using his lifeless body as cover.

I didn't see the fallen log until I nearly collided with it. Feeling my way beneath its slippery bark, I released the soldier and squeezed beneath it. On the opposite side I finally lifted my head above the water and gasped.

Another crash of metal came from the bridge. As I watched, hidden behind the log, the truck rammed the tight space between two cruisers. Smoke rose from their squealing brakes. The soldiers fired at the windshield but Jesse persevered, and soon had punched through the barrier. I caught a glimpse of a gun out the window as he shot once again and sent a second soldier over the edge of the bridge into the water.

With a growl of the engine, he sped off. Two cruisers followed, blue lights flashing, sirens wailing. The other car didn't move, nor did any soldiers emerge from it.

The shore was just to my left and I slogged up the bank, hitting dry ground and stumbling up the steep hill. My side screamed where the scab had broken open again but I didn't stop. I'd lost my gun in the fall and had nothing with which to defend myself.

The trees were thick at the top of the embankment. My eyes burned, as did my throat—I coughed, gasped, coughed some more. The blanket of pine needles made the ground slippery, but there was no stopping.

Jesse had risked his life to create a diversion so that I could find Chase. I would not fail either of them.

I tried to make a mental note of the time. We'd driven at least four hours. Maybe five. Less than twelve remained before Three began bombing the bases.

Hold on, Chase.

A dot of dim yellow light in the distance guided my way. As I ran it grew brighter, larger, spreading its fingers around the trees until finally the source came into view: a brick industrial building, surrounded by a high chain-link fence rimmed by a spiral of barbed wire. For the first time I slowed, staying low, scanning both sides for any sign of movement. Nothing stirred on the moat of asphalt surrounding the structure.

There were no holes in the fence permitting easy access. I was going to have to crawl through the barbed wire.

The thin metal clattered against the support beams as I gave it a tug. The toes of my boots were too thick to fit into the small holes, so hurriedly I removed them and tied the laces together so that I could sling them over my shoulder. I ripped the shredded piece off the cuff of my pants and wrapped it around my hands. Then climbed.

The thin chain cut into my toes, but I had a better grip with wet socks than with my boots. Finally, at the top, I gently moved aside the wire and crawled atop it. The coil was stronger than I anticipated, and as I shifted my weight to the top it sprung back and jabbed into my left thigh.

I bit down on my shoulder, displacing the pain. The chain rattled all the way down the fence as I attempted to pull myself free.

The distinct suction of a door opening came from around a nearby corner.

My heart thumped against my ribs. Sweat dripped in my eyes. I threw one leg down, unable to stop the cry of pain as the barb sliced deeper into my skin, then released with a clatter of metal.

I reminded myself that Marco and Polo worked at night, but it wasn't even afternoon. I hurried down, unable to put weight on my left side. I hoped their recruit, New Guy, was here.

Footsteps came closer. From my peripheral vision came a blue uniform. I dropped to the ground, rolling back into the shadows against the side of the building.

From around the corner came a voice I recognized.

"If you'd have waited five minutes I would have opened the gate."

NEW Guy held open the heavy metal emergency exit door, leaving room for me to duck under his arm. When we were inside and the lock was set, I exhaled, but couldn't relax around him.

Inside, the room was alive with machinery, buzzing, clicking, revving. A hundred different noises that grated my raw nerves and made me twitch. The printing presses were spitting out neat piles of Statute circulars—my story—onto a black belt that carried them to the back of the room. A sudden urge to read one took me, but I stayed in place when New Guy pointed to my leg with a cringe. The barb that had punctured my skin had torn my pants, and left a sticky red circle on my thigh.

"Looks like you've seen better days." He handed me an ink soaked towel, hanging from a protruding hook on the wall behind him.

He was right. I was covered in mud, still half soaked with creek water and sweat, and bleeding from a half dozen scrapes. With more time I would have asked for a change of clothes and something to eat, but there wasn't more time.

"When do Marco and Polo get in?" I searched the immediate area, disappointed they weren't already here.

"Later," said New Guy with a twitch of his shoulder. "They'll be terribly disappointed they missed you. What are you doing sneaking in the back?"

"Long story," I said, speaking loudly over the machines. "I need a favor." It was a question I'd been prepared to ask friends, not someone I hardly knew.

"On behalf of our mutual acquaintances, I'm sure that can be arranged."

He seemed genuine. I reminded myself that Marco and Polo wouldn't trust just anyone—their lives depended on a reliable secret keeper.

"I need to get into Charlotte."

His chin dropped. "The Charlotte base you mean. The one with the prison."

"And the special guest visiting this week," I added. "That's the one."

"How are you going to do that? You can't just walk into a base."

It was hard to hear him over the machines, so I motioned to the office, but he blocked my way.

"I was thinking you could drive me," I said.

"Ha," said New Guy, wiping his brow. "Ha. They didn't tell me you have a sense of humor."

"In a delivery truck," I continued. *Like the one Billy jumped inside.* "All you need to do is get me in, I'll figure it out from there."

"They didn't tell me you were crazy, either." Before he could step away, I'd grabbed his forearm.

"Please," I begged. My loosely laid plan was falling to pieces. New Guy said something I couldn't make out.

I leaned closer. "Can we go in the office? I can barely hear you."

"We just took a shipment a few days ago," he said in a loud voice. "It'll look fishy if we show up between shipments."

"You can tell them you got special orders to deliver now," I said, desperation leaking through. "I don't know. Make something up."

He stared at me blankly.

"Please," I said. "We need to leave now."

New Guy's gaze lifted over my head in recognition of something behind me. My first thought was that more refugees had been deposited here to wait for transport, but as I turned I caught the guilt flash in his eyes and knew.

It had been a mistake coming here.

I bolted toward the office door but was too late. Wiry arms clamped around my waist and lifted me off the ground. My heel made contact with something soft, but though my attacker crashed to his knees with a grunt, I was not released. I screamed in rage, kicking a pile of Statute circulars that fluttered to the ground.

"Someone grab her legs!" New Guy shouted. I threw my head backward, connecting to his nose with a crack. Instantly I was released, but only a second before I was tackled to the floor.

"Get the bag. Get it!"

I froze, straining my neck to see the face of the soldier who'd taken me down. The perfectly pressed navy uniform seemed out of place. The gold name badge on his chest reflected the overhead light. Lips pressed into a thin line, he leaned over me, and I didn't see the person who'd helped Sean out of the fire or run beside me as the tunnels in Chicago collapsed. Not the broken, beaten prisoner tied to a chair outside the mini-mart. I saw the polished, green-eyed soldier who'd come to my house to arrest me. The soldier who'd confessed to killing my mother.

I saw Tucker Morris.

I hadn't realized I'd truly believed he was good until the moment I discovered he was not.

Then there was nothing but darkness as something rough slid over my face and tied snugly around my throat. My hands were bound behind me. I twisted, and my cheek hit the floor hard. I was shoved onto my stomach. My legs were yanked behind me and bound together at the ankles. I could barely hear over the noise of the machines and the blood rushing in my ears.

THE cloth bag over my head was thick and hot; with each inhalation the coarse fibers suctioned to my mouth and nose, bringing on wave after wave of panic. I couldn't see, I could barely hear. Without my senses I was disoriented. My body didn't know which way to bend and turn to get away, or when my attackers would strike next. Long minutes passed, and soon I was lifted and slung over someone's shoulder.

"Throw her in the back with the other two," I heard Tucker say. The air was forced from my lungs as I was flung to a cool, metal floor. The growl of an engine told me I was in the back of a truck, and a few sharp turns later I was rolling across the compartment, unable to stop myself.

Something hard came to rest on my back, pinning me in place. I arched against it.

"Hey," someone whispered. "Hey, Ember, you okay?"

I didn't answer.

"Polo?" asked the same voice. Marco. His voice was distorted, as if he couldn't breathe through his nose. "Polo, wake up, pal."

Polo didn't answer, either.

TIME seemed to stretch on infinitely. Minutes lost their meaning. Hours passed. I didn't know how long Chase had left. I didn't know how long I had, either.

I was shoved onto a hard chair with a straight back. I wriggled my toes, flexed my calves and thighs, trying to work the blood back into them. My hands, still latched behind me, were asleep, and the space from my wrists to my shoulders prickled with the sharpness of a thousand needles. I tried to slow my breath, to be ready, but my muscles were stiff from the long trip tied up in the back of a truck.

Footsteps drew closer, and I braced myself for what might come. A shot of strychnine, as the soldiers received in the holding cells in Knoxville. A bullet, like that which had taken my mother's life. The kind of beating that had broken Rebecca's spine.

The fear dissipated, and in its place came a cool, morbid calm.

Fingers loosened the tie around my neck and ripped away the bag over my face. Instantly I was blinded by the white light. I blinked rapidly, the tears streaming down my cheeks. The air was warm and smelled like a toilet had overflowed but finally I could breathe.

"Look at this, Captain Morris," came a strange, thin voice. "She cries." Someone touched my face gently and I jerked away, baring my teeth. "Seems as though she bites as well," he added.

Gradually the room came into focus. Gray stone walls, a dirty floor with a drain beneath my feet. Bright overhead lights, circular in shape, hanging from metal cords. A camera above the door, accusing me with its single eye. The man before me was barely broader through the torso than I was, and his sunken, sallow cheeks brought on the impression that he was starving. He looked about the same age as DeWitt.

"The infamous Ember Miller," he said, smoothing back a tuft of peppered hair. There were gold stars on the shoulder of his uniform—a sign of rank. He was someone of importance. "I have to admit, I wasn't even sure you really existed. Such a young girl, and so pretty, too. How you've managed to survive this long I'll never know. It's remarkable, really. Don't you think, Captain?"

Out from behind me limped Tucker Morris, shoulders pulled back, chin lifted. Involuntarily, my arms and legs jerked against their restraints. Had they been free, I would have gone for his throat.

He'd lured us to the safe house, tricked me into setting him free. I was glad Jesse had shot him. How I'd ever believed he was good seemed impossible now.

All I knew was this: if any harm had come to Chase, Tucker would pay for it.

I glanced around the room, finding another guard standing near the door. New Guy. His nose was busted—a colorful burst of red and purple—and when I stared at it he looked away.

"Such trouble you've stirred," mused the man. "Did you really think we wouldn't find out what you were up to?"

He caressed my cheek again, closer this time, so that I could see the wrinkles that pulled at the corners of his black eyes.

His hand dipped lower, down my neck, pausing to feel the pulse accelerating through my artery. I looked away, focused on Tucker. Focused on the red hot hatred burning through me.

"It's a good thing we stopped that little piece of anti-American propaganda before it got too far. Wouldn't want people getting the wrong information." He took a deep breath. "Where did you take those Article violators the traitors at the printing press were hiding in their basement, I wonder. North?" His fingertips rose up my jaw. "South?" They lowered slowly.

When the man's fingers found my collar I jerked back so hard the chair nearly tipped. Tucker rushed forward to catch me, and for the briefest of moments our eyes met. His lips parted briefly.

The man folded back my collar, exposing my whole left shoulder. With the same gentle touch he removed my necklace, then what remained of my bandage and tossed them to the floor. I whimpered through my teeth before I choked down the sound.

"Very nice, sergeant," the man said, feeling the raised scabs from DeWitt's knife, "You were right. She *is* connected. Despite what the other one says."

I forced myself not to react.

"Thank you, sir," said New Guy.

"What was his name?" asked the man.

"Jennings," said Tucker after a moment.

I jerked involuntarily at his name. He was here.

"Ah," said the man in charge. "You're probably wondering if he's alive."

I stared straight ahead.

"He is. And he will continue to remain so if you answer a few of my questions."

"Like I believe you," I said, despite myself.

"Reformation is built on honor," he smiled. "Had you completed rehabilitation, you might have known that."

I nearly laughed.

"How long have you worked for the rebel organization Three, Ms. Miller?" He lowered so that our gazes held a straight line. His breath was rank with onions, but his teeth were impeccably clean.

I turned my face away.

He stood slowly. Then wheeled back and slapped me.

My vision exploded in fireworks of color. The skin felt like it had been ripped off the side of my face. Tucker caught me again; I hadn't even noticed the chair had tilted over on two legs.

The man cleared his throat. "Captain Morris, your knife please."

Tucker released the chair and stepped toward the man, handing him the switchblade from his utility belt. I stared at the gun in his holster, willing it into my hands.

"No, no, you keep it."

Tucker hesitated, but the older man had already turned back to me. He swung my necklace in front of my face, a blur of silver and gold. Behind him, over his right shoulder, the camera stayed pointed in my direction.

"All right, Ms. Miller, we're going to make this quick, because as you undoubtedly have heard, I have a party to attend."

Chancellor Reinhardt, I realized. The Chief of Reformation. I nearly laughed. I'd made it into the Charlotte base after all. If DeWitt had only known I'd be within inches of the most hated man in the FBR.

"What is Three planning? Why issue this pathetic call to join the resistance and fight? And don't say my assassination, because you've already tried and failed."

I forced myself to smile. We'd heard of the attempt on his life when we were in Knoxville. What a shame that he'd recovered.

"You need to think about it. I understand. Captain Morris, was she an Article Four Violator? I forget these things."

Tucker leaned over me, the marks from the beating I'd thought he'd endured as a prisoner still marring his jaw. A bead of sweat dripped down his brow and splashed on my swollen cheek, and I focused on the single gold star pinned beneath his name badge. With one hand he held my shoulder still; with the other, he brought the knife to my skin and slowly carved a line into the flesh, close to the three DeWitt had left.

I didn't make a sound. But the adrenaline scored through my veins, making me shake.

"I'm going to ask you a second time, Ms. Miller. What is Three planning?"

I stared straight ahead. I thought of Chase, walking barefoot on the beach. Sneaking through my window at home. Combing his fingers through my hair.

Reinhardt sighed. "No, that's right. Article 5 violation. That's what Ember Miller was charged with."

Tucker leaned down again.

"I should have killed you when I had the chance," I whispered.

Tucker cut me again—a swipe crossing the others—and this time I did cry out.

"That must hurt," said the chief with a wince. "You know we've captured your leader, correct? Three is finished. There's no need to continue to protect him. He didn't protect you, after all." The chief crouched down before my chair. "He sold you out. He told us where your posts were hidden. He told us where to find your base in the Red Zone."

DeWitt couldn't be the one ratting out the posts. He'd only just been captured.

"Yes," said the Chief, as if reading my mind. "Aiden De-Witt's been in contact with me for some time now."

Don't listen to him, I told myself. I thought of Sean finding Rebecca, going to Mexico. I'd miss them.

"It was luck, really. We didn't realize Carolyn was his daughter when Captain Morris brought her to us for the sniper murders. She wasn't in our cells for more than a week when DeWitt called me on the radio. Funny how people pop up when you've got something they want."

Rebecca had told me the doctor and his wife had been hiding Article violators, and that when the MM came his daughter had supposedly been killed in the crossfire. He'd taken down five soldiers in response.

We're not so different, you know. They took my mom, too. For harboring the enemy.

I pictured Cara as I'd last seen her—broken and beaten and woozy with pain pills, but under that I saw a different girl, one who was young and pretty, with dirty blond hair. I saw how she might laugh without bitterness, and smile warmly.

I saw the picture DeWitt carried with him.

He had traded so many lives for his daughter.

In my silence Chancellor Reinhardt groaned, annoyed. He followed my burning gaze to Tucker. "I'm sorry, it must be diffi-cult seeing Captain Morris again after all you've been through. Perhaps there's something you'd like to say to *him* if not to me?"

Tucker stepped back, staring straight through me without any acknowledgment of what we had been through together. He folded the knife and put it away.

I had plenty to say to him, but I kept my mouth shut.

"Nothing? After he set up a fire in Knoxville that killed so many of your friends?"

My teeth began to ache from pressing them together so tightly.

"Not even after he led us straight to the Chicago resistance? I haven't a clue how you made it out of *there* alive." He chuckled bluntly.

"I'm not sure how he made it out, either," I muttered, jutting my chin at Tucker.

A tight-lipped smile darkened Reinhardt's hollow cheeks.

"Some people are willing to die for their cause, isn't that right, captain?"

"Yes, sir," said Tucker.

My interrogator folded his hands behind his back. "I wonder, Ms. Miller, if you are one of them." He stared at me for one bone-chilling moment with his black ferret eyes, before heading toward the door held open by New Guy. Tucker followed.

"Is that what you told the insurgents?" I asked.

They both paused.

"Yeah, I know about that," I said. "And I know you paid off their families to keep them quiet about it. They must have been in a pretty bad spot to take money from you."

He laughed, but behind his back, his hands were folded, and they tightened, making his fingertips turn white.

"Don't think I haven't heard that before," he said, turning slowly. "*Reinhardt preyed on the poor. He promised their families would be taken care of if they served their country, gave their lives in the ultimate act of patriotism. Then blamed the acting administration for the war they started.* Is that the way the story goes?"

I felt the blood rise in my cheeks. "That's about right."

"You see, you can't tell me anything I don't already know."

"You're wrong." My voice was hoarse.

They both paused.

"You keep acting like Three is one man," I said, a reckless bravery controlling my words. "You're wrong. There's thousands of us. There's more of us than there are of you."

Despite everything I'd seen, despite everything DeWitt had done, I clung to this. I did because my life depended on the secrets I knew, and if I gave them up I was as good as dead.

The cuts on my shoulder stung. "*We carry them,*" DeWitt had said, "*because they remind us we are not alone.*" I was not alone. Chase was with me. My mother was with me. Jesse, and Sean and Rebecca, and everyone else who had been wronged by the MM was with me, and that filled me with a freedom he couldn't understand.

Tucker did not turn around. As he stared at the door, I watched his fists clench and release.

"No, Ms. Miller," said Reinhardt. "There is but one man with a thousand hands. Cut off his head, and his limbs lose their purpose."

"I guess that's why we keep coming after you then," I said.

His lips pulled thin, and grew dark white. Then he inhaled loudly through his nostrils and smiled. "Yes, that's why." On his way out, he added, "I'll be back later to check on you, Ms. Miller. We'll see how much you have to share then."

The door closed, locked in place by a deadbolt.

MINUTES passed, stretched by my impatience. Dark thoughts gathered at the edges of my mind like storm clouds, but I kept them at bay, refusing to give in. I twisted my wrists within the cuffs, straining to pull my numb hands through the metal rings. My skin grew raw.

"You did well, Ember."

I looked around, but the room was still empty.

"I'm officially losing my mind," I said quietly.

A soft chuckling could be heard, and then the voice, weak and crackling, came again. "It's Aiden. I think I'm in the room next to you. Or maybe below. It's hard to say."

I'd never heard him refer to himself by his first name before.

My gaze lowered to a drain in the floor where the sound had emanated.

"You heard everything," I said.

He waited a moment. "Yes."

If I was honest with myself, it was good to hear his voice; it didn't make me feel so alone.

"Is it true? Did you sell out the posts?"

Another moment passed. "I don't suppose it matters anymore, does it?"

"Endurance wasn't empty."

"I know."

"The safe house wasn't empty."

Down the hall, someone was yelling. The guards responded, harsh words and the clang of metal hitting metal. I couldn't make out what they were saying, and somehow that made me even more afraid.

"No," he said finally. "It wasn't. Once the Bureau knew the location, there was nothing we could do."

Without blowing the mission. Even now I was afraid to speak it out loud in case someone was listening.

"Our people at the mini-mart. They were all dead when we got there."

My hands hurt, like pins and needles digging into my skin. They'd been tied too long; I could barely feel my fingers.

"I'm sorry to hear it," he said.

"Are you?"

He chuckled humorlessly. "In medicine they call it triage. Prioritizing where to allocate your resources."

"Prioritizing who lives and dies, you mean."

"Yes," he said. "Essentially. I made a call. We didn't have enough people to send."

Even with everything else, I was relieved to hear he hadn't sent a team to execute them, as Chase had suggested. But the fact that we'd both considered it made me question our purpose all over again.

"What are we doing?" I asked. So many lives lost. They hit us, we hit them back, but in the end, what would we gain? The removal of the MM only mattered if it was replaced by something better, and right now Three didn't seem much better. I hoped the old president had something better in mind.

"Protecting our families. Our mothers and our fathers," he said, just as he'd told me in the cemetery before he'd given me the three scars on my chest. "Our sons and our daughters."

But it wasn't all the sons and daughters he fought for. It was one daughter. His. Cara.

"They let her go, you know," I said. "I saw her. Alive."

I could hear his breathing then, and only after a moment realized he was weeping.

"Thank you," he said quietly.

A moment later there was a screeching of metal.

"Let's go," I heard a muffled voice say. DeWitt didn't answer, but from the sound of it he was pulled from his cell and taken away.

I was alone.

CHAPTER
23

THE deadbolt slid back, and the door pushed inward.

Sweat broke out on my brow. I tried in vain to jerk my hands free. All I could think of was my mother. This was how she'd spent her last moments, too. In a cell, awaiting a grim fate.

Tucker entered the room. He hobbled toward me quickly, wincing, one hand gripping his thigh where he'd been shot.

"Well if it isn't *Captain* Morris," I said.

He moved behind me, favoring one leg, and I did everything I could to make it hard for him to grasp the cuffs that bound me in place. The cuts on my shoulder burned like fire as I twisted away.

"Hold still," he ordered.

A second later the latch popped, and my hands were free. As he knelt on the floor to remove the restraints around my ankles something beyond my control took over. I dove on top of him, bringing the chair to the ground with a crack that echoed off the walls. My thumbs wrapped around the soft tissue of his neck, but were uselessly numb from so many hours confined, and he peeled them away easily.

He rolled, and ended up on top of me, pinning my shoulders

in place with his knees. My legs twisted, still attached to the chair.

"Hold. Still," he repeated.

"Where's Chase?" I gasped. "What did you do to him?" I bucked my hips in an attempt to dislodge him, but he sat on my chest, crushing the air from my lungs.

From his pocket came my necklace that Reinhardt had torn off, and he held Chase's mother's ring directly over my face.

"You want me to tell you, hold still."

I stopped.

Slowly, Tucker eased back and released my legs. I snatched the necklace up and hurriedly put it back in place over my head.

"You have two minutes before surveillance comes back on," said Tucker. He lowered to my ankles and again, the metal popped. "Then the control station will see you on the camera feed."

My gaze flicked up to the box in the corner. "Can they hear me?"

Tucker shook his head.

"Where is he?" I stood, rubbing my hands together.

"He's being moved. Everyone on this floor is being moved. You included." He seemed to read my mind and added, "What are the chances that you'd escape twice on my watch."

The door rested on the deadbolt. He hadn't let it close completely.

"Where are they taking him?"

"The party. The chief is about to show us what happens to terrorists."

It was like the rehab hospital in Chicago where they'd kept Rebecca. The circus, Truck had once called it. Where they exploited the injured to deter noncompliance.

Us, he said. Because he was one of them. One of the soldiers.

But he was helping me. At least I thought he was helping me.

He checked his watch.

"Give me your gun," I said.

"Not this time." But he reached into his belt, and withdrew the knife he'd used to carve into my skin. I snatched it out of his palm and paused, trying to figure him out.

"Did you really start the fire in Knoxville?"

He didn't answer.

I swallowed. "And Chicago. There were so many people in those tunnels."

Tucker flinched. "I didn't have a choice."

"You expect me to believe that." He was probably going to tell the MM where all the bases were, too, if DeWitt hadn't beaten him to it.

"I don't expect you to do anything," he said.

The rage within me swelled, but a deeper fear, too. Before me was a person capable of enormous destruction.

I followed him, and unable to help myself, reached for the gun in his holster. Before I took another breath I was pressed against the wall, his body flush against mine, his forearm against my throat.

"What are you, stupid?" he said. "You want him to make me kill you, too?"

Fear shimmered through me, lighting my skin with goose bumps. The Chief of Reformation controlled Tucker, that much was obvious. The cuts on my shoulder were only the beginning.

"Why are you letting me go?"

"I don't know," he said through his teeth. He shoved me against the wall again. "Why do you care?" His voice broke.

"Tucker," I rasped, unsure what to make of the battle raging inside of him.

He pushed me harder against the wall, until my spine cracked and I scratched at his hands.

"You think we're so different?" he asked. "You think your cause is so much better than mine?"

I stood on my tiptoes, trying not to panic as the edges of my vision went blurry.

"The FBR saved my family," he said. "It saved my life."

"It killed my mother," I said, kicking his shin uselessly. "*You* killed her."

"I followed orders," he said.

"Stop," I managed.

"I followed orders!" he said again, as if I didn't understand. As if *he* didn't understand.

"You helped us rescue Rebecca." I didn't know why I was disagreeing. I had my window to escape; I should have been long gone. Soon the bombs would hit—I didn't even know how much time we had left.

"Shut up," Tucker said.

"Whose side are you on?" I stared at him, watching a vein rise in his forehead. A sound of misery came from his throat.

"Why couldn't he just listen, like everyone else? Why did he have to ruin everything?"

The buzzing in my ears paused as his grip loosened.

"Who? Who ruined everything?"

"He was my friend," he said, letting me down abruptly.

"Chase," I realized. I tried to picture them in training together. Partners, before Tucker had betrayed him.

"They would have killed him because of you." He jabbed a thumb into his chest. "I tried to help him. I only turned in those letters he was writing you because he wasn't listening.

Those fights our officers put him through were going to kill him. And then when they took your mom, I was the one who did what had to be done. What he couldn't do."

Tucker's words came fast, like a faucet he was unable to turn off, and I fought the urge to cover my ears and drown them out. The misery rolled off him, thickening the air in the room.

"He would have done it for me if our places were switched."

"No, Tucker," I whispered. "He wouldn't have."

Tucker stared at me, green eyes filled with self-loathing. "No," he said, with a short, pitiful laugh. "Of course not."

As if he'd forgotten, he checked his watch and threw back the door.

The hallway was empty. He broke into a run, and I followed close on his heels. At the end of the corridor was a security room surrounded by thick glass, and within a young soldier was typing rapidly behind a large black monitor.

It was a trap. I slammed to a halt, already backpedaling, but the soldier looked up and met my eyes. With his hair cropped short, I almost didn't recognize him.

"Billy," I whispered. "How . . ."

A buzzer sounded, and the door beside the station popped open. Tucker ushered me through.

"He was in the mess hall when I got back from the Red Zone," explained Tucker, unable to meet my eyes. "He said he snuck in with an extra security detail for the chief's party."

I touched Billy's arm, just to make sure he was real. He must have thought Tucker was attached to the resistance, not one of the real soldiers. I didn't tell him differently. If he had known Tucker had been the one to start the fire in Knoxville, I doubted he'd be helping now.

"Tucker marched right in here and told the two guys working they'd been reassigned and I was taking over." Billy smirked. "Can't believe they went for it."

"Focus," said Tucker.

Billy turned back to the monitor and began typing furiously on the keyboard.

"You really don't know when to quit, do you?" Tucker said. "There's a radio report playing on a back channel we picked up last night. Some woman named Faye talking about reading the Statutes and fighting the FBR. She says she's seen you herself."

"Faye Brown," I said. Felicity Bridewell was actually reporting on something worthwhile. Something that put her life at risk. Something about me, just like before, when we'd been on the run.

Of course that something was probably going to mean my painful death, but still. The bitterness I'd felt for her warped into appreciation.

"Yeah, well, everyone's probably heard it by now," said Tucker.

"The cameras in the cell are back on," said Billy. "Hallway cameras back on . . . now." As I watched, the screen before him flickered, then stabilized. A gray, grainy feed came through, and I shivered, thinking of the images of Chase and I that had been taken in the hospital in Chicago.

"Have you seen Wallace? Chase? Any of our guys?" Hurriedly, I looked from screen to screen. Every cell, including one with a metal chair tipped on its side, was empty. Even DeWitt was missing.

Billy shook his head. "I saw Marco and Polo. They didn't look so good."

"Do you know where they were taken?"

"To the party, I think. They went out through the recreation yard to the base."

Guilt surged through me as I thought of Marco and Polo's capture. Maybe New Guy had been the one to turn them in, but I still felt bad for everything I'd asked them to do.

I hoped they did not suffer long.

Billy was still typing, tongue now sticking out of the side of his mouth.

"What are you doing?" I asked.

"Oops," said Billy with a grin, striking one final key with his index finger. "Looks like the locks on cell block A through D aren't working so well anymore."

More black and white images popped into view on the screen to my left—these of hallways, and doors tentatively being pushed open from the inside.

I ruffled a hand through Billy's hair and he waggled his eyebrows at me.

Tucker pulled a contraption off the wall—a rope noose attached to a long pole, maybe five feet in length. I took a step back as he loosened the rope to create a larger circle.

From somewhere beyond our cell came a dull roar. The party to celebrate the Chief of Reformation's victories over the fallen resistance posts had begun.

"Look." Billy pointed to the central camera feed, where two soldiers armed with semi-automatic weapons opened a door.

"We're out of time," said Tucker.

Silently, and without delay, we followed him out of the booth to a hallway, where he stopped just before turning the corner.

"You're my prisoner, understand?" When I nodded, he placed the rope overhead and tightened it around my neck. He stood back, gripping the length of the pole, and despite the fact that I had allowed him to do so, I felt a hot prickle of shame inch down my spine. To anyone that saw, I was no more than a rabid dog on a leash.

"Hands behind you," Tucker said. "Head down." He looked at Billy. "You think you can handle her?"

Reluctantly Billy took the end of the pole.

"Sorry, Ember," he muttered.

We walked straight down the hall, Tucker holding my wrists, Billy pushing me forward from behind. My shoulder was still exposed, the cool ventilation making my new cuts feel raw and dirty. A few turns, and we came to a juncture where a guard behind a glass shield buzzed us through without question.

Night, and the heavy smell of moss greeted me, along with the roar of a crowd I could barely discern beneath the hair that fell forward over my face. Our time was nearly up. In just a short time, this place would be destroyed.

"Tucker," I whispered. "What time is it?"

"Past your bedtime," he said. "Now shut up."

In silence we continued through a grass paddock—the recreation yard—toward a fence. Just beyond it waited a sea of soldiers jeering at a site beyond the scope of my vision. My limbs grew cold, and my wrists began to tremble.

"We'll have to go around them," said Tucker. "Once we're out of this gate there's an alley between the buildings that leads into the back parking lot. That's your best shot."

"How do I get into the party?"

His fingers dug into my forearm. "Forget the party. This isn't the Knoxville holding cells. This place has real security. And it's tripled because the chief's here. Even if you find him, you'll never get out of here alive if you don't go now."

"Let me worry about that."

He made a noise of disgust. "I don't understand you."

But I wasn't sure that was right, because locked in one fist was a knife he'd given me.

"You should go," I told him, though everything in me

screamed that it was wrong. "Get out of here. You're better than this."

He stared at me for one long moment. Finally he shook his head.

"I'm really not."

The noise of the crowd grew louder as we approached, and made my bones turn to slush. So many soldiers—their voices snide and condemning. I did not know what I would do should they turn and attack. The rope pressed against my throat, as dictated by Billy's firm hold on my leash.

We came to a high metal fence where an armed guard looked down from atop a watchtower.

"You're late," he said. "They just took the last one through."

"Doesn't look like it," said Tucker condescendingly. He released my wrists to flash the gold star on his chest up at the soldier, who immediately turned to a control panel to his right.

"Sorry, captain. Gate's opening now, sir."

The back row in the crowd turned as the gate rolled back on its wheeled track. Some of the men, drunk with excitement, smiled slickly.

"All right," one said. "I didn't know there'd be a girl mixed in."

"Out of the way," said Tucker.

"Yes, captain," they responded. He lifted his chin while I lowered mine. If it wasn't for the cold sweat making his grip on my wrists slippery, I would have thought Tucker was enjoying his newly earned status.

The majority of the crowd was still focused on something happening beyond them though, and as I looked on I saw what had drawn their jeers.

A line of prisoners, their faces covered by black bags and hands bound behind them, waited to get into the building.

Some were badly injured and barely upright but were forced into motion by the chains that bound each man's ankles to the person before him. The soldiers threw handfuls of dirt and rocks on them from across the last barrier of fence. Some were attempting to spit on them; a few succeeded in hitting their mark.

"Wallace?" Billy said behind me.

I lifted on my toes, trying to see over the others, but I could only catch glimpses through the churning sea of uniforms and flying dust.

A second later the pole fell behind me, choking me, and my hand flew to my throat.

Billy was gone.

CHAPTER
24

TUCKER wasted no time snatching up the fallen pole. He gave me a sharp jerk, one which made the air lock in my lungs and my eyes nearly pop out of my head, and I fell to my knees. In a hurry, I lunged up, gasping, searching for Billy, but he had disappeared into the sea of blue.

More soldiers began to turn around, pointing and laughing at me. I couldn't escape it. To them I was a freak; I felt like a freak. I was exactly what they had made me.

At that moment, the front of the group erupted into cheers. The door to the building had opened, and the guards watching the line began to order the prisoners through. With all the attention directed back on the door, Tucker pushed me to the right, leading me against the fence to a narrow juncture between two gates. If I hadn't already been told an alley was there, I never would have seen it.

"No," I said. I had to go with the others. I had to reach Chase. Tucker didn't understand—none of this mattered if Chase died tonight.

Tucker twisted the pole, tightening the noose even further. As we approached the entrance, he pushed me within, and the weight on my neck grew heavy once again as the metal pole was finally released. I turned around, but he was facing the crowd.

Giving me a chance to escape.

Quickly, I shed the leash, and flung it to the ground.

"You have to go," I said. "By midnight this place will be flattened."

"Get out of here," he hissed over his shoulder.

I stared at his back for one final moment. A feeling close to what I'd felt before Harper had tried to kill Chase in that hospital in Chicago came over me. An unfilled well of potential. An inability to stop a train wreck.

I turned and ran.

As I neared the end of the alley I saw the parking lot Tucker had mentioned. A hundred cruisers, navy vans, and buses filled the lot, with soldiers in groups crossing to an entrance on the other side. I looked for anyplace I might sneak in but found none.

A caravan of government cars stopped one by one at the gate before being allowed inside. As I watched, three soldiers emerged from a check station and began to search a van. One examined the undercarriage with a mirror attached to a long handle.

The other two soldiers opened the doors and assisted half a dozen girls outside. They were dressed like the girls I'd only seen in my mother's magazines from before the War. Short, tight skirts clung to every curve. One of the girls' tops was see-through; the others looked as though they'd been scavenged from donation bins, and ripped and tied to create a new style all their own.

Cara's last words came alive in my mind: *If you're breaking into a base, make sure you dress the part.*

The girls were patted down, giggling at the wandering hands

of the guards, and permitted entry through the gate that buzzed open. Overhead, the light was fading. Night would soon arrive.

No time left, my thoughts echoed. *No time left.*

A clicking sound came from overhead, and without another thought I hit the ground, covering my head. Behind closed eyes I saw the ruins of the safe house. The burned bodies.

No time left.

The parking lot lights flickered on.

Shaking, I rose, damp with sweat. I laughed to myself—a crazy sound, even to me. Maybe I had a little more time after all.

The girls were approaching the entrance to the base. There were more now—maybe fifteen or eighteen—moving together as a group. Smart, I thought, when the sharks were already beginning to circle.

Without another thought I ducked behind one of the cruisers and ran to the second row of cars, situating myself between two vans. I could hear the girls laughing now, shouting their taunts to the soldiers, who whistled and catcalled back.

I needed to break into that group; if I made it to the middle, I might be able to get into the building without anyone noticing my shredded, muddy, bloodstained outfit. Just as I was about to chance joining them, I caught my reflection in one of the vans' side mirrors. My cheek was still an angry red, like my neck where the Lost Boys' rope had rubbed. But my gaze drew lower, and my knees weakened, because on my shoulder where I'd been marked a member of Three were now two more slashes, these ones ugly, gaping, condemning. Five hash marks, forever branding me an Article violator.

The MM found a way to twist everything.

I covered it quickly with my torn collar, knowing the red stain on the fabric would do little to hide what lay beneath.

The group drew closer, moving through the rows of cars to-ward the entrance. I stood, still unseen, but before I could join them one of the girls—a redhead with a shiny blue skintight gown—dropped something that rolled across the ground in my direction. Her heels clacked against the asphalt as she chased it.

"Hey!" I called softly. She looked up, rose, and tucked the tube of lipstick back into her purse.

"Someone there?" she asked tentatively, fluffing her hair. She glanced back to the group, continuing on without her.

"Over here!" I said. She appeared around the backside of the van, her eyes widening in surprise.

"Girl." She whistled. "They already worked you over good, didn't they?"

I covered the wound on my shoulder with one hand and tried to look meek. It worked—she moved closer, until we were both out of sight from the front gate.

"I need to get into that party," I said.

She crinkled her nose, stretching the dark freckles across her cheeks. "Haven't you already had enough? I mean, the pay is good, but it ain't *that* good."

No time left.

"I'm sorry." I withdrew the knife from my pocket. The blade was still stained with my blood. "I'm going to need your dress."

TWO minutes later I was jogging toward the entrance of the building, unsteady in the girl's high heels and trying in vain to stretch the fabric to cover both my bra and my thighs. I'd left her my clothes beneath a car two rows away. If she wanted them she'd have to crawl out half-naked and get them. I got the impression she wasn't stupid enough to call a soldier's attention to help—she'd have to wait until everyone was inside.

Under other circumstances I would have felt bad about that.

As I neared the entrance I opened her clutch and searched through the contents. Lipstick, eyeliner—things my mom had kept hidden beneath a loose floorboard underneath her bed. Contraband items, apparently deemed acceptable by the MM when it came to their parties. I thought of Sarah the first time I'd seen her in Tent City. A pretty girl in a pretty dress, pregnant and naïve, and in desperate need of safety. I hoped she would find it now in Tampa.

The last of the girls was being checked before going inside. I watched her remove her shoes at the door guard's request, and hold her arms out to the side as he patted her down. He checked her purse, but left her shoes alone.

As subtly as possible, I bent down and slipped off the high heels. I dropped the knife into the toe of one, and carried them by the strappy heels toward the door.

At the door, a soldier with pudgy cheeks and an extra chin smirked at me, running his thick tongue over his bottom lip. I kept my head lowered, trying to look coy as I cocked one hip out to the side, but was tense beneath his wandering stare. I might as well have been naked, so much of me was exposed. The dress was barely long enough to hide the puncture wound in my thigh where I'd gotten stuck in the fence at the printing plant. At least it covered my shoulder.

Behind him on the wall was a clock. The time was 10:37 P.M. Less than an hour and a half until midnight.

A bead of sweat dripped down the side of my face. I didn't have enough time. We weren't going to make it.

I had to try.

He stood and slid his heavy hands over my shoulders, back, stomach, lingering in places that made my muscles twitch and my stomach turn. I tried not to stare at the shoes, which I'd set on the ground beside me, even when he separated my toes.

"Good. No needles," he grunted. "No razor blades up top, I hope." He thrust a hand through my hair, eyes pausing only a moment on the welt on my cheek.

When he was satisfied, he opened a metal box on a podium beside him, and I forced myself to apply a layer of lipstick in the way I'd seen my mother do when I was young. My hands were trembling. I hoped I was hitting the right spots.

"Two now, two at the end of the night. Pending your work is satisfactory." He handed me two slips of paper—rations vouchers—which I stuffed into the handbag.

"It will be," I guaranteed. I slipped on the shoes, waiting until he looked away to slide the knife back into my purse.

I followed the crowd until I caught sight of the group of girls who had come in from outside. They ignored the men in the hallway, seeming to have their minds set on something else. I watched the way they walked and tried to swing my hips as they did. I placed one hand on my waist and stuck my chest out. Despite my best efforts to look confident, my ankles would not stop wobbling in the stupid high heel shoes. I hurried to the back of the group and clung close to the others while the soldiers called for me to give them a chance.

"Are we going to the party?" I whispered to a skinny girl with short, black hair. Her eyes darted around the hall, never landing on mine.

"First timer?" she guessed.

I tried to smile.

"Piece of advice." She lowered her voice. "Officers give good tips, but they think they can do whatever they want for it."

I checked to make sure the knife was still in my purse.

A girl in the front gave a giddy yell and clapped her hands, and soon the others had joined her. My heart beat faster, keeping time with the cadence of their applause. We were ushered through two double doors, which gave way to a large courtyard, brightly lit by fluorescent overhead lights.

I was bumped and jostled on my way toward the center, and held onto the girl beside me so I didn't fall. Around us swarmed more soldiers than I had ever seen in one place—more people than even in the Square in Knoxville. The closer we got to the center of the courtyard, the denser they were packed and the louder they became. I lifted my eyes overhead as a roar took the crowd. Surrounding us on all sides, and stretching up at least ten stories high, was the rest of the Charlotte base.

Each floor had an inner track that allowed viewers to look down into the courtyard. Soldiers lined the railing, gawking, raining their cheers down into the courtyard. I couldn't help but be awed by their numbers—thousands, maybe more. All the soldiers each region could spare, here to celebrate the FBR's victory.

This was where Three would attack.

Finally, we reached the center of the courtyard, where several rows of chairs surrounded a square chain-link cage. Two soldiers dragged a man's limp body out of the gate while those nearest called for the girls to join them. On a high platform to the right was a table, and seated in the center was the Chief of Reformation. He was flanked by two soldiers on each side, men like him—older, with stars on their jackets. Surrounding them was a blockade of guards standing shoulder to shoulder, leaving a distance of ten feet between the crowd and the table.

A few of the officers pointed in my direction and I immediately lowered my head, fearing I'd been caught.

"Send the girls up," called the chief. "And refill these drinks!"

He slammed a glass down on the wooden table while those nearest to him laughed. The party had already begun.

A few of the bravest pushed to the front of the line, and after being patted down climbed the steps up to the platform. Most of the other girls hung back, making their way through the three rows of seated soldiers that surrounded the cage.

On the opposite side the prisoners, their identities hidden by the black canvas bags over their heads, were dragged to a stand. Still latched together, they stumbled across the cement paddock in front of the cage gate. The soldiers on the floors above booed and shouted their insults, a hateful melody that made my ears ring.

Two men from the line, beige prison uniforms already clinging to their backs with sweat, were thrown into the center of the arena. I tried to get a closer look as those in the seated rows stood to watch the spectacle.

"Traitors!" called a man nearby.

"Dogs!" shouted another.

The hiss of a microphone cut through the noise, and then the chief's sinister voice, amplified from the speakers positioned at the corners of the courtyard, filled the night air.

"My fellow soldiers, a week ago, these two men wore the same uniform as the rest of us."

The crowd hurled their insults.

"They claimed allegiance to the Reformation. To the president. To everything we work so diligently to protect."

My chest rumbled with the deafening roar of the soldiers.

"They betrayed us. All of us. Without reformation they are nothing but animals, with no structure, no higher purpose, ready to bite the hand that feeds them. Without order they turn on each other, and tear each other apart."

Two soldiers ripped the bags off of the prisoners' heads at

the same time. They blinked at the harsh overhead lights and tried to gain their bearings as their cuffs were removed.

One had dark skin, the other, light. I froze.

"Fight!" chanted the crowd. "Fight! Fight! Fight!"

The few stories I'd heard of Chase fighting in Chicago refreshed in my memory. The thought of him being forced to do battle for the entertainment of others disgusted me all over again. As I looked around, a new pity slashed through me, this one bright and sour. Violence and brutality to teach compliance, to enforce morality—that was the MM's way.

At first Marco and Polo drew together, back to back, as if they might fight whatever came their way. *I'm sorry,* I thought. Sorry they were here, that they'd been caught, that I'd even thought of the Statute hijacking. They had made their decisions long before me, but I couldn't help but feel responsible for this.

"Only one of you is coming out," said the Chief of Reformation.

Marco glanced over his shoulder at Polo. His partner's lips were moving fast, saying something I couldn't make out over the shouting. And then Marco, already injured, hobbled away, turning so that they were facing each other. Polo tried once, twice, and then one more time to get close to him, his arms open and pleading, but each time Marco jerked back.

"Fight!" demanded the crowd.

The men began to circle, Polo's steps quick, Marco's strained and awkward. Polo was still trying to reason. Even from where I was standing I could see that he still didn't understand.

"Fight!"

I shoved through, getting closer to the fence. Close enough to hear Marco say, "I'm sorry, brother."

He attacked Polo as though he felt no pain, and as they fell to the ground the courtyard erupted in cheers.

I watched, frozen, unable to look away. It was a trick. They had a plan. Marco would no more hurt Polo than I would hurt Chase. I told myself this even as Polo's nose broke, as his blood soaked the floor of the arena.

Marco fought like a man possessed. He punched, screamed, and even cried, and as Polo's body went still under him a moan, filled with despair, tore from him.

The soldiers had to drag him off of his friend. And even as they did, he refused to let him go.

"Brutal!" clapped the chief, no longer magnified by the microphone. "Absolutely brutal!"

At a nod of the chief's head, one of the soldiers removed his weapon, and shot Marco in the back of the head.

My knees gave way and I fell back into the first row of soldiers. A man caught me around the waist and latched me in place on his lap. I could barely struggle; the horror had rendered my muscles useless.

"Likes a close view, does she?" came a voice beside me.

"Guess so," grumbled the man I had fallen into. I turned my face to see Tucker's green eyes blazing back into mine. His lips brushed my ear. "You must have some kind of death wish."

I tried to get up but he held me in place.

"What do you think is going to happen here?" he demanded. "You're outnumbered two thousand to one."

"To two," I said, but he only scoffed. "You can't just sit here and watch our friends die."

He tightened his grip. "You think I have a choice?"

"You always have a choice."

The prisoners shuffled forward; another was being brought toward the ring.

I strained my eyes through the chain-link, focusing on the man in the front. He was thin, bowed through the back. There a tattoo on his wrist that snaked up his bare forearm into beige prison uniform. His ratty hair was long to the shoulders, spilling out from beneath the bag covering his head.

I watched, speechless, as they unchained Frank Wallace from the others and dragged him toward the ring, but before he could get to the gate another of the prisoners attacked one of the guards. A fight erupted, and those closest to me stood again, blocking my way. Tucker latched me under his shoulder as the guards rushed in to manage the prisoners. We were only ten feet away, close enough to see the prisoner who'd started the fight. To see that the bag over his head had fallen free.

The noise went silent. The lights grew dim. Every man between us wavered in my vision.

There, on his knees, two guns pointed at his head, was Chase. His shoulders heaved up and down, and from his nose came a trickle of blood. When the soldiers had brought Wallace to the ring, they must have released the ankle chains that bound all the prisoners together, because Chase was now separated from the others who were being forced to lie face down on the ground.

Chase refused to lower. He looked up into the faces of the soldiers with cold defiance in his stare.

But when his eyes found mine, his lips parted, formed the word that tore me apart.

"No."

And in that moment I felt it. The certainty that we would not escape this place. That we would die here.

The sob rose in my throat.

"*I'll find you,*" I had told him once, "*and I'll bring you back.*"

I held on to his gaze as though it were my life raft. He rocked back on his heels, and tilted his head, and there was a grief blanketing his shoulders so heavy it nearly paralyzed me.

"Hold on," I whispered.

I reached into my purse for the knife. If I could create a big enough diversion, he might have a chance—at least he would be able to run. If I was fast maybe I could get away, too.

It was a slim chance at best, but I'd made it this far. I couldn't give up now.

On the platform, the Chief of Reformation was waiting for a man to test his drink. He grew impatient, slamming one fist on the table. Finally, the man, red in the face and blinking, nodded, and passed along the bottle.

My palms grew damp as I prepared for what I would have to do.

Tucker's arm, now at a diagonal across my chest, tightened. He was still watching Chase, scarcely breathing, and didn't let go, even as I attempted to peel back his fingers from my waist.

"What are you doing?" I whispered.

Across the ring, another soldier had climbed the platform steps. Stocky and balding, he bent low to deliver a message to the chief. Slowly, Reinhardt lowered his glass and nodded. A catlike grin split his face and he shook his head as if in disbelief, and stood.

He raised his hands, and a hush took the crowd. It began with those closest to him, and then, like wildfire, the silence caught, racing through the courtyard, climbing the walls of the building until no one made a sound.

Glancing skyward, I couldn't help but wonder how I was still standing. The time felt liquid, flowing by like water in a stream. It had to be after midnight. Maybe there had been a problem with the attack. Maybe Three had failed. Either way, I focused on the task at hand: getting on that platform.

"Don't move," Tucker said between his teeth.

Again the microphone's hiss cut through the air.

"Fellow soldiers!" began the chief, the metallic ring distorting his voice to give it a strange, robotic quality. "The way of the soldier is not always easy. We are ever challenged. Tested by those who would stand in our way." He paused. "If ever you need validation that your chosen path is indeed the one of righteousness, tonight is the night."

From the opposite corner of the courtyard came a unit of soldiers leading a man on three separate leashes, not unlike those Tucker had placed around my neck. His face was hidden, his wrists bound in front of him, attached to chains that latched to his ankles, but even at a shuffle he still managed to walk tall with his shoulders back and his chest open, as if daring someone to shoot him in the heart. A path cleared as they approached the ring, and in the quiet I could hear Wallace's voice, crackling with dehydration.

"Let him go, you . . ." He was silenced with the blunt end of a rifle. A young soldier with dark hair grabbed his bound wrists from behind and forced him to stand.

The prisoner was brought into the ring. It was then I noticed the slight limp, as though he favored one leg.

"I give you a member of the rebel group Three, caught just south of here attempting to flee our border patrol. Shall we show him what happens to those who try to outrun reformation?"

My stomach sunk. I willed it not to be true.

The soldier removed Jesse's mask, revealing the snake tattoo climbing his neck. I forced my heart to harden, to forget that he had sacrificed himself to save me, and instead focused on why he had done it. So that I could find Chase.

The microphone clattered as Reinhardt dropped it onto the table. Several of the officers attempted to stop him as he rushed down the platform steps, pushing aside girls and soldiers alike.

Now was my chance. Wriggling free from Tucker's grasp, I dashed around the outside of the ring. The chief was closer to the entrance, and made it in a moment before I reached him. I kept close to the gate, ready for the moment he stepped back out.

I was closer to the prisoners now, closer to Wallace, whose dry lips edged into a dangerous grin as he recognized me. Behind him, Chase was attempting to stand, staring at Jesse with shock on his face.

"You," Reinhardt said to Jesse. I doubted anyone past the first row could hear him.

Jesse spit on the ground and the crowd booed. "Did you miss me, Chancellor?"

"Can't say that I have," said Reinhardt. Hands clasped tightly behind his lower back, he approached Jesse, examining him slowly. He reached for Jesse's throat, and for a moment I thought he might choke him, but instead he ripped open his sweat-drenched collar, revealing three old scars, not unlike those I had carried before they'd been mutilated.

Whatever Three had done or hadn't done, I was proud of Jesse in that moment.

"Did you really think you could kill me?" asked the Chief of Reformation. "Was that the plan tonight? Amid all these soldiers, loyal to the cause?"

"Got pretty close last time," said Jesse with a cocky smirk. His gaze moved around the circle, pausing only momentarily on me, then on Chase, and resting on Wallace.

Reinhardt hummed his agreement. "So close I thought you'd died in the blast. Unfortunate for you that you did not."

A grim realization settled over me. Jesse had tried to kill Reinhardt—that had been the attempt on the Chief of Reformation's life when Chase and I had been in Knoxville. Everyone had said Three was behind it, even DeWitt had confirmed it.

Some of us saw what was happening, he had said. Dr. Aiden DeWitt, who'd *lost his girls*—his wife and daughter, Cara. Frank, aka Francis Wallace, who'd joined the FBR to enact change from within and ended up killing his partner to save a boy from the street. Billy.

And Jesse Waite. Chase's uncle. Who'd been framed by the FBR from the very beginning.

Three men.

The Chief removed the baton from his belt. Jesse threw his shoulders back.

"Do your worst," he challenged.

And Reinhardt did. He lifted the baton and smashed it down on Jesse's shoulder. As he fell to one knee, the chancellor hit him on the back, again, and again, until Jesse fell to his elbows. His chains rattled as he attempted to stretch against them, to break free.

"Stop!" I heard Chase shout. But no one heard his voice but me. The crowd had taken on new life, stomping their feet, cheering and clapping and screaming encouragement to their leader. My fingers latched in the chain-links, shaking it, feeling for a weak point to break through. As if it would do any good.

"Think you could kill me?" shouted the chief, the sweat dripping from his face. "*Me*? The arrogance." He struck Jesse's side. "The ego." A strike on his hip. "I have the president on my side." *Crack.* "I have reformation on my side." *Crack.* "I have *God* on my side." He fell back a step, the exhaustion clear in his body. "What do you have? *Nothing.*"

Jesse crawled toward me, not because I was there, but in retreat. His gaze met mine, and I saw him then, really saw him, for the first time. He wasn't cold and distant and protected by his sarcasm now. He was afraid, and tired, and there was regret in his eyes. I may not have been the one he wanted to see in that moment, but he locked on to me all the same, and I hoped he knew that he was not alone.

The chief kicked him in the gut, and a cold laughter from those nearby broke out. Jesse collapsed into the fence, the chain-links clattering against the supporting beam in waves. With tears blurring my vision, I pressed my fingers through the holes in the metal, feeling his back rise with each stunted breath.

There is but one man with a thousand hands. Cut off his head, and his limbs lose their purpose.

"Jesse," I whispered, and slipped the knife through the link beneath his knee. "I'll tell Chase what you did for him. I'll get him out of here, just like I said I would."

He nodded, just a slight movement of his chin.

Slowly, painfully, Chase's uncle rose. Something deep pulled him up, making him stand. Something powerful. Something indestructible.

"Yeah," said Jesse. "Well I have family on my side."

The chief laughed. A forced, mocking sound that only thinly veiled his fury.

Both hands still bound together, Jesse charged. Reinhardt planted his feet, threw his head back and laughed even harder, as if he was made of iron and nothing could ever defeat him. As they collided in the center of the ring his laughter choked off abruptly.

It was not until Jesse backed away that I saw the knife emerging from the left side of the Chief of Reformation's chest.

For several long seconds, the laughter continued. The soldiers roared, invigorated by Jesse's last stand. But as Reinhardt fell to his knees, the courtyard plunged into whispers. By the time he took his last, gargling breath, you could have heard a pin drop.

He fell face down in the ring of his own creation, and didn't move again.

Jesse closed his eyes, a look of peace on his face. I didn't watch him fall, but I heard the shots. A dozen, at least, before I finally heard him hit the ground.

There was one final beat of stunned silence, and then chaos erupted.

More shots rang out. Some of the girls near me screamed, and a soldier to my left was hit in the crossfire and fell to the ground. I shoved through the bodies, clambering to get closer to the ring and the prisoners. As I neared the gate where the soldiers were crowding, I was sandwiched between two bodies. I shoved through them, my dress ripping.

The chain-link fence slammed against the supporting beams, sending a high reverberating clang through the night.

"Dead!" men were shouting. "The chief is dead!"

It would only be a matter of time before they turned on the prisoners.

Finally I found Chase. He'd risen to a stand but the young soldier I'd seen managing Wallace was now behind him, facing the opposite direction.

"Get off him!" I screamed, and with all my strength, threw him aside.

Billy fell to the ground, a silver ring of keys skimming across the pavement away from us.

I cursed myself and dove after them, but another man snatched them up first. Wallace, his hands already free, snatched them up and raced for the other prisoners. Strong arms spun me, and in the next moment I found myself pushed down as Chase ducked the blow of a baton. The soldier was pushed into us, and Chase kicked him aside, barely staying upright.

"We have to get out!" I shouted. "Now!"

He didn't ask questions, he only nodded.

"Cease fire!" shouted one of the soldiers as another shot rang out. "We're too close! Cease fire!"

Soldiers were shooting soldiers in an attempt to kill the prisoners, but with so many bodies rushing the stage, we were packed like sardines.

"Help!" Billy was swallowed beneath a wave of blue. Chase dove in after him, never hesitating to give anyone in a uniform a chance to attack.

"Chase!" I screamed. I shoved toward where they'd disappeared.

A whistle reached my ears, a soaring, high-pitched song like the hiss of the microphone, only more distant, like a kettle of tea finally reaching the boiling point.

And then the world exploded.

CHAPTER
25

MY breath pulled in and out, in and out, like the waves at the ocean.

My vision was blurry, or maybe it was the cloud of dust surrounding me. Bright lights flickered, lighting the world for seconds at a time. It was difficult to make out my surroundings. Behind me was a hard surface, above me, some kind of warped chain fence.

As if someone was turning up the volume, the sound gradually increased until my chest vibrated with a rumbling, like the world was about to cave in on itself. Groans of pain punctuated the air, and above it all, the wail of a siren, low at first, but getting higher, and louder, just like it had during the air raid drills in the War.

In elementary school, the drills had come once a week. At the sound of the siren screeching over the loudspeakers, we were to duck under our desks, wait for the lights to turn off, and then run for the nearest exit. The teachers had made a game out of it.

Rabbit hides under a tree for Fox to hunt his prey.
Rabbit waits for dark, then rabbit runs away.

I thought of that now, as the blood pumped through my

veins and my eyes turned skyward in search of an aerial attack. But as I shoved up to a stand, I realized the attack had already come. The memories slowly returned to me. Jesse, killing the Chief of Reformation. Chase, just beyond the entrance to the ring.

I was missing a shoe, and the heel of the other had broken off. A pale layer of dust coated my skin, and I was bleeding from half a dozen scrapes on my knees and right arm.

The stage that had meant the deaths of Marco and Polo, of Jesse and the Chief of Reformation, and who knew how many others, had been flipped on its side, though it looked like it would cave in on me at any moment.

Sharp gravel dug into my feet as I stumbled through the cloud of dust in search of the prisoners. They were not far away, mixed in with soldiers strewn across the ground. Some stood, others toppled over or remained on their knees. Some—*most*— did not get up at all.

"Chase!" I rasped.

I picked my way through the bodies, finally finding him halfway buried beneath another body—a soldier, lifeless as a doll. In a surge of effort, I pushed him aside and to my relief Chase rose to his elbows and slapped a hand against the side of his head as if his ear was filled with water.

"What . . ." He looked up and met my gaze.

"We have to get out of here," I said. I glanced up, only to find a gaping hole in the side of the building. Where the stories of soldiers had climbed skyward, now there was only a pile of rubble. Half the base had been blown away.

"My uncle . . ."

"We have to go," I said.

Chase's face twisted in pain just for an instant before he packed it away with a curt nod.

I helped him to a stand, but he staggered. There beside us, on the ground, was the soldier I'd pushed aside. His blank eyes stared upward, unseeing, and a trickle of blood ran from the corner of his mouth.

"Billy?" I fell to all fours. I shook him, but he didn't move.

My mind struggled to make sense of what I was seeing. Billy was just here, just helping to free the others. He'd found the keys. He'd let me out of my cell. He could not be gone.

"Billy!" I shouted.

Chase's arms surrounded my waist and hoisted me to a stand.

"Can't say I ever thought I'd see you two . . ." Wallace trailed off as he saw the boy lying on the ground.

He crouched, and laid two fingers aside Billy's neck. His head fell forward.

"All right, kid," he said. "You did real good back there." He closed Billy's eyes. "Real good."

The sob in my throat choked out. The tears stung my eyes, but cleared them. Cleared away all the distractions, all the departures from the one road we should have been following the whole time. The road that led us away from *this*.

I looked at Chase and knew he felt the same.

"We need to get out of here," I said.

As if nothing else in the world mattered, Wallace carefully removed the boy's MM jacket, button by button, and gently placed it aside. I said his name, I begged him to come, but he acted as if he couldn't hear me.

The resistance leader who we thought had died on the rooftop of the Wayland Inn folded Billy's hands over his chest.

"That's my boy," he said. He straightened Billy's undershirt. "That's my boy," he said again.

An outcry came from the open side of the base, and we

turned just in time to see the men and women, dressed in civilian clothing, cresting the wreckage. The MM regrouped, and orders to stand and fight brought on a hailstorm of bullets.

Chase and I dove behind the stage, hearing the ping of bullets slap against its metal underbelly.

Wallace stood slowly, the MM gun from Billy's belt in his hand. He didn't seek cover as the bullets flew.

"We did it," he said, staring blankly into the battle.

Wallace was right. We had done it. Jesse had killed the Chief of Reformation, Three had broken into the Charlotte base. It should have felt like victory, but all I felt was loss and the gallop of my heartbeat repeating the same urgent message: *get out, get out, get out.*

I took one final look at Billy, and Wallace walking calmly to join Three as they attacked the remainder of the soldiers in the courtyard. Those in uniforms fell around us, fell from the high remaining floors that were still intact. Some surrendered and were taken prisoner. Some were not offered that option.

"Ember." My name on Chase's lips brought me back.

Now came the point of decision: to join Three's ranks and destroy the MM—to risk the chance at being destroyed ourselves—or to leave all of this devastation behind. Soon the choice would be made for us; a battle was underway and in a moment we were going to be caught in the middle of it.

"Follow me," I said.

Keeping low, we picked our way through a path of debris greater than the wreckage we'd seen inside the Chicago tunnels. Away from the fighting. My chin lifted; I didn't know if another bomb would come, but I wasn't about to wait and find out.

The two of us raced through the exit, down the hallway where I'd walked with the girls, toward the parking lot. As we neared the door, the patter of gunfire had us taking cover against the wall.

The buzz of the lights flickered on and off, grating on my raw nerves. Two shots embedded into the wall above us, then a third. Over it all, the siren screamed, constant and demanding. Outside came a cry of victory from the men and women of Three.

"You hear that?" shouted Chase. "That's the sound of you losing. If you don't want to die today, I suggest you get out of here fast."

A few seconds later we heard the clatter of retreating footsteps.

I kept close behind Chase as we exited the building. The parking lot lights had gone dark from the blast; some of the poles had been knocked over. Cars were crushed beneath them.

"There!" I pointed to the exit, but even as I spoke the terror punched me in the gut. The retreating MM troops had used this lot to regroup. A hundred or more soldiers gathered near the perimeter fence, their dark uniforms only degrees of shadow in the moonlight. They saw us at the same time we saw them, and instantly raised their weapons.

"Get back!" Chase shouted. We tried to return to the building, but now the retreating troops were pouring from the exit. When they saw their fellow soldiers they skidded to a halt, making one last play against the rebels fighting their way through the building.

We were caught in the middle.

"Under the car!" Grabbing Chase's sleeve, I dove behind the nearest van, furious at myself for not having grabbed a weapon from one of the fallen soldiers within the courtyard.

The sound of gunfire came from all sides. The interior of the base was on fire now and the smoke was tinged with electricity and something sweet. To the left of the base came the sounds of battle—the scrape of metal and a chorus of angry voices, yelling.

"The prison," said Chase, a grim look on his face.

Bullets sprayed around my feet and I tucked them close to my body, shaking with adrenaline, with fear, with anger that we were so close to freedom only to be pinned in place as target practice.

"I love you," I said to Chase.

He turned to me, a hard look on his face.

"Don't you give up." With that he stood, and disappeared around the corner of the van. I screamed as another shot embedded in the sliding door over my head. The MM had surrounded us. It was just a matter of time before we were discovered.

A great roar came from the direction of the prison—this one closer, shaking through my bones. I mustered the courage to peek around the side of the van, ready for the onslaught of soldiers, but instead found a wave of gray charging through the darkness.

Leading them was DeWitt. He carried a stick in one arm, raised high above his head. As he came closer I recognized the long pole with the looped leash.

It seemed possible then that DeWitt had planned to be here, now, to lead this wave of the attack. Somehow the prisoners had overpowered the guards. In the chaos I'd forgotten that Billy had freed them.

"Nice job, Billy," I whispered to the sky.

As I watched, half of the first line of prisoners fell. DeWitt crumpled, slowed, but then ran on again, urging the others to follow. Within seconds the clash of bodies and metal echoed against what remained of the stone base. I scrambled up, searching frantically for Chase. Eventually I caught sight of him, his prison uniform standing out in the night, running toward me from the now open gate.

Hope flooded through me. We were going to make it. We were going to live.

I didn't even hear the men behind me until it was too late.

The grip on my arm took me by surprise, and with a short scream I toppled backward.

"Stand up!" shouted New Guy. "Up on your feet!"

He wrapped his arm around my throat, using my body as a shield. Something cold and hard pressed against my temple, and without a doubt I knew it was the barrel of a gun.

Chase didn't slow; he ran at both of us like a freight train. We crashed to the ground, gravel scraping the palms of my hands as I tried to shove myself out of the way. From close by came the sound of a blunted shot, then a pained cry in my right ear. I finally succeeded in breaking away from between the two men.

New Guy, his nose still busted, and now with a scrape down his pale jaw, jolted up, leaving Chase facedown on the pavement. For one stunned moment none of us moved.

"Get up." Chase's leg was closest and I shook his calf. "Chase, get up!"

His arms bent at his sides as he attempted something that looked like a push up before collapsing back down on his stomach.

He's okay, I told myself. He took a hard hit. Got the wind knocked out of him. I crawled to his side and helped him roll over, watched as his dark eyes focused behind me, on the moon. Saw the dark liquid seep from his right side, just above his rib cage.

Time stopped.

We were a girl and a boy exploring a haunted house.

A kiss in the woods.

A ride on a motorcycle.

We were walking to school. Whispering across the space between our houses. Pulling hay from each other's hair.

We were pieces of the same puzzle.

But he was the boy from my dream, bleeding from a hole in his chest.

I couldn't move.

There was only my breath, too hard, and his, too strained. He cringed against the pain, and I filled his wound with my hands and my tears.

The fighting around us returned in a rush, blasting my eardrums. The soldier who had shot him, who had turned us in at Greeneville, was getting closer. I could feel his presence in the way the hair on my neck stood on end.

Without thinking I spread my body over Chase's, covering him, wishing I was made of steel and could stop a bullet. Two shots came fast. I closed my eyes, waiting to feel them enter my body, bracing against the fire they would bring to my flesh.

But when I opened them, Tucker was beside me, and New Guy was on the ground, motionless.

Lowering to a crouch, Tucker sheathed his gun and clenched a fist around Chase's shoulder.

"Shake it off, Jennings. It's just a flesh wound."

Around us, the battle raged on.

Chase opened his eyes fully, focusing on Tucker. And then in a surge of strength he sat up, and shoved me to the side.

"Get . . . away . . . from us . . ." he whispered.

"I saved her," Tucker explained.

You killed my mother, and all those people in Chicago and the safe house.

"He let me go," I said, placing my arms beneath Chase's.

Tucker had woken something inside of me. I could still save him, but we needed to get out of here.

Chase weakly shoved his old partner, who fell helplessly back on his heels. He looked shocked, like he couldn't believe that Chase didn't believe him.

"Help me!" I told Tucker. "He needs a doctor."

Tucker wound Chase's arm over his shoulders and, with a grunt, he stood. The noise Chase made was enough to make my whole body clench, but he didn't have the strength to object.

"There's a clinic north of here," said Tucker. "It's where they take soldiers who need more than the base medic."

I opened the sliding side door of the van. Tucker backed in, dragging Chase across the floor.

I jumped into the driver's seat, searched the center console. I threw a map over my shoulder, shoved aside a pack of batteries. Nearby, a man yelled out in pain.

"Keys," I said.

"In the visor," said Tucker from behind me. "The drivers leave them there when they're on base."

I ripped down the visor and snatched the key ring as it slid toward me.

"Hold on, man." Tucker had removed his uniform jacket and was trying to convince Chase to hold it over the wound.

"Let's go!" I shouted. As Tucker emerged I slapped the keys into his hand, then ducked in the back to kneel beside Chase.

Around us Three's soldiers fought side by side with the prisoners, defeating the MM troops. Their cries of victory sliced through me; they cheered for the deaths of others just as the soldiers had cheered the death of our men in the ring.

It was what we'd been fighting for. What we'd always wanted.

I slammed the van's sliding door and pressed down on the jacket over Chase's stomach. He groaned; the sound almost broke me. I couldn't stand him hurting like this. I couldn't do anything to fix it. The harder I pressed on the bandage, the more pain it seemed to put him in, but I didn't know what else to do.

The tires squealed. I glanced up as we cut through the parking lot. Tucker was carving a straight line toward the exit. Soldiers and rebels alike dove out of our way.

The gate was unlatched, but not wide enough for the van.

"Tucker?"

"Hang on," he said. The engine revved, then jolted forward, ramming hard into the side of another car sticking out in our path.

"Hold on!" I shouted to Chase as we punched through the opening.

Outside, on the road, men in uniforms were retreating, gunned down by the prisoners that chased them. A bullet pierced the back window, likely from one of the rebels—I'd forgotten we were in an MM transport—but though we swerved, we didn't slow.

Tucker had said there was a clinic north of here. I hoped it wasn't hard to find.

We finally hit a straightaway. Our speed increased. Chase forced himself up on one elbow despite my efforts to hold him down. His face was pale in the dark van, and gleaming with sweat.

He was staring at Tucker.

"He was in on it," he said between clenched teeth. "At the mini-mart. He knew."

"I know," I said.

"Did he really let you go?"

"Yes." I waited a beat, then pressed him back down. "Chase, keep talking."

"Why?" he asked.

"I don't know. I think . . ." Tucker swerved up onto the highway, following a sign with a white H for hospital. "I think maybe he's trying to make things right."

Silence.

"Chase?"

His eyes rolled back. Closed.

"Chase!" I screamed.

CHAPTER
26

I PACED through the small hospital room, ignoring the wet hair that dripped onto my borrowed scrubs. Tucker leaned back in an orange padded chair against the wall, his eyes drifting shut. Every time his head fell to the side, he jolted awake and rubbed his eyes.

"The doc come back?" He asked this every time he woke up.

I shook my head. For the twentieth time, I retied the waistband of my oversized pants. They were huge and wouldn't stay up.

Five hours had passed since we'd burst into triage of the small medical clinic demanding care. Four hours since the doctor on call, a man about Jesse's age with thinning hair and serious eyes, had performed surgery. I'd stayed in the room the entire time, convinced they might try to hurt him. Convinced they would just let him die. Even after the doctor showed me the three parallel scars on his shoulder.

Two hours ago they told me Chase would pull through and placed him in a recovery room. I'd finally agreed to take their clothes, clean myself off in the sink, and let a nurse dress my wounds. The doctor had given me a shot of penicillin in case any of them got infected. I'd never left Chase's side.

The rebels had taken over the clinic. Men and women I recognized from Endurance kept guard around the perimeter, while many of the prisoners kept watch inside. Tucker told me the staff was patching up MM officers—men Three would later make prisoners and use as collateral. He stayed close after that; he'd traded his uniform for scrubs and thrown the jacket in the trash. I thought maybe he'd make a run for it, but he hadn't.

DeWitt had yet to show up. Neither had Wallace. I wasn't hopeful either had made it.

While I watched Chase sleep, the slow, consistent beep of the monitors measured his heart rate. I kept one ear tuned to the hall, and when footsteps pattered by our room I tiptoed to the cracked door. Four rebels—the doctor who had completed Chase's surgery included—were gathered around an old black box radio in front of a window, where outside the sun was just beginning to rise.

I lingered in the background, ready to unhook Chase and move us on if I had to.

"Rumors of a massive explosion at the Chicago base have been confirmed," reported the familiar voice of a woman who liked to annunciate her words. "The detonations, which occurred just after midnight, were originally claimed as accidents—a misfiring from the base's weapons storage—but soon after, the prison and rehabilitation hospital also reported explosions, leading our sources to believe that this was in fact the work of rebels. The base has since been overrun with people carrying what look to be the Moral Statutes. The same is said to be happening at the FBR base in Knoxville, Tennessee, which fell less than an hour later."

I leaned back against the wall, mouth agape. Civilians overtaking the bases. Carrying Statute circulars. My story had reached people in time.

Jesse's words returned to me from Endurance: *"When a government becomes destructive, it is the right of the people to alter or abolish it."* It may have been my name on those Statutes, but it was the people who took action. A revolution had begun, and for the first time I finally felt as if my part in it was over.

"Since the attacks, former president Matthew Stark and members of his administration have released a statement calling for current political leaders to relinquish their power so that it may be rightfully returned to the citizens. He demands that officials explain their stance on the Expungement Initiative, a government protocol intended to reduce noncompliance by the execution of innocent civilians imprisoned for Article violations. President Scarboro has yet to comment on these accusations, or the recent claims that the late Chief of Reformation, Chancellor Reinhardt, offered bribe money to the insurgents during the War in exchange for acts of terrorism. Stark asks that citizens demonstrate tolerance and patience during this precarious time until peace can be established. With more on these stories as details emerge, this is Faye Browne."

I pictured the narrow woman with short, curly hair and wondered where she'd landed. I hoped she didn't plan on using her real name in public. That kind of thing could get you killed.

I snuck back into the room, pulling the chair close to the side of Chase's bed. Gently, I threaded his fingers through mine. Too cold. Normally he was like a furnace, but since we'd arrived he'd been unable to warm up. I pulled the blanket higher over his bandages, careful not to put too much pressure on his chest, and kissed his shoulder.

Tucker was chewing his thumbnail and staring at his boots.

"I never gave my C.O. those posts," he said quietly. "I gave them Knoxville and Chicago. I told them where to find the sniper, then told all of you she was dead. I even gave them the safe house when we were in Greeneville. But after the bombs in those tunnels, I stopped. They thought I was dead anyway."

He scratched his short hair down over his forehead, and I thought of how distraught he'd been after we'd survived the bombs in Chicago. He'd probably never thought the MM would take the place down with him still in it.

"I thought I had to. I thought, I don't know, I was doing the right thing."

I snorted at this.

"The right thing," I said, listening to the beep of Chase's pulse on the monitor. "What's that again?"

Raised voices in the hall drew our attention, but lowered a few seconds later.

"What happens for you now?" I asked Tucker.

He dropped his hands over his knees. "Not sure."

I regarded him carefully. He wasn't the same guy I'd first met at my house during my mother's arrest, what felt like years ago. He didn't even look the same. His green eyes weren't as sharp as they had been, and he slouched as though he could barely hold up his shoulders. He was beaten, lost, and on his own. But despite that, he felt real, more real than I'd ever seen him.

I didn't know what that made us, but that didn't scare me anymore.

"Welcome to the other side," I said.

He looked up at me, over Chase's still body, mouth twisting in a small smile. Before I could think about it, I smiled back.

The plastic pillowcase cover beneath Chase's head made a crinkling sound. He drew in a long, deep breath, blinking, and then turned his face to me. I waited out each torturous second as the confusion passed. There was much to tell him—about Jesse, about what I'd just heard coming from the radio—but we would talk about that later. For the first time in a long time, later felt like a real thing.

His hand, still in mine, rose to my cheek, an IV tube trailing after it.

"Welcome back," I said. "We're in a clinic. I'll get the doctor."

Tucker jumped up. "I'll go." He rubbed his hands on his sides as if not sure what to do with them, and then turned and left the room. His gun was left on the orange chair.

"I guess we made it." Chase's voice cracked, and he licked his chapped lips. "All of us."

Hearing him speak made my heart clench, and a small yes was all I could manage.

His hand lowered down my neck, to the place on my collar where the shirt couldn't cover the corner of white that stuck out from the V-neck. The heat of his palm pressed through the bandages, and I held it there, close to my heart.

"How'd you get your scars?" he asked.

The tears rose within me like a soft rain—quiet at first, dampening my face, making tracks down my chin to finally fall on my borrowed shirt. And then they came heavier, drenching my insides, muddying every memory into one painful pool and then finally washing me clean.

He pulled me closer and I curled up beside him on the bed, careful to stay clear of his wounds. He stroked my hair and kissed my brow, and I promised myself that nothing could ever come between us again.

A second later I heard the shot.

I bolted from the bed, instinctively dropping low. Behind me, Chase was trying to push himself up. The monitor beeped faster, catching up to my own jagged pulse. As a commotion in the hall raised, I snatched Tucker's gun and flattened myself against the wall just within the door. Ears ringing, I glanced around the corner.

At first it looked as though Tucker was leaning against the wall, head drooped forward as if he was still nodding off, and for a split second I wondered if I'd made up the sound. But then Tucker's hands, folded high on his chest, opened, and I saw then the dark red stains on his palms.

I ran toward him, following his shocked gaze down the hall to where Wallace stood, a team of men and women crowded behind him. They stared at him, as if waiting for orders.

Tucker fell forward, and his knuckles turned white as they gripped the metal bar against the wall behind him. I grabbed him just as he was sinking to the ground, the thin fabric of his borrowed scrubs ripping in my fists.

Wallace walked toward us.

"I should have listened to you from the beginning," he said to me. "You told me he would turn us in. I didn't listen." There was a strange, absent quality to his voice, like all the life had been sucked out of him.

"Tucker?" I whispered.

I couldn't hold his weight, and soon we were both on the ground. His head lay on my knees, his fingers scratched uselessly at his throat, as if an invisible hand were choking him.

"Tucker," I said again.

He choked, sputtered, red blood brightening his lips. Then a shudder. Then a stillness, like a long sigh before falling asleep. When his eyes found mine I wasn't sure what they saw, but he smiled, just a soft, subtle tilt of his lips.

"Guess I was too late," he said.

And as the life left him, as his body went limp and his hands fell to the floor, I did what I never thought I'd do. I cried for him.

The doctor awaited Wallace's approval before tentatively approaching. He pressed two fingers against Tucker's neck, just for a few seconds, then shook his head.

I looked up at Wallace. "What have you done?"

His brows furrowed in confusion, as if the answer should have been obvious.

They took Tucker's body to the back parking lot with the others who had died after reaching the clinic. Three had separated the area in two; on one side, the soldiers were thrown, their bodies discarded like sacks of garbage. On the other were the prisoners and members of Three who had fought to take down the Charlotte base. They were covered with sheets and laid side by side.

I didn't know what would happen to either side, but I made the freed prisoners carry Tucker's body to the side with the rebels. I wiped his face clean and covered him with a sheet myself. It was the least I could do after all we'd been through.

As I stood over him they brought out Dr. DeWitt, and laid him beside Tucker. One bad turned good, one good turned bad. In the end it didn't matter. We were all the same.

Chase and I stayed through the following night. As the hours passed, the clinic was flooded with rebels who'd survived the battle. The hall was soon overwhelmed with injured fighters, some badly burned, some with broken bones, many—too many—with gunshot wounds. The hospital staff ran from patient to patient, and for a while I helped where I could: passing out bandages, holding people still while the nurses and doctors stitched them up or made them comfortable enough to pass without pain, all the while feeling that aching pressure inside of me to move on.

The doctor told us about an old woman who lived nearby who was friendly to the cause. Before dark on the second day, one of the orderlies helped me move Chase and three other injured rebels to her home, a nearby farm with a collection of hand-painted signs lining a privacy fence that stated: BEWARE OF DOG. For six nights we hid in her basement while Chase recovered. She brought us food and water, antibiotics the doctor could spare, and word on the resistance.

At night we listened to Faye Brown's reports.

By the end of the first week, nine bases had been overrun by civilians. The soldiers that survived the riots had fled, were turned, or simply disappeared. And in every city where a base had fallen, hijacked Statute circulars were found, clutched in the fists of those who fought.

The old president came down from his hiding place in the mountains and began making speeches—Faye even got a special interview with him. The FBR's days were numbered, he said. It was time they laid down their weapons and accepted the inevitable. Democracy would return to the United States. The Statutes were history. We would rebuild again. All things that sounded good, but had yet to happen. He didn't condone the violence, but didn't lie about knowing Three, either. He sounded a little different on the radio than the man who'd showed me his son's favorite books. Stronger maybe. Not like an old man.

On the seventh day I was helping Chase into the passenger side of the MM van when a beat-up silver car pulled through the gate into the back of the farm. The man who unfolded himself from the driver's seat looked to have aged ten years since the Charlotte base had fallen. His ratty hair was now clean, tied by a shoelace at the back of his neck, but more gray around the temples.

"I heard you're leaving without saying good-bye," said Wallace, leaning against the side of the blue van. His fingers tapped a rhythm against the metal beside his hip.

I wasn't sure how he'd found us. In the past week I'd been careful not to use either of our names, nor give any information that might indicate who we were.

"We're leaving," I confirmed.

"Don't suppose I can convince you to stay. There's still a lot of work to be done." He looked up to the sky, like someone might after feeling a raindrop.

"We can't stay," I said. Chase's hand slid into mine, a move Wallace noticed.

"Yeah," said Wallace. "Well, if you change your mind, you'll always be welcome in my camp."

I almost asked where that would be, but guessed that he probably didn't even know yet. He was the last remaining leader of Three, a soldier of the cause, something I now realized I might never truly understand. I did know this, though: the blood on his hands—Tucker's blood, and Billy's, too—would never wash away. He would carry it the rest of his days, and maybe for that reason alone he could never stop fighting. It was the only thing left that could make his actions make sense.

I stepped toward him and shook his hand. He pulled me into a hug and I patted him awkwardly on the back.

"Take my car," he said gruffly, placing a tarnished silver key in the palm of my hand. He scratched the back of his neck, refusing to meet my gaze. "There's two full cans of fuel in the back. Not much food, but enough water to get you through a couple of days at least. And there's a map in the glove box. The border patrol in South Carolina has all been pulled in to support the existing bases. You should be able to get into the Red Zone without too much trouble, though I'd still stick to low-traffic routes." He hesitated. "Consider it payback for kicking you out of the Wayland Inn. Not one of my brighter moves, I guess."

I blinked, unsure how to respond as he reached out his hand to take Chase's.

"Your uncle was a good man," he said.

Chase tilted his head. "You knew him?"

"I knew him," Wallace said with a smile. "I knew him a long time ago, before the War." He looked like he might say more, but didn't.

There was still a lot I had to tell Chase about Jesse. We had a long drive ahead of us, miles and miles to talk.

"What was he like back then?" he asked.

"Young and stupid." Wallace laughed. "The most reckless of the three of us. He'd start a fight, and I'd go in after him, and then Aiden had to bail us all out."

Chase glanced at me. "Aiden DeWitt?"

I squeezed his hand.

"If Jesse didn't like something, he'd fix it. Fix the whole world if he could have. In the end, I guess he did. You should be proud of that, son."

I closed my eyes, thinking of the way he'd risen, broken and bloody, to stab the knife I'd passed him into the heart of the Chief of Reformation.

"I am," said Chase.

Wallace scuffed his heel on the ground. "You remind me of him. Once you get your mind set on something, you take it to the very end."

My lips turned up in a smile for the first time in a week.

"Good luck to you both," said Wallace. "Maybe we'll see each other again sometime."

But as he walked away, I knew we wouldn't.

EPILOGUE

SUMMER in the south wasn't as hot as I thought it would be. Each morning, the breeze came in off the ocean, and each afternoon the thunderclouds built overhead and cracked open for a short time before stretching thin and melting into the evening sky. Just before dark, the world seemed to bound back: the air smelled like fresh soil and the birds broke their silence—a last reminder before the dark of the life that surrounded us.

But early morning was my favorite time. The quiet before the day, just after the rise of the sun. In worn-out sneakers, cutoff shorts, and one of Chase's T-shirts, I walked down the beach, keeping to the crunchy sand left over from the high tide.

The docks would be quiet today. Most people stayed at the compound—an old Air Force base that had steadily grown over the past months. The runways had been bombed during the War, but the rows of housing were still intact, and now served as an evacuation center for those still fleeing from the interior. Sanctuary, it was called. An entirely self-sufficient community, complete with its own hydraulic power station, water desalination plant, and school. More than a few Lost Boys went there.

After the bases had fallen, the MM had destroyed all existing long-distance explosive devices. Uncertain who to trust within their ranks, they erred on the side of safety, assuring that their people, and ours, were no longer at threat of an aerial assault. In the last three months President Scarboro had received countless death threats and more than one attempt on his life. This, along with the death of his Chief of Reformation, had apparently been enough to force a treaty with Matthew Stark's camp—at least that was what we heard on Faye Brown's news report broadcasted nightly at Sanctuary.

I would believe it when I saw it.

It wasn't long before I came to the docks. Along the bank opposite the clear blue water, a grove of Cyprus trees appeared beneath the high overarching palms. I walked beneath the heavy boughs, the sound of the ocean growing faint behind me. The air grew rich with a sweet, heady scent, and the thin branches that had fallen crackled beneath my feet.

I made my way to the center tree, glancing beyond it, just for a minute, to where an old road broke off before bridging across the bay. Turning my attention back to the tree, I slid my hands around the smooth gray bark until I reached the indentations.

LORI WHITMAN, it said. Already the wood had puckered and accepted its new tattoos. Looking up, I saw a new ribbon had been tied around the lowest branch, a token from the last visitor.

"Hi, Mom," I said quietly, letting the breeze blow through my hair. I didn't feel her loss as sharply as I did before. The pain was still there, though more of a dull ache, a sadness.

My fingers traced the letters, then came to rest on the silver ring with the small black stone hanging around my neck. My someday promise. Laying beside it, the Saint Michael's medallion—for luck.

I traveled to the next tree, tracing another name: Jesse

Waite, and below it, three hash marks that Chase had carved there.

I moved from tree to tree. Billy. Marco and Polo, back together on one stout branch. Lincoln and Riggins from Knoxville. A soldier named Harper in Chicago.

Tucker Morris.

I stopped there, as I always did, unsure what to feel. Maybe someday I would come to peace with the role he had played in my life. I might accept what he'd done and his twisted logic behind it. The anger and the pity and the questions would all die down, and I would know him as a boy who'd been hurt by his family, who'd found a new family in the FBR, and who'd done what he thought he had to do in order to survive.

Perhaps he'd been right when he'd said we weren't that different.

From behind came the low groan of a motor, and with one final good-bye, I turned and made my way toward the water. The sand gave way to a cracked concrete walkway, which rose above the lowering beach and stretched twenty feet out into the waves. In the distance, a boat approached, its silver hull gleaming in the sun. A smile tugged at my lips, and soon I was jogging toward it.

He was standing at the front of the boat, his hair shaggy past his ears, his skin darker than I'd ever seen it. As the boat slowed and drew closer, he moved to the side and grabbed a pile of rope from the deck, flinging it across the divide to where I waited.

"Take your time, why don't you," I said. It had only been four days since Chase had left, but might as well have been weeks.

"You miss me?" A grin turned up the right side of his mouth, and as the engine went dead, he tied off his side of the rope using only his right hand.

It had only been three months since the gunshot that had almost taken his life, and though the medic at Sanctuary had given him a clean bill of health, I still worried at the way he favored his left arm.

I finished knotting the first rope to its anchor on the dock the way Sal, the carrier to Mexico, had taught me. From the back of the boat, a short, shirtless man hopped over the siding and finished the task in half the time it had taken us.

"I missed Sal," I said. The carrier grinned, dimples deep in his cheeks, and whistled my way.

"*Te amo*," he called, gripping his heart dramatically.

"I see how it is," said Chase, tying off another rope. My stomach did a small flip as the breeze flattened his damp shirt against his chest, revealing the ripples of muscle beneath.

"How'd it go?" I asked.

After Chase and I had arrived at Sanctuary, we'd volunteered to help the carriers transport refugees over the border. There was a time we'd considered going ourselves, but we'd never made it. Now I ran the check-in station in Tampa, and Chase served as the liaison on the Mexican border.

"Just as planned," said Chase, swinging his long legs over the side and finally toeing the dock. I reached to help him automatically, habit from the early days after his injury when he needed it.

When his feet were firmly planted, his hands rose, cupping my face. I touched him, too: his rough cheeks, the straight line of his jaw down to his chin. His gaze found mine and held, and I remembered dozens of times I'd felt the world slow, just like it did now.

When I was six years old and he'd walked me home from the haunted house up the street. The first time he kissed me,

in the woods after he'd been in Chicago with Jesse. In my bedroom, the night before he was drafted.

A tent in the woods. A truck in the Red Zone. An abandoned building the night before we'd gone for Rebecca.

A barn loft in Endurance.

And now. I would add this to my collection, and carry it
with me always, as he had once carried my letters, as I now carried his ring. Our someday was now, not some distant point on
the horizon. Almost losing him had taught me that.

He smiled—that small, secret smile he saved just for me.

I wet my lips, preparing for him to move closer, wrap me in
his arms, and kiss me, but a second later I was twisting through
the air and landed with a heave of breath over his shoulder.
Frantically I gripped at his back.

"What are you doing?" I screeched. "Put me down!"

He walked to the edge of the dock. Through my mess of hair
I could see the water softly slapping against the algae-stained
concrete, ten feet below.

"No, wait," I said. "Wait, hang on."

"Didn't miss me, huh?"

"I missed you!" I giggled, legs bicycling uselessly through the
air. "I missed you, all right?"

I hit the water feet first, a half second before he jumped in
after me. Sputtering to the surface I found him grinning from
ear to ear, and soon we were splashing each other, kicking
through the waves toward shallower water. When my feet could
touch the ground, I launched across the space between us and
tackled him.

He didn't let me go.

The water was warm as a bath, and as I shoved my hair back
he pulled me close. My legs wrapped around his hips and his

arms around my waist. The collar of my shirt swelled open in the water, and he kissed the corner of my scar. The mark forever reminding me that I was, under it all, an Article 5.

Somehow, when Chase's lips pressed against it, I was proud of what it stood for.

His mouth rose up my neck, a path of saltwater kisses that found my lips and left me flying. My blood heated, and I inched closer, tightening my grip around his neck.

"Get a room!" called someone from the shore.

Chase smiled against my temple as we pulled apart. On the beach was a horse with white stockings, and on her saddled back sat Rebecca, her blond hair already growing back to her shoulders. Against her leg leaned Sean, cackling at his interruption.

He cupped his hands over his mouth. "Are we going to get breakfast or what?"

I giggled into Chase's ear. "If you ignore him, he'll go away."

With that, Chase turned back, and kissed me again.

ACKNOWLEDGMENTS

Writing this is harder than I thought. Five years ago I was convinced I would never be published; I'd accepted that this dream of mine was going to forever remain my little secret. And now Chase and Ember's journey is over (at least my part in it), and I'm thanking the people involved with making this trilogy a reality. It's a teensy bit emotional.

I am so grateful to the team at Browne & Miller—Joanna and Danielle—for everything they have done for me, but most especially for pulling a poorly written query letter from the slush pile and seeing potential.

I'm enormously lucky to have Melissa Frain on my side—I can say for certain Sean is, too. Without her, I would probably, be drowning, in a river, of commas, and poor Sean would probably be sulky and, well, less cute. She's a rock star editor—the bee's knees, the cat's pajamas (but please don't tell her I said so, I'd never hear the end of it).

The people at Tor have been ever amazing from the very beginning of this series. Kathleen Doherty, thank you for your kindness and support. Alexis Saarela, you are absolutely the best publicist I could ask for. Seth Lerner, these covers have made the books. Well done and thank you.

I couldn't have done any of this without my husband. I'm not sure I would have wanted to. There are certain people who just make you want to be your best self, and I will be thankful every day of my life to have found mine. As I write this, my son is attempting to scale the bookshelves—I take this to mean he'll be a reader. It's hard to believe it was only eleven months ago I was frantically trying to finish the last scenes between contractions. If anyone thinks the end of *Three* is too scary, blame labor. If you feel hopeful, as I hope you will, blame my son. He's taught me all about it.

Once upon a time, I met another local author for bagels at a Panera in Louisville. I should have known that first day that she'd end up being my biggest cheerleader. A special thanks to Katie Mc-Garry for holding my hand through this entire journey. We did it, Katie! Can you believe it?

And finally, thank you to the ladies at Jazzercise who sweat extra hard with me when I was in revisions, to the bloggers and authors who have been so supportive and inspiring, and to the people who have written me letters about Chase and Ember, about books, and about your own struggles and triumphs. I am deeply humbled, and grateful for you all.